The
Physic Garden

Catherine Czerkawska

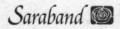

Published by Saraband
Suite 202, 98 Woodlands Road
Glasgow, G3 6HB, Scotland
www.saraband.net

ISBN: 9781908643513
ebook: 9781908643520

Editor: Ali Moore

Printed and bound in Great Britain by Clays Ltd, St Ives plc.

MIX
Paper from
responsible sources
FSC® C018072

3 5 7 9 10 8 6 4 2

In loving memory of Julian Czerkawski

and

for Alan, with love

'The gard'ners year is a circle as their labour, never at an end.'

The Scots Gard'ner, John Reid, 1683

'Bookes (Courteous Reader) may rightly be compared to Gardens; wherein, let the painfull Gardiner expresse neuer so much care and diligent endeauour; yet among the very fairest, sweetest, and freshest Flowers, as also Plants of most precious Vertue; ill fauoring and stinking Weeds, fit for no vse but the fire or mucke-hill, will spring and sprout up. So fareth it with Bookes of the very best quality, let the Author bee neuer so indulgent, and the Printer vigilant: yet both may misse their ayme, by the escape of Errors and Mistakes, either in sense or matter. If then the best Bookes cannot be free from this common infirmity; blame not this, of farre lighter argument, wherein thy courtesie may helpe vs both.'

Florio's translation of Boccaccio's Decameron, 1620

CHAPTER ONE

Taking the Bees

The first time I saw Jenny Caddas, she was taking a swarm of bees. It was late June of 1802 and I remember that it was warm, which is not always the case at that time of year in Scotland. Sometimes the frost can still nip your nose and your freshly planted seedlings even on a June morning. But not that day. That day the sun beat down on my unprotected head. I had come away without my hat, so anxious was I to be out of the town, away from the college. The bees hung in a small tree, a dark, dense shadow, a single mind, full of their own narrow purpose. You could hear them. You could almost feel them like a vibration in the air. She had the skep in one hand and a short-handled brush in the other, and she was stalking them, fearlessly, without veil or gloves, while her wee sister looked on from the cottage door with her thumb in her mouth and a doll that was nothing more than a moppet, a vaguely human-shaped bundle of rags, clutched in her other hand.

'Will I help you?' I called, on impulse, and she turned, distracted from the work by my voice, but her head still inclining towards the drowsy swarm. They mustn't be allowed to escape. But you never knew when they would fly, suddenly purposeful, heading towards their new home.

'They send out scouts,' my father had once told me. 'Looking for a suitable place. You have to take them before the scouts come back. Before they know where they're going.'

The lass looked me up and down, assessing me swiftly, and nodded. 'Alright then,' she said, so I put my bag down in the long grass at her gate and went forward, although it was my father who had always taken the bees when I was a lad, and – as he was fond of commenting – I myself who had eaten the honey. But I must have observed him as closely in this as in everything else because, although I was feart of the stings, it came easily enough to me, and I was stung only the once. Besides, she knew what she was doing, and I did as I was told, which was to slice off the branch, gently and carefully, with the knife I always carried for taking cuttings or sawing through difficult roots. The swarm was too intent on their queen so that in a moment, before they knew what was happening to them, they were imprisoned in the basket, and she was brushing the remainder after them, which they didn't seem to mind at all. Then she swatted a few stragglers away from her face, shaking her head, and her hair flew out in flaxen strands. She was a pretty enough lass of about my own age, but – and I distinctly remember thinking this as well – her hair was a marvel.

She sorted the bees first, introducing them to their new home, talking to them, settling them with her voice, which was low and musical when she spoke to them, and then she came back to me.

'Were you stung?' she asked briskly. Not so low, nor so musical. It was plain to me that she was more fond of the bees than of lads like myself.

'Only my finger.' I was sucking at my hand, tasting the salt of my own sweat on it. Bee stings are sore, though, and I could feel it spreading up through my arm, a wave of poison in my blood.

'Come in,' she said 'I have something will sort that.'

She shooed her sister away like somebody shooing a hen, and the wean moved down the garden, skipping and hopping every few steps, but slowly, dreamily, engaged in some world of her own. It was always the way of it with that lassie, as dark and mild as her sister was fair and bold. Head in the clouds, Jenny would say, and it was true enough.

I went inside, into a room that was a kitchen and parlour all in one, with a fire in the grate, a well-swept floor and a couple of larch chairs. There was a big spinning wheel – a walking wheel they call them, where you stand up and move back and forth with the yarn – and box beds in the wall with cheerful woollen blankets covering them, tucked in very tight and smooth. I can picture all this, even now, and the moon-faced clock, wagging friendly at the wall, its slow tick tock in the background, the simple wooden dresser with a row of spice drawers along the back and a few best blue and white plates and dishes standing on the top of it.

I remember it because it was so much like our own house, except that this was much neater and cleaner and there was the smell of grasses and green things about it, and that was what attracted me. It smelled like home only better. She had bunches of herbs and flowers from the garden hung about the room to dry. Some of them must have been there since the previous summer while some were freshly picked. The astringent scent of them filled the place. There was lavender, catmint and callamint, camomile and pennyroyal, rosemary and yarrow, meadowsweet, ladies' bedstraw and bitter wormwood and all kinds of other plants that I could name, all of them, and I daresay I could name them still if I took my time and gathered my thoughts and my memories about me.

She sat me down in a comfortable chair with a faded patchwork cushion in it. Later, I found out it was her father's special seat. Then she fetched vinegar on a clean rag and bathed the wound, which was getting angry now, for all that I had nipped out the sting with my teeth. Bees sacrifice themselves when they sting you, which perhaps explains why you are more likely to be stung by a wasp, which can sting and go on stinging, once, twice, thrice in the same place, than by the poor bee who does it only *in extremis*. Then she brought down a pot of some dark brown tincture from the top of the big press in the corner and dabbed it on the wound. It smelled most fiercely of beeswax and she said it was of the bees' own making, but it would take the fire out of all injuries, burns and stings and scalds alike, and she was right, because it was wonderfully soothing, although it stained my skin yellow where she dabbed it on.

Then it was time for introductions, a little later than is normally thought polite. She told me her name was Jenny Caddas and she lived with her father, Alexander, who was a weaver. There was a handloom in the weaving shop to one side of the cottage. That was where he worked, he and a lad called Gilbert whose job it was to wind the wool onto the pirns for him. A dreamer who was aye getting things into a fankle, she told me, scathingly. Alexander was away in town on business, collecting the raw materials for his trade, and he had taken the lad with him to do the fetching and carrying. Her mother was dead, so there was just herself and her wee sister, Anna, and the man of the house, Sandy Caddas. Gilbert lived nearby and came in to work for his master each day. I told her that my name was William Lang and I was a gardener.

'Are you looking for work?' she asked, obviously wondering what I was doing wandering the lanes in the warmth of a June afternoon, and at that I remembered my bag and leapt up to find it. It was still where I had left it, in the long grass outside her gate. She was curious to know what was in it, so I showed her all the specimens. They were much like the things she had drying in her own kitchen, but more of them: valerian, nightshade, swallowwort, scurvy grass, thistle and so on, wrapped up in damp linen to keep them fresh. I found that she could name them as well as myself. She knew the Scots, not the Latin names right enough, though she knew a few of those too, which surprised me somewhat. I told her what I did and where I did it and who for, and I think she was impressed, because she must have thought me very young for such a position. I wanted her to know that I was not too young to be the college gardener in the great town of Glasgow.

I had a feeling of pride in myself and my own accomplishments but fleetingly wondered why it should matter what I said of myself when I was in the house of a country lass merely, and her opinions counted for nothing. I was, it has to be admitted, a wee thing brash back then. It also has to be said in her favour that she ignored my presumption and treated me very kindly for a complete stranger who had come into her kitchen and proceeded to brag about himself.

She gave me a drink of ale and a piece of oatcake with honey spread on it and then she called her sister.

'Anna! You'd best have something to eat.'

The child came drifting in, still in her own world, but took the sticky bannock anyway and crammed most of it into her mouth, clutching the makeshift doll in her other hand while the crumbs fell to the floor. A daring hen – seeing them through the open door – took the chance of an unanticipated meal and pecked them up. Anna eyed the hen with pleasure, while she chewed the remainder. Jenny Caddas shooed the bird outside and then looked at me over the top of the wee one's head, more mother than sister. She gave that broad smile she had, raising her eyebrows and grinning at me, and I saw the way her teeth were very white and her eyes lit up with the smile as well. The hair, the flaxen hair, was still a wonder to behold.

'She is a trial to me,' she observed. 'For she has little interest in food, unless it be sweet and can just be held in her hand.'

'She doesn't look ill fed to me.'

'Small thanks to anyone but her sister.'

Anna stared from one to the other of us, finished chewing her bannock and skipped off into the garden in pursuit of the hen.

Jenny Caddas refilled my cup. She seemed disposed to be friendly. Perhaps she was glad of the unexpected interruption to her day. She wore a plain, blue, Indian cotton dress, very much patched and mended, and I remember she had wrapped a good woven shawl around her shoulders, although the day was warm and it kept slipping down, but perhaps the shawl was meant to disguise the poverty of the dress. She told me later it was not her best, but her working dress. Her feet were bare and dusty. There were two patches of sweat under her arms, because she had been stalking the swarm and exerting herself. There was a faint scent of it off her, not unpleasant, just the scent of activity. And she said,

'Well thank-you for all your help, kind sir.'

I asked her, did she ever get stung herself, not because I really wanted to know, but because — what with the ale and the honey and the sight of such a bonny lass — I didn't want to have to walk out of the house. I didn't want to get on with the work I had been sent to do, the work of collecting plant specimens for the students of botany, for the young gentlemen of the college. She said no, not very often, and when she did she hardly felt it.

'Is that true?'

'That's the way of it, William.' (How pleasant it was to hear her say my name like that!) 'You either get worse, much worse, so that even a single sting will make you ill and might even kill you, or you get so much better that the stings are nothing at all, but like midgie bites just.'

'Aye well, this one feels much worse than a midgie bite,' I told her, holding out my poor, injured finger to her. It was throbbing away for all the tincture she had put on it.

She said, 'What more can I do for it? Are you expecting a kiss? Like my wee sister?' She smiled and blushed at what she had just said, and it was the bonniest thing to see.

She was one of those lassies who laughs often. She couldn't seem to help making light of all kinds of things. She liked fine to please people. She looking at me with shining eyes, as though at that moment everything, myself included, was a cause for laughter. Which it was for her, then. It pains me still to think of it, how the whole world was a cause for laughter with her, and how maybe that very innocence played its part in the events that followed. She was not ignorant, you must understand that. Never ignorant. She had more knowledge of plants and the remedies that could be made from them than most of the young gentlemen for whom I had been sent to gather specimens. Women generally did; it was the auld wives who knew about plants and their health-giving properties. But as for Jenny, there was an innocence about her, as though she aye expected the best of people. A lack of suspicion. I see the same thing in my grand-daughter, and it would break your heart, so it would.

I was twenty and I thought I had never seen such a fine lassie in all my born days. When I think about it now, more than fifty years later, I would say that she was still the loveliest thing I ever laid eyes on, worn gown and all, and that thought sits heavily on my heart, like a pain in my chest, like a pain deep inside me. I should not have begun with Jenny you see. I should not have begun there. I should have started the tale elsewhere and earlier. But I wanted to write about her, the way you want to talk about what you love. Loved. I wanted to bring her to life in words the way I would once have made seeds, bulbs, roots and tubers grow into plants, the way a few green shoots could grow and stretch out and blossom, the way affection grows and blossoms, although you never see it happening, no matter how closely you try to follow the movement of it.

All the same, I should have started the tale earlier. Perhaps I should have begun by telling you about my father, Robert Lang, who had been college gardener for many years, since I was just a lad. Or with myself, who loved green and growing things even as a boy. Or with Thomas Brown, who had come to teach botany at the college, a few years before I met Jenny.

But I think that would have been the hardest beginning of all. So instead, here I am, telling you about Jenny Caddas and her swarm of bees, the way she smelled of sweat and honey, and how her hair flew about her head and caught the light, a tangle of flax in the sunshine.

CHAPTER TWO

Doctor Brown

I had better get on with it. I had better leap straight in and call him by his name although, even now, it pains me to bring him to mind. You see, I saw Thomas Brown before ever I knew Jenny. The first time I met him was in the year of 1799, when the century was old, in the college garden at Glasgow. My father was still in life. I was not yet seventeen years old, but very strong, and I flatter myself that my father could not have done without me, although he would have been the last person to tell me so himself.

'Why praise a lad for what should come naturally to him?' was his habitual refrain.

Doctor Brown, as I had to call him then, for he was much my superior in station, if not in years, had just been appointed as a substitute lecturer in botany at the behest of Professor James Jeffray, a clever man whose interests, notoriously enough, all lay with dissections and surgery. Jeffray had no patience with plants and their uses, but he was engaged to deliver botanical lectures to the young gentlemen and it was a sore trial to him. Thomas Brown had been recommended to him as a suitable replacement. It was commonplace enough, in those days, for one professor to ask another to stand in for him. The college was canny with its money. Any salary was to be met only from fees paid by students, so the success or otherwise of the venture depended very much on Thomas Brown's popularity. And Jeffray, of course, would not be out of pocket, whatever the outcome.

On that particular day – and dear God, it could have been yesterday – Doctor Brown came into the garden where I was working, held out his hand to me and shook mine, although it was grimed with soil, but it was aye grimed with soil and I was soon to discover that he never minded. He was not a man to mind things like that.

'You must be Robert Lang's son,' he said, smiling at me with what I later learned was characteristic warmth. Even then, I thought him a charming man, although in Scotland that particular virtue will earn you the suspicion of your fellows rather than any more positive judgement.

'Aye. My name's William. William Lang.'

He was one of the gentry, he was one of the teachers, and I was shy of him. I think I must have seemed a wee thing surly, because of my diffidence, but he was never a man to let things like that influence him either. He had a habit of speaking to you face to face, of looking directly into your eyes, and you could see that you had his full attention.

'Your father tells me that you know everything there is to know about plants.' He said it with a twinkle, knowing it was a great exaggeration. And I was very surprised to hear that my father had been in any way fulsome in his praise of me. But that was always his way and the way of many a Scotsman, I think. He will brag about his son to a stranger but would die sooner than give him a word of praise to his face.

It would be true to say that I loved trees and plants, but more, I was interested in them. Right from the time when I was a lad, running at my father's heels and getting under his feet, I would ask him about this or that flower, this or that herb, a hundred times a day. And patiently, he would tell me whatever he knew about how things grew and where best to plant them. He knew how to propagate things, how to treat growing things as individuals, how to tend those that were delicate and needed extra care. He would tell me what kind of soil this or that plant liked best, speaking as though they were people.

'He will thrive in sunlight. He likes best to grow in shade. He loves to be damp, but he will die if you keep his roots wet.'

This is the kind of thing my father would tell me, characterising all that grew and, like a good son and a good gardener, I would store the advice away for future use.

So when Thomas came to me and shook my hand, I agreed with him that I had a certain amount of knowledge, more perhaps than most of the young men who toiled about the garden, doing only as they were told, season after season, without enquiring too closely why they were doing their work in this way rather than any other.

'But I could learn more, much more.'

'Then I think you may be able to help me. You know that I'll be lecturing in botany in Professor Jeffray's stead?'

I nodded. I had already heard as much. 'Will you be needing specimens, sir?'

'Yes indeed. I had thought to take them from the physic garden but ...' He trailed off, wrinkling his nose.

'The poor physic garden ...'

'Is in a parlous state. The smoke from the type foundry, I take it?'

'Aye. It blights all that is planted there.'

The stench of the fumes from the type foundry, which the university had permitted to be built next to the old physic garden, covered all the leaves and flowers in a foul-smelling, oily deposit that few plants were robust enough to resist. We knew just how destructive the foundry was, my father and I, for we had experimented in all kinds of ways in an effort to improve matters. Nothing worked for very long. The fumes were just too virulent.

He sighed. 'It is a shame the foundry was ever sited there, a damned shame that permission was ever given, but I suppose one cannot expect Faculty to understand about trees and plants, eh? Can we, my friend?'

CHAPTER THREE

Books

My dear, late wife used to tell me that love was the answer. My habitual and, no doubt, irritating response was always that I was not even sure of the question. But the older I grow, the more convinced I become that love, whatever it may be, is not the answer at all, or only part of it, and maybe friendship, enduring, unconditional and undemanding, is a better alternative.

Thomas.

There, I've written his name once more. And without flinching at all this time. Practice will no doubt make perfect. Doctor Thomas Brown was already married to Marion Jeffrey from Edinburgh when he began teaching at the college. I thought at first that she might be some relation of our Professor Jeffray, that the marriage might have been an astute step on the academic ladder. But when I knew him better, he pointed out that the names were spelled differently, that Marion Jeffrey came from an old Edinburgh family and there was no kinship between them.

I remember Marion – long departed this life – as a handsome and forthright young woman of decided opinions, and a good match for Thomas, or so I thought, although one can never really know what goes on between husband and wife. The most unlikely and mismatched couples can be blissfully happy, while those who seem made for one another can suddenly confide their misery in the marriage, or so I have learned over the years.

At some point in our acquaintance, Thomas invited me to make use of his library, to read whenever and whatever I wished. At first I was very reluctant to avail myself of this privilege and later, although I grew accustomed to visiting his house, I was always diffident about being there. Marion did her best to put me at my ease, but I was neither flesh nor fowl nor guid red herrin' as my father would have put it, especially when there were visitors in the house. I felt as though I did not belong in that company, but only a few years earlier, the great poet Robert Burns had had something of the same problem. The Edinburgh nabbery, the gentry, found him to be a man of intellect, but were surprised and entertained by it, astonished that he had the accomplishment at all.

I often think Mr Burns and myself might have had a great deal in common if we had had the good fortune to meet and talk about our respective experiences. Burns wrote convincingly and lovingly about the flowers of his native heath. I cannot even now read the lines, *oft hae I rov'd by bonny Doon, to see the rose and woodbine twine; and ilka bird sang o' its luve, and fondly sae did I o' mine*, without it bringing a lump to my throat, which is a very daft notion after all this time.

But then, I believe the poet's father was a gardener too, and it was that work which first took him to Ayrshire where Rab was born. How very like me, as my wife would have said, to notice this one fact about him, that he was the son of a gardener. But it would be true to say that whenever he wrote about enduring affection as opposed to the heartbreak of unrequited love, it was friendship, male and female, that he valued more than all else, and so – I think – do I.

Gardens and books. I cannot write without mentioning them. But of the two, books have played by far the larger part in my life. Books have, in some sense, been my life. But they have been my sorrow as well as my joy. It has taken me long enough to get to it, but here it is. On my writing table. This precious book, *The Scots Gard'ner* by John Reid, has come home to me at the end of my life, as was the intention of the sender. I hardly need to open it, for I find that I still have much of it by heart. The words come rushing back to me, as when we would recite the names of trees from it, or quote passages, turn and turn about, making a daft game of it.

'Laburnum, horse chestnut and the bonny rowan,' he would say and I would reply with, 'dogwood and guilderose, sweet briar and turkey oak.'

Sometimes it would be the names just, because we both took pleasure in saying them aloud, but sometimes it would be whole passages.

'Choose your seeds from the high, straight, young and well thriving,' he would begin.

'Choose the fairest, the weightiest and the brightest, for it is observed that the seeds of hollow trees whose pith is consumed, do not fill well,' I would quote back at him.

'Or come to perfection,' he would continue. 'Go on, William!'

'It's a mischief in many people that ... that ...' and then I would hesitate, and he would finish for me, 'that accompts all ridiculous that they have not been bred up with or accustomed unto.'

'So it is with trees in some respects and so it is with men who think themselves superior,' I would finish, triumphantly, and we would laugh, as though at the accomplishment of something quite wonderful, although what that could be, other than the foolish indulgence of our own high spirits, I do not know.

It is this same book, The Scots Gard'ner, that lies on my table now, alongside another volume, a manuscript book with yellowing pages covered in the neat handwriting that I still recognise as Thomas's own. This was his commonplace book, the book in which he copied his correspondence, drafting out the letters he wished to send and sometimes copying down the letters that came to him in return, although often enough, to save time, he would simply slip the original letter between the pages. Besides that, he would make notes of important purchases or simply of things that interested him. It is a fat book, covering many years, because I think that there were long periods when he neglected it and others when he was at pains to record many things there. So I know what I will find. But also, I do not know what else I will discover there. And I feel my skin flutter in apprehension.

I half wish he had not sent me either of these books, but it must have been on his express instructions, else how would such personal documents have been included in the parcel? It was once a bonny book too, this commonplace book, but time has made a *moger* of it; there are many loose leaves and stains where some liquid has been spilled on it, and I can hardly bear to tease the pages apart because I know that the words will bring back yet more memories, perhaps more than I can bear.

There is, of course, yet one more book that I should mention. But I am not ready to write about that one yet. Do you know, when the parcel first came, when I guessed that he must be gone from this life, I commenced wondering which book it contained, what manner of book he had sent me? It was like standing in the teeth of a strong gale. I could not catch my breath for a moment or two and found myself trembling, my teeth chattering, even as I opened the wrapping. I cannot tell you how vastly relieved I was to find that it was not what I had feared. I should have known, for the parcel was not large enough to contain that book. All these years, and I have never seen another copy, thank God. But if I had, if it had come into my shop, in all its terrible beauty, I think I should have cast it into the flames, and I can never bring myself to destroy any book willingly, which explains why there is so little free space in the shop or this house. But it did not come. So here I sit with this unexpected gift from my one-time friend. Here I sit in the last sunlight of the day and run my fingers over the cover of first one volume and then the other, and wonder if I can bear to remember him.

⊞ ⊞ ⊞

I have avoided thinking about Thomas these many years past. Most days I sit here peacefully among my books and papers, reading or writing. When I look out of the window at the front of the house, I can see the naked stone figures that adorn the new building opposite, like a frozen imitation of sensuality. Their eyes gaze coldly outwards to the sky, not at each other, and there is no affection in them. Neither love nor hate, neither joy nor sorrow do they know, will they ever know. But they too have a quality of peace about them.

This parcel, with its carefully written direction, arrived only a few days ago. I recognised it immediately as his hand. I would know it anywhere, even after all this time. My son, Robert, placed it before me.

'Look,' he said. 'This has come for you.'

He would have waited until I opened it, wishing to satisfy his curiosity, but I sent him off on some errand. I could not do it with anyone else standing by. And they are used to my eccentric ways now and do as they are told. Keeping the old man happy in his dotage. Humouring him.

'Give him a good flower folio or a natural history and he'll be occupied for hours.'

I know what they say of me, smiling, with a mixture of affection and exasperation. My sight is not what it was but my ears are quite unaffected. I have not yet turned foolish. Or no more foolish than I ever was.

What is the point, I wonder, at which friendship topples over into love? Can it be measured? Would it be a convenience to know with certainty, so that one could say, thus far and no further, because beyond this point, I will be in danger of an inconvenient madness? And how could it ever be measured? When I reflect upon these things, I still, after all this time, and all these years later, feel a sensation like a physical pain, somewhere in the centre of my chest, where the heart is said to lie. If I am honest it never goes away, this pain. It never for a single day leaves me.

There now, that's said. And it is such a striking confession that it surprises even me. And yet I know that it is not real, or not real in the sense of being engendered in blood and bone, not real in the sense of being measurable, although the flesh responds as though it were. It is, I think, as frozen as the passion that remains locked into the breast of that stone god out there. But there is no physic will ever cure it now and, besides, that garden is dead and gone. It is an old malady and one that I must just go on living with, as I have lived with it this long time past.

CHAPTER FOUR

The Silken Balloon

A few years ago, I found myself looking among old records in the college library. They would not have known who I was. I am a different man now, in all but name, and they would never have made any connection between the raw under-gardener I once was and the crabbit old bookman with the cautiously radical reputation, whom they had asked to catalogue some of their manuscripts. But there I was, ensconced in my favourite position among books and papers, and I found myself comparing the written hands of the various gardeners who had been employed to oversee the college gardens over the years. It was an interesting exercise and not only because one could easily track the sad decline of the physic garden through its pages. My father had been appointed as college gardener in the year 1784, two years after I was born, and there was his signature on various agreements and bills of sale. It was strange to me to see his hand. It brought him so vividly before my eyes. He was not at all confident with a pen, though better than his wavering predecessors. And better still with a spade, as he used to say.

He wrote his name laboriously, as though the letters were somewhat unfamiliar to him, or as though his fingers were stiff, which I'm sure they were. Most gardeners succumb to rheumatism in the end. His salary was ten pounds a year, so the records

21

told me, and he had a house for which he paid no rent. It was not, I remember, a good house, neither wind nor watertight, but it was a roof over our heads and we made the best of it. He was to look after both college and physic gardens with all that that entailed. He could harvest and sell the grass from the college garden but in return for that privilege, he must pay back his ten pounds as rent for the land. But when he undertook other work, such as taking down a bridge over the Molendinar Burn, or laying new pathways, he would be paid extra accordingly. Which meant, I suspect, that he was always over-extending himself, promising more than he could deliver.

He had married my mother, Margaret Tarrant, a quiet girl from Helensburgh, sent into service in Glasgow, which was where they met. He was an under-gardener by that time and she was a parlour maid. Attachments between servants were frowned upon but that didn't prevent them from happening. Still, respectable society, in the shape of masters and mistresses as well as mothers and fathers, continues to try to control the desires of the young. The urge to control nature is almost as strong as the urge to procreate. Almost but not quite.

They were wed a short while before he was made college gardener, perhaps on the expectation of his acquiring the position, and I was born a year later. My mother, Maggie, as she was always called, was a good-natured woman who quickly ran to stoutness and was perennially short of breath. She was prone to anxieties, easily beset by nerves and yet she smiled a great deal in an effort to please. Perhaps her experiences in service had affected her but she never spoke about them. I remember when my sister Bessie went into service, our mother was very keen that the place should be 'decent' as she put it. Whatever those tribulations were, she survived them, and I think she was very fond of my father.

There was a story always told in the family about me, her first-born. Although my mother was far gone in pregnancy, my father had, perhaps unwisely, coaxed her out of the house to watch the Italian balloonist, Lunardi, the Daredevil Aeronaut as he was known, ascending into the grey Glasgow skies over St Andrew's Square. My father (and I find this incredible but he must have been very much in love – it is the only explanation) had already paid the extortionate sum of two shillings, one apiece, to take her to see the balloon, where it was being exhibited in the choir of St Mungo's Cathedral, the only public building in Glasgow big enough to contain it. It was suspended there, floating above the choir, magnificent in pink, green and yellow silk.

'Enough,' said my mother when she told the tale afterwards, 'to make quite a hundred fine spring gowns. And such beautiful stuff!'

Having seen the balloon, my father was anxious for a glimpse of the flight, and he persuaded my mother to come too. But Lunardi was a great dandy. 'I thought his balloon very marvellous but I did not take to *him*,' observed my father, dourly.

All did not go smoothly. A local worthy known as Lothian Tam managed to get entangled with the ropes and was lifted some twenty feet into the air, yelping like a dog, before Lunardi cut through the rigging and the unanticipated passenger fell to earth, to the mingled horror and entertainment of the crowd. He tumbled onto soft ground, luckily enough for him, and lived to relate the story and cadge a free drink or two on the strength of it in many a Glasgow ale house. My mother was among the spectators and she always swore that it was the shock of the sight that sent her into labour. She was confined immediately afterwards and I was born a few hours later. She had, I believe, some idea of naming me Vincenzo in the balloonist's honour, but my father would have none of it, although he did buy her a Lunardi bonnet with a straw brim and a fantastic balloon-shaped crown, which I'm told she wore to my christening. She kept it in a box for many years afterwards, as a memento of the occasion, until one day she found that mice had nested in it, whereupon it was consigned to the midden. I have sometimes wondered if the circumstances of my birth did not lend a certain sense of adventure to my nature, much as children with strawberry marks on their faces are said to be born to women who have consumed too many fruits, late in pregnancy. All nonsense of course and besides, my father's influence would bring me back to solid ground as surely as our very own Icarus, poor Lothian Tam, came tumbling down.

Over the course of some years, Robert and Maggie had seven more children. I had a comfortable enough childhood, for we were generally well fed and well clothed. My father was a man of great energy and enterprise and always seemed to make the very best of what he had, even if it meant that he was constantly overworked. There was hardly ever an evening when he was not exhausted, sinking into his chair beside the fire, the chair that nobody else was allowed to use, with my mother pulling off his boots and rushing around with warm water for his calloused hands and ale in a pewter pot to slake his thirst, until the meal should be on the table.

'Ah Maggie! Maggie!' he would say, stretching out his legs, 'That was a hard day!' and she would look up at him and, setting the boots to one side, she would run her hands tenderly over his poor feet. I mind those naked white feet yet. They made me uncomfortable, although I couldn't have explained why. Perhaps it was that he was such a force in our lives, and yet his feet seemed so vulnerable, so defenceless.

'There now,' she always said. 'Drink your ale and take your rest.' This exchange between them was the same, every working night, for all the years of their marriage. Such familiarity is, I suppose, one of the chief comforts of the married state.

I find, somewhat to my surprise, that my own signature has changed greatly over the years. Back then I can see that it was fine and firm and stylish, with those confident high-flying loops on the W of William, on the capital L of Lang and a big flourish on the final 'g'. Now, time and experience have transformed it into a spidery scrawl.

❏ ❏ ❏

24

While I was working alongside my father and even before I began to gather specimens for him, I spoke to Thomas Brown quite frequently. He must have been in his mid-twenties then, which seems a mere lad to me now, although I thought him a good deal older than me at the time. I remember his thin face, his high forehead, the curly hair just a wee thing too long, his pale grey eyes that missed nothing. He had a reputation in the college as a clever man with an excess of high spirits when he had taken a drink. But mostly, he seemed wiser than I was, and made me feel raw and untried. Yet all that was down to me and not him, because I cannot remember that he ever patronised me or indeed did anything to make me feel uncomfortable in his presence. The fault, if fault there was, lay with me. I was in awe of him and somewhat afraid of him, his learning, his self-possession, his wit and what seemed to me very like wisdom.

He had studied medicine at Edinburgh and was working as a doctor in Glasgow because – so he told me during our increasingly friendly conversations – the growing population and prosperity of the inhabitants of that city would provide excellent opportunities for him. His father was a banker with an interest in surgery. Even then it seemed an odd combination to me, but I was to learn that all kinds of professional men were fascinated by the novelty of surgery, the prospect of cutting open the human body to ascertain what went on inside and what could be done to alter it. When Thomas was just a lad of six, his prosperous father had built himself a new house at Langside, near Glasgow, and that was where he had grown up, but upon his marriage to Marion, he had rented a property not far from the college, which was where he lived and had his consulting rooms.

Thomas's professor at the college, James Jeffray, was an anatomist first and foremost, and his mind was all fixed on the intricate workings of the human body. Plants held no fascination for him, as they did for Thomas and myself. He considered their medical applications to be little better than a string of old wives' tales, so he was very ready to farm out his summer lectures in botany to Thomas.

'And so I decided to make of it what I could!' Thomas told me. He was very confident in those days. There was a spring in his step, a liveliness in everything he did, and people were attracted to him. Somewhat later, while our friendship still flourished, he told me that he had possessed a youthful self-love which was a good substitute for experience. He thought that he would do very well indeed at the work, better certainly than Jeffray, who was known to be but a tedious exponent of botany and given to reading aloud long lists of plants and their properties, very slowly and drearily, so that the young gentlemen might copy them down, practically breaking their jaws with yawning as they did so at the sheer mind-numbing weariness of the undertaking.

I had heard tales of those lectures of Jeffray's – how the lads would take food and strong drink into classes and commence throwing bread pellets at each other and once, a young Highlander, the son of some minor laird, smuggled a tame rat in under his blue wool coat and let it loose in the room to the consternation of Jeffray who couldn't abide vermin at any price. The professor leapt onto the desk calling for somebody, anybody, to fetch a dog to catch the rat. The scholars would do anything to relieve the monotony.

Perhaps because of the force of contrast, Thomas's lectures were wildly successful, so successful in attracting students that, as the century turned, he was given a permanent appointment. There was still no payment from college funds of course. I doubt if he needed the money, or not in the way that we needed it for winter warmth and the avoidance of starvation, but his lectures were certainly attracting students and with them came fees.

His knowledge and enthusiasm drew them in, but his wife Marion used to say that his propensity for making dubious jokes helped. The students were young men of a robust nature, rustic for the most part, as unversed in the liberal arts as I myself, the only difference between us being the accident of birth. There was always an admixture of Highlanders, the sons of small landowners who scarcely understood English, never mind the Latin tongue in which some (but not much) of their learning took place. And they were all raw, with not a thought in their heads, most of them, beyond ale, oysters and a pretty woman. Thomas would lecture to them in a mixture of English and Scots. They came to his classes with relief at understanding something, stayed because he entertained them and – in spite of themselves – became interested in what he had to tell them. His enthusiasm for his subject, coupled with his natural charm, lent him an irresistible eloquence.

I don't know why it seems so important to me to lay all this out now, so late in the day, to clarify it in my mind. I suppose I'm looking for beginnings, for the start of those events that were to change my life. An outsider, seeing the course of my life in retrospect, would never see what I see, understand what I now understand. If I would describe my subsequent prosperity, my work, my marriage and my beloved family, I have been more blessed than might have been supposed, and there are many who would envy me. I have had my tragedies, it's true, but a great deal of good fortune has also befallen me. There is nothing now about the public perception of my life which would give anyone to understand that things have been otherwise than smooth and rewarding. I have been, I would say, a very lucky man. I am lucky still in what has turned out to be a happy life.

But there cannot, surely, be a single person, man or woman, who, looking back on a long life, carefully lived, does not have secrets buried deep in heart and mind. Secrets, regrets, moments of joy so intense and so acute that to confess them seems at once a shame and an urgent necessity.

CHAPTER FIVE

The Commonplace Book

I wait until the house is very quiet before daring to look through Thomas's commonplace book. I wait for an afternoon when the family are all away on business of their own, the children imprisoned with their dominie, all save my wee Jenny who is sleeping, having exhausted herself with running after her new spaniel puppy this morning. My daughters-in-law are paying afternoon calls, one of my sons is down in the shop and the other about the town on book business. When I have heard the last slam of the door, when I am reasonably sure that I will not be interrupted, when I can almost feel the house sighing and settling around me into its afternoon torpor, only then do I slide the commonplace book across the table and tease the pages gently apart.

As I thought, it spans a great many years, a large folio, bound in calf, a fat book with plenty of loose leaves, copies of letters, notes and cuttings tucked into it here and there. The first thing that falls into my hands is a detailed 'receipt for the very Best Raisin Wine', written in a faint scrawl which is certainly not Thomas's own. His hand was small, almost cramped. It always surprised me to see such a crabbed hand emerge from such an expansive personality. The receipt covers several pages, recommending Smyrna raisins for Madeira wine, Malaga raisins for Spanish wine, and so on. There follow all kinds of specifics including the cost of making sixteen gallons of good wine with one hundredweight of fruit, producing sixty-four bottles at less than sixpence per bottle. 'There are many delicious wines to be made with gooseberrys and currents mixt with the raisins,' the writer tells us. 'But be sure to use none but good, sound fruit, for bad raisins will never make good wine.' And it strikes me that this might be a maxim by which one might live one's whole life. If only one could be sure of getting good, sound fruit. But there are some fruits that decay from the centre, while maintaining a glossy outward appearance. How can you ever know?

Right at the bottom of the last leaf of the receipt, Thomas himself has added a note. 'My grandmother's. Her blackcurrant wine was very good.' It takes me by surprise, that little addendum in his preternaturally neat hand. I have a sudden vision of him, sitting beside his fire, in his library, opening a cobwebby bottle and pouring its contents carefully into two thin glasses, one for me and one for him, the glasses so fine, their intricately twisted stems so fragile, that I am almost afraid to handle them, never mind drink from them. The wine is very dark and has the scent of fresh blackcurrants. It is remarkably strong, and, when I drink it, I can feel it coursing through my blood and clouding my mind with a sudden intimation of pure happiness. Memory twists inside me like a knife. I set the book down and rest my head on my hands for a while. I cannot look at it.

I cannot let it alone.

I turn to the last few pages. I find myself at once curious and apprehensive. But Thomas seems to have conceived an interest in the mineral world in his later years, and I am disappointed to find that there are only inventories of various specimens along with their prices and very little else. I learn from these that he paid eighteen pounds for a seven-ounce specimen of gold and one pound twelve shillings and sixpence for a meteorite from Sowerby. Twenty-one specimens of red stilbite ('a most magnificent collection,' he adds, 'perhaps unrivalled') cost him all of thirty pounds. In 1851 he had his whole mineral collection valued at one thousand seven hundred and fifty-one pounds. The precision of this — I must confess — astonishes me, but the lists of glistening chunks of rock, for which he had acquired such a passion, fall dry as dust upon my eyes and make my head ache. How did he come to this? How did my Thomas come to this? In much the same way as I came to books, perhaps? And were we both taking refuge in something safer and more predictable than the world of living trees and plants?

Hesitantly, I make my way back through the book, back through time, through those years of our estrangement. Many of the entries are concerned with life in the countryside. From some ten years ago, dated 1845, there is news of the death of the local minister's wife. 'Mrs Kennedy died at six o'clock on the morning of 27th March and was buried on the following Friday.' There is a copy of a note to the 'Directors of the Farmer's Annual Ball' from 1836, to the effect that Thomas is 'exceedingly sorry that it is out of his power to do himself the honour of attending the ball this night'. There are requests for subscription funds. One for a 'subscription for a monument to Robert Burns' catches my eye as does another for 'Alexander McKinnon, in Spring Row, who has suffered from having his machinery destroyed by accidental fire on the night of 29th June last and from a consideration of the honest and upright character he has uniformly maintained, and of his enterprise in establishing and carrying on the bleaching business to the satisfaction of the public, we deem it is our duty to assist him in the expense of repairing his machinery.' Fire seems to be a regular hazard in the country, as it is here in the town, for only a few months later a lady has had her 'two good cows consumed by fire' and seeks his help, which seems to have been readily given. As why would it not? A kindly man still, you see.

There are lists, some of them land values, some of them to do with the finances of the school, which Thomas is obviously helping to support. There is a piece of correspondence concerning a poor woman who is 'evidently in indigent circumstances and will in all probability soon become an object of charity' and another seeking written permission to travel unhindered about the parish so long as the bearer shall 'keep the straight or postroad'. That one, in particular, gives me pause for thought, brings back unpleasant memories, but I pass over it, moving back through the pages.

There are many references to the weather. 'This day snowed from the north and covered the earth four inches deep. More snow during last night. I rose about nine o'clock this morning. There is a strong wind from the north east with a very thick snow and drift, which continued until the evening incessantly. I never saw so deep a snow in general, although I have seen much greater weather.' And earlier, much earlier than the lists of mineral specimens, but dating perhaps from his first years in the countryside, there are a few lists of plants and trees acquired for the gardens of his uncle's house. But they seem half-hearted at best, or am I imagining things? Well, perhaps not, for I turn over a leaf and see another list, which includes various interesting specimen trees. Beneath it, he has drawn two broad, dark lines, the pen digging into the paper, and there I see the words, 'Such as William might have appreciated.'

My own name, boldly written down there, comes as a great shock to me, even more perhaps than I would have anticipated. I have to pour myself a small glass of whisky. I sip it slowly and when my heart has stopped racing I go back to the book with shameful eagerness, but there are few other references to me. I find copies of such letters as he wrote on my behalf with his own neat corrections. I find the letter that I wrote at his behest, with similar, more extensive corrections overlying my own scrawl, tethering my flights of fancy to the page like Lunardi's balloon in the cathedral, but I find nothing else either to excite or sadden me. There is, incautiously I'm sure, a quotation from a document which appeared all over Glasgow in 1820, a call for men to 'rouse from that state in which we have sunk for so many years, we are at length compelled from the extremity of our sufferings and the contempt heaped upon our petitions for redress to exert our rights at the hazard of our lives', but it is copied without comment of any sort, as a historical curiosity merely, although it was a call to arms for which many suffered the extreme penalty.

There had been a series of terrible harvests throughout the whole country, the Corn Laws had affected the price of bread and many poor working people were destitute. There had, of course, been riots. Those in authority were so alarmed by the threat of revolution that punishments were severe and repressive. Glasgow had attracted destitute people from the Highlands, from the Western Isles and from Ireland, people who had some fixed idea – or should that be desperate hope? – that a man prepared to work hard might make his fortune here. Well, some did. I can't deny it. But many of them were soon disillusioned. Those who managed to secure employment in the burgeoning mills and manufactories were housed, fed and clothed but they were also physically exhausted in a way that the likes of Sandy Caddas seldom had been, and they were often injured by the new machinery. For those who could not find work, more often through age and infirmity than from any idleness on their part, conditions were even worse. The minister might preach against the vice of slothfulness, but I was aware of a kind of widespread and abject poverty that, even throughout my most difficult times, I could hardly have dreamed of.

So it was that groups of self-styled United Scotsmen sprang up, advocating reform. The pamphlet or proclamation that Thomas had incautiously copied out was in the nature of a call to arms, although most would now judge that it was a false and deliberate provocation on the part of the authorities. It allowed them to charge any who responded to it with high treason. Many Glasgow weavers, unaware of the duplicity, answered the call, among them two young men, Andrew Hardie and John Baird. They were ultimately sentenced to be hanged, beheaded and quartered, their bodies mutilated far beyond the doubtful ministrations of the anatomists, a savagery that even now revolts me.

Two things there are that further disturb me on this quiet afternoon. At the very end of the book, there is a letter, folded and tucked in upon itself and addressed to me. 'For William, to be read after I am gone,' it says. But I have read enough and I put it away for the moment, sliding it into the private drawer at the back of my desk. Besides, I can hear the house coming to life around me, the sound of pots and pans in the kitchen, Jenny's light footsteps on the stair with the pup scurrying in her wake, its toenails slithering and scratching on bare wood. Then, in my haste to close the book, I cause a draught of air, and a few dried leaves float from between the pages and settle on my table. They are skeletons, light as thistledown, all colour and goodness long gone from them, leached away from them by time. At first, I don't know what they are, or where they are from, but I think their presence among the pages of this book is no accident. Suddenly, the sight of them gives me such a pang of sadness, such regret, that it is all I can do to contain it. I want to cry aloud with the pain of it. But, of course, I do no such thing. I scoop them carefully together, fold them among the loose sheets of one of the letters and replace them from whence they came.

CHAPTER SIX

Perpetual Motion

The physic garden was dying. Thomas Brown and I were in agreement about that. When he asked if I would gather specimens for him, the state of the physic garden lay at the heart of his request. In fact, the state of the physic garden lay at the root of all that occurred over those next few years. There had been a slow but steady decline for a long time past and the miserable end of this once beautiful and productive garden was inevitable.

It all began with Alexander Wilson who was made professor of astronomy in 1760, but he was already the official type founder to the university. This was his main trade; astronomy was but a pastime with him. These academic disciplines were often hobbies for men who made their real living elsewhere. Much, I suppose, as Thomas would have said that his real work was medicine, even while he was lecturing in botany. Professor Wilson soon petitioned Faculty for permission to build a type foundry in the grounds, a convenience for himself, since he was about to become resident in the college. Without reference to the gardener – for who ever would think to consult a common gardener on such a matter? – they allowed the foundry to be built on a small plot of land next to the physic garden.

The type foundry was much more important than the physic garden. The university needed printing of all kinds and it was an expensive business, as I now know only too well. I always feel that there is a certain irony in the nature of my later profession: fate winking at me from behind her hand, so to speak. But life does sometimes seem to throw these strange coincidences our way. The first venture must have been very successful because they quickly allowed it to be expanded, and a second foundry was built beside the first. From that time onwards the garden deteriorated a little more each year.

My father had been working as college gardener while I was toddling about the place and getting up to all kinds of mischief. I spent my childhood running about the gardens, paddling in the burns with the other lads, guddling for the wee silvery fish that swam there, or catching them with nets and letting them go again. I was supposed to be helping my father, although perhaps hindering might be a better way of describing it. But he tolerated me and encouraged me in about equal measure. He was a good, God-fearing man, if a little dour.

I remember one time when I was running like the wind on an imaginary errand of my own. Oh I was well away, my feet scarcely seeming to touch the ground. I think I had some vague idea, without knowing anything save that these countries lay beyond the great river and the sea, that I might run to Africa or the Americas or some such place, that my legs might carry me over the water and beyond. I was brought down to earth from this engaging fantasy when I collided with a professor, who was donnering down one of the pathways, deep in thought, his black gown flapping behind him. He was a small man and I ran right into his belly and for all that he was small of stature, his belly wasn't that wee, I'm telling you. They were well fed, those professors.

I fairly bounced off him, and the collision released a cloud of snuff from his waistcoat. The impact took the breath from him and from myself too, and I fell over. I remember sitting there with my arse paining me, and my hands digging into the cold grit of the pathway, looking up at him staggering backwards with his mouth in a round 'o' of astonishment. I don't know which of us was the more surprised. My father had seen the whole thing and he came galloping over with his spade in his hand, brandishing it like a weapon. He was all for giving me a beating there and then, and I think he might have been tempted to use the flat of the spade to do it, so great was his wrath, compounded by embarrassment at his own son for being the perpetrator of such a crime. I expected it and thought my arse would be sore all over again. But the old man wouldn't have it.

'Na, na, na. Leave the wee man alane, Mr Lang,' he said. 'Let him be. He was merely doing what boys do.'

'Aye,' said my father drily. ''Cause naethin but trouble! Will ye let me hammer the deil oot o' him Master? Will ye?'

He was hovering there, wondering whether to drag me to my feet or brush the professor down or what to do next. The professor surprised us both by letting out a wheezy chuckle, like a laugh that has gone rusty from lack of use. As perhaps it had.

'Na, na, Mr Lang,' he said again, shaking his head. 'Leave the lad alane! It's whiles a pleasure to see a wee lad runnin' within the walls of this solemn auld place – and doin' it for the joy of movement!' he added. 'My, my, but it's the closest thing to perpetual motion we'll ever see, for all their wild propositions and experiments with wheels and vast quantities of mercury! Look to the lads, that's what I say! Look to the lads!' and off he went, still chuckling to himself.

I didn't understand a word of what he was saying about perpetual motion and mercury, neither of us did, although I found out all about it later, when I had more books in my possession, and how it was a sort of holy grail among scholars. But he seemed to be in high good humour, as though he had enjoyed the whole incident. While my father was gazing after him in some astonishment, I scrambled to my feet and took myself off before he could change his mind and give me a beating anyway for the good of my immortal soul.

◻ ◻ ◻

My father's predecessor, Sandy Adams, had been a fine gardener who had taught my father all that he knew. Adams's enterprising wife had set up a shop in one of the rooms of their house in Blackfriars Wynd, just outside the college. There, she would make herb ale (said to be a great tonic for the blood) and would sell it, along with all kinds of medicinal herbs, both dried and fresh, and distillations of these herbs, including cinnamon and peppermint as aids to digestion, lime flowers for the apoplexy and vertigo, elder with all kinds of curative properties, as well as common mint and pennyroyal, which, although its oil is very poisonous, will keep the flies away from your larder if you but place a pot by the door in summer. We still do that here in this house. There would, of course, be seasons when the produce of the physic garden was abundant, and I think Adams must have sought and gained the permission of Faculty to use the surplus as he saw fit in the service of his other business.

By the time of Sandy Adams's death, however, the type foundry was already exerting its malign influence and the garden was in decline. My father was a young married man by that time, steady and reliable, but already with considerable experience in the college gardens, and Faculty had no hesitation in appointing him in Sandy Adams's place. When I grew old enough to become a real help to him, my father never tired of telling me that he judged the physic garden to be in a dreadful state. After his appointment as head gardener, he had attempted to remedy it and immediately ordered forty cartloads of dung for dressing the soil. I mind the stink of it yet for I played my part in shovelling it into and out of wheelbarrows. You could shovel all day long and the heaps never seemed to get any smaller or smell any sweeter.

Throughout my childhood, the botanical garden, as my father called the physic garden, became a constant cause for complaint. It was the focus for all his woes, a sad accompaniment to a thousand conversations. I would sometimes be sent to fetch him in when his supper was on the table — invariably broth, bannocks, a little crowdie with salt, since he was a man of regular, even monotonous habits – and more often than not, I would find him foraging among the herbs, studying leaves and blossoms for signs of injury. But you didn't need to look too closely to see that the garden was sickly, leaves yellowing and falling before their time or shrivelled, their growth stunted, so many plants afflicted with some dreadful malaise. It was a vegetable plague and just as deadly as the epidemics that from time to time would ravage the human population of the town.

Professor Hamilton, although I have small recollection of him, must have begun lecturing in botany around that time. He had studied under the celebrated anatomist William Hunter, in London, and so came with a reputation for an interest in dissection, that is, slicing into real, albeit dead human bodies, to find out what goes on beneath the skin. Professor Hamilton was a good friend to my father and when the post of college gardener became vacant, he thought that my father would be a very suitable person to fill it and recommended him to Faculty.

My father and Professor Hamilton used to have frequent discussions about remedies for the problem, much as Thomas Brown and I would later spend many hours wrestling with possible solutions for what was becoming an intractable state of decay. But I doubt if their relationship was anything other than formal. My father was the kind of man who knew his place and would offer due deference to men whom he thought of as his superiors in intellect and station, if not in the eyes of God. All men were equal in the eyes of the Lord. He would say that and I must suppose that he believed it. But although Professor Hamilton was youthful and gracious, he would have expected nothing less than respectful compliance with all his wishes, and my father would have thought this right and proper.

I have seen some of Professor Hamilton's lecture notes. Like many another before him, he was convinced that plants gave off noxious substances by night, vapours inimical to the human frame, a belief which has persisted to this day. My late wife herself believed it, my daughter-in-law still does, and my grand-daughter is not even allowed her posy of wild flowers in her room at night, although I myself remain unconvinced of it, perhaps because I slept in close proximity to all kinds of vegetable matter for a very large part of my youth, and apart from the occasional twinge of rheumatism and a little deterioration of my eyesight, have remained as active and healthy a man as it is possible to be.

Rather, I feel, it is the noxious effluents and vapours of such as the type foundry and numerous other manufactories, which have been established in our town, which destroy our trees and shrubs and flowers, which poison our rivers, which will, I do believe, ultimately destroy us all, for are we not made of the same organic matter? When the plants begin to die, we should look to ourselves and our own health to follow them into putrefaction.

Now, Glasgow is indeed growing and flourishing, but not in any way of which a gardener would approve. Not to put too fine a point on it, the town which, in my youth, was a place of many gardens and still full of the scent of flowers, now stinks to high heaven. The waters that were clear, in which the fish swam, over which the birds flew, are livid and sluggish as they flow through the town. The green leaves turn yellow and sour, even as they unfurl on the tree. The bark that should be silver or brown is as caked with dirt as the stones of this old house and even the statues on some of the new buildings, the gods and angels, already have a thin overlay of soot.

I have to remind myself that I am no longer a gardener and need not care for such things. But old habits die hard, and I do not like the smoke and the fog and the soot, even though I seem miraculously immune to its ill effects. There is nothing left of the dear, green place that Saint Mungo loved, and he would recognise no part of it. The folk of this town grow as stunted as the trees. They are pale and cough a great deal, and I think it was not so in my youth, no matter how hard the privations that the poor had to endure then. But progress must have its way, as my sons are always telling me and perhaps they are right.

My father and Professor Hamilton made strenuous efforts on behalf of the physic garden but they were sadly thwarted by Faculty itself, for a third type foundry was soon built. Everyone knew what the effects of the smoke and fumes would be but nobody was prepared to make a decision to save the garden. And so we limped on in this fashion until Professor Hamilton himself took ill and died. He was then only thirty-two years old. It was in May of 1790 that Professor James Jeffray was appointed to the Chair of Botany and Anatomy in his stead. But in the type foundry next door they were melting lead, tin and antimony. You could taste them on your tongue. Like Canute, and just as helplessly wise, my poor father stood among his plants, head bowed before the onslaught of the incoming industrial tide.

CHAPTER SEVEN

The Anatomist

Professor Jeffray had a fondness for wild experimentation and sensational ventures. His anatomical lectures were well attended because he was a great showman where these were concerned. But as I have said, his botanical lectures, which he was supposed to give in the summer months, were tedious affairs, blighted by his own lack of interest. A little while after the affair of the rat, he proposed that Thomas Brown undertake the lectures in his stead. Brown's first course of lectures was successful and in May of the following year, he was appointed to teach botany in the university 'so long as it shall be expedient'. The arrangement suited both men. But it meant that neither could afford to offend the other too much, although I cannot think that Jeffray was a man whom Thomas would have chosen for a friend, had circumstances been different.

Thomas, I have already begun to describe for you and now that I have made a start, I am afraid I shall write even more of him. Memories jostle my pen: the way he stood, his habit of rocking back and forth on his heels, the way he walked through the gardens with his head in the air, which gave him a haughty look, completely belied by his ability to focus all his attention on you, staring at you with those pale, clever eyes, as though your every word was important to him and for all I know, that may have been the truth. My words may have been important to him at that time.

But I am somewhat at a loss to bring James Jeffray clearly before your sight because my judgement of him is clouded by subsequent events. He died only a few years ago. He had been professor of anatomy for fifty-eight years, and must, in that time, have contributed a prodigious amount to the study of medicine. Back then, as a young man, he was impulsive, intelligent, experimental. All these things. Mercurial. You could never quite pin him down.

There were those who called him a mere sawbones, myself included at that time, albeit in private, and only when I was in conversation with Thomas Brown. There were those who thought he was a genius. Perhaps both judgements were true. Most of his qualities would seem to be admirable. And yet, there was something repellent about his demeanour, or I always found it so. There was something about his ruthlessness in the pursuit of knowledge that gave the observer – this observer, at any rate – a certain feeling of revulsion, like a premonition of dreadful things to come. And yet, he was in no way to blame. In no way at all.

Much later, after all was said and done, something happened that may serve to explain both Jeffrey's genius and my misgivings. You will no doubt have heard the tale. I was not there. Oh no. I was certainly not there. And somehow, I do not think that Thomas would have been there either. Not by then. He would have learned his lesson all too well by then I think, and he had even resigned as lecturer in botany a couple of years earlier. But Professor Jeffray's courses in anatomy were still exceedingly popular. The numbers who enrolled annually were sometimes as many as two hundred. And as with botany, samples were required. But these were not things that could be gathered by young lads venturing into the countryside on fine days in June. Jeffray needed human specimens. And he needed them to be dead. Not surprisingly, there was some difficulty in obtaining subjects for demonstration. Executed criminals were fair game, but there were few such in Glasgow at that time. I would never have called this a law-abiding town, but murder was still something of a rarity.

However, in 1818, one Matthew Clydesdale, a weaver from Airdrie, was arrested and charged with murdering an old man in a fit of drunken violence. I suppose Clydesdale was neither better nor worse than many a working man who indulges a little too freely and loses his temper, but in this case the results were tragic. Clydesdale was a big man, and his much older victim could not defend himself. He fell down, banged his head on a flagstone and died. Clydesdale was brought to trial in Glasgow, found guilty of a murder, which was never, I think, his intention, and sentenced to be hung, with the additional judgement that his body was to be anatomised afterwards, a slightly more merciful version of the old, barbarous custom of hanging, drawing and quartering which was generally meted out to Scottish patriots by their neighbours, and latterly to young men such as Andrew Hardie and John Baird, tricked into acts of treason. There had not been a public execution, or indeed any execution for murder, in Glasgow for ten years. As I said, this is by no means a law-abiding town, but murder was still enough of a rarity to be cause for comment, speculation, curiosity. It was by no means the only offence for which the penalty was death. Robbery was also a capital offence, but the additional sentence of being sent to the anatomists was generally the prerogative of foul murderers. Unless one of the professors tipped the wink to the hangman, and there were no close relatives with a prior claim on the body, relatives moreover who were ready to defend it from those who might come to dig it up again in the night. There was a highly lucrative trade in resurrected bodies at that time, certainly enough to encourage a few unscrupulous individuals to cut out the inconvenience of natural death and burial and facilitate the provision of fresh bodies themselves.

Many people came to watch the execution that late autumn day. It was a regular day's entertainment. I remember the crowds, although I myself kept well away from the jail square and the Saltmarket where the gallows had been erected in front of the brand new High Court building. There was ale for sale and spirits and all kinds of comestibles and sweetmeats. It was a grand

43

spectacle, so people told me afterwards. The children loved it, and if it taught them a lesson in good behaviour, so much the better. One mother actually said that to her ragged brood within my hearing as she herded them towards the High Court! The authorities even had to post soldiers by the timber footbridge over the river, lest the crowds overwhelm it with their numbers and caused a catastrophe as they struggled to get a better view of proceedings. More fodder for the anatomists I suppose.

There were two hangings that day. A youngster called Simon Ross was hanged for theft, and I believe the poor lad took a long time to die, twitching and struggling on the rope, a truly dreadful procedure to behold. Clydesdale's end was much quicker. He was by far the bigger man and the weight of his body must have pulled him down and broken his neck and hastened his end, thank-God. Once they had been pronounced dead, Clydesdale was taken down, placed in a cart and trundled up the Saltmarket, across Trongate and into the High Street, to the university college. Poor young Ross was handed over to his grieving relatives and buried somewhere in the Ramshorn graveyard, so the anatomists did not get their hands on him then, and his grave was well guarded, so that they would not get their hands on him afterwards, either. The resurrection men who were hard at work procuring corpses for scholars would have been sorely disappointed.

□ □ □

The anatomy theatre was very crowded. I suppose that some who had watched the execution came to watch the dissection. We are wont to talk of nature red in tooth and claw, but there are few creatures of the natural world so lacking in sympathy for the fellow members of their own species as human beings. The dog will fight his enemies to the death, but, on the whole, will spare the lesser canine who submits to him. Even rooks will mob the hunting hawk to protect their own kind. The casualties of the overcrowded rookery are few, and then only when the young tumble from the nest. We are more like insects, I think, but even they eat because they must and that for the greater good.

The anatomists who received the body of the unfortunate Clydesdale were Jeffray and Doctor Andrew Ure, who seemed to have a touching not to say daft faith in the possibility that he really could reanimate a dead body and bring it back to life. James Jeffray, I'm absolutely sure, held no such illusion. He was no fool but he was quite prepared to experiment with galvanisation – the application of the mysterious current to the corpse – in an effort to observe the effects of such stimulation on the human anatomy.

One of the customers at our bookshop, Hugh Brodie, a Glasgow watchmaker who had a somewhat unlikely passion for the works of Horace Walpole and Ann Radcliffe, that is, for gloomy castles and distressed damsels and mysterious murders, came to the shop specifically to tell me all about it. I suppose it fed his taste for the bizarre. When I pointed out that reanimating a murderer might be something less than advisable, he became quite angry with me.

'There's no need to tak' that tone wi' me!' he said, as though I had deliberately affronted him.

'What would they have done if he had lived?' I asked, amicably enough. 'Would they perhaps have hung him all over again, do you think? And what would the legal position have been in such a case? Would it have been permissible?'

He departed, muttering and shaking his head, and that was a customer we had lost, but I found I didn't care. Besides, the question was not such a foolish one after all, for I later learned that Ure had attempted to answer it for me.

'This event, however little desirable with a murderer, and perhaps contrary to the law, would yet have been pardonable in one instance, as it would have been highly honourable and useful to science,' were his exact words.

Useful to science. Ah yes. How many execrable acts have been justified with those glib words? How many will yet be justified? But I repeat that I do not think that Jeffray anticipated any such result.

The way it went was this. The men first dissected the body. There was no flow of blood. Clydesdale was well and truly dead. But they wished to expose areas where galvanisation might be applied. The connecting rods were fixed to heel and spinal cord whereupon Clydesdale's knee flexed so violently that he appeared to kick one of the assistants in the ribs, thus causing the man almost to fall over, in a somewhat ironic recreation of the actions that had brought the weaver to this pass in the first place.

Then they connected the rods to what they called the phrenic nerve and the diaphragm. Ure thought to restore breathing to the corpse and, indeed, according to written reports at the time, the 'chest heaved and fell. The belly was protruded and again collapsed.'

Tiring of this, at last, with the corpse showing no signs whatsoever of reviving permanently, they applied the current to the forehead and the heel, encompassing the whole man, as warlocks are said to do when they make their followers swear allegiance to Satan. Then they varied the voltage.

Expressions of all kinds appeared to flit across the murderer's features in a terrible imitation of life. He seemed, by turns, enraged, horrified, despairing, amused and desperate. It was at this point, I believe, that several of the spectators turned sick and were forced to leave the theatre in order to vomit in the street outside. One gentleman fainted and had to be carried out. However, some of the students, of a more sanguine disposition, were distinctly heard to clap their hands, whistle and cheer, as such young gentlemen invariably will. The corpse remained resolutely dead, although to make doubly sure, Jeffray despatched him again with a scalpel, slicing right into his neck and almost decapitating the unfortunate weaver in the process.

Clydesdale's corpse was eventually released to his wife. She, poor woman, had given birth to a son less than a month before the assault that was to result in her husband's execution. I do not know where the body was buried, although executed murderers were usually laid to rest under the courtyard of the High Court building, with the weight of the forces of law and order pressing down upon them, presumably to stop their restless ghosts from troubling the populace at large.

There can have been few murderers, however, who proved to be so resolutely, finally, unarguably dead as Clydesdale. Where galvanisation and the combined skills of two professors of anatomy had failed, even the saviour himself might have faltered, Lazarus notwithstanding. But I am an old man and must be allowed my fun, if fun it can be called. A gruesome joke, certainly. And I tell this tale only to bring Jeffray before your eyes. He was this kind of man, you see, quite ruthless in the pursuit of learning. The great mass of people may well approve of him and find his actions both explicable and even praiseworthy. It is universally accepted that the pursuit of knowledge is a very fine thing. And Clydesdale was, after all, a common murderer.

□ □ □

All of that came later and at the time I knew only that I found Jeffray and his obsession with anatomy disturbing. During the years when we were friends, Thomas would sometimes say to me that observing the way the human body worked was like seeing a machine, a complicated machine, where everything was dependent upon everything else.

'So much sickness and misery,' he would say, 'is caused because the machine that we call our body breaks down. If we could only repair that machine, William! If we knew how these things worked. If we could effect adequate repairs, then so many lives might be saved, so much misery avoided!'

It was a sign of the times. There was a positive rage for machinery, for mechanisms that worked and could be fine tuned and repaired when they broke down. It was one reason why the pursuit of perpetual motion was so much in vogue. The type foundry was one such mechanism that was admirably suited to its purpose. But the problem for the new manufacturers was so often that their human operatives broke down beyond hope of repair, crushed, exhausted, sickly as the plants in my garden and certainly far more ill nourished.

When Thomas said to me that it would be a blessing if one could learn how to repair the human body, I could not help but agree with him. He respected Professor Jeffray well enough. To be sure, he would sometimes say, 'Oh, Jeffray is such a showman!' and there would be a slight air of disapproval even from him. Yet there was always the implied 'but' in such remarks. 'But the work he does is worthwhile. But he is a fine surgeon. But anatomy is the way of the future.'

I believe now, with the benefit of all too many years of hindsight, that there was a connection between the aspirations of the new manufacturers and the desire to learn how to mend the human body in the abstract. And I doubt if there was anything very philanthropic about it. It was, rather, a matter of good business sense. Machines might run endlessly with the application of a little oil, a small adjustment here or there, so why not people? The poor factory weans could work fourteen hours a day, but those who did the full stretch soon fell ill, crippled by calamitous fatigue as much as by the constant collision of wood and metal with poorly formed bones. If machines could be fixed, then so could people. Rest and nourishment were costly alternatives. Surgery might come cheaper. This was their motivation, or so I believed and still continue to believe, although I cannot accuse everyone of an equal cynicism. And I cannot accuse my friend Thomas Brown of desiring anything but the general good of mankind, although for a long time I blamed him, ferociously and bitterly.

By the time Jeffray was performing his experiments with the reanimation of corpses, I had learned other, more subtle and yet more terrible lessons. And so had Thomas Brown. Which serves to explain why neither of us wished to witness the galvanisation of Matthew Clydesdale. His was, as it turns out, the last body to be sent for public dissection, the authorities having a little more compassion, or perhaps a little more distaste for the subject, than either of the distinguished medical men involved.

CHAPTER EIGHT

My Father and My Family

One way and another, the turn of the century was a terrible time in Glasgow. There had been shortages of even the most basic foods, oatmeal and potatoes, and there had been riots in the town, since when folk can barely afford to eat, they become weak but they also become desperate on behalf of their children. Food may have been in short supply but alcohol was freely available. A proliferation of 'tippling houses' gave working men a respite from all the misery. But when desperate folk have a drink inside them, the least thing will set them off, like a spark on tinder-dry moorland. Troops had been called in to disperse the crowds and had behaved with predictable brutality. Many arrests were made and people were transported to the colonies.

My family and I were by no means as badly off as some. We had the produce of the gardens to sustain us and my father had had the foresight to plant extra vegetables in our own cottage garden, but all the same, times were difficult. He had been working hard and the weather was dreich and drear as it so often is in January, that most difficult of months when the sun hardly seems to rise before it is setting again. He had been employed in taking down the old stone bridge over the Molendinar Burn, because it was becoming dangerous. The work was exhausting. I know because I helped him with it, but he would not rest. The payment was to be some twelve guineas, which was a great sum of money to us.

'It is a fine opportunity!' he said to my mother. 'Enough to see us through the rest of the winter. We'll put it by and only use it when we have to.'

It was in his nature to over-exert himself. He never could bring himself to believe that anyone else could do a job as well as if not better than himself. Before that, we had been employed in laying out new walks in the garden, carting and spreading gravel to improve the pathways, so that the scholars and professors might take the air when the weather improved. But when we began work on the bridge, the wind was cold and the sleety rain was intense. I remember looking at my father's blue lips and noticing the tremor in his legs and thinking that he did not look as he should.

He insisted on carrying on with the work, but when I paused for breath, I saw that he was bent double, clutching at his chest and panting for breath. He leaned on me and I managed to half drag, half carry him back to the house. We got him into the box bed in the wall, the two of us, my mother pulling off his muddy trousers, for he was too weak and in too much pain to manage it for himself. I looked at his legs, which seemed very spindly, and the hair on top of his bowed head, which was thinning, showing the shiny pink scalp beneath, and wondered at myself for not noticing how frail he had become. My mother stroked his head, much as she would caress her children, and I saw that her hand trembled.

'Will I fetch Doctor Brown?' I asked.

Afterwards, I realised that I should just have gone for him anyway, but my mother hesitated. I know he would have come at my request. Later, he was angry that I had not sought him out there and then.

'Why did you not come for me instantly?' he asked. 'There might have been something I could have done! You must know me well enough by now, William, to be sure that I would have come at your request.'

But when my father came to himself a little, he would have none of it. He said we could not afford doctors, what were the likes of us doing contemplating calling them in and when I said that I did not think we would have to pay Thomas Brown, who had always treated me kindly, he frowned and said he would rather die than take charity from any man. Which is what he did, a few days later, when the pains returned with even more ferocity. My mother, who had been swithering, as she invariably did, between her own sensible inclinations and obedience to her husband, blamed herself.

But how like him to want to keep going until the end of a particular job. 'Never leave work half done,' he would tell me. The maxim has stayed with me and yet I haven't always followed it. I think now, there are times when it is better to leave a little to be done another day. Which is one of the good things that Thomas taught me.

'Don't kill yourself, William,' he would say, with a smile. 'You'll get twice as much done if you don't rush at things but take your ease now and then.'

At that time, I believed everything my father told me, and would work as though some demon were behind me, urging me on, which was always the way of it with him. Truly, the demon was himself. I have seen it since in many men, and often in men more than women. Women work because they must, but they seem to know how to ration their energies and when they lose a little of their health and strength, they blame it on time, not on others. They may lose their strength but they do not lose themselves in the process. Men grow old and are by no means as full of energy as they once were. They seem to lose something of themselves and blame it on those around them. It is as though their only value is in what they do or what they once did, and not in what they think or what they might have achieved within the span of their years.

I have tried very hard not to make that mistake. I try to value what I have made of my life and to give myself due credit for my achievements. I loved my wife to the end. I love my sons, although it is not in the nature of Scotsmen to say so very often. I love all my grandchildren and that is permissible. We are by no means so embarrassed by such an admission. But I will also confess that I love none of the others quite as much as I love my little lass with the flaxen hair and that, I have come to realise, is for reasons over and beyond herself, although she is as sunny-natured a child as you could wish to find.

❑ ❑ ❑

While Faculty cogitated about replacing my father, I found myself supervising the completion of various pieces of work that he had begun, which meant that at least some of his payment could come to me and could be handed on to my mother, for the benefit of my brothers and sisters. But all the same there were many bills to be met, including his funeral expenses.

I was strong and confident, for sure, but too young to know how little I really knew. And as the eldest son, I found myself in the unenviable position of having to support my widowed mother and my younger siblings. My poor mother, who had always seemed to expect something of the sort, a born pessimist I think, made it clear that she was relying on me to fill my father's exceedingly muddy boots when it came to providing for the family.

Our worries were so acute because there were so many of us. While my father was alive, I had not realised just how difficult it was to feed and clothe so many. I had been very ignorant, and he had been content to shield me somewhat from the harsh realities of his life. But when he was gone, I soon came to understand why he had been irritable and morose on occasions. My only wonder was that he had remained so cheerful for the most part, so optimistic, so hopeful for some unspecified future prosperity. I found myself loving and honouring him more in death than I had in life, and regretting that I had not been able to tell him so.

There were eight of us, of whom I was the eldest – a great number to provide for at any time, let alone one of general poverty and deprivation. My younger sister, Bessie, barely fifteen years old, was already in service at the house of one of the more wealthy college professors in the town. He was a great man with a number of business interests that were far from scholarly, but respectable enough. She was employed as the scullery maid, which means she was a skivvy, responsible for everything from raking out the ashes in choking clouds and lighting the fires in the morning, to emptying the chanties from under the beds. Her first job after lighting the kitchen fire and setting the porridge pot on top of it, so she told me, was to wake the cook, which was no easy task, given that Mistress MacTaggart was fond of a dram or two before bed. Thereafter her days were as long and full and quite as exhausting as my own. She must undertake everything from gutting the breakfast fish to peeling potatoes, with her hands made red raw by the icy water, from scrubbing the kitchen table until the wood turned white to cleaning the pots and pans, but at least she was well fed and she had a roof over her head, so that was a relief to all of us. She was a good-natured lassie and we loved her dearly, but my mother and I were relieved that she, at least, was off our hands.

Next came the twins, twelve-year-old Jean and Susanna, 'great big lumps of lassies' my mother used to call them, which drove them wild. They were old enough to do some sewing, which kept them occupied and brought in a few pence each week, although they lacked both skill and concentration, as my mother also used to say, lamenting their awkwardness. More often than not she had to launder their work when they were finished, simmering it with soap in the copper, since it was so grubby and sticky from their fingers, and then pressing it with a smoothing iron. But they could stitch a plain seam, and that was useful. Susanna's eyesight was not good, which was some excuse for her clumsiness. Jean was careless and a wee thing selfish. She liked animals and was always to be found playing with a mischief of kittens under the table, or coaxing the fox terrier that belonged to one of the professors into our garden with bits of cheese, for which it had a passion.

'I wouldn't care,' said my mother, 'but we can ill spare the cheese. She feeds it enough to make a good supper for herself and her sister. And she is normally so greedy, but that dog must take precedence!'

It was true that what they lacked in concentration they made up in appetite. They would have eaten us out of house and home. My father always said as much, although he never begrudged them a mouthful of bread or a cup of milk. But when times were hard, as they were now that my father was gone, they had to make do with less, and 'we're starving' was their constant complaint. But they were good humoured withall, and always laughing.

I had, besides my sisters, Bessie, Jean and Susanna, three younger brothers, James, John and Robert. James was old enough to do his bit about the gardens. Nine years old and he could wield a spade with the best of them. He was wiry but very thin and the sight of his spindly shoulders bent over the spade would – so my mother sometimes said – make her heart ache for him. Mine too, although I wouldn't admit as much. She would try to feed him up, putting extra bread on his plate, an extra spoonful of porridge in his bowl. But he was stronger than we realised. My father had been keen to see him schooled, as I myself had been taught to read and write, but James was a poor scholar at the best of times, and his learning had been limited to the occasional lesson from the old dominie who had once taught me, and who would try to wrestle words and numbers into his bullet head for a few pennies, when my father could spare them.

Of the two youngest, John was but four years old when my father died, and Rab was a little lad of two, just toddling about, both of them too young to do much more than I had at the same age, although I found employment for Johnnie, who was something of a favourite with me, in scaring the birds, whenever I had planted seeds in the garden.

Rab was the runt of the litter. He did nothing but cling to my mother's skirts and hinder her from doing her work. He was a sickly soul, with a terrible cough, day and night, and with the snotters always hanging into his mouth, green candles my mother called them, dripping down from his poor nose. She worried about him, but then we all did. When food was scarce, she would go without herself so that he could eat. He liked to nibble the bread and sip the broth off her dish, but his appetite was small, so it was no great hardship. And for all that he was sickly, he was mostly uncomplaining, except when the earache beset him. Those twin organs would become so inflamed that he had trouble hearing and he would keep us all awake at nights, sobbing, 'Mammy, mammy, my ears are that sair!' On the whole, though, Rab was a brave wee boy and Johnnie made much more of a fuss over the least little upset. When he was stung by nettles in the garden or when he accidentally dropped a rock on his toes while he was trying to help me, you could have heard his wails and cries all over the college.

Most tragic of all, my mother was heavily pregnant with her eighth child when my father died. He never lived to see the baby, named Janet, and she did not survive him by many months, so my mother felt herself doubly cursed. For my part, I could not help the uneasy sense that the infant would have been just one more mouth for me to feed. I cannot say I was relieved at her death. I mind even yet her waxy face on the day she died, like a spent candle end, and my mother's sobbing, low and persistent, for night after night, but all the same, I cannot deny that it was easier to provide for seven than for eight.

◻ ◻ ◻

After Janet died, my mother was very low in spirits. 'We shall starve, William,' she kept saying. 'Starve or freeze! Starve and freeze.'

I didn't think we would freeze; there was an abundance of dead timber in the gardens, and it was there for the taking. But money for food was another matter, and she was right. I had been thrust into my father's shoes with scant experience, and my head fairly buzzed with wondering how year after year he had managed to bring in the income that had kept our little ship afloat. I began to understand his weariness and how he had squeezed every last ounce of productive time out of his days. Once the money from the work on the Molendinar bridge was gone, we would barely have enough to keep body and soul together, never mind to give the younger children a modicum of education.

At last, having racked my brains for ideas, I recollected Sandy Adams, the old gardener, and his wife's successful apothecary venture. I suggested that we might follow their example, rent a front room in one of the properties adjacent to the university and set up our own apothecary business there. I thought that my mother could run it, much as Mistress Adams had assisted her husband.

My poor mother, however, was no Mistress Adams. She was so bemused by the sudden death of my father that she could say nothing but, 'if you say so, son!' which was certainly the wrong answer, because I knew as much about the business of being an apothecary as I knew about the subject of women, love and marriage in those days, and that was precious little. But then, we are all full of wild and unrealistic aspirations at that time of life. It would be a poor world if the young did not have their dreams. Anything seemed possible to me, and I was too foolish to realise that my mother was still stunned by her twin bereavements.

I mourned my father with a sorrow that frequently took me by surprise, took the breath from me. Sometimes when I was digging in the garden, I would fancy that he was standing just behind me. I would turn round, expecting to see him, and find nothing but empty air where he should have been.

'Put your back into it, son,' he would have said. I could almost hear him say it. Then the grief that dogged me would seize me by the throat, and I could feel the tears start behind my eyes.

I felt that the most fitting tribute to his memory would be for me to make the best of things for his widow and my brothers and sisters. Pursuing my dream of financial independence for all of us, I forged on with the apothecary plan. When a moneylender came to our door, I let myself be persuaded into borrowing a sum of five pounds, to lay down as rent on the proposed apothecary shop, to fit it out and buy in some supplies. They have an uncanny ability to sniff out need, and this man had, no doubt, heard of my father's untimely death.

'Young man,' he said. 'You'll not regret it. And I wish you every success with your new venture!' he added, as he walked away, no doubt sniggering up his sleeve at my naivety.

It was not a clever move. I was very foolish. I thought I knew everything about life, but I had not the smallest measure of wisdom. Not at that time.

CHAPTER NINE

The Water of Life

After the death of my father and my infant sister, I threw myself into the work that had killed him with renewed vigour, out of a sort of defiance against fate itself. I moved earth, cleaned out the Molendinar, took down the old stone bridge and did some work on the new one. There was rebuilding and planting up of the banks of the burn to be done with such plants as would spread and bring some stability. I hoped that if I could convince the authorities of my capabilities, then – although I was only eighteen years old – they might agree to make me gardener in his stead.

It was at about this time that Thomas Brown singled me out for his particular friendship. He had always been disposed to be kindly to me. I had begun to collect specimens for him during the previous spring and summer. But now I saw a very great deal of him as he walked about the gardens, even at times when the weather was particularly inclement. He didn't seem to mind. There were days when, had I not been engaged on all kinds of renovations, hefting stones like a convict, I would most certainly have been indoors, toasting my toes beside the fire, but Thomas seemed impervious to cold, rain, sleet or even the occasional flurry of snow.

He was a very striking man. He would stride along with the air of having his head in the clouds. He had a rather stern face, which belied his essential good nature. He had curly hair,

which he tied back with a ribbon, and grey eyes that he sometimes felt the need to strengthen with a pair of round spectacles
that sat somewhat incongruously on his nose. He was slender,
but gave the impression of a certain vigour and capability. His
hands, when you looked more closely at them, were something
like the hands of a working man: strong and a wee thing calloused and freckled. He was nothing like most of the professors who would wander about the college gardens, deep in
scholarly thoughts, as though they were not quite of this world.
Nothing like the professor who had called me a perpetual
motion machine, and excused me a beating because of it. There
was a fey look about some of them. I thought they hardly even
noticed me but it was not in the way the nabbery would deliberately ignore you because you were one of the lower orders.
No, it was more that their minds were so wholly elsewhere
that they saw nothing: not the young scholars who regularly
created mayhem among the trees and flowers, not us gardeners
who were always trying to curb their excesses without seeming
to insult them, not even the sight of a pretty maid would have
disturbed them in the middle of their cogitations. Except that
Thomas Brown was nothing like that. You got the feeling that
Thomas noticed everything.

He always passed the time of day with me and stopped to watch
me working, but there came an afternoon when there was a woeful,
thin sleet, borne on a snell wind which battered it into our frozen
faces, and on that day, he watched for a while and passed a few pleasantries, and then he came up to me and offered me a silver flask.

'Here,' he said, holding it out to me.

'What's this?'

I squinted up at him, my face stinging, my eyes watering. It was
such an extraordinary occurrence that I thought he wanted me to
do something for him, that he was giving me orders of some kind.
I didn't realise at first that he was actually giving me his flask.

'Drink it and see!' he said.

I put the flask to my numb lips and swallowed. I remember the intense shock of it to this very day. There was an explosion of peat smoke, spring water, seaweed and honeysuckle in my mouth – my first taste of a good whisky from the islands.

He grinned at me and nodded. 'Go on. Take another swig. It'll put a bit of life in you. Colour in your cheeks. You look so cold, William.'

'That's because I *am* cold. But this is very good.'

'Oh I know.'

'Where does it come from?'

'Ask no questions and you'll be told no lies.' He sat down on a low wall, close beside where I was working in all the sleet, huddled his blue wool coat around him and took a swig from the flask himself. It struck me that he didn't even wipe the bottle before he put it to his lips and that small gesture of complicity touched me.

'Actually,' he continued, 'one of my students is island born. He comes from the Isle of Islay, out in the west, and he brings this elixir to Glasgow with him. To remind himself of home, I expect. He calls it the water of life. "Can I give you a wee sensation of the water of life, Doctor Brown?" he said to me, once. The next time he went home he brought me rather more than a sensation. Afterwards, I found out that the name of his house means the Place of the Still in his own highland tongue.'

Thomas Brown was so free and easy with me that it was impossible to feel embarrassed with him and yet it was not an everyday occurrence for one of the professors to be sitting on a wall conversing with a gardener and sharing a drink with him. No, it was not an everyday occurrence at all.

'Tell me,' he said. 'William. I may call you William?'

'Aye. That's my name.' In my surprise, I think I must have spoken brusquely, but he ignored my rudeness.

'And you must call me Thomas. Will you do that?'

'If that's what you wish.'

'I do. I was very sorry to hear about your father. You should have sent for me when he fell ill.'

'I would have, but when he came to himself he would have none of it, and we didn't dare disobey him.'

'It must have been a great shock for you and your mother.'

'It was a great shock for all of us. He was a good man.'

'And a fine gardener.'

'Aye, he was that too.'

He stood up briefly and held out his hand to me. I shook hands with him in return, aware that my own were very grimy, as they had been the first time we met, when I was a lad of sixteen. Once again, he didn't appear to notice, or to mind if he did.

Then he offered me the flask again and when I had finished, he took another pull for himself. The spirit was coursing through my blood like a spell, warming my limbs, and making my head swim. I was not at all used to strong drink. My mother wouldn't have it in the house for any save medicinal purposes. Perhaps it was the spirit which made me suddenly so free and easy with him, so lacking in my habitual diffidence.

'A drop of that every day would banish the winter for sure,' I told him. 'And how are things with you, sir?' I added, feeling that some politeness was expected of me.

'Things are going very well indeed,' he said.

I nodded. I knew all about him. The students loved him. I would hear them complaining and grumbling about this or that professor, but of Thomas Brown, after his last series of lectures, I had heard nought but good.

'I think at least some of my success is down to you and your knowledge in the field,' he continued. 'Tell me, William, have they offered you the position of college gardener yet?'

I was surprised that he even knew of my situation.

'No. Not yet. I've been working as hard as I can, completing all the work that my father started, but they haven't made up their minds yet.'

'Well they should. They won't find another man here with such knowledge.'

'I'm only completing what my father began, sir.'

'Maybe I can write to them on your behalf.'

'Would you do that?'

'Aye. I don't see why not. Though it would be better if I per-suaded Jeffray to do it instead. He has far more influence than I do. I'll see what he says.'

'Thank-you, sir.'

'Don't *sir* me so much. Thomas. My name is Thomas just. And that's what you must call me. But tell me, what would you do if you had a free hand here?'

I didn't hesitate. 'Plant more trees,' I said. I stood upright and eased my aching back. The sleety rain had stopped and a blink of watery, winter sunlight was filtering into the garden. He smiled at me. He had a smile that would have raised the dead. Even, I think, Matthew Clydesdale.

'Ah,' he said. 'A man after my own heart then?'

'How come?'

'A man who loves trees as much as I do.' He swept his arm around about, encompassing the expanse of the college garden. 'Not enough planting, Thomas. We could remedy that, between us. You and me. What would you say to placing a big order for trees? A grand new planting. Where would you go for them?'

'McAslan and Austin,' I said, without hesitation. They were nurserymen and the best in town. They knew their business. That was what my father had always said and he had been right.

'Yes. I know them. My father – when he built the new house – he bought a fine selection of trees from them. And what would you buy, William?'

'What would I buy? What would I *not* buy, given a free hand? A huge variety. New kinds of trees as well. I mean new for this garden. My father was a conventional man in many ways, as were they all, all those old gardeners. Limes, beeches, elms, poplars and thorns. He saw no further than that. They are fine trees in their way ...'

'But you would have it different?'

'Oh yes. Those and more. I love trees. But I think I would purchase something that might grow more quickly, as well as all of those.'

'Such as?'

'Flowering cherries for the springtime, maybe the guilderose as well and larches.'

'Oh aye, there would have to be larches. Are you fond of larches, William?'

'I love the larch and the way it moves! The way it sways and the beauty of it even in the winter. And the shapes it makes in the sky.'

'It seems you are a poet when it comes to trees, William!' He was looking at me with a hint of a smile at my enthusiasm, but I could see that he was not mocking me, although I could not read his expression. 'And what more?' he asked.

'Weeping willows and hollies. I think we need more hollies here.'

'But they are not swift growing.'

'No. But the birds are glad of them in winter. And besides, they brighten the place up at a dreich time of year.'

'Ah!' he nodded, understanding. 'And you don't mind the birds taking shelter in the garden, William?'

'No. They rid the place of so many unwanted visitors, slugs and snails and the like, that I rather think they should be encouraged. It was my father's opinion too, although there were many who disagreed with him.'

'Go on. What else? Have you anything more exotic in mind?'

'Why yes. I would plant dogwood, the service tree, and the turkey oak. But there are other trees and shrubs from the Americas which I have seen in the nursery at McAslan and Austin. Trees to make your mouth water. The wayfaring tree that some call the hobblebush is so beautiful. And the sugar maple and the cockspur thorn.'

'You know your trees it seems. And all their magical names.'

'I know my plants too, but I love trees best of all growing things. Especially those that we know will long outlast us. I like the idea of living things that were here for many hundreds of years before us and will be here for many hundreds of years after.'

It has often been my thought that there is a kind of immortality in the planting of trees, and I may have had an inkling of that sort even then, although I couldn't have put it into so many words for him on that day.

He drew out the flask again and we took another dram, the two of us. There were three professors walking by, deep in conversation, three corbies all dressed in black, and they cast a suspicious, sideways glance at us but Thomas ignored them. Who could blame them for their curiosity? It was an uncommon sight, not just that a professor and a gardener should be speaking together on equal terms but that they should be sharing a nip of whisky from a flask. That was unheard of.

He said, 'There is a yew, at Fortingall near Aberfeldy. I have seen it, William, and it is – to me, at any rate – one of the great wonders of the world. It is as old, they say, as Jesus Christ himself, and it looks it too. They have propped it up, much as one must support a venerable old man. And there are limbs on it that seem more stone than bark. More petrified than living tissue. I was never so taken with anything in my life. I could only think what memories must lie buried deep within every tiny part of it, if one could only find a way of accessing them, but perhaps in doing so one would only kill the tree and that would be unthinkable.'

'Aye it would.'

'I should like for you to see it some day. I think you would feel the same.'

'I think I would.'

▫ ▫ ▫

I have never yet seen that tree, although I have seen two of them in the gardens of Kelburn Castle, down in Ayrshire, which are said to be very old. But not as ancient as the Fortingall Yew. In fact, this is the first time I have thought about it in many a long year. It occurs to me to wonder if – old and venerable as I am myself, a living fossil of times past – I might yet be able to make the journey north and view it. It would be a difficult journey to be sure, but I am still fit and well for my age, and one of my sons might be persuaded to accompany me. I think it would be a pilgrimage of sorts, but would I be doing it for myself or for Thomas? I can't say.

'How many trees do you think it would take to renew this sorry place?' Thomas asked.

'The physic garden or the whole garden?'

'Oh, the whole garden, for I fear the physic garden may already be beyond redemption! Don't you agree with me?'

'It may be so. Well then, it would need some twelve dozen of trees and flowering shrubs to make a difference. So much money. But it would make a difference you know. And I think the professors would be glad to see them.'

'It would gladden my heart, certainly. I'll tell you what, William,' he said, getting to his feet, 'Will you make out an order for McAslan and Austin? Can you do that?'

I thought he was asking me did I have the skill of writing again. I bridled with indignation and said, 'Sir, of course. You know that I learned reading and writing when I was a lad. My father made sure of it. And when you give me a list of plants, do I not read it as well as any scholar?'

'I don't doubt it.' He smiled at me again. 'And will you stop "sirring" me, man? I was not enquiring about the measure of your learning. I only meant are you brave enough to write down all that you would want to plant here, no matter what the cost?'

'It would give me pleasure to imagine it, even if they deny me at the last.'

'Then do it. Make an order and cost it out fully and let me have it. I'll see if I can get Jeffray to take it to Faculty on your behalf. He owes me something, after all, for I have done him a great favour by taking the botanical lectures off his hands. And if they don't allow all that you wish, but give you the gardener's position instead, I'll pay for the trees out of my own pocket. There now!'

I think I must have stood there with plain astonishment on my face.

He smiled at me, his face full of kindness, slipped the flask back into his pocket and went on his way, whistling a cheerful air.

I made out that first order, and the authorities allowed it. I made out a supplementary order in late January and again in February. They allowed all of them. God knows how Thomas managed it, but I believe it was only down to him. He was a man – as my mother put it – who could charm the birds out of the trees if he so wished.

Over the winter I made a gravel walk from the new bridge to the Observatory House, and planted up trees throughout the college garden. I worked with a will, and the result of all this was that I took up my appointment as gardener, in my father's place, at Candlemas of 1801, which was a great relief to all of us at home, in that we would continue to have a roof over our heads and something of the wherewithal to keep us in food and fuel.

I still don't know what magic Thomas worked on Faculty on that occasion. But I think that he must have enlisted Jeffray's aid. Because Professor Jeffray was already a man of considerable influence. He liked Thomas very much but what is more to the point, he needed Thomas. Without him, he would have to return to lecturing in his loathed botany. However it was, I became college gardener and was able to go to McAslan and Austin and select my trees, although the old man there treated me like a boy still. Oh he called me Mister Lang, right enough, but you could see him thinking, 'He isnae a patch on his faither. He's no hauf the gairdner his faither wis. I kent his faither, and he's no the same man at a'.'

All the same, he must have known that my father would never have ordered the likes of the wayfaring tree from him. It is sometimes called the hobblebush, *Viburnum alnifolium*, with the most elegant white flowers you ever did see. We planted that and the cockspur thorn, which has glossy leaves and pretty flowers and even prettier berries. And we established the sugar maple, which I think was always my favourite, Thomas's favourite tree too, tall and fine and beautiful, like an autumn sun shining on a chilly day.

CHAPTER TEN

Gathering In

When spring came round, and when the new planting was done, Thomas again asked me if I might find the time to go out and about into the surrounding countryside and gather specimens for the students.

'I know how busy you are, William,' he told me. 'But it would be such a favour to me, if you could oblige me in this. And there is nobody I would trust quite as much as yourself in this matter.'

The truth was that I had no free time whatsoever for such a venture and no business to be doing it. Between the garden and the apothecary business, which was already failing, indeed which could never truly be said to have got started, I needed all the time I had for myself and my work. But I could not bring myself to deny him. He was that kind of man, so generous, so persuasive, that you wanted to please him. And besides, I think I wanted to do it for myself. There was that about it that satisfied something in me, something over and beyond the daily grind of digging and hoeing, of weeding and pruning. It was a pleasure of the mind as well as the body: to be entrusted with seeking out certain plants, to be using all my skills to find them and, once found, to preserve them for him. But he surprised me even more by his next suggestion.

'Why don't you come to my lectures?' he asked.

'How could I attend your lectures, sir? A common gardener.'

I could not get out of the habit of calling him 'sir' no matter how hard I tried.

'Oh, I think you're a very uncommon gardener, William. But why not? I think you might find them interesting.'

I could think of a dozen reasons why not, most of them to do with money or the lack of it. 'Sir, your students must pay and I could not afford to pay you!'

'Well, perhaps we could come to some arrangement. You supply me with botanical specimens and I'll be happy to waive my lecture fees. Would that persuade you? It seems fair enough to me!'

I told him that I would think about it and I did think about it, perhaps more than was good for me. I was so hungry for knowledge at that time and the learning he offered me gleamed in my mind's eye, enticing me like some exotic fruit.

⊞ ⊞ ⊞

That spring and summer, my mother pottered about with a small quantity of withered herbs, trying, like *Whuppity Stoorie* in the tale which my grand-daughter loves, to spin them into gold, but with far less success than that legendary fairy woman. Meanwhile, I would walk for miles in the sweet countryside outside the town, taking my leather bag and my squares of damp linen with me, and I would collect plants in great quantity, all that Thomas asked for and more: angelica, aromatic and tender in the spring, dog violets and windflowers, campion and ramsons. There were young nettles with many medicinal properties, not least the virtue of purifying the blood, followed by foxgloves in high summer, marching armies of them, poisonous and beautiful, although Thomas told me they had some medicinal uses. I harvested pink and white yarrow and cuttings of the sweet honeysuckle that grew, a buttery tangle in all the hedgerows. I gathered chickweed, scurvy grass, thistle and valerian, nightshade and wormwood, feverfew and sweet cicely and calendula. The names were poetry to me, an incantation on my tongue, a worship more potent than any prayer intoned by the minister in the kirk.

Then I would bring them back and present them to Thomas. I would hand them to him as my grand-daughter brings me the treasures she finds in the garden, the chuckie stanes and feathers that she sometimes gives me, and I would bask in the enjoyment of his gratitude, much as she is certain of pleasing me, whatever she brings. And if that sounds plain daft to you, I can't help it. One smile, one nod of his head, was enough to make my day.

All the same, there were times when Thomas would be distracted. He would be talking to me about botanical specimens or even enquiring after my family and he would be interrupted by some passing professor or scholar with a pressing question. His gaze would slide away. 'One minute, William,' he would say and turn aside from me. I cannot even now tell you why I would feel so unreasonably bereft, angry even, unless it was a premonition of things to come. There was nothing in it. And yet I would be suddenly chilled, as when the sun goes behind a cloud in the middle of a warm day. Perhaps it was simply that I found our conversations so precious. Interruptions were terrible to me. I was always hanging on his words, like poor Lothian Tam on Lunardi's balloon. And when he withdrew, I would find myself plummeting to earth. I would pick myself up, and tell him that I had better get on with the work I was being paid to do. He could see that I was not best pleased and I think it irritated him but he always contrived to leave me with a smile.

I'll not deny, a large part of the pleasure I took in it sprang from his gratitude. The warmth of the man. The way he would shake my hand like a friend. He was only a few years older than me, but he was born to quite different things and I was young enough to believe in heroes. His students were right. When I could spare the time to attend his classes – not half as often as I would have liked – I found that he was an exceedingly good teacher, lively, knowledgeable and generous. He treated me no differently from the way he treated the other students, even though they would cast scornful glances at me and make unkind remarks. In fact, I would have said that he treated me with even more warmth. He was, at that time, a god in my eyes. I would have gathered more than prickly whins and nettles to please him. I think I would have gone deep into the underworld for him at that time, a surrogate Orpheus in pursuit of his Eurydice.

❖ ❖ ❖

As far as I remember, the day that I first met Jenny Caddas was the same day that he gave me the book, although I know that memories can be deceptive. They sometimes slide together and no two people will have the same remembrance of the same event, each one convinced that he is right. But the two events are conjoined in my mind. It is the same book that lies before me now, on my desk, the book that came to stand for all that we shared. I was tired and footsore on that day, and later than I had intended because I had lingered longer than I should have at Jenny's house. I had arranged to meet Thomas in the college garden but he was nowhere to be seen, and I thought he might have given up on me and gone home to his house in the town, so I sat down on a stone bench, opened my leather bag and began to unwrap the plants, making sure that I had all that were required and that none had suffered too much on the way back to town. I became so engrossed in the task that I never heard him as he came along the path in the dusk.

He threw himself onto the bench beside me. 'You've got them all?'

'Aye, most o' them.'

'I knew I could rely on you,' he said.

I stretched out my legs. I was tired, but only in the way you are when it's almost a pleasure to you: not real exhaustion, so much as the kind of weariness that induces sound sleep. 'I've foraged three miles and more from the town and walked three or four times that much.'

'I know it's demanding, William.'

'No' just walked either. I've been chased by dogs with sharp teeth and lads with stones and an auld wifie with a ladle and she was much the worst of the three!'

It was true enough. People in the countryside, especially so close to the city, were suspicious of strangers, seeing robbers and vagabonds everywhere. And perhaps with good reason for we lived in lawless times and still do. The dogs that guarded the cottages were prone to nipping at your heels on sound preventative principles and even the young lads who were marauding through the fields, meant to be tending to the crops and scaring the birds, would toss a stone or even a boulder at you as soon as look at you. But the old women were by far the worst and even if you were to stop and ask for directions or a drink, they would likely hunt you from their doors with whatever was to hand, be it a besom or a garden rake. Jenny had been unusual in being so friendly, but I flattered myself that maybe she had liked the look of me and that was the reason why she had – against her better judgement – allowed me to help her and invited me into her house.

'I'm so sorry,' said Thomas. But he looked amused rather than genuinely apologetic. He brought out his flask and offered me a drink again. It had become something of a habit between us, and my reward for all my efforts on his behalf.

'Have you ever tried it?' I asked him.

'Tried what?'

'The distillation.'

He shook his head. 'No, no. I haven't. Don't put ideas into my head.'

'You'd have the knowledge right enough. As a medical man!'

'I would. But I don't have the time. And I'd rather not fall foul of the exciseman.'

'Ah weel, it would be one way ...'

'One way of what?'

'Of getting some siller.'

He frowned. He didn't have to ask why I needed siller. He knew.

'Your apothecary business?'

'It is going badly. You would hardly credit how badly.'

'Oh, I think I would.' He sounded sad rather than angry.

'Disastrously' would have been a better word. My mother could hardly stir herself to tend to the shop after she had seen to the needs of the younger children. There was money owed to the moneylender. Even now, with high summer approaching, there were not enough herbs and plants to supply the shop and the botanical lectures. Not in the physic garden and not even with what I gathered for Thomas. He could use all that I could fetch him and more. Why had I ever started on such a venture?

My only excuse had been my desperation about money when I had been unsure as to whether I would win the gardener's position. And my mother had merely done as she was told, submitting to the will of a young man, too daft to know better, submitting because she was still smitten by grief. If my father had been alive and had suggested such a thing she would have persuaded him otherwise. But then he was a sensible man, and he would never have suggested such a thing, nor permitted me to indulge in it. He knew his own limitations and mine.

'Do you not have enough to do with your time, what with the garden and all these?' Thomas gestured at the plants. 'I doubt if you could keep up to this and your apothecary venture and attend lectures as well.'

'I cannot keep up to them. That's the problem. And my mother is no hand with the herbs.'

I wondered later if he was worried about me or worried that I would not be able to gather specimens for him. But to give the man his due, I think he was already aware of the difficulties and was trying to find a way to help me.

'It is not an easy trade, you know,' he told me. 'Even for those who are born to it. It is not just a question of plants, but of scholarship. It tends to run in families, with folk passing the learning down from one to another over the years. And often it is the women who are the keepers of such knowledge. Folk talk of auld wives' tales, but the auld wives can be repositories of profound learning and should not be dismissed out of hand. Or so I have always thought.'

'I thought my mother would learn. And I hoped that my young sisters would help her.'

'Your foolish sisters?' He glanced over at me with a smile that was both rueful and foxy, making me smile too. 'When you have told me that it is a moot point which is the more lazy of the two, Susanna or Jean?'

'It was stupid of me.'

'Not stupid. I would never call you stupid. But over-optimistic maybe.'

'It's what the old gardener before my father did, you know. He and his wife took a shop and his wife made all kinds of remedies with the spare herbs from the gardens. It was a very successful venture I believe.'

'Aye but that was maybe back in the days when the physic garden was in a better state than it is now. And perhaps his wife already had the skills.'

'She had.'

'It worries me that you are tied into such a venture. I wonder if there is anything that I can do to help you.'

'I doubt it. You may be a fine botanist and a better physician, Doctor Brown, but I cannot see you making distillations and medications for me, and I fear my mother will never learn to do it.'

I had hoped that the apothecary business might be a way of adding to our meagre income over the summer, so that we could survive enough winters for the lads to be sufficiently grown to earn money on their own account. For Rab to grow strong and healthy. For wee Rab — as I thought of it in my darker moments when I lay awake, turning things over and over in my mind — to survive.

The moneylender had come to our door, asking if there was anything he could do for us, sniffing out the needy like all such parasites who prey on the poor. I had taken the money, and had negotiated with the owner of one of the properties adjacent to the university for the use of his front room as a shop. But, more often than not these days, it sat empty and dusty, while my poor mother found one excuse after another not to be there. And I could not do it for her. There were not enough hours in the day for me to do it.

Even when she was there, she did little more than footer about the place, boiling up evil-smelling potions that fermented in their bottles and occasionally exploded, sending shards of glass and foul smells everywhere. Nobody would ever pay her money for these things and I would have been afraid to sell them lest the cure prove infinitely worse than the disease and ultimately kill somebody.

The best thing she ever made was a variety of ale from the tips of the young nettles, and, later in the year, a sparkling beverage conjured from the creamy elderflowers that were everywhere to be found, the elder being a most prolific tree at seeding itself in this part of the world. Both of these were palatable and could – I suppose – be deemed to be health giving. But this was plain cookery, kitchen brewing rather than medicine and she felt herself on surer ground, as she also did when adding the green shoots of ramsons, with their strong flavour, to white cheese, making a delicious concoction that had been a favourite with my father.

Thomas had offered to pay me extra for my excursions into the countryside on his behalf but I was reluctant to take anything from him and he knew it. I think it was why he had suggested I attend his lectures. I was afraid of spoiling our friendship. We never felt like servant and master, but I had an inkling that if I allowed him to pay me, it would subtly alter something between us. Maybe I was wrong. Now that I have been in business for so many years, I can see that it is possible to have a good financial relationship with a man and yet be on friendly terms. But back then, it seemed that we were negotiating some precarious pathway, feeling our way into a friendship that was rare for both of us, and I wanted to do nothing to upset the balance between us.

CHAPTER ELEVEN

The Gift

That evening, with the sun slanting into the garden and my mind full of thoughts of Jenny, I watched Thomas lifting the plants, handling them carefully, sniffing here and there at some herb, rubbing a leaf between his fingers. I can close my eyes and I am back there. I am in my flesh as it was then, healthy and vigorous, with all my senses acutely aware and the blood of youth coursing through my veins.

In the distance, somebody was singing in a high, clear voice. It might have been a girl or a young lad, his voice unbroken. It was impossible to tell, but I remember a sudden awareness that the sound was immeasurably beautiful, enough to bring a tear to the eye. I think I was in that state of exhaustion that provokes sentimentality. Nearby, a few scholars were playing at a game of ball, laughing and calling to each other. The sounds seemed to echo off the old buildings in the warmth of the evening, making a canticle with the swallows that circled deliriously among the stones.

'These are very good,' he said. 'But best put them away before they dry out. I wonder if we've got enough?'

'To be honest with you, Doctor Brown,' I said with emphasis, 'I've lost count. And I'm very loath to go out again the day!' I felt suddenly very tired but it was the thought of all I had to do, of all who relied on me, that exhausted me and not the walking I had done that day. It was as much fatigue of the mind, I think, as the body. 'How many students did you say?'

'Thirty,' he said, with a grin. 'And I have no intention of sending you out again the day. And I've told you before, my friends call me Thomas, Mr Lang.'

'Aye, but what would Faculty say. The gardener hobnobbin' with the nabbery!' Whisky always loosened my tongue. Afterwards I would look back on my own effrontery with something like shame, but it never seemed to bother him. He never seemed to think the worse of me for it.

'Faculty wouldn't approve,' he said. 'But what would Faculty know of plants or herbs and their uses?'

'Or gardening for that matter!'

'Very little.'

'Which is why the professor is glad to have you lecturing in his stead. Otherwise he would have to make shift to do all this for himself.'

'It's true. Jeffray has no great love for botany.'

'No, he's a regular sawbones.'

Thomas regarded me narrowly. He already knew my feelings about dissection, the students and their professors who all seemed so ghoulishly attached to cutting up bodies in the name of science.

A necessary evil, Thomas called it, during our frequent debates on the subject. I remained unconvinced.

'Each to his own,' he said. 'But they are never so glad of me that they will pay me. I get only what the students are prepared to give, you know.'

'All teachers should be paid so!'

'Then some of them would die in poverty.'

'Much the same as the rest of us. But not you, I think. They would pay you readily enough. And besides, my heart bleeds for you.' But I said that last under my breath. Sometimes, like now, when I was footsore and weary, I was possessed by rage at the difference between us, at the fact that his idea of poverty was – for me at any rate – riches beyond the dreams of avarice. And because

I was relaxed and friendly with him, I felt at liberty to say so. Or almost.

'What did you say?'

'I said my heart fair bleeds for you!'

'Ach, I'll not quarrel with you!'

It was what he always said. He never would quarrel with me. Even at the bitter end of our friendship, I think he resolved that he would not quarrel with me.

'Will you not?'

'No. Not today or ever, William. But why are you so angry with me all of a sudden?'

'I am not angry with you, but I was thinking that they should never have let the type foundry go ahead. And building it so close to the garden as well. And if Professor Jeffray was more interested in plants and less obsessed with anatomy ...'

'Printing must always take precedence over planting. In the college, at any rate.'

'Aye, but if they are offering the young scholars botany lectures, they need plants. Thirty specimens of every plant on your syllabus? What do Faculty know of plants and their classification? What do they know of green and growing things, if it comes to that?'

'That's what I like about you, Will,' he said. 'Never let the uncertain truth get in the way of a good sound prejudice.'

He had taken to shortening my name sometimes, a gesture of familiarity and affection. I was 'Will' to nobody but him, not even my mother, nor ever have been since, not to a single soul.

' What's uncertain about it?'

'The truth is that we probably need both. Gardens and books. And anatomy. We need that too. We dissect plants so why not the human body? Which is, after all, only another growing thing. Whiles, a very green and growing thing.'

I thought he was making mock of me, but gently, as was always his way.

I stared at him, thinking that we would never agree on this point. He was right, of course. I could see that. I can see it now. But

I could never feel it, in my heart, in my blood and bones, and that was the trouble. I repacked my bag and handed it over to him. He would store the plants in cool, damp conditions until his lecture, the following day, and give me back the bag for my next expedition.

I brushed the earth from my hands.

'Aye, but which bodies?' I asked. 'Which bodies do you cut apart?'

'Whichever you can get, I suppose,' he said, light-heartedly.

I thought it best to change the subject then, too tired to think of further arguments, so I said only, 'I helped a lassie take a swarm of bees today!' Besides, Jenny had been on my mind. I wanted to talk about her, the way you do when you like somebody, and I thought that I should not mention her to my mother. Not yet.

'Did you?' he asked with interest. 'And was she bonny?'

'Well I thocht so. She was standing there with her skep and the swarm was, oh it was a muckle big swarm, hanging in the hedge like this great … you could hear it … like this creature, this living creature just hanging there. And she was tall and slender as a birk, barefoot and all. I cut the branch for her. It's mair of a problem when they're clustering on a fence post or at least that's what she was telling me.'

'I don't think I've ever taken a swarm myself.' He was really interested now, not just humouring me.

'Have ye no? Well I expect you've aye got a body to do it for you. Some gardener or other!'

'And how many swarms have you taken yourself, Will?'

He was determined to ignore my contrariness. Determined to keep his temper.

I started to laugh, in spite of myself. 'None! And that's the truth. My father used to do it, and I would watch him.'

'Did you get stung today?'

'Aye. Just the once.' I held out my finger to him.

'Poor William!'

'The lassie said that when she's stung, it never even hurts her. She cannae feel it!'

'Now that *is* interesting,' he said.

'It's a blessing for her.'

'But I mean as a doctor I find that interesting. Why should that be, I wonder?'

'Some folk get very ill.'

'I know. I've seen a man die from a single bee sting. He swelled up and couldn't breathe and there was nothing to be done and so he died. And yet you tell me your lassie never feels a thing?'

'She says she likes bees and the bees like her fine.'

'Well, maybe love is the answer, William.'

'You can tell where they've been,' I ventured. 'The bees. That's what she tell't me and she's right. I have seen it myself without being aware of what I was looking at.'

'What do you mean?'

'What flowers they've been at. You can see it on them, whether they've been at the meadowsweet, or the heather, which is much darker, or the balsam that makes them look like wee white ghosts, flittin' about.'

He was staring at me in the twilight, and I had the strangest sense that he was holding his breath. Then I heard him give a little sigh.

'I didn't know that. Or at least I never thought about it until today.'

'Me neither. Whiles it just needs a body to point something out to you and then it all falls into place!'

'Aye, William. It does.'

Even in the gathering dusk, I could see that he was looking at me with affection and an intermingling of pride. It was the way my mother sometimes used to look at me. Or my father, when he thought I couldn't see him watching me.

'She said if you're feart of them, they sense it. Maybe they can smell it on you. You have to tell them, ken? You have to tell them a' things. Births, weddings, deaths, you have to let the bees know about them. And she's right for I tell't them when my father died. My mother said I had to. I felt like a great gowk daein' it, for the hives were all silent, but I tell't them all the same.'

Unexpectedly, he slipped his arm around my shoulders. It was as strong, as muscular as my own, not like the arm of a gentleman, but more like the arm of a man who works hard for his living.

'You miss your father, don't you?'

'Aye, I miss him. Why would I no'? It's been a hard row to hoe for us since he died.'

For answer, he steered me back to the more pleasant topic of Jenny Caddas and her beehives. 'So you took the swarm?'

'Aye and we took it back to the bee bole in the wall and when it was set there, she took me indoors and put this remedy on my sting and gave me an oatie bannock with honey on it. She's a bonny lass.'

'So I gather.'

'We were talking for a long time. But her wee sister was there. It was alright. There was naethin' wrang in it.'

'I never thought there would be. I'd trust you anywhere, William. And with anybody. What about her parents?'

'Her mother's deid. Her faither's a weaver and he was away on business. She's Jenny Caddas, and you should have seen her hair. It's that bonny. As pale as flax.'

'She seems to have made a deep impression on you, Will!'

'She has.'

We sat in silence for a moment.

'And will you be seeing her again?'

'Aye well, I thought I might pay her a visit. Now and again. If I have plants to find.'

'Then I'd best send you off hunting for more specimens!'

'Aye, maybe you should.'

I had the inclination to talk about her and go on talking about her. You'll know the feeling yourself. When you find somebody that takes your fancy, you want to spread the word. It's like something inside you that aye wants to come bursting out and there's a strange comfort in saying their name aloud. Jenny, I wanted to say. Jenny Caddas. Oh it was not that she was any great beauty, in spite of the lint-white hair, but she had the right face, the right face for me. I think Thomas understood me well enough.

'So what does she do, this Jenny Caddas,' he asked me. 'Beyond keeping house for her father and minding her wee sister? Or is that work enough for a lass?'

'The cottage was full of bundles of herbs, drying. She knew what was what. She kent the names as well as myself. Not the Latin names, though she had a few of those. But the good old Scots names. She kent them all.'

'Not mutchwort and dog's bedstraw then?'

'No!' I started to laugh.

What Thomas did not know of the old Scots names he would ask me or, occasionally when he was lecturing, make up on the spot. He had confessed to this when I expressed my complete ignorance of a 'wee white flower called mutchwort' and another named 'dog's bedstraw'.

'I invented them on the spur of the moment,' he said. 'I just could not help myself. Sheer devilment. Did you see how laboriously they copied the names out? Not a single one of them, although they all have a fine conceit of themselves as scholars, not one has thought to question me. Only you, my friend. Only you!'

When I had seen Jenny's herbs and heard her speak about them, the thought had crossed my mind that she might be able to help with the apothecary shop. It seemed a wild idea when I hardly knew her and, on reflection, I was sure that her father would never permit such a thing, but all the same, I added it to the heap of dreams and daydreams with which I beguiled my days and leavened my nights. Always a dreamer, you see, and at least some of those dreams have become a reality for me, even if others have been dashed under my feet.

'She sounds like a clever lass. Intelligence is a rare thing in any woman, let alone a lassie with flaxen hair!'

'You're mocking me. And her.'

'Only in the kindest way, Will.'

'Well, I'll allow I was smitten with her.'

'So it seems!'

I knew that I should be getting home to my mother. She would be fretting about me. She did not like me going on these excursions to the countryside. She had not set foot out of Glasgow for many years. I think she had some idea that I was going off to strange foreign parts and that I might be set upon by footpads and robbers. Well, it was a possibility, though God knows what she thought they might rob me of, since I never carried anything with me save a piece of bread and cheese, my leather bag of specimens, my pieces of linen and the knife that I used for cutting them. They were doomed to disappointment if they thought they were going to get rich by robbing me. But my mother confessed that she worried about me until I was safe back home again, as though I had been a child, like my brothers. I was more in danger from the auld wives with their besoms, who seemed to want to sweep me away from their doorsteps, than I ever was from thieves and highwaymen.

Thomas stood up to go but then clapped his hand to his pocket and said, 'I almost forgot. I have a gift for you!'

'A gift? For me?' I could not hide my surprise.

'Aye. A man of my acquaintance had this for sale, and since it made me think of you, I thought I would buy it for you.'

He handed it to me. I was so astonished that he should think of giving me something that I almost dropped it. The parcel was loosely done up in cloth and I unwrapped it. It was an old book. Even then I could see that it was very old. I found out later that it was written more than a hundred years earlier. If I have an embarrassment of books about me now, I am still something of a rarity in that respect and back then, the only book which was ever to be found in the houses of the poor was the Holy Bible, with sometimes a separate New Testament for taking to the kirk on a Sunday.

I am staring at it now, that book, and the scent of the years is on it, that magical, musky scent of old books, as familiar to me as the scent of the beeswax polish my wife used on our furniture, the polish my daughter-in-law still makes and uses. *The Scots Gard'ner* it is called. By John Reid. 'Published for the Climate of Scotland.' I turned the leaves then, just as I am turning them now. 'Gardens, Orchards, Avenues, Groves,' it says, 'with new and profitable ways of Levelling and how to Measure and Divide Land.' It was printed in Edinburgh, by David Lindsay and his partners, at the foot of Heriot's Bridge, in 1683.

I tried to hand it back to him. 'You cannot give me such a thing!'

'Why not?'

'Because it's too precious. I'm only a gardener, Thomas.'

'And who else but a gardener could best benefit from a book on gardening? Have you any better suggestions?'

'No. But it's so old. And so beautiful.'

'Then treasure it and enjoy it. Besides, I have my own copy. I took mine from my cousin's library in Ayrshire. He had no use for it, and I wanted to read it. When I saw this, I thought it would be fitting that you should have a copy too. You can read it, and we can compare notes if you like.'

'I suppose we could do that.'

'It is written with such love. There is poetry in every line of it, and I think that you will like it as much as I do. I have not given it lightly, and you deprive me of nothing by accepting it. In fact, you will give me nothing but pleasure. Men who love plants as you love plants, men who also like books as you like books, they are few and far between and must always be treasured when found.'

So I took it. I took it home and put it on the top of the dresser and warned the younger children, under pain of a beating, that they must not touch it under any circumstances. Whenever I had time and light, I would take it down and read it and reread it until I had it almost by heart. Thomas was right. There was poetry between those pages. My brothers and sisters would watch me reading, but none of them would go near it or even ask me about it. Only Rab, as he grew older, would come creeping up beside me and run his fingers over the letters, but I never minded him. He was a gentle lad and I thought that one day, if he survived, he might love books as much as I did. Nobody else touched it. Not even my poor mother, who viewed it as one might a magical talisman. She was afraid to touch it but would sometimes say to me, 'only move the book, William' when she wished to polish the dresser.

CHAPTER TWELVE

Needlework

That afternoon, Jenny had told me, as I did not tell Thomas, not then anyway, that she also took in sewing. It was not the plain sewing that my poor plain sisters struggled to do. No. This was fine stuff and sometimes it was embroidery in white thread on muslin so that it looked just like costly lace: flowers, ferns and sprigs, in stitches so fine that you could barely distinguish them one from another with the naked eye.

'It was my good friend and neighbour, Nancy Mackenzie, who taught me to do it,' she told me. 'And Nancy was taught the skill in Edinburgh by Mr Ruffini who was an Italian incomer. That was more than twenty years ago.'

'So Nancy is not a girl like yourself?'

'No, no. She is a widow lady. But back then she was one of Ruffini's girls or at least that is how she describes herself!'

Nancy had been an orphan who was taken in by the young Italian, taken off the streets when she was a child of ten. She had been taught to do fine whitework, along with a number of other girls he had decided to train up.

Later, Nancy had met and married a travelling weaver and they had come down to the west because the Glasgow weavers were beginning to make the very fine muslin which was needed for this work, using cotton carried up the long hard road from Manchester. The couple had settled near Glasgow town, but when Nancy's husband died, she had no recourse but to support herself with her needlework and with spinning for Sandy Caddas. She and Jenny had become firm friends, although there was such a difference in their ages.

'But then,' said Jenny, a little sadly, 'I was in want of a mother. My mother died not long after Anna was weaned.'

The care of the child had fallen to Jenny, but this kindly neighbour had taken some of the work off her shoulders and had, besides, taught her all that she knew of needlecraft. Now, as well as keeping house for her father and drying plants from the garden to make what remedies she could, Jenny would spend hours doing this embroidery, whitework on fine cotton or coloured sprigs, tiny flowers neatly worked on silk for ladies' dresses and men's waistcoats and the like.

'Really, I should be spinning for my father,' she said, with a smile. 'But he says that my work fetches more money, which is true, so he would rather I do the fancy stitching. He pays a couple of women in the village to do the spinning for him. Sometimes Nancy takes it off his hands as well because her eyesight is not what it was, not for the fine work she used to do.'

She had shown me some of her embroidery, just a small panel of a waistcoat that she was working on for one of the local gentry, and I thought it very marvellous. Perhaps because she knew so much about the flowers themselves, she seemed to have a talent for painting pictures with her needle. The stitched flowers were as real as any I have ever seen. I thought about my sisters, about Jean and Susanna, but I couldn't ever see them being able to do more than hem a petticoat and even that with difficulty.

It has sometimes struck me, watching my wife or my daughter-in-law working away with a needle – although my wife was certainly the more skilled of the two – that there is some strange and elusive connection between these things, embroidery and weaving and the flowers that gardeners grow. The big shawls that the weavers of Paisley make nowadays, with their curving ferns and masses of flowers, sometimes seem to me to be like gardens woven in cloth. They have the appearance of a flower border in high summer, the same jumble of dazzling colours. Then there are the delicate floral sprays on the lace that prosperous brides wear, or the white sprigs and flowers of Dresden or Ayrshire needle-work on fine muslin. It strikes me that all these things, whether the province of men or women, have much in common with the work that some gardeners do. Or do I mean the results of that work? And if it seems over fanciful to say as much, perhaps I mean that we are nurturers only and they echo what we do, weaving it or stitching it into their world, pinning it down and passing it on for others to cherish, for those who come after, like Jenny Caddas, who had the skill of fashioning flowers with her needle as well as in her garden.

A world without flowers would be a poor world indeed, although I know, or perhaps I should say I used to know, many gardeners for whom the growing of fruit and vegetables was para-mount. I think my father was one of their number. They cared little for flowers and grew them only to please their mistresses, considering them an inconvenience. It was the same with trees for some of them. They hated to let trees and shrubs grow tall, because they fancied that such things would overshadow their car-rots, their skirrets and their scorzonera. They were men, I think, who were more comfortable wielding an axe or a pair of sharp shears. Too high, too untidy, too intrusive. That was their judge-ment. But it was never mine.

◻ ◻ ◻

During those few years of my friendship with Thomas Brown, I was torn between the pleasure I took from his company and my growing affection for Jenny, both of which were tempered by my almost constant worry about lack of funds and what that might mean for my family. There were too few hours in the day and too many jobs, far too many jobs, to fill them. It made me tetchy and ill tempered. With Thomas, I felt I could relax and speak as I saw fit, not bothering to curb my tongue, conscious that he would always make allowances for me. With Jenny, though, I had no inclination to be anything but gentle. The more time I spent in her company, the more enchanted I became by the sunny mind that seemed to illuminate her smiling face. Her cup was always half full, never half empty. More often than not, it was full to the brim with life and the pleasure she took from small things. Oh I do not mean that she was never cross or tired or irritable, for she could be all of these things when her sister was a trial to her, or her father's demands on her time exceeded her capacity to fulfil them. She could be wilful when she chose and she was never afraid to challenge me, much as my sisters were never afraid to put me firmly in my place.

I think she regretted the loss of her mother deeply, the older she grew. There was always too much to be done about the house, in the garden, with the plants she harvested, with her needle. I understood that well enough, for I suffered from the same problem myself. She did what she could and sang about her work and was marvellously contented with her lot for most of the time. The best way I can describe it is to say that she filled the cottage where she lived with as much good nature as it was possible to find in a poorly educated country lassie – which was, after all, exactly what she was.

Later, I found myself regretting that I had not made the most of my time with her. I was very much absorbed in my own troubles and did not have the wit or the imagination to see that she could not always be as cheerful as she seemed. I would go to her for solace, and she would listen to my complaints, patiently offering what suggestions she could.

'We just have to make the best of things, William!' she would tell me. 'After all, look at what we have. We're doing work that we enjoy, most of the time anyway. We're earning enough to keep body and soul together. What more could we ask for?'

Well, I could think of plenty more, but I had to acknowledge that there was some truth in what she said. Still, the students were a sore trial to me. The gardens were meant to be for the benefit of the professors and lecturers. But the young scholars would often gain access to them. There were times when all manner of rascals, much the worse for strong drink, would maraud about, creating mayhem. I caught one of them, a young gentleman who should have known better, setting a fire under my newly planted wayfaring tree, a delicate shrub that had cost a very great deal of money. I shouted at him in no uncertain terms and in language that would have brought a blush to my mother's cheek. It didn't go down very well. He threatened to report me to Doctor Brown and when I stared him out, he said he would tell his family.

'I'll have my father horsewhip you!' he said, but his threats cut no ice with me.

'You're very welcome to try it,' I shouted and advanced on him, but he ran off before I could exact retribution. The ground was damp (when is it ever not damp, here?), and I stamped the fire out and restored order. He was a spotty wee lad with a shifty look, which could have described any one of a dozen or more, and I doubt if I would have known him again among so many. Some rich man's son, no doubt. They cared nothing for my gardens, not one of them.

I think I equated them in my mind with the professor whom Thomas had replaced, the sawbones who loved to pull things apart to see what lay beneath, what made it all work. It reminded me of the time I had once dismantled my mother's cherished kitchen clock, an object which was very much prized and which, as a young lad, I had thought to take apart to 'see how it worked'. To my horror I had not managed to put it together again at all, and my outraged father had had to pay a watchmender to fix it.

'But once your professor has done that, once he has destroyed a body to see how it functions,' I observed to Thomas during one of our all-too-frequent debates on the subject of surgery, 'can he put it back together once more?'

'In working order?' he said.

'Aye. Like a clockmaker.'

'After a fashion. I think that is what he aims to do, eventually. As long as there is a little life in it still. It is one thing to mend a broken body and quite another to raise the dead!'

'Well, you can pull a plant apart and it'll whiles grow again. But if you pull the blood and bones and sinews apart, you cannot reassemble them any more than you can reassemble the swallow's nest when you have howked it down from a barn wall. Or the laverock once you have taken her breath away. She will never sing again.'

'Will, I think you're a poet. And I can't disagree with such passion,' said Thomas, his hand on my shoulder. 'And you may be right, of course. But all the same, I believe somebody might do it some day. The swallow's nest is just that — a thing of clay, a shelter for a small time. '

'And is that not what our bodies are?'

'Aye they are that and more. But who knows better than you that when you cut yourself in the garden, the skin will generally knit together? Our bodies have that about them that allows them to heal. And so perhaps we can find a use for those properties to repair them inside as well as out.'

'And do you believe he might do it, your professor?'

'Well, it is his passion. But no, I think he just wants to see how it all works. And there's a greatness about that, you must admit. A greatness about him. It's just that people can't see it yet.'

'I can see that he'd no' be above a wee bit of raising the dead from their last resting places at any rate.'

'I don't think he would go so far,' said Thomas.

'Do you not?'

'He's been a good friend to me and mine.'

'Only because you're saving him from what he most dislikes.'

'That's true enough.'

We were walking in the gardens, looking at the newly planted trees and wondering whether they would thrive, in spite of the depredations of spotty wee scholars with bonfires. They were growing, after a fashion, those that were far enough away from the malign influence of the type foundry, but I sometimes felt that the whole college was becoming an island amid a sea of filth. The filth emanated from the manufactories and the rank jumble of houses that was creeping ever closer to the old buildings, like malignant weeds clustering around the base of some venerable tree.

The trees and shrubs were one more thing that brought us together. I had little interest in growing vegetables myself – a strange confession for a gardener, I know – but I think Thomas felt the same. He was interested in the many different varieties of apples and pears which could be grown, especially since pears were said to have many medicinal uses, but the practicalities of supplying the college tables with the likes of seakale and spinach held no interest for him or for me either. There were hothouses in the physic garden where we attempted to grow vines, and I would set Johnnie to tend a plot for ourselves, to provide curly kale and so on for our own use at home. A great handful of curly kale and a loaf of bread will make a little meat go a very long way. But that, I think, was the sum of my interest in such things.

CHAPTER THIRTEEN

Pineapples

My father had been a very fine gardener, although he was no botanist. He was, however, a member of the Free Gardeners, a brotherhood to which I never aspired, although there were some aims and ambitions of which I most certainly approved, and approved them the more, the older I grew. But I was never a great one for joining secret societies, no matter how beneficial they might have been for myself.

I was somewhat surprised to find that Thomas was not a member of the Free Gardeners either. It was supposed to be – and largely was – a group of working men who had joined together, 'for their mutual benefit and support', as the constitution termed it. But I was uncomfortably aware that the gentry, the nabbery as I used to call them, before they became my customers (and I still do call them that in the privacy of my own home), were much inclined to join the Free Gardeners as well.

It was supposed to be a magnanimous gesture, a sort of condescension to what they thought of as the lower orders, that the gentry would go along to meetings alongside their common gardeners. They were always made very welcome, even though, as my father once said in an unguarded moment, they could be 'gey patronising'. It was the reason why I never availed myself of the opportunity while I was yet a gardener, although men who had known and liked my father had certainly issued me with more than one invitation.

'Will you come?' they would say. 'You'd find it very helpful to you in all kinds of ways.'

But I knew I would not be able to put a curb on my tongue in the face of such patronage on the part of the gentry, and it seemed foolish to go out of my way to make enemies, so I simply told them that I had too much work, which was true enough.

As far as the gentry attending meetings went, there was much more to it than their supposed generosity. They liked to know what was going on. They liked to keep a finger on the pulse of the working man and the things that he might be about. They were terrified of revolution, at the tail end of a revolutionary century, and they would go to meetings and listen out for sedition. They were, all of them, well aware of what had passed in France only a few short years before and nightmares of the guillotine haunted their feather bed sleep.

They seemed to have taken a collective decision to spy on the lower orders, lest any should be fomenting sedition. And who can blame them? I would have done the same thing myself in like circumstances. My father would probably have denied that it was the case, crediting his masters with more generosity of spirit. He was always respectful of his betters, although it did him little good in the long run. It was bred in the man, in blood and bone, much as a clever plantsman will breed certain qualities into a fruit or vegetable. And it must have been born in me too, except that something changed me and I don't just mean later events. Even as a lad, I was aware that my father was worth ten of the men to whom he was forced to doff his cap like an underling, and I hated it. It was one of the reasons why I admired Jenny's father. As Sandy Caddas once declared, the weavers would bow before nobody, not even the king himself, were he ever to come down among them.

My father would go out to his Free Gardener meetings on a regular basis, but I never found out what he did at them, although I was very curious.

'Ask nae questions and you'll be tell't nae lies,' he used to say. And off he would go with his long apron, his talk of Jack in the Green, his book of ritual, laboriously written down. He kept that volume well away from prying eyes. After his death, I hunted high and low for it, fancying that at last I would find out what was written in it, but I could see neither hide nor hair of it. When I asked my mother about it she said that somebody had come to the door, offering her the sympathy of the Gardeners and a little money that had been collected at a meeting, 'for the benefit of Robert's widow and children'. The same man – having sat for a while with my mother, passing the time of day and enquiring after each of the children in turn – had asked her if she knew where my father's book of ritual might be kept. It was lent only and should be returned to the Free Gardeners from whence it came, but only if she could lay hands upon it at that moment, and she was not to think of troubling herself about it.

'Well,' she told me, 'I knew where it was, right enough, because your father always kept it in the same place, under his pillow, and I was so grateful to them for their contributions and their kindness that I fetched it at once, and gave it to him. Did I do the wrong thing, William?'

I could not, in all conscience, say that she had done the wrong thing. And besides, there were more small sums of money forthcoming from the Gardeners over the years, so I am sure she did the right thing, but I would dearly like to have known what was written in that book, and it is one volume which has never been through my hands in all these years that I have been dealing in and with books.

God knows what daftness they got up to, nor why men in particular are so fond of their secret rituals, like lads at play. It has sometimes occurred to me that women are far too sensible to indulge in such nonsense, but encourage their menfolk in these pursuits with the sole aim of getting them out from under their feet. And we men dutifully oblige. But the meetings served some purpose in that they would also exchange knowledge, gardening knowledge of the sort to be found in the book which Thomas had given me. And it was helpful, because I suppose there would be some among them who could neither read nor write, or perhaps who struggled, could maybe manage an order for plants but that was all. It would be very helpful to them if their fellow gardeners could pass on the detailed and intimate knowledge that was needed to nurture plants and the ground from which they sprang.

I know what the sum total of my father's ambition was, though, because he told me. He wanted to grow a pineapple.

'Ah,' he would say. 'That would be a very fine thing. To have a hothouse. To grow pineapples. Or even a single pineapple! Let's not be greedy about this, William.'

I told Thomas about this in an unguarded moment. I think he could see that I was inclined to scoff but he was never one to mock those who loved their work.

'Not a bad ambition,' he said. 'Not a bad ambition at all. I have heard far worse.'

'The good lord knows what he would have done with it if ever he had succeeded.' I glanced at Thomas. What did I see in his face? Mild disapproval perhaps? He was my weather vane at that time and I would temper my behaviour to his responses.

'But I suppose it was a harmless enough ambition for a working man to have,' I added, seeing that he so obviously expected me to defend my father.

'It was a grand ambition,' said Thomas, decidedly. 'Have you ever tasted a pineapple?'

'No. I imagine it might be something like an ordinary apple.'

'Oh no,' he said. 'Nothing like that.'

'Then you have tasted one?'

'Aye, once or twice. They are sweet beyond sweetness. I tell you, William, if the fruit of the tree in the Garden of Eden had been a pineapple, not all the angels in the heavens could have kept Adam and Eve from tasting it. And thinking paradise well lost! So don't mock your father's ambition. Perhaps he had tasted the fruit at some time and that was what inspired him.'

'He never said. But then we never asked him.'

'They are ambrosia and their juice is like the nectar of the Gods. It runs down your chin and leaves the scent of itself on your fingers.'

'Is that true?'

'Oh aye. But I am told that they are devilish hard to cultivate here in Scotland.'

'I'm sure they are. I wonder if I'll ever grow one?'

'Would you like to try?'

'I'll try anything that will buy me a measure of satisfaction. Or money. I take it they are very expensive.'

'Very.'

'But mostly, I think I would do it for my father.'

'It would be a fine tribute to him. My uncle has a pineapple house,' he added thoughtfully. 'In Ayrshire.'

'His gardener must have the secret then.'

'I think so.'

'My father would have been envious. But if he had managed it himself, he would have been the envy of the Free Gardeners as well.'

'Did you never want to go to the meetings with him? Were you never curious about what they got up to?'

'He said he would take me when he thought I was ready. He died before he could do it. Or before I was ready. And afterwards I thought I never would be ready. All the ritual, all the nonsense that seems to have grown up around it! I have small curiosity about it and I think I never will have.'

Even allowing for the fact that, in later years, I attained something of a reputation as a radical publisher, a dangerous reputation at times, I never attended meetings, never allowed myself to be persuaded to participate in unwise demonstrations of solidarity. I did not disapprove of them, but I knew that they were not for me and stuck to my principles. If a man brought me a pamphlet and if it was well written, I would print it. Sometimes, if I thought the words might be deemed inflammatory, I would do it in secret and distribute it in equal secrecy. Ostensibly I dealt in rare books, particularly those concerned with natural history. That was the face I presented to the world at large and it was as true as any other. As far as any other beliefs were concerned, and I had plenty, I made no grand gestures and believed nothing I was told, taking nothing on trust. Thomas did that for me at least. He imbued me with a desire to question all things.. Meetings were open to infiltration you see. There were men whose job it was to rouse revolutionary passions and lead good men into terrible folly. I and my family steered a course through some very stormy waters, through times that saw better men than me transported or executed. I sat on a number of fences. In secret, I did what I could, but I did it with great circumspection, knowing that more than myself were involved, that there were others, my wife and my family, who were relying on me to behave sensibly. If I were transported or worse, I would be of use to neither wife not child, and all of us would be wrecked on the reef of my own folly.

So even back then, I was circumspect and I never did join the Free Gardeners.

'I'm sure you're right,' said Thomas, whenever we talked about it. 'And yet it's what men do.'

'Indulge in such nonsense? More shame to them.'

'It gives them a modicum of certainty in an uncertain world.'

'Ritual or no, he was a practical man, my father. He would never have tried to set up an apothecary shop. He would never have fancied himself a botanist. He would never have ached to know more about plants and their properties. He was just a gardener. A fine gardener, but still. Pineapples. That was where his ambitions lay. And maybe he was all the better for it.'

'He would never have treated me with your familiarity,' Thomas observed.

'No he would not. He could not have brought himself to do it.'

'And consequently he would never have been the friend to me that you are.'

'No. He knew his place and kept his family from starvation. Perhaps I should decide to do the same.'

'You're a botanist, William, whether you like it or not.'

'Aye, and that's my tragedy. I love it all, the Latin names, and the properties of plants and the uses and the growing of them and the way some plants grow where others do not and the beauty and the poetry of it. Much good may it do me!'

He said nothing. There seemed nothing else to be said.

CHAPTER FOURTEEN

In Debt

By the end of summer, and in spite of all my hard work, matters seemed to be coming to a head. Faculty members were complaining about the state of the garden, at first mildly, but then vociferously. The professors who liked to walk there were beginning to look with disapproval on the general untidiness and decay they found. And of course, they blamed me. It was whispered that I was too young and inexperienced for the position, that I was lazy, neglecting my duties. The truth was at once simpler and less open to remedy. I had bitten off more than I could chew. I had rushed into the apothecary plan without realising just how difficult it would be for my mother. Meanwhile, I was struggling more and more to keep up to the work in the gardens and to keep Thomas Brown supplied with plants.

When I look back on it now, I see that what I probably should have done was to stop obliging Thomas. I should have told him that the garden must be my first priority, with the apothecary business and my mother coming a close second. If I was going to go roaming the countryside, I should have brought back such herbs as my mother could have used to make medicines. In fact, I could have bought them for a few pence from the likes of Jenny and if I had asked her, I think that Jenny might well have taught my mother some of what she knew.

But I didn't do any of that. I couldn't do it. I made all kinds of excuses to myself, but the plain truth was that whatever Thomas asked, I would do. Perhaps he should have seen how I was struggling. Well, I'm sure he did because he tried to do what he could to remedy it. But he was blind to my real problems. He believed that he could educate me, shape my mind, bring me out of myself. But I think my daily struggles to make a living were quite beyond his understanding, as the daily struggles of the poor always are beyond the full understanding of the wealthy, even those who have come from poverty themselves. Our memory for such things is as short as that of women for the pains of childbirth.

He did help me though, I can't deny it. And in doing so, he laid the very foundations of what I have become since. He introduced me to a world beyond the garden, a world of books and learning. He made me what I am. But all that came at the expense of the work I was engaged to do in the college, the work I should have done to assist my mother. And for that, I blame him, but I blame myself more.

▣ ▣ ▣

Without my father to support her, my mother was sinking day by day into a sea of misery. Thomas gave me some medicine which he said might help to lift her moods of unremitting gloom, and so it did, when she could remember to take it. But I think it was Thomas's attention that made her feel better and when he was gone, she would fall into gloom again. She trusted him as a doctor, but she was uncomfortable with our friendship. I felt guilty because I thought I was not the pillar of strength my father had been, but Thomas would say, 'How can you be, Will? You're a young man and her son. Her natural impulse will be to protect you. You want her to lean on you but you can never replace her husband.'

The medicine helped, but even that made her fret because we had not paid for it. I told her that I obliged Thomas enough with all my hunting for plants on his behalf, but it made no impression on her.

'We should not be beholden to him,' she would say. 'It is not right and no good can come of it. Your father would not have approved of it.'

This was still her touchstone, the standard by which she judged everything: whether or not my father would have approved. And perhaps she was right.

As well as my mother's health, I would consult Thomas from time to time about my young brothers. The lads had commenced some schooling, but we had to pay a share of the dominie's living, his food and his fuel. James McClure kept a damp schoolroom outside the college, large enough to house a few scholars of small means. He would turn a blind eye to payment some of the time, but he was not a rich man himself. His clothes, which were the garments of a bygone age, were all threadbare and snuffy. The boys made fun of him until he would lose his temper and pull out an ancient leather tawse which he barely had the strength to wield. He was the man who had taught me some years previously, and I liked him very much, but at the same time, I found him a pathetic figure. He was reduced to teaching the sons of poor men, and yet I believe in his youth he had once had the potential to be a great scholar, a potential that he had dissipated by an over-fondness for spirits, tobacco and gambling. He smelled to high heaven of smoke and whisky. But he could be an inspirational teacher when he found a boy who had the sense to listen to him.

'Dear God,' I said to Thomas 'The man's wig is losing more hair than his own head.'

Thomas let out a great splutter of laughter and almost choked on his whisky. He said, 'You're telling me that your brothers have a dominie whose wig is going bald!'

I started laughing too. It was comical right enough and the poor old dominie might well be a figure of fun, but it was no joke when we couldn't afford for the weans to go to the schoolroom more than once a week. There was never enough money and there was never enough time either.

In a panic, I sought Thomas's advice about our plight, especially the complaints about the garden. There was nobody else I could take my troubles to, and he confessed that he was aware of the grumbles in Faculty and had done what he could to counter them.

'You cannae grow trees where the air is filthy,' I said. 'No matter what I do, no matter how much care and attention I gie them, they aye look as though something has burned them. I try. I try my best.'

'I know you do.'

I pulled a few scorched leaves. 'Maybe I should show these to Faculty. Try to make them see what the type foundry is doing to my plants.'

'Maybe you should.'

'Naethin lives here!'

I remember it as though it were yesterday. 'Even the birds,' I said, 'Even the birds sometimes fall from the branches, bundles of bone and feather. There's no telling why. Well, nae doubt your Professor Jeffray would dissect them and find out and draw pictures of them afterwards.'

'The slugs survive,' Thomas observed, picking one off a leaf and then dropping it and squashing it beneath his foot.

'Oh aye, the slugs always survive.'

We walked on together, more than a little downhearted by the sight of so much destruction.

'And how does the apothecary business go now?'

'Disastrously,' I admitted. 'My mother is not really able to do the work and I don't have the time to help her.'

'I feared that might be the case.'

'Then you should have told me so. Before I started on the venture.'

'I did tell you it was unwise.'

'But you didn't tell me it would be ruinous.'

'I thought you might be offended by the advice, William.'

'I wouldn't have taken offence. Not if the advice came from you.'

'Well, maybe not. But what will you do now?'

'I don't know. Faculty are complaining that I don't spend enough time on the garden. And perhaps they're right. My mother is struggling. Jean and Susanna are no help, although they should be. But they are haunless as ever. They break pots and spill distillations and are better off out of it. Bessie is a capable lassie, but she has her ain work, and they keep her hard at it. We seldom see her.'

'What about your brothers? Could they not help more?'

'Och they are ower young yet. James works as hard as he can and since he is no scholar, and never will be, he's better off in the garden, doing as he's told. Johnnie is a thoughtless lad just, and Rab is as sickly as ever.'

'What would be best for you? I mean what would be the best thing from your point of view? Can you tell me that?'

'If I could pay back the money we borrowed for the room that houses the shop, I would put a stop to the whole venture. My mother would go back to keeping house, and the girls to their stitching. And then perhaps without that worry I could go back to doing what I am paid to do in the garden.'

I didn't add, of course, that so much of my time was spent gathering plants for him and not in the garden at all. And he didn't see fit to mention it either.

He said, 'How much do you owe? Is it a great sum of money?'

'Great enough for me. We borrowed some five pounds and although I have paid a little back it has grown to six pounds now. I cannot lay hands on such a sum. Not without going hungry for weeks.'

'Why did you not borrow the money from me in the first place, William?'

'Because I didn't know you so well, back then. And besides, I would never have asked you for so much. You must know that. It would have been beyond me to ask you. It would be beyond me now.'

'Will you let me help you?' He seemed unusually grave. I stared at him but his look was unfathomable.

'How do you mean? What could you do?'

'You've been such a help to me this summer and yet you won't take regular payment.'

'You let me attend your lectures.'

'I look for you but I seldom see you.'

'I come when I can. The garden takes up so much time.'

'Then will you let me assist you now? I can give you six pounds with very little trouble to myself. You know that. The only thing which has hindered me from offering it until now has been the knowledge that your pride would not let you accept it. If I give you the money, you can pay off your moneylender, let go of the shop, and give your mother peace to grieve for her man and cope with her children without having to worry about work she cannot do.'

I was speechless for a moment, all kinds of feelings warring inside my head: gratitude, affection, discomfort at my own foolishness. Then I found my tongue. 'It's tempting, I'll allow. But I would think shame to do it.'

I had the words of my father nipping my ears. 'Never borrow from your enemies,' he had told me. 'But still less should you borrow from your friends, for it is the soonest way to ruin a good friendship.'

I think Thomas could see that I was wavering, and he hurried to press the point home. 'There's no shame in a friend assisting a friend. Particularly when the mere accident of birth means that one has more financial resources than the other. And it would be far better for you to be beholden to me, your good friend, than to some rascally moneylender, if that's how you insist on seeing it! William, I would gladly give you this money as a gift from one friend to another. You know that.'

He put it so plainly and simply that it was impossible to be offended by the truth. The offer was tempting. But my pride still hindered me.

'I would borrow the sum, so long as you treated it as a loan and not a gift and allowed me to pay you back as and when I could.'

Whatever makes it acceptable to you, William. Pay me back or not, just as you choose. I'll not harass you for the sum, but if, in the future, you feel able to pay me, then please do so.'

We shook hands there and then. And later he paid off the moneylender himself, so that there should be no arguments with the man about the terms of the agreement. The rogue might have threatened me, but there was something about Thomas Brown that inspired a fear of unpleasant consequences, even in such villains as that. I think my mother was more relieved than she would ever have admitted to me, but she certainly told Bessie as much on her next visit, and Bessie related the same to me.

It must have been all of fifteen years later, when I sent ten guinea notes, drawn on the Royal Bank of Scotland in Edinburgh, being the sum loaned, plus a deal of interest, to Mr Thomas Brown at his house in Ayrshire. I had debated long and hard between my wish to be done with the debt and my fear (or should that be desire?) that he might take the repayment as a friendly overture, as an attempt to make contact with him again. But there was no reply, and now I don't know whether I was relieved or disappointed or perhaps a little of both. At that time, I was fully occupied with my business and my family and I hardly permitted myself to think about him at all.

I know only that today, when I flicked through the leaves of this old book, that sits here on my desk, I found the old bank notes, pressed between two pages. Untouched.

I looked at the text, and read, 'The black cherrie is a tree that I love well. There is a sort at Niddrie Castle whose fruit is preferable to any cherrie. I take it to be a soft heart cherrie but it's a great bearer. Gather their stones when full ripe, eat of the fleshy part and lay the stones to dry a little.' That's what the words said.

I took the notes and folded them back into the book at that exact place. This room is dusty at the best of times, but most particularly in the early autumn when the weather is cool and dry, and the fire is lit again. My eyes water. I must needs take a linen handkerchief and wipe them, rubbing at them until they are red and sore.

CHAPTER FIFTEEN

Jenny's Remedy

I love spring best of all the seasons, but who does not? Even now, when I am in the winter of my years, spring brings a lifting of the heart, a return of the sense that anything is possible. Fluffy willow catkins and hazel lambstails appear as if out of nowhere, even in the town gardens. Back then, when I was working at the college, I would give my brother James and the other under-gardeners enough work to last the day and take myself off with my collecting bag on my back. Without the encumbrance of the apothecary business to worry about, my mother was much more cheerful. With my worries about her eased, I thought that I would be able to organise my gardening and my collecting duties more efficiently.

As soon as I had gathered what I thought was a fair number of specimens, I would contrive to drop by Jenny's door, preferably at those times when Sandy Caddas would be away from home. She used to wait for me at the side window from which she had a pretty good view of the path to the house. I'm sure she took pleasure from my visits. She would feed me freshly baked cakes or oaties and soft cheese, and mugs of her father's ale, and sometimes she would let me steal a kiss or two when there was nobody to see. One week slid into another and I was blissfully happy. I must have been, because time passed so quickly and the blue, white and pale lemon of spring flowers imperceptibly gave way to the more vibrant colours of summer. Then I would find her gathering bundles of the lavender she grew in the cottage garden, and hanging them up to dry.

'I'll take some of them into the town and sell them just as they are,' she said. 'But some of them will have to be rubbed and the flower heads stored. So you can make yourself useful!'

I helped her to do it and it was a pleasant, highly scented task. Then, Jenny and her sister would take the lavender and stitch it into muslin bags which could be placed among linens to keep the moths away. Some of these she would use at home and some would be taken into town with the bunches of lavender to be sold there. Lavender has many useful properties and she said that deterring moths was the least of them. Some of it she would make into lavender water.

'It's a very good remedy for a headache and if you sprinkle a few drops on your pillow you'll sleep soundly and your dreams will be pleasant. Take some for your mother!' she would urge me. She was a generous lass, wanting to share all that she had in the way of remedies and knowledge.

'How come you know these things?' I asked her, a little indignant that a lass should have a head so stuffed with things of which I was quite ignorant.

'I had them from my mother,' she said.

'But you said she died while you were young.'

'Aye, but I was a quick learner! Besides, she would make it all into a kind of game, so it was a pleasure, even though I was but a child. And she wrote some of it down for me.'

We have them still, those receipts. I could lay hands on them if I wanted to, hardly a book at all really, but a sheaf of papers for this and that remedy, most of them scrawled on precious scraps of paper, covering every surface, the spelling erratic, the directions cryptic.

Besides lavender, Jenny would grow pot marigolds in her garden, like so many miniature suns, shining among the other flowers. These have always been a favourite with me and she shared my affection for them. They have a lovely, peppery scent but she told me they had other valuable properties. She would make an ointment out of the petals and it was said to be very good for cuts and grazes and suchlike injuries. She gave me a pot of it to take home with me, and I used it whenever I cut my fingers in the garden, which was pretty often, and she was right. It was wonderfully effective for preventing infection.

Thomas saw me using it one day, after I had torn my hand on a rose bush. I am very fond of roses and always have been, most particularly the little wild rose of Scotland that scrambles among the walls and hedges of this country, deceptively delicate but resilient where other plants will fail. They always remind me of Jenny, with her light hair. They are lovely but, quite unlike Jenny who would not willingly have harmed anyone, they are malicious plants. They seem to wait until you turn your back on them and then they pounce on you, no matter how hard you try to avoid them. I was more cut about with roses than with anything else, even nettles, in my whole career as a gardener.

'What's that?' Thomas asked when he saw me applying Jenny's marigold ointment to the latest crop of punctures and grazes. I explained that it was something my friend had made for me, and he asked if I might procure a pot or two for him, since I obviously thought it efficacious, and he would try it as an experiment on his patients. He offered to pay for it, so I got Jenny to make a few pots for him. He came back to me for more, as much as she could supply, because he said it was extremely effective. Jenny and I joked that in due course, we might be able to resurrect the apothecary idea, with a little help from Thomas. Because this was a real skill she had and, as Thomas said, there was always a call for simple remedies that worked, especially for sailors and the like who might have no recourse to more complicated medicines during their long voyages.

'One day,' she told me, 'One day we'll maybe go into business for ourselves.'

'Do you think so?' I would have been reluctant, all the same, having tried and failed so comprehensively.

'Well, I think I would have the skills, especially with you to help me. But we would have to find another, better garden than your physic garden to supply us with plants. We'd have to grow things ourselves. Have a ready supply of the right herbs.'

I remembered my father's predecessor, and how successful he and his wife had been in similar circumstances, and it didn't seem too fanciful to think that one day Jenny and I might manage it. The unspoken assumption in all this, of course, was that we would always be together. We skirted around the idea all the time, cautiously, both aware of what a momentous commitment that might be, aware too that neither of us had the necessary resources. But I was young and strong and full of hope for the future.

▣ ▣ ▣

She had not met Thomas at that time, but she had heard about him, because I spoke about him often. In fact, I think I spoke about him rather too much for her liking.

'Thomas, Thomas,' she said. 'I hear this Doctor Thomas Brown mentioned on all sides! Is he the fount of all knowledge? Can he truly be right about everything, William?'

She was laughing as she said it, but there was a germ of truth at the heart of her complaint. I did defer to Thomas on most occasions and about most things. Over the years, I have noticed that this is a fault of men more than women. We think our heroes can do no wrong, while clear-eyed women seem able to love theirs in spite of their faults. If he told me something, I believed him. If he advised me to do something, I usually found myself obeying. And yet it was not in my nature to conform. But at that time, I think if he had told me black was really white, I would have agreed.

When my Jenny wasn't working with her plants or in the garden, she was usually to be found stitching away at her silk or her muslin. She had it in a circular wooden tambour to keep it straight and whenever one of these broke I would contrive to make another for her out of a hazel wand. The needles she used were very fine and the thread too was so fine that it was a tricky task to thread the needles. She would give Anna, her wee sister, a penny to rub beeswax on it, and coax it through the eyes, keeping several needles threaded at once to save time. When the weather and the season allowed, she would sit outside the door on a boulder, deliberately rolled there for the purpose, and she would stitch away in the sunlight. She said it was hard on the eyes otherwise, and in any case it was hard on her neck and shoulders, always bending over like that, staring at the tiny flowers and sprigs she was creating, like an artist with his brush.

I can bring her before my eyes yet, the curve of her neck, the fragility of it as she bent over, and the curls where she caught up her hair, coiling it onto her head to keep it out of her eyes. She had shapely arms and surprisingly sturdy hands with stubby nails, hands which could achieve miracles. The work was exquisite. I have never seen anything like it before or since. You would have sworn it was fine lace, but it wasn't; it was embroidery. And at the centre of the flowers were even smaller centres, each with its own design, a minute cobweb of threads as though some tiny spider had been hard at work there. Some of the work would be made up into lappets for ladies. Sometimes it might go for baby gowns, for the infants of the rich, who liked their children to appear as fashionable as themselves.

This was not, you must understand, the Ayrshire needlework currently very much in vogue and advertised in all our newspapers, especially here in Glasgow, but an older design, albeit very similar, the same that was brought by Mr Ruffini to Edinburgh from his native Italy. For that reason alone, I think Jenny could command a high price for her work. There was so little of it to be found here in the west at that time. This explained why she devoted so much of her time to it, and her father encouraged her. He liked to see her working out in the garden, taking the fresh air and sunlight as well. His philosophy was that, 'folk aye need claithes', by which he meant that the work of the weavers would never disappear. I don't think he foresaw the advent of the enormous weaving machines that would supersede his cottage industry within a generation, driving the weavers from their own homes where they were kings, controlling their work as they chose, and into the hands of the factory owners who regulated the lives of their workers in every particular. Or if he did foresee it, he dismissed it as an impossibility. Nobody, he thought, would be able to reproduce the quality of the work done by a weaver, labouring diligently under his own instructions. And perhaps he was right. But that is, I'll allow, quite another story.

▣ ▣ ▣

Once or twice, Jenny would rush out and intercept me and tell me that her father was in the weaving shop from which he might emerge at any moment, and we had better not be seen together in the house. Then we would walk a little way away and sit among the trees, just talking, just passing the time of day with daffing and laughing the way lads and lassies do and have done since time began. Once or twice she let me take her hand. When I kissed her, it was very cautiously because it was such a new thing for me to kiss a lassie. Her lips were dry and warm. The touch of them made me feel strange. I had the clean scent of her breath in my nostrils, honey, which I think she had been eating, and something else that made my heart pound and my ears sing. Then I looked up and saw her sister standing watching us, with her doll clutched in one hand and her thumb in her mouth. She had grown somewhat since that first day when Jenny had taken the swarm and she had looked on. She was watching, aye watching us, her eyes large and dark, hazel eyes, nothing like her sister's bright blue. Jenny looked around and saw her too. She rose up swiftly and flew over to her.

'You don't say aethin' aboot this! D'you hear me now? If you say aethin' at a" — she cast about her for a sufficiently horrible threat — 'I'll tak' Maisie,' (for that was the name of the wee rag doll) 'I'll tak' Maisie and put her at the back of the fire. There now!'

I thought the child would greet but she did nothing of the sort. She tucked Maisie safely under her arm, stuck out her tongue at her sister, turned around and flounced off down the path. I don't think she believed a word of the threat but the gravity of the situation must have struck her forcibly, for as far as I know, she didn't tell.

Gilbert was a different matter. Gilbert was the boy who worked for Sandy Caddas and I think right from the start he disliked me. I don't know whether it was because, young as he was, he was over-fond of Jenny or because he sensed my dislike of him. He was twelve, a scrawny, undersized lad who lived nearby with his mother and came to work for Sandy every day. He looked ill fed, and sometimes there were bruises on his face and his arms and shins. I knew Sandy treated him well enough so could only assume that his mother, or perhaps her man, who was Gilbert's stepfather, was not above giving him a beating or a kicking. I didn't enquire too closely. In fact, I ignored him as far as was possible. I'll allow I didn't like him much. I know I should have felt sorry for him. I *was* sorry. But he irritated me. He sniffed constantly, his face was covered in raw blemishes and he had a way of grinning, like a dog will grin at you with curled lips, to avert a beating. He was very polite to me, to my face, calling me Mr Lang, but there was an edge to the way he said the words, and I thought that if he could do me an ill turn, he probably would. I found him repellent. Jenny was always kind to him, and perhaps that too disposed me to dislike him. But she had a deal of sympathy for him, defending him more often than not. Sandy Caddas kept him very busy and we seldom had more than a glimpse of him, trailing after his master, or working with him at the loom and being roundly — albeit only verbally — abused when he got the threads in a fankle.

CHAPTER SIXTEEN

Whitebeam

I think at that time I was as happy as I have ever been, before or since. Having got rid of the unwanted encumbrance of the apothecary business, I was working hard in the garden, learning more of my trade with each passing season and growing in confidence. I had complete charge of the physic garden as well, although the allowances for plants and manure were made to Thomas, who promptly handed them over to me, to spend as I saw fit. I think we both knew that there, at least, we were fighting a losing battle. Besides, we had another and perhaps still more serious problem.

A little over twenty years previously, the anatomist William Hunter had died in London and, in view of his old associations with the place, he had left his entire collection to the University at Glasgow. It was the result of a lifetime's interest in many aspects of scholarship, minerals and archaeology included, and it contained books, manuscripts and artworks, as well as all kinds of anatomical curiosities.

'It's worth a fortune,' observed Thomas. 'And they will be very glad indeed to have it, but it is something of a poisoned chalice.'

'Why?'

'Well, I wonder where they are going to put it all?'

I think he already knew what their plans were and had been reluctant to tell me because he also knew what my reaction would be. Hunter had been so concerned for its preservation as a single collection that he had left a massive sum, £8,000, an amount of money which was almost beyond my comprehension, so that the university could build a museum to house it. There was to be a lecture hall as well, both for the benefit of students and for the general public to gain admittance and 'enlightenment', as he put it in his will. The museum would have to be built but, as usual, this would not be without a certain amount of debate.

I had learned by then, after so many years of labouring alongside these men of intellect, that nothing whatsoever could be done in the college without a good deal of argument. If these people were, by some miracle of transposition, to be precipitated into the real world, the world outside those venerable walls, I am convinced that they could never survive. They would not be able to so much as decide what to eat for supper, or whether they should change a shirt or wear it for one more day, so reluctant were they to determine anything without what they called 'informed debate'. With so many opinionated people gathered in one place, it was inevitable I suppose. And who am I to complain? I had spent all my young years in and around the college and it must have influenced me too, even if the harsh realities of earning bread for the table and fuel for the fire were foremost in my mind each day.

During those first years of my appointment as gardener, Faculty was still much occupied with arguments over the siting of the museum. These seemed to be centred upon whether the teaching of anatomy and midwifery should be kept separate from the housing of Hunter's great collection. Some wanted the two to be amalgamated into one building, while others argued that the elegance of the museum would definitely be harmed by the inclusion of facilities for the teaching of anatomy which was at that time and still is, for all I know, a dirty, smelly and far from elegant occupation. Parallels with butchery spring all too easily to mind. Also, not to put too fine a point on it, many of the professors considered the students to be wholly undesirable, a necessary evil, an inconvenient interruption to the real business of scholarship.

Besides, the mob outside the college walls (and who more alarming than the Glasgow mob, in full cry!) were known to be readily inflamed by any suggestion of grave robbing. And they invariably associated anatomy with the unlawful 'resurrection' of bodies for dissection. Always allowing for a certain amount of exaggeration, they were probably right in their assumption that the anatomists were so desperate for corpses upon which to practise their new skills, that they would seldom seek to question the provenance of the cadavers on offer. They would simply take the goods the gods provided and do what they wished with them.

Eventually, the authorities decided upon the physic garden as a site for the museum. It was fully enclosed, which would allow them to protect their precious collection from any possible incursions by the unwashed of the city who might wish to protest about the violence being inflicted upon the dead in the name of progress. The fact that the building reduced an already besieged physic garden to something the size of a pocket handkerchief didn't seem to concern them. But the way in which the new building ate into the already meagre and polluted area of the garden meant that I had to spend even more time foraging about the surrounding countryside for specimens for Thomas's lectures.

I must say that I enjoyed these excursions more, the more my knowledge grew. Occasionally, Thomas would even find, or perhaps he would make, the time to accompany me and we would scavenge about quite happily together, like lads let out of school. He taught me all he knew of botany in the field, and I was a regular sponge and absorbed everything he cared to tell me.

Once he brought bread and cheese, and we ensconced ourselves down beside a burn in the hills, somewhere to the south west of the city. We ate our makeshift meal with the song of water on stone as an accompaniment, and then we lay flat on our bellies, side by side, watching the eddies and dipping our fingers into the icy waters that had come tumbling down from the narrow, birch-filled glen behind us, but which were now flowing more smoothly between flat sun-warmed stones.

'Can you guddle for trout?' he asked, brushing crumbs from his hands into the water.

'Aye. Well, I know how to dae it, but I would not say I am a master of the art.'

He nudged me, grinning. Although the water was cold, it was a warm day and before we knew it, we were in our bare feet, wading cautiously into the burn and standing there in companionable silence, peering down into the water. Neither of us caught anything that day, but I mind yet the fishes rising to the crumbs and flies on the surface, the breeze that lifted our hair, the scent of grasses and the sight and sound of swifts and swallows, soaring and diving all around us, hunting those same flies, their high, sharp calls piercing the air.

At such times I would find myself torn between disappointment that I would not be able to visit Jenny, and the absolute pleasure of his company. Not once did he suggest that I should introduce him to Jenny on those occasions. He never even mentioned her, and I never raised the matter either, much too happy to be his companion and confidant for however short a time, regretting only that such occasions were so few, so far between.

⊞ ⊞ ⊞

All the same, I was surprised when he suggested that an excursion farther afield might be in order: a journey to the island of Arran, which I had never even seen at that time, although its peaks and glens are clearly visible from the coast to the south and west of this city, when they are not obscured by all-too-frequent clouds and mist. But then I had never had occasion to travel so far. He said that we should be away some time – a week or more – and he made me read a volume from his library by one Martin Martin in order, I think, to tantalise me as much as to inform me.

It was called *A Description of the Western Isles of Scotland*. I have a copy of it in my own library now and often find myself rereading it, although it was written more than a hundred years ago.

Martin had visited the Isle of Arran and reported, among much else, that there was a 'valuable curiosity in this isle which they call Baul Muluy, that is Molingus his stone globe'. This Molingus was, I believe, very nearly a contemporary of our own patron saint Mungo, living only half a century later, and dying a martyr to his Christian cause. Martin describes the globe in some detail.

'It is a green stone, much like a globe in figure, about the bigness of a goose egg. The virtue of it is to remove stitches from the sides of sick persons, by laying it close to the place affected; and if the patient does not outlive the distemper they say the stone removes out of its bed of its own accord. The natives use this stone for swearing decisive oaths upon it.

'They ascribe another extraordinary virtue to it, and it is this: the credulous vulgar firmly believe that if this stone is cast among the front of an enemy they will all run away and that as often as the enemy rallies, if this stone is cast among them, they will lose courage and retire. They say that MacDonald of the Isles carried this stone about him and that victory was always on his side when he threw it among the enemy. This stone is now in the custody of Margaret Miller, alias Mackintosh. She lives in Baelliminich and preserves the globe with abundance of care. It is wrapped up in fair linen cloth and about that there is a piece of woollen cloth; and she keeps it still locked up in her chest when it is not given out to exert its qualities.'

'I should like very much to see that stone and test its medicinal properties,' said Thomas, with a laugh.

'And do you think it would be efficacious?'

'Who knows what might happen if there was a belief in it? If I were one of the credulous vulgar, who knows what it might do for me?'

'Perhaps we could bring it back with us and cast it before Faculty.'

'Perhaps we could. But you will come with me?'

'I'd like nothing better. But what will Faculty say if their gardener goes jaunting off on a sea voyage?'

'Oh, Faculty have already agreed,' he said, airily. 'And all without the assistance of Baul Molingus. I have already asked them. You see this is in the nature of a collecting trip. Our first real collecting trip together, William. And perhaps the first of many more to come. I hope so at any rate!'

'How did you persuade them?'

'There is a tree grows on the island. A whitebeam of great beauty and interest, which is only to be found there. It is the *Sorbus pseudofennica* or Arran service tree, although I have also heard it called the bastard mountain ash.'

'I've never heard of it.'

'No, you would not. It was discovered only a handful of years ago, in Glen Diomhan at the north end of the island. In essence this tree seems to be some rare product of the rowan and the whitebeam together. I should like to see it, to draw its leaves, to bring a small specimen back with me if I could.'

'It would never survive in the physic garden.'

'No, it would not, although I have not said as much to Faculty. But perhaps my uncle's garden in Ayrshire might be a better home for it. Will you come with me, William? I should very much like to have your company.'

❑ ❑ ❑

It was a very long time ago, and now I am hard put to it to write the details of that voyage. I remember it more as a series of pictures, like a man looking at illustrations in some fine old volume. My mother fussed most dreadfully, I know that, and I'm sure she thought we would both be drowned and that she would never see either of us again. You would have thought we were sailing halfway round the world, rather than across the sea to Arran. She begged and pleaded with me not to go, but wild horses would not have prevented me.

I know that we took a gabbert from the Broomielaw down to the coast, and I have an image of the tall Merchants' Steeple on the skyline and the smoke of the city behind us, with the women doing their washing on the banks of the river as we went past. From the port, we could see the Isle of Arran lurking on the horizon, all misty peaks and troughs, like the blessed isle of the ancient Celts. Wearing borrowed oilskins against the weather, we embarked on a small sailing vessel which carried us over the Firth of Clyde. Thomas pointed out to me that the mountains are said to be in the shape of a sleeping warrior who will awaken when he is needed, but I'm afraid I couldn't see it myself. Besides, although the firth was reasonably calm, I was very sick and disorientated, especially when we reached the mid point between the mainland and the island, and each shore seemed so very far away that the long horizontals on all sides, with the dazzling height of the sky above and the heaving green waters below, made my head spin. I was imagining all kinds of monsters down there. Once or twice, there would be a swell on the surface, and we would see some great creatures swimming by. The sailors said they were called basking sharks. They roamed these waters in profusion and were harmless enough creatures, being quite without teeth, except that they could overturn your boat if you did not keep a sharp lookout for them.

We had brought food with us, and Thomas, who seemed quite indifferent to the motion, encouraged me to eat. 'An empty stomach does the mal de mer no good at all,' he told me. 'You must eat and it will settle you.'

Not a morsel could I manage, and the movement of the vessel induced a dreadful dizziness and stupefaction, followed by a dry retching which was most unpleasant. I felt chilled to the bone and utterly miserable. The sailors laughed at me behind their hands until Thomas spoke sharply to them, whereupon they looked sheepish and ignored me. I had begun to think that my mother had been right after all, that we never would arrive, but so dreadful were the sensations induced by the motion that, for a while, I confess I didn't care whether we arrived or not. Death seemed a good and desirable option.

Then – quite suddenly so it seemed – the misty distances resolved themselves into land, we were in the lee of the island, the air had the scent of grass and other growing things upon it, and miraculously my sickness evaporated. I felt quite hungry.

We spent several days on the island, being offered hospitality, food and comfortable beds in one or two good houses, although what Martin Martin had pleased to call the 'natives' were poor enough and for the most part went barefoot and spoke in the Gaelic tongue. Our hosts were minor gentry, people of consequence with whom Thomas seemed familiar: a minister of the kirk and, later in the week, a younger son of some old highland family whose son attended the university. They were not ostentatiously rich. Their houses were not large and were overcrowded with children and dogs, as well as family servants who seemed more like friends and who might, so Thomas said, be impoverished relatives, but they lived contentedly enough and they possessed books which they seemed to prize. Thomas would never introduce me as his gardener, but rather as his friend and fellow botanist, and I would always concur. If he was happy to call me that, what reason did I have to argue with him? Nobody questioned him. I minded my manners, but these were island folk and they made me welcome, quietly and without fuss.

We were fortunate in the weather: it was one of those long, fine spells with which this coast is sometimes blessed. At such times, you can never imagine any other kind of weather, but fall into the way of thinking it will persist, which it never does. The skies were blue with skeins of thin, white clouds chasing across them from the west and if ever rain came, it seemed to leap right over the island, to fall on the mainland beyond. We walked throughout the days gathering specimens as we went, or simply observed what grew where. In the evening we were entertained by our hosts with good plain food. We ate well, more meat than I had eaten throughout the whole of the previous year I think: pies stuffed with mutton, venison haunches and stews, for the island is home to a great many deer. We drank French wine, sometimes watered, sometimes not, and once or twice we were served tea out of fine porcelain cups, all of which must have been imported from the city. The lady of the house seemed inordinately proud, both of her cups and her tea, which she kept locked away in a little wooden box.

In one of the houses, the more crowded of the two, we were asked to share a big down-filled bed, with cool linen sheets, up in the attic at the very top of the old house. I think they would not have put us together had we been servant and master, but as they thought we were friends, they had assumed that we would not find the arrangement inconvenient. I confess I was embarrassed by Thomas's proximity. Just at first. I had slept with my brothers all my life, but this seemed very different.

At some point in the short, summer night, I awoke and listened to the scurrying of mice, partying behind the walls, and to the eerie calls of some unknown seabird flying overhead. It was a lonely sound, a high double note that pierced the darkness and made my heart sink, without any discernible cause. It brought before my eyes a vision of endless seas and dark shores and the sadness of some creature seeking, but never finding, its mate. Then I became aware of Thomas's even breathing beside me. He was fast asleep. I would only need to reach out in order to touch him. I could feel the warmth of him from where I lay, smell the faint sweat of his body, the peat smoke that clung to us both. I felt all unreal, as though I had been transported to some other universe where the normal laws of this one did not apply, so strange did my situation seem at that moment. I think I put out my hand towards him, but he sighed, stretched a little in his sleep and turned away from me. I lay on my back, counting his breaths until I too fell asleep.

On our daily excursions, he would stride ahead, and I would follow him. It was always that way round. He would lead, I would follow. He would talk, I would listen. But you must not think I resented him for it. I was entirely happy in his company. It was as though an enchantment had fallen on me, more surely than on those old enemies of the MacDonalds, defeated by the Baul Molingus. My mother, my siblings, my work in the gardens, even Jenny, faded from my mind until they seemed impossibly remote. I believe that for those few summer days, as never before or since, I lived entirely in the present, with Thomas as my treasured companion. It was a glimpse of paradise and I existed, for that short space of time, entirely without regret for past mistakes or fearful anticipation of future sorrow.

As the week progressed, I found myself wishing that it would never come to an end.

I sat one night, rocking a little back and forth before the fire that our hosts had lit in our attic room.

'What's wrong?' he asked.

'I wish we could do this more often. That's all.'

'But there will be more voyages and more excursions for us. Perhaps even farther afield. Why should there not be? We work well together, do we not?'

'We do.'

'We are good companions, we two. I always thought it might be so and now I know it for sure.'

As for the declared purpose of our visit, we found the Arran service tree. Thomas sketched and took specimens of its fine green leaves, its slender branches, its small, hard fruits. The day before we were due to leave, we dug up a sapling, from where it had been clinging to a cleft, on the side of a glen at the north end of the island. I advised him to take a little of the earth that had nurtured it and this he did, potting it up to preserve it for the journey.

The sailors said it was as well we were leaving, because the weather would break within a few days. How they knew such things I couldn't say, but they were right, because by the time we were safely back in Glasgow, there were strong winds and rain blowing in from the west, and the voyage seemed like a dream, a magical, never-to-be-repeated experience.

Thomas had me plant his tiny specimen tree in a bigger pot, and it seemed to thrive, although I had half expected it, like the fairy gold of the ancient tales, to wither and die, leaving only a handful of dried leaves. Later he took it off with him to Ayrshire, and I suppose it must have lived, because I think I recognised those few skeleton leaves slipped into his commonplace book, recognised them all too clearly. Fairy gold after all, and just as transitory.

CHAPTER SEVENTEEN

Weavers and Sailors

Upon our return to the city, seeing how hard it was for me to obtain books, Thomas said, 'Would you like to have the use of my library, William?'

'I'd be glad of it,' I told him, frankly, still basking in the ease induced by our voyage to the west.

I was free to browse there from that day on. He would even have let me take books away with me, although I was reluctant to do so, since I felt that our house was too smoky and too thronged with lads and lassies, my siblings and sometimes their companions, to be a safe haven for the precious printed word.

Besides, I enjoyed my occasional snatched hour, seated beside the fire in his house, with the luxury of being able to take down and read whatever book I wished. I was much taken with his many volumes on botanical subjects, Gerard's *Herbal* and the works of the great naturalist Carl Linnaeus, chiefly his *Materia Medica*.

Thomas's wife, Marion, was very kind to me on those occasions when she found me in her library. The servants were less so. I think his housekeeper was very conscious that she had a common gardener in his dirty boots, however diligently I might clean them before my visits, cluttering up one of the most important rooms in the house, and I sensed her unspoken animosity whenever she came into the room and found me there. It was in every clearing of her throat, every flounce of her skirt, every hostile glance. I would have removed those same boots out of respect for Marion's carpets, but was always torn between shame at my boots and shame at appearing in my much-darned woollen socks. In short, I did not know what I should do and nobody seemed to want to tell me. The housekeeper might have advised me, but she was too respectful of her employer to go against his wishes in any way, and Thomas had obviously told her to treat me with every politeness. All the same, she found many small ways of demonstrating her disapproval: banging doors, rattling drapes or sending servants up the back stairs and into the room to rake out the fire, filling the place with noise and clouds of ash while I was reading.

There came a day when Jenny suggested that it would be a good thing if I met her father. After all, as the college gardener, with friends among the gentry, I was a lad o' pairts and I had prospects. She felt her father might approve of me as much as anybody who had come courting her, although he could perhaps have wished for a more prosperous match for his Jenny, one of his fellow weavers who might in due course set up his own weaving shed, and make a good life for her. A gardener would be a poor comparison with such as these.

'I chose my moment well,' she said. 'I waited until he had finished his evening meat and ale, and then I told him that I had met a nice young man and had some conversation with him. I asked him if I might invite him to the house and he said I could.'

I sometimes think, now I am older and wiser, that he must have known all about us and been simply biding his time until Jenny should pluck up the courage to tell him of our friendship, which was clearly beginning to verge on courtship. Perhaps he had made enquiries and found out who I was and what I did. It is most certainly what I would have done myself in the same circumstances. I have read my *Romeo and Juliet* and am well aware, even without my wife's wise words on the subject, that forbidden fruits taste the sweetest. And what gardener doesn't know that seeds germinate best in the dark, struggling to reach the light?

He was a wise man, Alexander Caddas, taciturn and a wee thing cautious, not a man to make friends too readily but not a man to let them go either, once made. The more I knew of him the more I found to like about the man, although I'll confess that the first time we met I was tongue-tied and racking my brains to think of something to say to him that might win him to my side.

I sometimes wonder if Jenny's sister, Anna, didn't let slip something about my visits, although she always denied it. Or perhaps jealous Gilbert had seen fit to mention it, although I can't imagine Sandy Caddas paying much attention to any such tittle tattle on the part of his young apprentice. Whatever the real story, he was cautious of me just at first but by no means as disapproving as he might have been. He shook hands with me and welcomed me into the house, which was already very familiar to me, although I had to pretend otherwise. Because Jenny's mother was dead and gone, the task of finding a suitable husband for his precious elder daughter had begun to weigh heavily on his shoulders. He was not in any way demonstrative, but I noticed the way he laid his hand on Jenny's shoulder, the way he absent-mindedly stroked her hair, the way his gaze flickered this way and that between us, assessing me in the light of his daughter and all that he wished and hoped for her.

I flatter myself that he liked me well enough on that first meeting. He questioned me about my work, and seemed impressed that I had been made gardener at such a young age, but seemed more impressed when I said it was all down to my father. I added that I would rather have been working with him yet, and learning what I could from him, than having the whole of it on my shoulders, which was the plain truth. But I suppose I was canny too, because I was trying hard to impress him with my general worthiness. I don't know quite what I aspired to. There was small chance of my marrying for some years. My father had married on less, right enough, but his own parents had been dead and gone by then, and he had but one elder brother, John, for whom my own brother was named.

My uncle John had been a sailor and a legend in our family. On the scant evidence of my voyage to the Isle of Arran, I could see that I had not taken after him in matters of seamanship. I remember him visiting us just the once, when I was very young. He had brought not only the aura of tar on his blue cloth jacket, but a plain grey parrot that sat on his shoulder and enlivened our house with strange utterances in a variety of languages, interspersed with the occasional cackle of mad laughter. My mother was terrified of it and thought it an embodiment of the devil himself, but I found it very wonderful. Its name was Apollyon, a name that I only later discovered meant 'the destroyer'. It would climb down from my uncle's shoulder and walk across the kitchen floor, its intelligent eyes roaming the room in search of human prey. It seemed to have a great fascination with feminine attire and would tweak my mother's skirt up to show her petticoat if it got the chance, scandalising her and frightening her in equal measure. She blamed my uncle for teaching it such behaviour, but he said that it was very old, that parrots lived far longer than men, and he had got it from a shipmate who had fallen too ill to look after it. Who could say which previous owner was responsible for Apollyon's execrable manners?

The scent of tar filled the cottage. I have only to get a whiff of it now, tar and wood and canvas, the scent of ships, you can smell it down the Broomielaw any day, and I'm back there, a young boy still, listening to my uncle John and my father talking, while John scratched Apollyon's head and the bird seemed to be following the conversation, looking curiously from one to the other. I had seen nothing like John until that time. He swayed from side to side when he walked. His face and forearms were the colour of polished mahogany and he wore his hair in a pigtail. Apollyon would sit on his shoulder and peck gently at the plaited hair, which seemed to be a mark of affection with him.

John and Apollyon brought with them a breath of foreign lands and strange people and I remember being enchanted by both of them. Bessie was still at home when John came visiting but she found him disturbing and the wee ones were frankly afraid of him. James was but a wean and barely remembered him afterwards. Johnnie and Rab weren't even born, although I suppose Johnnie might have been on the way, which would explain my parents' choice of his name. Uncle John sat and drank with my father and told stories of his time at sea, and we listened. He spoke of the constant noise, the creaking and groaning of timbers and the endless movement of the ship accommodating herself to the waves.

'Were you sick?' I asked him. Even then I knew that the motion of the waves could make you unwell.

'Oh aye, I was sick right enough. But I soon got used to it. Most folk do!' he said. 'Just at first, when you step on dry land again, the earth moves under you like a restless horse. But as soon as it stops doing that, you know that your sickness will be over and done, and that's always the way of it. I haven't had the sea sickness since. But if you stay on land for too long, back it will come again, so I never stay ashore for very long!'

I questioned him closely, to the point where my mother tried to hush me, but he only said, 'No, no. Let the lad alane. Why wouldn't he be curious?'

He spoke of ship's biscuits and weevils, which you had to eat or you would starve, of rats the size of dogs and cockroaches as big as your hand. I saw my mother flinch and turn pale, my father watching him quietly, with a wee smile, just as though he had heard this kind of thing before.

But he also spoke of the scent of exotic flowers and lush, loud forests where strange birdsong was to be heard and whenever he did that, Apollyon nestled close, as though he understood. He spoke of men who were enslaved, and how he would never sail on that kind of ship, because even a working man had his honour. He spoke of insects that bit and could kill you – a man might die, raving, only a few days later – and of stranger things yet, sea creatures that you saw when you were on watch by night, large, swimming creatures that you could put no name to, but which came to investigate the boat. Some of them were whales, but some of them might not be, and God alone knew what they might be, these monsters of the deep. And he spoke of fire on the water, the droplets that shone as though there was light in them, even without the moon to illuminate them. And at last, he spoke of remote paradise islands, where the people were kind beyond kindness, and where nobody seemed to go hungry because the land supplied all that was needed in the way of food and drink, a land where the cold winds never blew, and where even the rain was warm. It was in places such as these – and here he hesitated, gazing at my mother – that the lassies were very bonny and wore flowers in their hair and 'whiles not much else'.

I saw my mother frown at this, and my father raise his hand, and glance over at me, as though to warn his brother that young ears were listening, and no more was said about the lassies with flowers in their hair. Nevertheless there was enchantment in his every word, and I remember thinking, even then, that it would be a fine thing to travel, to go across the seas and feel those balmy airs, to smell the scent of as yet unknown plants and bring them home with you, even at the risk of dying of outlandish diseases.

He stayed the best part of a week with us and seemed to have siller in his purse all the time – something that was a great wonder to us, for we had grown used to counting every penny. He bought fruit for Apollyon, which the bird would hold in its claw to eat as a man will hold a piece of bread. He would fetch sweetmeats for us and posies of sweet violets for my mother and before he left, he presented her with a bonny silk shawl, which he said reminded him of the shawls he had seen on his travels. He bought a second-hand fiddle for himself in the town as well.

'Perhaps some other sailor was forced to pawn it to pay for his bed and board,' he told me, with a grin. 'Ah weel, it's found a good hame wi' me! I'll mak' it sing! And it'll soon be off on its travels once again.'

'Did you never have a fiddle before, Uncle John?' I asked him and he said, 'Oh aye, but I broke it over some man's head in the Carolinas, some man that was beating his woman in the corner

129

of a tavern. She was screaming blue murder and he was swearing and beating her with his fists and I brought the fiddle down over his head and knocked him clean out with it, but it broke into a dozen pieces. I thought it a good sacrifice to make, for all that I half regretted it back on the ship, on a long sea voyage, with naethin' to play, and naethin' to pass the time!' He winked at me, a prodigious wink that screwed up the whole side of his face, and I thought he was very wonderful.

He played us a jig and something that he said was a hornpipe. Apollyon seemed to enjoy the music and jumped up and down as though he was dancing in time to the rhythm. But at the end of the week my Uncle John packed up his tarry canvas bag, took his fiddle and his parrot with him, and went down the Broomielaw in search of a ship. That was the last we ever saw of him and his wonderful bird.

He died a few years before my father. A laboriously written letter from a shipmate brought news of his death in some terrible storm in Biscay, when he had gone overboard, falling from the rigging. I mostly forgot about him, although I have to say I remembered his tales and his parrot, long after the look of his face had faded from my mind in all but the most general particulars: a pair of bright blue eyes in a sun-scarred face, a stranger who seemed more like a foreigner than a blood relation.

He had been my father's sole surviving relative at the time when my father and mother were married, but I was in quite a different situation. I had my widowed mother, my brothers and sisters to provide for as well as myself, and there seemed little possibility of my being able to support a wife for some years to come. The best I could hope for would be to put the younger lassies into service somewhere, if I could find anybody foolish or tolerant enough to take them on, and to see what I could do for the younger lads as and when they reached working age. I was pretty sure that James would become a gardener like myself and I worried that Rab was so delicate that he might not live to make adult, never mind old bones, but most of the time my family were the cause of a sort of general worry. All I could do was work to the best of my ability and hope that sooner or later, some solution would turn up that would allow me to marry, set up house and start a family of my own. But I had no notion of what that eventuality might be.

I do remember my first proper invitation to Jenny's house, though, and I'm grateful to her father for avoiding those very obvious questions about my prospects and, instead, speaking of my brothers and sisters and my mother, with a good deal of sympathy at her bereavement. He asked me all about the college garden and what we grew there and why, so that I found myself on solid ground and could answer all his questions with knowledge and enthusiasm. I remember having to be very careful not to let slip that I had spent rather more time with Jenny than we were owning up to. Her blue eyes lifted to meet mine from time to time, with a mixture of warning and amusement, and Anna opened her mouth every now and then to say, 'But William usually ...' and then stopped because her sister had administered a sharp poke in the ribs or a kick under the table. We thought we were doing very well indeed.

Some time later, I realised what fools we were, and what a kindly man Sandy Caddas must have been, to let us get away with it, to tolerate the string of small lies with which I abused his hospitality. But he let it all go and welcomed me in as Jenny's acknowledged suitor and, for a while, we were very happy indeed not to have to dissemble any longer about a friendship which seemed to be growing closer with each month that passed.

CHAPTER EIGHTEEN

Fevers

Quite early in our acquaintance, Thomas persuaded me and my mother that my brothers and sisters and myself should be inoculated against the smallpox, which was then a great trial to the whole country but particularly in the cities. A most terrible illness it was, killing vast numbers and scarring where it did not kill, particularly among the needy. It was no respecter of persons and the children of the gentry were as much at risk as any other, but it did seem to strike at those who were poor and ill fed, and who were living as we did, fairly crammed together in small, damp houses.

'I'll come to your house to carry out the procedure,' he said. My mother was very dubious about the whole enterprise but finally allowed herself to be persuaded. She wanted to undergo the procedure too, out of a sense of loyalty to her children. We knew that it was a risky business, for all that Thomas tried to reassure us. There were tales of people who had contracted the disease itself from the preventative. But Thomas told my mother that there was no need for her to be inoculated. If she had not, so far, caught the disease, then she would in all likelihood not catch it now. He was right. It would be true to say that it was very largely a disease of the young, I suppose because those who survived possessed some property which must repel the sickness.

I remember her pacing up and down the kitchen the night before, saying, 'If only your father were here. He would know what to do. He would know whether it was the right thing to do or no.' Eventually her respect for Doctor Brown – and my persuasion – overrode her natural suspicion of anything new, and she trusted him enough to allow him to treat all her children, even wee Rab, who was her baby and her golden boy.

It was a great novelty for us at the time, although I think it is much in use nowadays and so may not be quite the strange experience that it was for us. On the day when Thomas came to do the procedure, he passed a few pleasantries with my mother and then assembled us in the kitchen. We must have been a strange sight, lined up with our arms bared, like participants in some secret ritual, with my mother hovering about, wringing her hands with anxiety on our behalf. He brought a packet out of his pocket and said that the *matter*, which would do the business, was in fine cotton thread therein.

He took a small bit of the thread, saturated with this *matter*, between the thumb and forefinger of his left hand and a lancet in his right hand. At the sight of the sharp instrument, Johnnie set up a great wailing.

'Don't be such a baby!' said our mother, but she herself looked like to cry in sympathy and I saw her lip trembling.

'Hush now, Johnnie Lang!' said Thomas, quite sternly for him. 'Are you not planning to be a big, brave sailor one day? And look at your sisters. They are not making such a dreadful noise. Will you be shamed by the bravery of a pair of lassies?'

Johnnie bit his lip at that and quietened down somewhat.

Thomas dipped the lancet in the cotton thread and, with the point of it, made two dots about two inches apart on the arm of each of us. It looked to me, for I watched him with interest, like a strange kind of needlework. He dipped the lancet in water and then in the cotton thread and onto our arms again.

James and Johnnie began to make a great fuss again, as the punctures were made, bawling and crying that it was 'sair' as was their wont. I think they were more feart than they let on, and fear always seems to increase pain, or so Thomas remarked quietly in my ear. Rab was stoical about the whole process, although he gave a little start when Thomas introduced the lancet into his arm, but he said stoutly that it was 'not so bad after all'. The girls — following Bessie's example, for she had come home to undergo the procedure — declared that it only tickled a bit and giggled and fidgeted with their feet. The lassies were right. It was a mild discomfort only, just at first. We were to stand there with our arms exposed to the cold air for about three minutes till the thing was almost dried up, and it was plain to see that, where the dots were, there was a red mark, growing vivid almost instantly, like the sting you get from a midge bite or a nettle.

Thomas's advice was that we must eat meat at dinner if we could (a rare enough occurrence for us at any time) and then abstain from it for a little while after, which was no hardship to us for the same reason. He prescribed a powder of calamine for night time, and in the morning we were to take water gruel, as much as we could eat. The small irritation continued on our arms for some time, and the wee ones felt worse than we did, becoming hot and fractious for a spell, but that was the whole of it. Thomas said that we should be safe from the disease for some years afterwards, although the process might have to be repeated in due course.

My superstitious mother could not fathom how it came about and confessed to me afterwards that she thought it was a kind of magic. Thomas seemed very excited about the whole thing and I asked him to explain the process to me, for I did not think it could be magic.

'Those who work in the countryside, most particularly dairymaids who spend much of their time among cows, almost never contract the smallpox,' he said. 'We believe they have somehow been exposed to some similar but less virulent illness among cattle, and — much like your Jenny with her bee stings I suppose — their bodies have grown familiar with the sickness and never seem to fall ill with it afterwards.'

'But how did they discover the procedure? How did they find it out?'

'Some doctors decided to take a little of the matter from the sores on the cows that were ill but seldom died of the disease, and introduce it into their own blood.'

'Was that not dangerous?'

'Oh very dangerous indeed, since they would have no idea of the effects. It was significant that they never took the smallpox either, and neither did any that they similarly inoculated. There is that in the blood which must learn to recognise the sickness in some way and reject it from making inroads into the body. That is as much as we know. But we are learning, William, we are learning all the time.'

Afterwards, we had few ill effects. My mother need not have worried. Rab ran a fever for some time, to be sure, but Thomas came back and bled him a little. He instructed my mother to sponge him down with tepid water, and he was soon quite well again.

◼ ◼ ◼

This procedure, which we had great faith in, serves to explain why, when I took a severe chill in the rainy weather at the tail end of 1804, I had no fears that my illness might be the smallpox, and I was confident that I would soon shake it off. I believed myself to be a strong young man. At that age, you never consider any alternative. My father had had the weight of years on his back, but when you are in your twenties, you know that you are immortal and invincible, if ever you spare a moment to think about such things at all. During that winter of 1804 and right into January and February of 1805 I felt constantly unwell. The air rattled in my chest, and a horrible, dry cough woke me up five or six times in the night and saw me sitting bolt upright in the box bed with its high piled pillows, fighting for every breath.

My mother, thoroughly frightened by my pallor and shortness of breath, fussed over me, cooked beef broth for me and made me wear flannel next to my chest. I kept going for as long as I was able with all the work that needed to be done in preparation for the winter season in the garden. And then there was structural work to be undertaken, paths to be laid and walls to be built, as well as all kinds of pruning and cutting. I think she must have had my father and his death very strongly in her mind at that time. The garden might lie fallow over the winter, but that didn't mean that there was any less work for the gardeners. I couldn't shirk it, no matter how unwell I felt, although James told me to rest, he and the other lads would get on with things. I knew they were but haphazard workers when unsupervised and felt I had to be there as much as possible, to make sure they were doing exactly what I had told them.

The weather was cold and very wet. It is the constant rain that keeps the fields green throughout the whole year in these parts. But in the town, the rain clouds seemed to make the filth and fumes from the type foundry hang low in ragged, oily vapours. My breathing became even more painful, and each breath would set me off coughing all over again, as though the air itself was irritating my lungs. Which perhaps it was. I was more often than not soaked through to the skin by the time I got into the house at night and I never seemed able to rid myself of the ill effects. I would think I was getting well after a day or two's rest, but then I would go out into the gardens and the next night would wake up shivering and sweating and coughing all over again. Everything was a trial to me. I thought sometimes that my legs would not hold me up for one instant longer. One cough would spawn an army. I would be racked with them, bent double, sucking in air and expelling it until my ribs ached.

Thomas had been away on family business for a few weeks. On his return, he missed me in the garden. I had not told him of my plight, or not the whole of it, keeping it from him out of a curious reluctance to admit to my own weakness. At last, he sought out James and asked what was wrong with me. Whenever I could contrive to visit her, Jenny would send me away with a jar of honey, and now Thomas sent a message with James, in which he advised me to take a little rum or whisky if I could get it, with the honey and some lemons. Whisky was available in the town, as was rum in plenty, but I could no more afford to buy lemons than I could afford to buy books. These fruits were very plentiful in Glasgow at that time, coming in on the vessels from foreign parts, and Thomas had all kinds of acquaintance aboard these ships, because sometimes he would acquire plant specimens from the captains, men whom he paid to find such things for him. But lemons were much too costly for me.

The gentlemen's clubs of the town still make their Glasgow punch with rum from the Carolinas, brown sugar which is seldom in short supply and lemons. There is a way of making it, just so, with a sherbet compounded of sugar and lemons and water – the quality of the sherbet dictates the quality of the finished punch – and once made, you add rum to taste. I would never have deemed it a health-giving drink, and my mother had a positive aversion to spirits, but Thomas said that a type of this drink, made with Scots whisky, might do some good to my poor wheezing chest and even if it did no good whatsoever, it would make me feel better. Then, Thomas arrived at the door with a whole bag full of lemons.

'Just what the doctor ordered, Mistress Lang,' he told my mother, who seemed tongue-tied by the very sight of him, let alone his unexpected gift.

She viewed the bag of sweet-smelling lemons as some exotic fruit, which they were to her of course, as they were to all of us, and was inclined to use them one quarter slice at a time, in an effort to make them last. I was sitting in front of the fire with a woollen blanket wrapped around me. My teeth were chattering, my hands and feet were icy, though my head was hot, and I felt strange and otherwordly altogether. Thomas saw me and seemed very concerned. I remember his sharp intake of breath, the way he practically ran across the room. He sat down beside me and put one hand on my forehead and then took hold of my wrist with the other. He said he was counting my heartbeats and that I was much too hot and the pulse, as he called it, was rather fast. There was some comfort in the touch of his hand and I found, to my immense shame, that I didn't want him to let go. I felt like a wean and, in my debilitated state, I wanted only to close my eyes, lean up against him and go to sleep, secure in his warm presence, as I had done in that feather bed, on the Isle of Arran.

I think my mother would have been horrified to see me so familiar with a man she considered to be the gentry. As it was, I felt the shameful tears prickling at the back of my eyes. My throat was swelling up with them too, and I turned away lest he should see my weakness. Well, I'm sure he *did* see my weakness, for when I looked back, he was gazing at me steadily with a mixture of compassion and concern. He moved to crouch a little in front of me, so that my mother could not see. His fingers moved down from my wrist to my hand, and he squeezed it once, very firmly, which brought the tears to my eyes all over again, and then he let go.

'Ah, William!' he said. 'My poor William. You should have sent for me before this!'

He tucked the blanket more closely around me and told my mother to mix the lemons up with honey and some whisky, which he had brought with him in a silver flask. He supervised the task, tut-tutted at the way she was scrimping with the lemons, made her cut them in halves and squeeze them generously into the drink. Then he told her to mix an equally generous quantity of honey with the lemon juice.

'Don't skimp, don't skimp,' he said. 'Mistress Jenny Caddas is not short of honey, I'm thinking!'

He watched while she heated it over the fire and then he added a large measure of whisky with his own hand and brought it over to me in a cup.

'Drink it slowly,' he said. 'But drink all of it.'

I did as I was told. I would have drunk whatever he put into my hand at that moment. He could have prescribed poison for me, and I would have taken it gladly.

Because of the inoculation, I did not fear the smallpox, but I was terrified that I might start coughing blood, which would have been a sure sign of consumption or something equally fatal. We had seen whole families fall victim to the disease and drop off the bough, one after another. One of the old gardeners had buried seven children and his wife as well, although he himself had survived unscathed in body, if not in mind.

I seemed constantly debilitated and yet there was no respite from the work, and I worried that I was neglecting the gardens and that complaints would surely be made against me. Thomas said I was not to worry, but was just to think about getting well again. If there were any complaints he would write to Faculty on my behalf and all would be well. And I believed him. I trusted him completely. Why would I not? He had given me no reason to do otherwise.

Whether it was the whisky toddy or some other medicine that Thomas prescribed for me, or what my mother called his 'healing hands', by the time the milder spring weather came in, I was beginning to feel stronger and more myself.

After the gift of lemons she became quite besotted by him, although such things as inoculation had never inspired a similar admiration.

'You look a little better,' said Thomas, when next he visited. 'I confess I've been worried about you. But the sooner you can go out into the countryside again and get away from this wretched city for a few hours, the better it will be for your health.'

He was right of course, although I still had some misgivings about the amount of extra work involved in gathering samples for him. I had been head gardener for some four years, and was beginning to feel very comfortable with the job, was beginning to feel that I knew what I was doing. But all the same, I realised that complaints were still being made about the state of the gardens and the fault was deemed to be mine and mine alone.

CHAPTER NINETEEN

An Uncommon Gardener

I believe some of the complaints about me were instigated by Professor Jeffray and, looking back, I sometimes wonder if his disapproval of my friendship with Thomas Brown lay at the root of them. He had noticed the familiarity between us. Who would not have noticed it? Thomas never hid it. I think Jeffray found it incomprehensible that a man of Brown's standing in the college as well as in the town should be on friendly terms with a mere gardener. That Thomas thought I was no common gardener (as he was often at pains to tell me and anyone who would listen) only served to irritate Jeffray the more. He could not understand it, and I think it inspired a kind of revulsion in him. But perhaps the fact that Thomas could be on such easy terms with everyone – scholars, professors, gardeners – irritated him even more.

'Would it not be better to send one of the common gardeners foraging for specimens?' Thomas remarked. 'That's what the professor said, William. And I said a common gardener would be quite ignorant of the places where he might find the wild plants necessary and that such a man – quite unlike yourself, William – would be unqualified for the task of field botanist. I said that I needed an uncommon gardener.'

'Well, thank-you for your kind words. But I don't want to antagonise the man.'

'And neither have you. You can leave all that to me! I admire him in many ways, but I am not afraid of him.'

I had no option but to neglect the college gardens at times. More than ever, I was feeling that there were not enough hours in a day. I was overstretched and not quite in full health yet. Moreover, I was always trying to supplement my meagre income with the sale of crops from a few plots of land leased from the college, plots which I was supposed to tend in my spare time, but I had none.

Besides, I had constant troubles with the younger scholars, who seemed to be intent on making my life a misery, marauding about the gardens when they should have been studying, particularly during the winter months. In winter, the rule was now that the students were allowed to use the gardens. This had been introduced in an effort to encourage them to take air and exercise, but they were — not to put too fine a point on it — a rabble, or so it seemed to me who had the job of curbing their unruly behaviour, without having any real authority over them. When they had over-indulged in ale or, much worse, in rum punch or whisky toddies, they were uncontrollable. They would start fires and fights in about equal measure and the damage to trees and plants was extensive. Besides all that, I knew I was fighting a losing battle with the type foundry, and so I swung between the two extremes of pleasure and despair.

Things came to a head in the summer of 1806, when Thomas took it upon himself to write a letter to Professor Jeffray on my behalf. I think he was alarmed by some of the vitriol that had been coming my way. I must say I was both grateful to him and touched by his obvious regard for me. Mind you, when I first read the opening — he let me see the missive before he sent it to Jeffray — I almost lost my temper. And I can quote it, because it is here yet, in the commonplace book which he sent to me but a short while before he died.

I am very sorry, he had written, to start with, that the College is dissatisfied with William Lang's behaviour and I am much afraid that it has been improper in many respects.

'Improper?' I said, indignantly. 'Improper?'

We were in his library at the time. He had just finished drafting out a fair copy. He blotted the letter and handed it to me to read. 'Why don't you read on?' he said, mildly.

'In what respects has my behaviour been improper? What have I ever done that was improper in your eyes?'

He had the good grace to colour up. 'Nothing,' he said. 'In my eyes, you have done nothing improper, not could you. And I've asked you to read on.'

'So why say it?'

'You don't understand.'

'I understand all too well. You, even you, have to give them ...'

'... what they want to hear, my friend. Precisely.'

'Even if it means stretching the truth?'

'Even then. But with the best of intentions, I assure you.'

'I once thought the college was a place of truth. A place where great men of learning sought the truth. That was what my father used to tell me. That was why he so admired the place.'

'Well so it is.'

'But only when expedient.'

'William,' he said, 'My dear Will, come down off your high horse for a moment and read the rest of the letter for God's sake.'

So I did. And very kindly he spoke of me as well, for it went on in this vein: I can only say that I have no fault to find but every reason to be completely pleased with him. The Botanic Garden is so very barren that its produce can scarcely be of any advantage to a lecturer on Botany such as myself. William is therefore under the necessity both of collecting plants himself in the fields and in neighbouring gardens, ('To say nothing of helping lassies with swarms of bees,' he added, with a smile) and of trusting to the exertions of the under-gardeners. William has always been active and intelligent and you must know that a common gardener, ignorant of the names and places of growth of the wild plants, would be entirely unqualified for the office of assistant to the Botanical lectureship.

I hardly knew what to make of it. It was not what I expected and I found myself moved by it.

'So that's what I am?' I asked. 'Assistant to the Botanical Lectureship.'

'Aye, you are.'

'Well all I can say is, I'm very upset that it isn't a paid position.'

'It would be if I had my way. But you will take nothing from me!' he said, indignantly.

'I know. I know.' I carried on reading.

William unfortunately engaged in the business of an apothecary but this imprudence is now over and I know that he has lost so considerably by the speculation that he will not again engage in a similar one.

'I had to say that for the simple reason that they have mentioned it on every possible occasion since, heaven help me!' he remarked, as though to pre-empt my objections, but I was beyond objecting. In fact I was touched by his obvious partiality and the fact that he did not mind declaring as much to Faculty.

The college ought to calculate whether the emoluments derived from the office of College Gardener be sufficient to maintain a man with his family in this city where the expense of living is so high. If the college should make the situation comfortable I have little doubt that William Lang would be much better qualified for it than any common gardener that it could employ.

'I am hoping,' he observed,' that they might be persuaded to pay you for your endeavours as my assistant. But read on to the end.'

His health has been bad for some time past but it will probably be soon completely restored. Since his father's death he has maintained a mother and educated or supported his brothers and sisters, which unquestionably ought to have some influence on the College in his favour.

'So what do you think?' he asked when I had finished. I set the letter down on his writing table.

'I think it is the most amazing mixture of reason and appeal. I don't know whether to feel flattered or angry.'

'Oh William. Make up your mind to be flattered. I have to do the best I can for you and it's no use appealing to their better natures for I am not at all sure that they have any. I am simply trying to make your case as best I can.'

So that's what I did. I made up my mind to be both grateful and flattered, and for a little while at least, the letter seemed to appease them, much as a bag of bones will appease a pack of hungry dogs. I went on collecting plants for the botanical lectures and visiting Jenny whenever I could. Her father welcomed me. Her sister had so far unbent towards me that she would creep up beside me and take my hand now and then. Sometimes she would say, 'Can you fetch me some paper, William?' Paper was at a premium in our house as well, but I would beg it from Thomas, who always had a ready supply. Anna wanted it so that she could draw pictures on it, which she was exceedingly fond of doing, not just flowers and landscapes and suchlike female pursuits but little sketches of her sister, her father, even myself when she could get me to sit still for long enough. I have them still. I am not inclined to look at them very often. But all the same, fate had taken a hand. I had not the slightest inkling that my carefully constructed castles in the air, all my dreams of a bright future, were about to come tumbling down around my ears.

CHAPTER TWENTY

The Christening Cape

It was during the summer of 1806, that I first introduced Jenny to Thomas and his family. Thomas and Marion already had one daughter, but Marion had not long given birth to their second child, a son this time, naturally enough named Thomas for his father. Thomas was to be his only son, although there were two more girls.

However, at the time I am writing about, Thomas and Marion must have anticipated the birth of a succession of strong sons, and they wished to have a fine christening cape made for this new and precious infant who had almost died, but had been brought back from the brink of death by his father's care, and was now a very bonny, thriving baby. There was already a gown in the family, inherited from the Edinburgh side, perhaps the work of one of Mr Ruffini's many orphan girls, but Thomas had promised his wife something new for the baby, an heirloom for the future. Marion was no great hand with her needle, but Thomas was prepared to pay handsomely and, through me, engaged Jenny to undertake the task. They had not yet met at that time, although I had spoken so often about Jenny to Thomas and Thomas to Jenny that they must have felt as though they already knew each other. I had certainly shown Thomas one or two examples of Jenny's beautiful work: an embroidered muslin handkerchief that she had made for my mother and a sprigged waistcoat that she had asked me to deliver to the city merchant who had commissioned it.

That spring, when I was just recovering from my illness, Jenny came to the college with her father, who left her at our house while he went off on business about the city. He often did this nowadays and it was, so my mother said, a mark of the growing trust and respect that lay between us. Thomas had bought silk fabric in blue and cream and a selection of brightly coloured silken threads for the project, on Jenny's explicit instructions and at great expense. I believe such excellent fine silks and gossamer thread for embroidering come from the land of China, although I had only the sketchiest notion of where that was at the time.

I looked for it on the globe of the world in Thomas's library and I was quite stunned by the size of the place. It caused an instant's dizziness, while my head was transported to wide foreign landscapes where unknown flowers and plants grew, flowers and plants that Jenny told me were used to dye the silks with colours which were quite unknown in Scotland, where the woollen cloth was more likely to be coloured with the natural subtleties of the Scots landscape: heather, whin and the dun of peat bog.

'Is she telling me the truth?' I asked Thomas.

He smiled at me. 'She's no fool, your Jenny Caddas, but then what else would you expect from a weaver's daughter? They aye know what's what! And she's right. The silkworms, which are not worms at all, but insects, make the thread that makes the silk, and flowers and plants are used to make the most wonderful dyes. There are many interesting plants, medicinal and otherwise, that come from the land of China. They were a highly civilised people when we were still living in caves!'

'Can that be true?'

I sometimes think I must have seemed such a simpleton to him but my innocence never seemed to annoy him.

'Oh, as true as I'm standing here.'

And then he remarked, as he invariably did, 'One day we might go there together!' and I could picture us travelling the many miles across the world in company, as other collectors had done before us, bringing back a thousand magical plants to enrich the botanical collections of Scotland and England. Some of these collectors, so he told me, had even started out as gardeners, very much like myself.

I am not sure that I ever believed in the possibility of even one such voyage. But like the heavenly paradise that the minister preached about each Sunday, the very idea of it was a constant incitement to work hard, to win his praise. I would go so far as to say that the biblical paradise seemed a pallid and colourless place by comparison.

That day, he had left the parcel of silks at our house from where Jenny was to pick it up. Although I was still acting as intermediary, it was a matter of chance, merely, that they had not yet met. Her visits to my house and to the college garden had not yet coincided with Thomas's. Even working through the light spring and summer nights it might take her a few months to complete the cape. Thomas had left her a sum of money as a deposit and had said that there would be a handsome payment once the garment was completed. She didn't want to accept even that small payment in advance until she was sure that he was satisfied with her work, but he insisted, and her father – ever the realist – had told her to 'haud her whisht and tak' the siller'. What good was pride when they needed bread for the table?

That day, Jenny took the silks and a neat new pair of shears away with her. She had particularly asked for these because she feared that the big shears that her father used for trimming off the long floaters at the back of the cloth, when his weaving was finished, might mark the delicate fabric. While the days were long and light, she commenced work on the exquisite garment, which was intended to become an heirloom for the whole family, and which did indeed become a family treasure for all I know. They may have it still, for how could it be otherwise? But I can imagine that Thomas would not care to have looked at it very often. I can imagine that Thomas would not like to have looked at it at all, although it would have been too precious to be destroyed or even given away, and it may have been that he had to smile at his wife and dissemble and pretend that he still valued it as much as ever.

How often have I blamed myself for what happened? Times without number. I know it is not rational to think so. I know that things happen as they must. What's for you won't go by you, as my mother, with her auld wife's wisdom, used to say. I wish it had not been so. I wish things could have been entirely different. But they weren't. And if they had been different, I would not be the man I am today. Which is a disturbing thought, as though the minister is right when he stands up and declares that God's plan is laid out before us, and we are powerless to change it. It is only how we respond to events, that alone is what we can alter, in that alone resides our free will.

I sometimes wonder, as I sit here in the enforced idleness of old age, what my life might have been like if I had indeed become a famous plant collector and botanist, the esteemed friend of Dr Thomas Brown. But that thought too induces a kind of dizziness in me at the largeness of it, much as the map of China did all those years ago, and I cannot bear to think about it for very long.

⊞ ⊞ ⊞

If the truth be told, I spent a couple of weeks of that summer of 1806 on rather poor terms with Thomas, even though I carried on finding plants for him. It might never have happened if I hadn't got into the habit, especially while I was recovering from my illness, of spending as much time as I could in the library at his house, reading mostly about plants and their properties, but sometimes indulging in my growing taste for traveller's tales. The servants, all except the fearsome housekeeper, had grown used to me and let me in without a murmur, showing me to the library and leaving me to spend my time as I saw fit.

Marion was either with her children or out and about in the town, paying visits to her friends. Thomas would be teaching or seeing patients, although sometimes he would come and sit with me in friendly silence and read or write, and those were the most congenial times of all. The first time this happened, I made as if to leave him in peace. Our arrangement was that I would use his library when he was absent.

He smiled and said, 'No, no. I have come to keep you company. It's good to read and study in friendly company.'

I found that he was right. We were at ease with each other and I think we both welcomed the occasional interruption when one or other of us had discovered something of interest or, more frequently, when I had questions for him. He was a good teacher and seemed pleased to give me the benefit of his wisdom.

He was one of the best respected doctors in the town and the ladies of fashion flocked around him. It must have been a very lucrative trade for him, although it didn't strike me at the time. But I had seen it with my own eyes. Or at least heard it with my own ears. Sometimes when I was at his house, which was also where he had his consulting rooms, I would sit beside the library fire, in the threadbare armchair that was Thomas's favourite. It actually had the scent of him, his tobacco, his hair oil, on it. From time to time the family cat, a fat and indiscreet tabby, would come and drape itself round my shoulders like a warm cloak. Thomas had named her Messalina after some strange, classical fancy. 'Deadly' was all he would say when I asked him who the original had been, although I later found out a good deal more about her, none of it very savoury. This shoulder hugging was a dubious favour the animal also tried to bestow on Thomas himself, although he was a less compliant victim and would wrestle the cat to the floor, where it would roll about with claws extended in protest.

I think Thomas's female patients envied the cat. I would be sitting there with my mind on a favourite volume of botanical studies, memorising the properties of plants, absorbing all these wonderful illustrations, when I would hear a pair of young ladies or even a twittering group of them, like a flock of fieldfare, descending on the house, arriving to 'see the doctor'.

Often enough he would visit them in their own homes, but they seemed to like to visit him as well. I think they made excuses to see him because the excursion provided them with some much-needed excitement. They were the wives and daughters of merchants, men of consequence in the city. They were invariably dressed in the height of fashion, fantastic costumes that Jenny and my sisters would have been ashamed to wear, topped by the most foolish hats you ever saw, with immensely tall feathers in them, more foolish even than my mother's Lunardi bonnet. They never looked remotely unwell.

Thomas seldom if ever spoke to me about his patients and certainly never mentioned specific complaints. Once he said, 'all these lassies, half their trouble, you know, is that they have too little to do and far too much time to brood. A minor ailment, which would be as nothing to a girl who had to work for her living, looms very large in their lives because there is nothing else to occupy their thoughts. The devil makes work for idle hands and idle minds too.

'These things affect their minds as much as anything else,' he continued. 'Even the smallest imagined slight begins to loom very large for them. Their affairs of the heart concern them constantly. They have headaches and flutterings. They come seeking a measure of concern, of kindness, and – once you give them a little attention – these complaints evaporate into the air as though they had never been. But they need something to occupy them. They need to read, even if it is only novels. I'm sure your Jenny has no imagined complaints.'

'No. She would not have the time.'

'And from what you tell me, she would have far too much good, sound, common sense.'

'I'm sure you're right. But maybe you judge these young ladies too harshly. What choice do they have?'

'None. And I'm wrong to be impatient since they give me and mine our daily bread. But all the same, I do grow impatient with them. A little.' He laughed. 'You know, William, sometimes, when

150

I am in the middle of these consultations, it feels as though I am being bitten to death by midgies!'

I remember thinking how I wished that my mother, my sister Bessie, or Jenny Caddas had the troubles of these women instead of the weariness, the many aches and pains that beset them, the callouses and racking coughs, the weak eyes from overwork in damp rooms, the fatigue that was the result of poor food and little rest. I would look at my mother from time to time and think that she looked all spent, her skin sagging around her eyes, her teeth beginning to loosen in her gums. It wasn't Thomas's fault. He was not to blame for the injustice in the world, and he often gave his services to one of the charity hospitals in the city in an effort to relieve the woes of the truly poor. But it was the prodigious gap between rich and poor that struck me as it never had before, or not in this way. The college was a chilly, dusty old place and many of the professors who lodged there cared little for personal comfort. It was only when I was admitted to Thomas's house and experienced what I thought of as its opulence that I became fully aware of how ill-divided was the world in which we lived. I saw the way in which the rooms were always warm and clean and comfortable, the way in which food seemed to appear on the table as if by magic. Well, there was no magic. It was down to the never-ending hard work for small reward of women like my sister, Bessie. I saw that those who are born and bred with even a modicum of wealth can have no idea of what it means to be poor. They say that money does not bring happiness and perhaps that's true. But I tell you this. It is easier to be unhappy and rich than it is to be unhappy and poor.

CHAPTER TWENTY-ONE

William Hunter's Book

It was only a short while later that a certain occurrence overshadowed our friendship for a time, much as a poorly pruned tree may affect the tender growth beneath. It was a fine day. I remember that. I had been wandering all over the surrounding countryside the day before, in search of specimens for Thomas. And I had been hard at work in the garden when I returned. It was that time of the year with long light nights, warm and damp to boot, when things would grow so quickly that if you neglected the gardens for only a few days, they would be out of control and twice as hard to manage. I had worked with a will, and then, leaving James to finish off, I had cleaned myself up and gone to Thomas's house, to give myself a much-needed respite. The library seemed to me like an oasis of calm and cleanliness in the midst of the world full of mud and rampant, albeit not always healthy, growth, which I was always struggling to contain.

Usually I went to the shelves where Thomas kept his botanical books. Linnaeus was my bible in those days and I was working my way through his classification of plants, learning them as I went. *The Scots Gard'ner* I still kept at home, and had it almost off by heart, referring to it constantly in my day-to-day work about the college. But today, for some reason, I felt too weary for learning and instead found myself sifting through a heap of books, new acquisitions that had just arrived and which were sitting neatly on the library table where the servant had placed them, awaiting Thomas's attention. Among them was a very large and unwieldy folio with a fine cover that proclaimed it to be an expensive volume.

The name caught my eye first. William, because it was my namesake. And Hunter, because that seemed familiar. William Hunter. My father had spoken of William Hunter and I knew that the museum that was in the process of stealing a large portion of my physic garden was being built to house the extensive collection which William Hunter had left to the college.

I also knew that Hunter had had an interest in natural history, among other things, so my attention was instantly captured. I thought it might be some illustrated volume of plants to rival Linnaeus. Well, it was a picture book. But it was like no picture book that you would ever want to see. I remember the title very well now. It is burned into my brain. It was called *The Anatomy of the Human Gravid Uterus*. I saw it and realised that this must be one of Thomas's medical books, although I didn't understand the title at all, not at that time. I laid it flat on the blotter – it was a very large and unwieldy volume – and began to turn the pages, carefully but with simple curiosity, all unaware at first of exactly what I was seeing. Well, they say curiosity killed the cat, don't they?

I have to admit that the book was very beautiful. By which I mean that the pictures were quite astonishingly accomplished. I know more about it now. I know that it is a serious book, written by a serious man, with nothing at all frivolous about him. It was illustrated by a talented young Dutchman. His name was Rymsdyk and he was a man of genius. It was a great work of scholarship, which probably helped to save many lives. I know all that and am willing to acknowledge it. Time and experience have mellowed me to some extent. But I still cannot bear to think about that book, because useful and beautiful as it may have been, may still be, I find that the thought of the misery and tragedy lying behind it clouds all else. I cannot help myself.

It was words and not pictures that caught my eye first. Perhaps it was the oddness of them. 'A woman died suddenly when very near the end of her pregnancy. The body was procured before any sensible putrefaction had begun. The season of the year was favourable to dissection.'

I turned over the page and saw, dear God, I saw such a picture as I hope never to see again. I never have and I have been a dealer in books for these many years past. But that day, there was a compulsion about it. Like Orpheus losing his Eurydice on a glance, like Lot's wife who could not prevent herself from looking, I was helpless to control my own impulse to see. I gazed and gazed and I think there was something in me that was turned to salt for ever after, some sweet innocence lost forever.

When the bird falls from the bough, it can never be made to fly again. My head went spinning and I saw the song birds falling, tumbling through the cold air. I felt physically sick. Never, never to fly again. I remember Thomas saying later, 'An interesting book. Very. And Hunter was a difficult man by all accounts. Clever but difficult. He believed that anatomical illustration must be very precise. That one must touch as well as see.'

And I thought, 'Touch? Dear God in Heaven!'

'William, the book is a masterpiece,' he went on. 'The illustrations are amazing.'

Well, they were amazing, but not in the way he meant. The pictures you see. I can hardly bring myself to describe the book even now, even though there was a terrible beauty about it all. They were, in the main, pictures of women, their legs spread wide, bones and bellies, with their insides laid out for inspection. And the weans, Christ, the weans, the wee babies, were there too. Not so wee either, for one woman had a full-grown infant nestled inside her. I can call it to my mind yet, although I do not choose to do so very often. It comes to me in nightmares. The baby lies with its face hidden, half covered. One surprisingly mature hand is tucked in by its face, the hair damp, the knees drawn up, so little space is left to contain it in the womb. The skin is soft, malleable, with the bloom of life still on it. You could marvel at how the artist has captured the sheer beauty of these children, the shelly ear, the dimpled fingers, the limbs fully formed, plump and pliable.

There was such beauty about it that I was captivated by it, until I realised, until the thought struck me all of a sudden, that for a man to record it so lovingly and in such detail he must have seen it, and for a man to have seen it (and perhaps even to have touched it) both mother and child must have been stone cold dead. Not just dead either, but so lost, so cast out, that not a single soul cared enough to claim the bodies, to mourn them, to give them a proper burial. Instead some cold authority was content to consign them, like common murderers, to the anatomist's table. It was this dual perception of repugnance and beauty that made me tremble with emotion. I did not know how to deal with my feelings.

Fascinated, in spite of my revulsion, I turned the pages. One page was full of drawings that looked like so many hives or wasps' nests hanging there, and I realised that these were the wombs themselves. There were drawings of the exterior of the womb with what I realise now must have been blood vessels, but to my eyes they looked very like drawings of trees with trunks and branches, or of exotic plants clambering over rocks. There was something of the vegetable world about them. There was a whole series of bellies, laid open for inspection, and in some of them the child was grown, while in others it was a puny thing, as scrawny as a fledgling fallen from its nest, but still most recognisably an infant.

And there were other things I could not recognise at all, gatherings of tissue like mushrooms on a log, shapeless things, the stuff of nightmare, flesh and blood divorced from its human host.

I think I saw then that the minister who not only spoke of paradise, but also preached hell fire and damnation in the kirk on Sundays, telling us of invented horrors, of demons and suchlike creatures, was wrong. Because sometimes evil is entrancing. And sometimes it needs no perpetrators, no devil whispering enticements to this and that transgression. Sometimes evil is simply present and takes your breath away with its bold and beautiful brutality.

There were no faces of course. Perhaps that would have been too personal. Or perhaps the artist didn't care. They were just torsos. Anonymous women's bodies, vessels without arms or legs or heads. But some of the infants had faces, for sure, dead infants inside dead women, looking as though they slept merely.

'A woman, immediately after a natural labour, grew faint without apparent cause and died within the space of two hours,' Hunter had written, and 'A woman who died of flooding in the ninth month of pregnancy.' Further on, he pointed out that everything had been examined in the most public manner, which was deemed to be a very good thing. He foresaw that in the course of some years he might procure in this great city (which was, I take it, London, not Glasgow) 'so many opportunities of studying the gravid uterus as to be enabled to make up a tolerable system'. Finally, he observed that in a work that had already become too large and expensive, it was thought proper to omit the internal anatomy of the child.

I gazed and gazed. And felt, God help me, my body stirring in response to the nakedness that lay before me, that part of a grown woman which I had never seen before. I slammed the book shut and rushed out of the library, out of the house and down the street, home to my little gardener's house, which was always full of weans and the smell of smoke, bread baking and ale brewing and dust, my house which suddenly seemed cleaner and more congenial than anything Thomas had to offer, than anything Thomas or his ilk might ever have to offer me.

We did not talk of it for a little while. I didn't want Thomas asking me about the book, so I avoided him as far as I possibly could. Oh I still went out into the countryside, still gathered his specimens, because it was the right time of year for the work. And when I was doing it, I took refuge in Jenny's house, but I didn't tell her about the book either. How could I? It did not seem to be a fitting subject for a young woman. It was not even a fitting subject for me! But I sent the plants to him by way of my brother James, which he must have thought odd, and I didn't go near his house, and eventually, a week or two later, he sought me out himself.

He seemed puzzled. He was evidently a little hurt by my neglect. He must have fancied me unwell again. Or perhaps merely occupied with Jenny. But the longer I left it, the more it must have worried him. I had avoided him out of embarrassment. I didn't know what to say to him and so I postponed any meeting with him.

CHAPTER TWENTY-TWO

A Quarrel and a Reconciliation

He came to me before I relented and went to him. I was working in the garden, working — as I had been for these few days
past — with a madness upon me. I had started building a wall and
was hefting stones about and throwing them down at the risk of
breaking my toes, in spite of the sturdy tackety boots protecting
my feet. My wall was not a good wall, and I do not think it would
stand the test of time, but the exercise seemed to help the feelings
of acute disgust that threatened to overwhelm me when I thought
about the book I had seen in Thomas's library.

Thomas came to me and I carried on working. He stood
watching me with his arms folded for a while, and then he said,
'William, my friend, will you stop for a moment and talk to me?'

I stopped and wiped the sweat from my brow, glaring at him.

'I have work to do. Can you not see?'

'I can see that. But you can surely spare me a few moments
from your busy day.'

He spoke so mildly, so patiently, that he made me feel clumsy
and loutish. I stopped what I was doing and brushed the grit from
my hands. He motioned to me to sit down and he perched opposite
me on one of the boulders forming the foundations of my wall.

I said, 'A woman died suddenly when very near the end of her
pregnancy.'

He frowned. The day was fiercely hot and we were both perspiring.

'What woman? I don't understand you.'

I said, 'You cannot see things the way I do. You never, never will. It's nae use.'

'Then explain them to me, my dear William. Let me at least try.'

He was shaking his head, puzzled, and I reflected that it was unfair of me to treat him like this, unfair of me not to explain. He obviously hadn't the faintest idea what it was that had so upset me.

'Your library. You gave me the use of your library.'

'Aye. I did. And was very pleased to see you there. You seemed to be full of enthusiasm until a couple of weeks ago. You were looking at the work of Linnaeus were you not? And as far as I know you were learning a very great deal.'

'I was.'

'And believe me, I was happy to see you there. To see you so contented. Enjoying my books and my house. Such hospitality as I could give you. But now you seem to have had enough of books, and perhaps enough of me, and I am wondering what has happened to cause this.'

'What do you think has happened?'

'I don't know. I'll allow I was disappointed, although whether in you or in myself, I can't tell. Perhaps you have become uncomfortable there?'

I shook my head. Speech seemed to have deserted me. There was a lump in my throat. I swallowed hard and looked away from him, trying to regain control of myself.

'Have any of the servants made you uncomfortable? I know fine that our housekeeper can be difficult. She often forgets herself. Forgets her manners. I have spoken to Marion but she knows nothing about it, nothing that might have occurred. And I have thought long and hard about asking you, William, for fear of offending you still further. Sometimes you have more prickles than a thistle and I cannot for the life of me grasp you.'

'No. No, they were most polite to me. They have aye been polite to me.'

'Well I'm glad to hear it. So what in heaven's name is wrong with you? What have I done or said to upset you?'

'You have done nothing.'

'Then in the name of God, tell me what ails you?'

'But there is a book in your library.'

'There are many books in my library.'

'No. I mean one book in particular. It is a book with pictures. Christ, sic a book! It is called *The Anatomy of the Human —*'

I saw and heard him draw in his breath sharply. Understanding.

'Ah. You saw that one, did you? It is a new acquisition for me. And it cost me a pretty penny, I can tell you, but I had to have it.'

'So now you know what upset me.'

'I had no idea you — or anyone — had come across it.'

'I could not avoid it. It was on your table.'

'The servant should not have unpacked it and left it out for all to see. The children might have come into the room.'

'You'll allow that it is a scandalous book?'

'Not at all William. Not at all. I'll allow no such thing.' He looked at me severely and I felt a tremor of anxiety, like when the dominie used to gaze at me sternly for forgetting my work.

'My dear William, I am a grown man and a doctor and I think that there is nothing scandalous about it,' he went on. 'But I would not have wanted any of the children or young servants to come upon it unawares. The housemaids, I mean. It is not a fit book for them, if only in that it might frighten and shock them.'

'It is not a fit book for anyone.'

'The book is a masterpiece. The illustrations are amazing.'

'Aye, they are that alright. And I was truly amazed by them!'

When I recollect what I said to him that day, he must have thought me daft. Very young and very foolish in my high-minded outrage. Yet he did not say so. Instead he took me seriously, engaged me in the debate, hoping to persuade me that I was wrong. Was I wrong? Well perhaps so. Or perhaps not. I confess that age has brought me no certainty whatsoever in this matter.

'Did you not find them so?' he pressed me. 'The artist was a young Dutchman. Rymsdyk. The contribution it made to our knowledge was immense. You could almost have believed that some of those babies – that they were –'

I spat in the dust. He flinched.

'Alive,' I told him. 'You were going to say alive.'

He shook his head, frowning, trying to see it from my point of view. 'I see that the book has distressed you deeply.'

'Distressed is not the word.'

'I'm very sorry. I had no idea.'

'I could not bear to look at it and yet I turned the pages and hated myself for doing it.'

He ran his fingers through his hair. 'Ah God, I didn't realise how it would look to you. I should have had more understanding, more sensibility.'

'But the pictures, man. Those poor women with their insides laid out for inspection. And the weans. It didnae distress me, man. But I'll tell ye this much. It offended me. It offended the heart of me.'

'All the same, William, it is a great work of scholarship. Can you at least allow that?'

'But they were pictures of deid women, Thomas! Deid women and deid weans. "A lovely and bitter cold day, ideal for preparing the young lady that died last night." That was what he wrote.'

'They were already dead. I am truly sorry for their predicament but nothing could be done to save them.'

'To save them? Could it no'? So how did they come there, I wonder? Were they cast out of their homes by good God-fearing men like us? How did they die? And how did Hunter and his artist come by the models for the work? Why did he do it, I wonder?'

'It was his life's work. And I happen to know that he lost money by it. He lost a fortune before he died.'

'Aye well, he may have done that. But I think he lost his soul at the same time.'

'You don't understand.'

'I understand well enough. It was his passport to fame and fortune and patronage. Much like our esteemed Professor Jeffray.'

'It may have been a consideration but I think he did the work for its own sake. I think the professor does too.'

'But such work. And does none of that matter? Did naebody think to ask these questions? And if they didnae, what does that say about the hale damn lot of ye?'

I could feel the anger rising in me all over again. I was hot-tempered in those days. I had a handful of wee pebbles, chuckie stanes just, and I threw them at the wall, venomously. The wall was so badly built that I had a feeling of surprise when it did not come tumbling down at once, but stayed where it was, each boulder leaning precariously upon its neighbour.

'He was a difficult man,' Thomas remarked. 'They say he could be a difficult man.'

'He was a butcher. It was a violation. The women were violated. Every precious detail of them exposed for public viewing. And all in the name of progress. Jesus, and your professor accuses *me* of impropriety.'

'I am so sorry, William. I had no idea you felt like this.'

'But why would anyone not feel like this? That's the wonder of it. Ach it's plain to me you see things differently. We see things differently, the two of us.'

'You have to try to understand that the knowledge he gained will help to save other women's lives, now and in the future. Nothing could save those women then. But I can and do help those who come after. I bought the book as a work of scholarship merely. You must know that.'

He was right of course. My head told me that he was right, but my heart could not agree with him or forgive him. Not at that moment. I was still possessed by a sense of outrage at the book itself and the tragedies that lay behind it.

'I know you do, and you are a good man. An honest man, that's for sure. But I don't believe your professor has quite such fine motives. He's nae fool, Thomas. I have small affection for him, and he certainly has nane for me, but even I can see that he is nae fool. He cannot possibly imagine that he will ever be able to reanimate a corpse and yet that is what he wishes to do.'

'Where on earth did you hear such nonsense? I have never heard the like. Certainly Jeffray has never spoken of it.'

'I hear the students talk. How can I not hear them? They pass me every day and treat me as if I were a tree, so little attention do they pay me. Even in your classes they do not talk to me, but regard me with suspicion, like the interlowper I am. Your man must know what they are saying, and yet he surely cannot believe it is desirable, or even possible.'

This was well before Jeffray's experiments with galvanisation. They were all to come, and yet there was much speculation in the college about the man's ambitions and already some crazy talk of bringing the dead to life. The scholars were, of course, very taken with the idea and talked about it in hushed tones, but with an underlying excitement that scandalised me.

'No. I don't think he does believe that,' said Thomas. 'But fame would be a kind of immortality and even the best of us may have thoughts about that. Oh, he will do it right enough. Sooner or later. Not resurrection, of course. But the imitation of it. Movement without breath. Animation without life. He will attempt it, by way of experimentation. If he can get his hands on the right body.'

'Who would give the body of a loved one for sic a cause?'

'He's waiting for a criminal. He's waiting for a hanging.'

'But who would want to resurrect …'

'A murderer? Who indeed? But then, you've said it yourself, it isn't possible. He knows it isn't possible. What he will put on is a show, like a puppet master, like a man playing God.'

'Aye, a trick such as will make him famous for all time to come.'

'Well, I'll allow there is something distasteful about that. But it is a different class of thing altogether from Hunter's book. That was a work of true scholarship and is a different thing entirely! The two are not comparable in any way.'

'Aye, but who is to say that we arenae puppets ourselves with our creator jerkin' us this way and that at his will?'

He sighed and stood up. 'You're very angry, William, and it makes you unreasonable. I'm so sorry. I had no intention of upsetting you and I'm sorry for it.'

'Deid weans. Women with their legs spread wide for an artist to pin down on the page. And us down here in the garden planting our trees for posterity with the blissful illusion of freedom.'

I have no idea where such ideas came to me at that moment, but the words came tumbling out of me, surprising me, surprising him. He just gazed at me and shook his head, shocked into silence.

'You had better leave me,' I muttered. 'I must get on. I have work to do!'

He made a move away from me, but then turned, unwilling to leave me in anger. All of sudden, he held out his hand. He was half smiling, that rueful grin he sometimes had.

'Oh, William!' he said.

I could not resist him. There was something about him that was eminently persuasive, and besides I felt the ground shift under my feet and knew I had a fear of upsetting him, a fear that one day I would go too far, that he might really turn his back on me, withdraw his friendship altogether. I could not bear it.

I hesitated but only for a second or two and then put my hand in his. His palm was warm and dry and his grasp was strong. He shook hands with me and clapped me about the shoulders with his free hand.

'William, I can't quarrel with you,' he said. 'I simply cannot do it. I have such respect for you, for your strength of feeling. It's the last thing in the world I would ever want to do. To cause you pain. If I thought it might repair our friendship, I would take the book and hurl it onto the back of the fire. Such is my regard for you that I would do it. I mean it. Just say the word and in it goes!'

164

'No. You mustn't do that. It is a valuable volume and I would feel guilty at your loss.'

'Then you'll just have to find it in your heart to forgive me. I had no intention in the world of upsetting you so much.'

'There's nothing to forgive. Are two friends not allowed a disagreement now and then?'

He seemed ridiculously relieved. It struck me that perhaps he did value my friendship as much as I valued his. I think now, with all the benefit of hindsight, that I was somewhat unreasonable. I don't know if I really was as moral as I pretended to be, or if my shock at the sight of the book was some compound of pity and prurience that in turn made me feel guilty, good Presbyterian lad that I was.

Besides, I believed him when he said that he would cast the book into the flames on my say-so. In a curious way, it made me even more disposed to agree with him, made me wonder if perhaps he was right and I was wrong. My mind was all on the dreadful privations of the poor and the ways in which the fate of these unfortunate women was so hideously illuminated by the book. He was a doctor, a healer, and he would experiment with whatever methods might further his own learning, but it was all in a good cause. It struck me that his motives were of the purest form.

His next words confirmed these feelings.

'I promise, William, that I will use the book with care. I promise I will consider those who gave their lives to illustrate it. I promise I will use it to save other lives. Will that content you and even persuade you just a little?'

'You speak as if you are beholden to me in some way.'

'More than you know,' he said. 'More than you will ever know.'

'Then I am content.'

And so, we resumed our friendship. If anything, we were closer than before, knowing that we could disagree, might even quarrel like equals, but that it would never damage our regard for one another.

CHAPTER TWENTY-THREE

Sprigging

Later that year, Jenny declared that she had finished the christening cape at last. There was not one more stitch she could put into it and it was ready to be handed over to its new owners. I had been following its progress on my visits to her house and reporting back to Thomas. I found myself marvelling at her skill with a needle, which seemed to reflect her skill in her garden. If Rymsdyk drew and painted pictures on canvas and paper, then Jenny surely drew and painted pictures with her needle. Thomas and Marion had arranged the christening ceremony and issued invitations to their friends. Although he had seen samples of Jenny's work before he commissioned the cape, Thomas had still not met my Jenny.

'Why don't you ask her if she would be so kind as to bring it to your house, William,' he told me. 'I should like to congratulate the seamstress in person when I pay her, so I think I shall collect it myself.'

Jenny's father brought her to the door. I mind the day well, even at this distance in time. They set off early, travelling with one of the carriers on a rough and ready cart. She was carrying the garment wrapped up in a piece of pale silk to protect it from the dust of the road. Sandy Caddas had business in the town, taking finished cloth to the merchants who commissioned it from him. When Jenny was busy and he couldn't leave Anna under the supervision of their neighbour, Nancy, with whom he seemed to be on increasingly good terms, he had got into the habit of bringing her with him and leaving her at our house. Anna was obliging enough and would sit quietly doing whatever task my mother allotted to her, drawing when she could get paper, but chiefly helping with cooking or baking bread, in which she seemed to take a tremendous enjoyment, being much more adept at it than either of my younger sisters.

On this particular day, however, Mr Caddas had made Anna stay behind with Nancy. I think he was aware that poor Jenny was on pins, wondering whether the christening cape would meet with Doctor Brown's approval, and much too nervous to be bothered with her sister. My mother had been up early, cleaning the house from top to bottom in honour of the distinguished visitor. Thomas had become quite at home in our house and because he always turned the full force of his charm upon my mother, she was invariably pleased to see him. But she had never become exactly at ease with him. Instead, particularly after the gift of lemons, she would flutter about him as if he were royalty, a deference that irritated me but was none of his doing.

His occasional unanticipated visit would throw her into a panic. She would make him sit down in my father's old chair, and give him whatever we had in the house that she thought might be fit for a gentleman: new ale, old whisky if there was any, which was seldom, bannocks and honey, soft fruit in season. Once she presented him with a platter of ripe strawberries from the garden as triumphantly as though they had been jewels. I saw that she had selected them all so that their size and shape were completely regular, although I couldn't find it in my heart to comment on it. I understood her partiality. And to give him his due, Thomas accepted all this adulation – for that was what it must have seemed like – with his usual grace and good-natured diffidence.

I sit here in the sunlight and find myself remembering him the way he was then, with no thought of the old man he would have become during the years of our estrangement. There is a sense in which that old man does not exist for me. When I see myself in a looking glass, I am always faintly surprised by the face that stares back at me. Who is this wrinkled stranger who seems to me very like the turtle that my wee Jenny so loves to look at in my illustrated volumes of Daudin's *Histoire Naturelle*? Where did he come from? And why is he usurping my body?

Did Thomas feel the same whenever he had occasion to glance at himself in the glass? And did he, I wonder, ever give a passing thought to me? Did he remember our friendship and grieve for it from time to time? I would give a very great deal to be able to travel backwards and see him one more time, really see him and not just with the mind's eye, which is a cold substitute for reality, however potent. I wish I could see him as he was then, striding into my house, bringing light and air and ideas with him. I find myself wishing we could have met again, just once. But maybe that would have been a disappointment. Because I never did see him again, this is how he is in my mind still, young and vibrant, my best and finest of friends.

There was something peculiarly attractive about him, but it was not any great regularity of feature. I would not have thought him especially handsome, but there was some way in which he seemed comfortable in his own body. He had a certain effect upon young and old, male and female alike, that was quite devastating. I thought myself reasonably handsome and Jenny seemed fond enough of me. The other girls I met in the streets around the college and on my excursions into the countryside seemed happy enough to flirt with me, but I had no illusions about myself. Thomas was different. For a while, I fancied it was just myself who was so taken with him, because of his obvious regard for me. We do tend to approve of those who are at pains to show us that they like us, particularly those we consider to be our superiors. But with hindsight, I realise that it was like that with almost everyone he met. He was a man whom many people loved on sight and almost without effort on his part.

Dear God, even the flea-bitten and ragged dog, the little beast belonging to one of the college porters, would come and fawn upon him when he walked about the gardens, licking his hand gratefully when he bent to pat its rough coat. And I'm still, after all this time, not sure what it was about him that provoked such affection. But whatever it was, I see now that it was dangerous. You would think about him in his absence and wonder what madness had seized you and why you fell in with all his suggestions, thoughtlessly, heedless of your own self interest. But fall in you would, even if you regretted it later. Which should explain a very great deal to me. Everything is forgivable in time. Well, almost everything.

All the same I want … what do I want? I think I want to put things straight. To put things right. To try to describe things as they were and as they are. Ah, but if by some miracle, I could be transported back to those early days, to the innocence and ignorance of that time when I was so fond of him, when I looked forward to our meetings as the high point of my day, when I trusted him completely, would I do it? If it meant forgetting all that had occurred since? Would I do that? If some magical creature appeared and granted me one wish, instead of the three that are more usual in such tales? Well, sometimes I believe I would. Which is both a shame and a revelation to me. With one proviso. I think I could not bear to lose my grand-daughter. I think I would elect to keep her, and in doing that, perhaps I would lose Thomas all over again. And I tell you, it would be hard, but I would have to do it.

Most of the time there was, I fancy, a certain calculation about him. It troubles me to think of it now. Perhaps he was all too aware of his power to influence, particularly where women were concerned. He must have realised it but he generally restrained himself. The trouble was, of course, that he had never yet met any woman, except for Marion, for whom he felt even the smallest regard over and beyond the normal pleasantries of everyday polite interaction. I believe he had known Marion since childhood, and they had moved very smoothly from friendship to courtship to marriage. But passion? The lightning strike that comes upon you in an instant? No, I do not think that had ever yet troubled Thomas. Or not to my knowledge, anyway. In fact, I flatter myself that he was more fond of me than of most other people.

He was well aware of the power of his personality and kept it very much in check. And although he influenced me and changed me and gave me thoughts and ideas that were a long way above the station to which I had been born, I'm convinced he meant nothing but good by it. I am certain that I would not be the man I am today, would not have had the considerable success I have had – albeit in an entirely different trade – without Thomas's influence on me, his generous imparting of all kinds of knowledge, to say nothing of the confidence that my learning gave me.

At that time, I cherished the idea that I might one day be able to work entirely for and with Thomas. In fairness I would say it was he who planted the seed in my mind. He would tell me tales about travellers who went to foreign parts: not just the likes of Linnaeus, who was our God at that time, or William Kent, Joseph Banks and William Paxton, but other men, such as Archibald Menzies, men who had started out as common gardeners like myself, men from comparatively humble beginnings, but with a thirst for knowledge and a sense of adventure, not so very far removed from my own. We would talk about the places my Uncle Johnnie had spoken of. Thomas would tell me how there were men who would sail overseas, not as tarry sailors, but as gentlemen or at least passengers, who would travel and collect plants which they would bring back for the gardens of the rich, or for various botanical gardens. He said that there were rich men who loved to collect such things and were willing to pay good money for them. In short, he opened my eyes to a hundred possibilities.

'It is not something anyone and everyone can do, William,' he said. 'It needs bravery, dedication and knowledge, a unique combination of skills.'

'Yes, I can see that.'

'And I think that we would make a good partnership, you and I.'

'Do you really believe so?'

'I do. I really believe it!'

So we would beguile the hours with dreams. For they were only dreams. But it seemed a wonderful prospect to me. And this was the foundation upon which the two of us constructed a whole edifice of impossibilities.

I had forgotten that Thomas was a dreamer at heart. For that short while, he turned me into a dreamer too. How could it be otherwise? I deferred to him in everything, so why not this? But the reality of the situation was that he had a wife and children, he was a Glasgow doctor and a professor of botany to boot. All his interests and responsibilities were in the city. He had money, but it was not a fortune of the order of, for example, Joseph Banks. And, more to the point, where on earth would he find or even make the time to travel overseas in search of plants, in his current situation?

Maybe later in his life he would have been able to do it, although I am not aware that he ever did. As time passed he transferred his affections from plants to fossils, from living things to their petrified remains. Perhaps he thought it safer that way. Perhaps with these at least, he could do no harm. I heard that he amassed a fine collection, but at second hand only, leaving others to do the travelling. Perhaps he should have done it much earlier in his career, if that was what he wanted to do. But he had not known me then, and I pride myself even now that it was our conversations and my enthusiasm that had sparked these ideas in him. If it was an unrealistic ambition for him, then how much more unrealistic for me, who still had a widowed mother and younger siblings to support, no money whatsoever to spare, and so much work that I barely had enough hours in the day to complete it all, a man who invariably slept the sleep of exhaustion when he finally retired to his bed?

All the same, I have since thought that if we had genuinely

wanted to do it, perhaps we would have found a way. There were other men with even fewer resources at the start and they managed it. So it comes to me that we didn't want it enough, while there were others who did, who had the imagination, the dedication and the confidence to bring their dreams to reality.

⊞ ⊞ ⊞

I must return to my story. My grand-daughter has been unwell, taken with fierce pains in her stomach. Illnesses can overtake the young so swiftly. In the space of an hour they can switch from robust good health to desperate sickness. We were all worried about her, but it turned out to be nothing more than an over-indulgence in unripe plums from a tree in a neighbouring garden. I have done the same myself and the repercussions can be most severe. Her mother fetched a hot stone bottle wrapped in a blanket and a cup of sweet peppermint cordial in warm water. I sat with her and sang to her until her symptoms abated. Now she is well enough to play outside in the low sunlight, although sternly warned away from the tree whose branches overhang the garden at the back of the house. And I am free to return to my tale, but curiously reluctant. I was in full flow. The interruption has disturbed me. I find that I don't wish to think about it any more. The thought of Thomas makes my heart ache and time will not cure me. But the story must be told, nevertheless.

There we were, waiting for Thomas to arrive — Jenny and myself and my poor, half-demented mother. She was restlessly rearranging things, pulling the threadbare curtains over the beds in the wall, which she had smoothed with unusual care that morning, moving his chair — or at least the one where she always made him sit — up close to the fire, flitting from the table where the christening cape was still wrapped up in its silk, to the fire-place, to the shelf where the best pewter was set out for the visitor's ale and a couple of wheaten cakes made especially for him and now smeared with enough of the best butter to serve us for a month. Rab, who had been unwell all that week, was tucked up in a blanket close beside the fire. My mother had even been ready to banish him, her darling, to the scullery or to one of the cold garrets upstairs, fearing that his coughing would disturb the doctor, but Jenny was so horrified by the very idea that my mother relented and let him stay.

God knows what Thomas would have made of it because he always liked to see Rab, always liked to question him about the state of his health.

'Anyone would think,' said Jenny, when my mother had gone out of the room briefly to fetch something, another cushion for the doctor's chair, a better cup for his ale. 'Anyone would think that we were expecting a visit from the king himself. Is this Doctor Brown such a demanding personage then, William?'

'No. Not at all. You'll see for yourself. But my mother worships the ground he walks on. To be sure, she does treat him as if he were the king. Perhaps better. He doesn't demand it, you know, but she seems to feel it's his due.'

'Well I wish she would stop it. It makes me nervous. I hope he likes the cape.'

I had seen her work and it was impossibly beautiful, the stitches so tiny and detailed that it was sometimes hard to distinguish them one from another with the naked eye. I have no idea how she managed it with human hands and eyes.

'Don't worry!'

And then he was there, coming in the door, cheerful as ever, and Jenny was suddenly shy, lurking behind me, hands folded in front of her, quite unlike her usual confident self. She was wearing a light cotton dress, very fine and pretty, her new best dress she said. I think her father had had it made for her in honour of the meeting. She wore a cream wool shawl with a narrow border of flowers down each side and a deeper border of exotic flowers and ferns woven at either end, in imitation of the fine Kashmir shawls that the ladies of fashion loved to wear, and that cost a king's ransom when brought from India. It was said that the wool from which these shawls were woven was so fine that you could thread one of them through a wedding ring. Jenny's shawl, which her father had woven especially for her, was fine, but not quite as fine as that. The local weavers were setting up in competition to the Indian shawl makers. I think Jenny's father, always a canny man where a business opportunity was concerned, was hoping that Thomas might see the shawl and make enquiries about it, but I'm afraid his attention was all focussed on Jenny and on the silk parcel containing the christening cape. As for Jenny, she seemed a creature of light and air. I was so proud of her. I thought her a princess, standing in her pale dress with her pale hair falling onto the dazzling shawl, there in our gloomy house.

'You must be the lady who makes gardens with her needle,' said Thomas, quite unexpectedly. Coming from anyone else, this compliment would have seemed ridiculously contrived and over-blown, but when Thomas said things like that, you believed him. You accepted what he told you as the truth, as no less than your due. She was standing just behind me. She gave herself a shake and came forward, smiling. He took her hand.

'I can't wait to see it.'

She went to the table, and carefully unwrapped the garment from its enveloping silk. I held my breath, hoping that he would say the right thing. She unfolded the cape and spread it out on the silk, which she had first laid on the kitchen table. Thomas stood back to look at the garment, drew in his breath and then let it out in a contented sigh. I saw that Jenny had been holding her breath too, and now she also sighed, faintly, echoing him, satisfied that the work was as perfect as she could make it.

It was one of the most beautiful things I have ever set eyes on, and to think that it had been made by a country girl, working in her father's cottage, was a marvel. I had never seen anything like it in my life before – but then, I never moved in those circles. Babies in my family were christened in whatever decent garments could be found for them, each handed down from the next eldest, and if the kirk was cold, which it invariably was, even in summer, they were wrapped in a simple woollen shawl. But of course this had been made for the precious son of a gentleman.

It measured some three feet from collar to edge and consisted of a double cape in Chinese silk. It was the colour of clotted cream or new butter with a quilted edging of sky blue and it smelled sweetly of the lavender with which she had stored it to keep the moths away. The work had taken her months, and they had delayed the christening because of it, but Marion wanted the very best and Thomas had been willing to go along with her. Most wonderful of all, the cape was hand-embroidered, sprigged with numerous flowers like the flowers which Jenny grew in her garden, like the flowers which we tried to grow, but could not, in the physic garden. They were the blossoms of spring and summer, as befits a baby: pinks, rosebuds, violas, campion, all in many different colours, small but accurate, made with love.

Thomas looked from the cape to the girl who had created it and I saw Jenny glance up at him in return. 'Is it alright?' she asked. 'Is it what you wanted?'

'Is it what I wanted?' he echoed. 'My dear girl, it's wonderful. Miraculous! I can't imagine what Marion will say. I'm sure she never expected anything half as beautiful as this. I know I didn't. William, why didn't you tell me what a genius this lass is with her needle?'

He examined the cape in the way he touched my plant specimens, delicately and with concentration, turning it this way and that in the light, looking at the way it was stitched, praising everything from the embroidery itself to the minute stitches on the blue quilted border. He was always wholehearted when something impressed him. There were never any half measures with Thomas.

Afterwards, when the garment had been safely folded away, he went over and put his hand on Rab's head, took his wrist, and questioned him gravely for a moment or two. He felt in his pockets and brought out a bottle of some tincture or other and told my mother to put a few drops in some fresh milk if she could get any, ale if she could not, and it would ease Rab's aches and pains.

Only then did he sit down, drink his own ale and eat his bannock with every appearance of relish. He offered a piece to me – which I accepted, although my mother had warned me to refuse – and to Jenny, who did refuse because, as she told us afterwards, she was still so nervous that it would have choked her. Then he washed his hands in a bowl of warm water and dried them on a fine linen towel I didn't even know we possessed, like a participant in some religious ceremony. Which for my mother, at least, it was. He shook Jenny by the hand, took up the cape in its parcel of silk and carried it carefully home. Before he left, he handed her a purse of money and when she counted it, after he had gone, she was surprised to find that there was a good deal more than the sum they had agreed upon.

'He had no need to do that!' she said.' Do you think it's a mistake?'

'He told me himself that he intended to reward you with more than you had asked for. But I did not know by how much. This is generous indeed, but then he is a very generous man.'

She danced around the kitchen, her high spirits bubbling over, spirits that she had been restraining during his visit. She hugged herself, kissed my mother, me, wee Rab, who blushed furiously beneath his pallor. She could scarcely contain herself.

'He liked it!' she said. 'He liked it, he liked it!'

'Why wouldn't he?' asked my mother, stoutly. For all her admiration of the doctor, she was very fond of Jenny. 'It's a splendid piece of work.'

'Do you think his wife will feel the same? Oh but what if she decides that she doesn't like it? What will I do?'

'Don't be daft,' I said. 'How could she help but like it?'

'I have lived with it these many months past. It always comes to me that I don't know whether the work is good, bad or indifferent!'

'It is a garden in silk. How could he not like it?'

She seized my hands at that and we danced a jig around the kitchen together, bumping into table and chairs, like weans. My mother smiled while Rab sat huddled up in his blanket, watching everything that went on with feverish eyes, and clapping his hands in time to some melody in his head.

CHAPTER TWENTY-FOUR

A Letter to Faculty

A few months after Jenny had finished the christening cape, Professor Jeffray sought me out in the garden. He normally gave the impression of being a jovial enough fellow, or at least that was the appearance he liked to cultivate, but this time he was frowning. I realised that he had deliberately chosen a day when Thomas would be otherwise occupied, a day when Thomas was, in fact, lecturing in his stead. My heart sank but I decided to put on a brave front.

He called me 'Mr Lang', to be sure, but he spoke with a certain edge to his voice, and very little respect. 'Mr Lang, I have to tell you that we are growing ever more displeased with the way in which you are undertaking your duties. Or rather not undertaking, but seriously neglecting them!'

'In what way am I neglecting my duties, sir?' I asked.

I looked around. It was very cold. There had been a hard frost in the night which had brought the smoke down, so that even now it lowered over the college. You could smell the sulphur off it. But so far as I could see, the gardens were fine and tidy. My brother had been working hard, I had spent every spare moment restoring order and the under-gardeners had done their best as well, mainly because, with the onset of winter, I had been at hand to encourage them or at least bawl instructions, interspersed with a little personal abuse when more than encouragement was needed.

He gestured around expansively. 'You must admit that you are not quite the gardener your father was.'

'We are never the men our fathers were, sir. We can never aspire to be their equal, but we can surely hope to learn from them.'

'And have you learned from your father, do you think?'

'I hope so.'

'You are much favoured by Dr Brown, I see.'

'I think he respects my knowledge. As a gardener. Just as I respect his knowledge as a fine plantsman and botanist.'

'Hmm.' He pulled a long face and it struck me that he looked very like a horse. I had a disastrous desire to laugh at him. 'He wrote a very fulsome letter in support of you,' added the professor. 'He seems to find you completely indispensible.'

'Not indispensible, sir, by any means, but I like to think that I am some use to him in gathering specimens for his lectures. Specimens that – as I'm sure you must be aware – the physic garden can no longer provide.'

'So you say.'

'It is the plain truth, sir. The type foundry blights the physic garden. You must know that. When you yourself were delivering the botanical lectures, you must have known that there were problems with finding specimens.'

'Ah yes. The botanical lectures. Old wives' medicine.' Again that sneer, an indication of disgust. He could see no use for botany whatsoever, that was clear.

'But even Doctor Brown was forced to admit in his letter to Faculty that your behaviour had been improper in many respects.'

'Sir?'

'Those were his very words, were they not? "I am afraid that his behaviour has been improper in many respects." That was what he said. And I'm afraid Faculty were less than impressed with your behaviour.'

'But I believe he also intimated that I might be able to work more effectively if I were better paid for what I do.'

'We would all do that, I'm sure, Mr Lang.'

'What would you have me do?' I could feel the rage rising in me. Somewhere inside me, at that time, was a hot-headed young man, but even then, his fires had almost been quenched by poverty, ill health and hard work. He is still there, buried beneath the weight of years and wisdom. I wanted to turn on my heel and leave the professor standing, but it would have been unthinkable, so I stayed where I was and hated myself for my cowardice. I did not bow my head, however, but gazed steadily at him, until he dropped his eyes to the turf beneath our feet.

'I would have you do exactly what the college is paying you to do!' he exclaimed. 'No more and no less. The gardens have been far from satisfactory this year past. And yet when first you were appointed, you spent so very much money on trees. I would never have permitted it, but others were swayed by Brown's eloquence. I would have thought that we might at least see the fruits of all that expenditure by now.'

'Sir, may I be allowed to explain?'

'Please do.'

'I thought, well we both thought, Doctor Brown and I, that if the garden was sick, which it was and is yet, the answer might be trees. We thought that if we planted trees, it might help to purify the air somewhat. We agreed upon such a course of action and Faculty seemed to see some sense in it.'

'Purify the air?' he scoffed. 'And tell me, Mr Lang, what would you know of such things?'

'I consulted with Doctor Brown. That was why. Because I did not know of such things, but he advised me. He fancied that the trees might breathe as we breathe and help to cleanse the filthy air in some way.'

'What nonsense is this? Trees are not people!'

'No, sir, they are not. But they are influenced in much the same way by the air that surrounds them.'

'Exactly. Which is why they are yellowing and dying are they not? A waste of good resources as usual. And some of them seem to be damaged beyond saving.'

'At least some of that is down to the young gentlemen.'

I couldn't help but say it, couldn't help but voice some of the anger I felt.

'How so?'

'They maraud about the gardens by night, breaking down trees and setting fires beneath them and God knows what else, in their drunken celebrations.'

'Then you should find some way to curb them. If you do not attempt to curb their high spirits, what else can you expect?'

'I? Curb their spirits?' I must have stared at him in open-mouthed amazement for he had the grace to look away again. 'Sir, they are very young, they are away from home and there seem to be few who will supervise them or even attempt to correct them. How can I tell them how to behave? If I do, they insult me, call me a common gardener, threaten me with dismissal. But they are responsible for a vast amount of damage and I will not be blamed for behaviour that I can do nothing whatsoever to address.'

He had to admit the truth of it. He could be a fair man when he chose, and I saw him nod, briefly. 'There is something in what you say, and I will raise the matter with Faculty, Mr Lang. But all the same, I see that you yourself often leave the young gardeners, your brother included, all unsupervised, while you go stravaiging across country hunting for plants for Doctor Brown. And it will not do, I tell you. We are paying you to be here, and here you must stay and work, or suffer the consequences!'

I said nothing. If I had spoken at that moment there would have been even more harsh words between us and I could not afford to antagonise him further. He glared at me and then walked off, gathering his gown about him. He had said his piece and now he was leaving me to stew in the indignant juices raised by his words.

▣ ▣ ▣

181

Later on, I told Thomas about the encounter. 'Good God,' he said. 'Are they at this again? What have you ever done to Jeffray that he should take against you like this?'

'I rather think that he dislikes me because you are so friendly with me and he considers it scandalous that a lowly gardener should form any kind of friendship with a doctor of medicine.'

'You're probably right. Not that you are lowly, but that our friendship scandalises him. But all the same, this could be serious for you, you know. You might write to them. Setting matters before them as they really are. I'll help you if you like.'

'Well, I'll have need of help, for sure, so perhaps you could tell me what to say, since I'm so unlearned.'

'William, I don't mean to insult you, but only to offer you whatever help I can in this matter.'

'Man, you're gentry and I'm no and never will be!'

But when I had calmed down, I took Thomas's advice and wrote a detailed letter to Faculty, stating my side of the case, not allowing the facts to be manipulated by the likes of Professor Jeffray. Once more, I can quote from the letter in full, because like so many things that I thought were gone forever, Thomas had written it all down in his commonplace book, copying the letter out in a fair hand, in among his expenses, his outgoings, his bills of sale, making a note of where and when it was written, who wrote it and how he had helped me.

I am reading my own words, which were half his words as well as mine, and I can picture us sitting together at his library table, labouring over the task. He told me I had a fine, neat hand, better and more legible than his own. The dominie had at least drummed that into me. I baulked at all that I had to say, at how much it was necessary for me to crawl before them, but Thomas encouraged me, not – he told me – because he agreed with them, but because it was necessary to 'keep them sweet'.

'Sometimes the ends justify the means. This is one such time.'

Gentlemen, I wrote, I have thought it necessary to lay before you a fair statement of facts respecting my conduct since my appointment as gardener to the University immediately upon my father's decease. Gentlemen, when my father was appointed Gardener it was then observed by several members of Faculty, that the wages allowed were not sufficient for supporting himself and his family and therefore they granted him the liberty of occupying his vacant time in that way he thought best for the advantage of his family.

The struggles my father had are well known; his salary being small and having an inclination for educating his children, he found himself in circumstances somewhat straitened, so that he was not able to make any provision for his wife and family. At the age of eighteen I was left the guardian and protector of a mother and six other children, seven until the death of my youngest sister, the sole provision for them being the salary you allowed me.

This was not strictly true of course. Bessie was already a young woman when my father died, but all the same, the rest were too young to be of any help, and Thomas said that it might be prudent to stretch the truth a little.

During the summer, when the botanical lectures are going on, the garden furnishes very few specimens. It is therefore required of me to collect elsewhere whatever plants may be necessary for carrying forward the lectures, for which purpose I have to traverse the country in search of plants; and that, Gentlemen, almost every day during the course.

A great part of my time is occupied in this manner. And oftentimes, after I have travelled two or three miles from town, I have been disappointed in finding the individual plants wanted and must again set out to some other quarter to find them. As the number of students last season was upwards of thirty, it became necessary for me to provide more than thirty specimens of each individual plant. And as several hundred Genera and Species were examined last season, a great proportion of my time must be occupied in this manner. For the truth of the above statement I beg leave to refer you to Dr Brown.

We had got so far with the letter when I said, 'What about the conduct of the scholars?'

He pursed his lips. 'Do you think you should mention it?'

'They are half my trouble!'

'But it may not go down well with Faculty. The scholars are their bread and butter, for all that they sometimes wish them gone to the devil.'

'I care not for their bread and butter. But I do care for justice, and I am determined to point out that the scholars do great damage to the plants.'

'Well, if you must, you must,' he agreed.

And gentlemen, I continued, During the winter season, when the students are permitted to amuse themselves in the College Garden, it really becomes very difficult to keep them from doing mischief of one kind or another. Which tends much to hurt the appearance of the Gardens. I have brought this matter to the attention of Professor Jeffray himself and he agreed that I cannot be held responsible for the damage.

However, Gentlemen, I shall, so far as I am able, endeavour to do all which my station may require. I am, Gentlemen your most Obedient and Humble servant, William Lang.

Thomas read what I had drafted, corrected and added to it, trying to achieve something that looked as though it might be wholly written by me. We were in his library with, as far as I remember, Jenny working at her sewing beside the fire. I have a memory of her sitting quietly there, listening to us wrangling gently about the text of the letter and sometimes humming some old melody under her breath. I have a memory too of being happy, in spite of the precariousness of my position in the college. Jenny was there because Thomas and Marion had engaged her to do some more needlework for them, an ornate waistcoat for Thomas and a sprigged gown for Marion. She was spending some hours each week in their house now and I think they were paying her well. When I could find the time, I would accompany her, walking the miles home with her and stealing a kiss or two on the doorstep. Her father would bring her and collect her when he could, but sometimes, when the weather was particularly dismal,

Thomas would send her home in his own carriage. Winter was fast approaching and the days were growing shorter.

'Do you know, I think I have a solution to all our troubles,' said Thomas, suddenly, looking up from where he was scratching away at my somewhat blotted original, erasing a word here and there, adding a suitably penitent phrase.

'What's that?'

'I think,' he said, glancing across at Jenny, 'That maybe we should have Jenny here stitch flowers for specimens for the students. Hers are so lifelike and real that I'm sure none of them could tell the difference and then we could use them all over again next season!'

Jenny looked up at him and smiled, white teeth, rosy lips and cheeks. I watched her hair, gleaming in the firelight and I remember noticing, momentarily, that she was changed in some subtle way. The only way I can describe it is to say that there was a gloss about her. She seemed burnished, shining with cleanliness, her dress neat, her shawl pulled about her white arms, her fingers no longer the fingers of somebody who worked in the garden but neat and nimble and – apart from the nails, which were still a wee thing broken – they looked like the hands of a lady. I noticed all this and was glad of it. They were easy on her in that household and she was thriving there.

I loved her dearly at that moment, and there is some part of me that has never stopped loving her. She was my first thought each morning when I awoke and my last thought each night before I fell asleep, however exhausted with the day's efforts. I would have dreamed about her constantly if I could have manipulated my sleeping thoughts, and I did dream about her often. I was full of hope for our shared future. I believed that, with Thomas's help, I had written so eloquently on my own behalf that my position as gardener would be safe. Jenny, ever the optimist, believed so too and Thomas declared that he was certain of a favourable outcome.

CHAPTER TWENTY-FIVE

Dismissal

It was not to be. Only a little while after they had received the letter, I was informed that Dr Jeffray had renewed his complaints about me and, of course, he won in the end. My appointment was to be terminated, although, mercifully, I was to be allowed a full year to make other arrangements and was also allowed to remain in possession of the land during that time. This meant that I could sell the grass and whatever else I could grow. My family would not be entirely destitute.

I think I had Thomas to thank for my year's reprieve. He had told Faculty in no uncertain terms that if they didn't see fit to give me time to find a new place of work and a new home for my family, he would have to consider his own position in the university. I was touched that he would put his livelihood at risk for me. But in truth, there was small risk to him in such a stand and he knew that they would never let him go. Even Jeffray had not expected this and was appalled at the thought of having to resume his botanical lectures again, when he had so much else to occupy him, so he was forced to swallow his prejudice and make some kind of grudging representation to Faculty on my behalf. Or so Thomas told me, relating the events with a kind of glee, pleased with his own machinations on my behalf. The result was that I was given my year's grace.

'Don't worry, William. We'll think of something,' said Thomas. 'There's plenty of work for a man of your skills and intelligence.'

'But not here.'

'No. Not here, that's for sure.'

'They've said that they will let my mother and the younger ones stay on in the house for a while if need be, even after the year is over, but I shall have to make some provision for them. I need work. Real work.'

'And what will I do without you to collect specimens for me?'

'I don't know.'

'If we can find you some gardening work in the town, perhaps you could continue, and I could pay you for whatever you provide.'

'Perhaps so.'

But I could foresee only more hard work and a neglected garden all over again. He heard the reluctance in my voice.

'You know I would like nothing better than to work for you, all day, every day,' I continued.

'And you must know that I would like nothing better than to work with you. But as yet I have no proper place of my own. This is a rented house with a small patch of garden and a few miserable apple trees with codling moth at the heart of all the fruit. As the younger son I am not a rich man.'

'Nor a poor one, either.'

He frowned. 'Well, as it happens, I do have an idea of sorts, but I am very unsure as to how you will receive it!'

'Tell me. What idea? I'm desperate, Thomas, and will consider anything.'

'Oh, this is a little better than a counsel of desperation, I think. You have often heard me speak of my uncle in Ayrshire?'

'Aye, I have.'

'He has a large estate there. Larger than he needs. His wife died some years ago. They rattle around that cold, old house, himself and his son.'

'And the house has a garden?'

187

'More than that. It has extensive grounds. A walled garden. A park. All you could wish for. I could have a word with him. I am something of a favourite with him. He is very cautious of his own health, although he is as robust as I am, but his son, my cousin, is very sickly, a little like your wee Rab, and I do the best I can for him whenever I am there. Would you perhaps think about travelling to Ayrshire? If I could get you a position there?'

'Of course I would. But how could I desert my mother and the boys? And it would be a long way away from Jenny.'

'I have already thought of that. There is a great deal of land, and you would not be head gardener or not yet a while, but you would certainly have a position of some seniority, William. Coming from the college, and on my recommendation too. You see, the head gardener is knowledgeable but old and rather frail. He needs help and my uncle knows it.'

'I would certainly go wherever there was work to be had, if only I could make some arrangements for those who depend upon me.'

'Well, perhaps there would be a house for your family. That is what I have been thinking. I know that there are cottages on the estate. And if none was suitable, one might be built. And I would be prepared to make the request on your behalf. Would your mother be willing to move, do you think?'

'I think she would. Needs must. Although it would be hard for her to be so far from the girls, Bessie especially.'

Jean and Susanna were both in service now. But I knew that Bessie would keep an eye on them. The more I thought about it, the more I liked the idea.

'Perhaps James could work in the gardens too. Or get work on a nearby farm maybe? Or is there a home farm, perhaps? He's strong and willing. And the wee lads would surely find seasonal work in the country.'

'I think they would. Do you want me to ask?'

'I'd be grateful. And will you ever be there, Thomas?' I asked, hesitantly.

He smiled at me. 'Aye. To be sure I will. I ride down there from time to time. If you are there, my friend, I will have even more reason to go! And I would be glad to speak to my uncle for you. He's very careful of his own health so he is always pleased to see me. There is aye something wrong with him, be it his head, his stomach or his legs. In reality he is as strong as myself, although I could not say the same about my cousin. But my uncle is fond of his garden. Almost as fond of his green and growing things as you are, William. Although if there is a fault with the estate it is that there are by no means enough trees. I think maybe we could persuade him to plant more. Broadleaves of all kinds, some native and perhaps some more exotic specimens.'

'I think I should like that very much. And what of Jenny?'

'Ah, Jenny,' he said. He paused, gazing at me with a quizzical expression. Jenny was still visiting his house often, still doing her fine sewing for the family. 'I suppose you have some thoughts of marrying your Jenny?'

'Some day. But if I wait as long as I may have to, I'll be too old to enjoy my wedding night!'

'Oh, William, we can't have that, can we?'

'I'm powerless to remedy it.'

'Well, it might be arranged.'

'How? I would be an under-gardener with no resources and a family to support.'

'You cannot waste your whole youth supporting your family, William. The sacrifice is too great. I won't let you do it.'

'I don't see how you can prevent it!'

'Listen to me. The older children are almost self sufficient. There is no reason why, once you are established in Ayrshire, you should not marry your Jenny – if her father will spare her – and bring her down to keep house for you. Your mother is fond of the lass.'

'She is. But two women in charge of one house?'

'Although you may not want to admit as much – forgive me – your mother is no longer young and will not always be there.

And who knows? Maybe we could persuade my uncle to find two cottages instead of one. In fact, I have in mind two wee houses that stand side by side, a little tumbledown and battered by the elements to be sure, but not beyond rescue by a strong young man such as yourself. And your brothers would help. There will be plenty of work at the big house for a young woman with Jenny's talents. Although we will be very sorry to lose her here in Glasgow. Very sorry indeed. But of course the connection will not be broken. No, it will never be broken. For I am in the habit of visiting the house often.'

▣ ▣ ▣

It all seemed possible when he outlined it to me. Not just possible, but desirable. Those big lowland estates were in the nature of villages. Even when the families who owned them were as small as was this one, consisting of a widowed man and his ailing son, they would offer shelter to a large household of servants, with a few poor relations thrown in for good measure. There were usually many cottages that had sprung up around the central house like so many mushrooms at the foot of some venerable tree. Tumbledown and damp and uncomfortable most of them were, to be sure, unless there was some enlightened landowner with an interest in building. But a deal of work would remedy matters and the house we had lived in for so many years was no palace either.

I began to feel that the future was looking quite rosy. Jenny and I had an understanding. Her father approved of me and thought that the college had treated me shabbily. Besides that, I knew that Jenny's father was now openly courting his neighbour Nancy and had even tentatively spoken of marriage. It occurred to me that it might suit him well enough to have at least one of his daughters off his hands. Anna was on good terms with the potential new Mistress Caddas (after all, she had spent enough time in her house) and could stay at home until she too found herself a husband or began to work at the weaving in good earnest. I think she was already a great help to her father and undertook much of the spinning that he had once put out to women in the village.

'What's for you won't go by you,' my mother always said, and I began to think that it might be true. I would miss Thomas if I did not see him almost every day, but even that ache would be tempered by the anticipation of seeing him whenever he came down to Ayrshire. He had intimated that we might be able to study together. That I would continue to have access to the library at the big house whenever I wished. Thomas's uncle liked his out-door pursuits, his hunting and fishing. He himself had small use for books, but Thomas had told me that the library was a fine one, much better than his own, full of historical curiosities and rare books, and he promised to beg permission for me to have the use of it whenever I wanted.

Even now, I sometimes find myself imagining that bright future as it might have been, wondering if I would have been as happy in the countryside as I had believed I could be. I think it might have been possible. Our dreams and plans were ambitious enough.

'Maybe one day my uncle will give me full control over the gardens,' said Thomas. 'In which case, we could plant a great many new trees.'

'An avenue of limes. Loud with bees. Can you picture it, Thomas?'

'And bee boles in all the walls for your Jenny. She would keep the bees happy, would she not?'

'So that the fruit trees and the grape vines would all bear fruit.'

'We might even travel, you know. To the Americas, to Africa. To Asia and beyond.'

'I don't think Jenny would approve of that.'

'Nor would Marion. But who can say what the future might hold? And if we must stay here in Scotland then we could at least make the best of a new garden.'

'I think you once told me they grew pineapples there?'

'Oh aye, they do. There is a big orangery which serves as well for pineapples. And an old walled garden which is very sheltered.

The climate is mild down there, milder than here.'

Then I'll grow pineapples for you. In memory of my father. Oranges perhaps. Peaches too. And plums and cherries. With pears and apples layered against the walls.'

'Blossoms in spring, fruit for winter. I fancy that one could even grow the tree fern there. And I have some idea of planting the Eucalypt if we can get it. Joseph Banks brought the first specimens back from Botany Bay. I have seen pictures only, but it seems to me that they grow like so many silver towers. If we can get them and nurture them, they will long outlast you and me. And you know that our wee Arran tree thrives there yet.'

'Ah, Thomas, we could plant trees like weans and watch them grow.'

'Trees like weans and watch them grow. Why not, William, why not?'

It was a fine plan. The thought of it, of all that we could have accomplished, still burns into me sometimes, a regret for all these unrealised schemes. He was such a hero to me at that time. But idols sometimes prove to have feet of clay. Oh men should not be worshipped, nor women either. They should be regarded only for what they are and trusted where trust is due. One should never expect too much. Expect no heroes, nor heroines. Life has taught me that truth, if nothing else. Love others. Do right by them as far as you possibly can. But never give all the heart recklessly. And never expect too much of any man.

CHAPTER TWENTY-SIX

Jennies

I noticed nothing wrong at first. Afterwards, that fact caused me many sleepless nights. Jenny and I continued with our courting. We met, walked and talked. I remember, even now, the grasp of her strong fingers in my own and the roughness of our two hands pressed palm against palm, although since she had taken up the sewing in good earnest, hers had become softer and whiter. We fitted together well, our footsteps went well together. Sometimes, we would walk in the woods at the back of her house and, in the privacy of the thickets of willow, she would allow me to slide my arm around her waist and kiss her. I am sure that she must have kissed me back, because I saw nothing amiss, although I had little experience of such things. We were handfasted after all and would be married as soon as we could. But afterwards I saw that she would only permit me, that was all. She did not exactly encourage me. She allowed herself to be loved by me. I thought she was virtuous, but perhaps I was wrong. Oh she liked me fine, I am sure she did, but she was not overcome with any great passion. Experience has taught me that.

Marion had asked her to do more embroidery, some of it for garments and some of it for the household, and when I went to the library to read, I would often find her there, sitting over her sewing where it was warm and peaceful. I think they were all mindful of her comfort at that time. There was a sewing room upstairs and it was there that she would cut out fabric, measure and arrange things, there that she would keep her shears, her silks and her needles.

While it was still chilly, before the advent of spring and even afterwards, well into summer, there was always a fire in the library and sometimes Marion would send her to sit there and sew. I think she was doing it as a kindness to me, throwing us together, and perhaps she fancied that she was giving us somewhere warm and comfortable to do our courting when we neither of us had much privacy at home. It certainly gave us time to be together. But I was often wanting to read, wanting to make the most of my limited hours in the library, and I'll allow her presence distracted me. But then she was always busy, stitching away at her gardens in silk and singing and smiling to herself as she worked. At that time I would have said that she was absolutely contented with her lot.

Sometimes the three of us would be there together, Thomas, Jenny and myself. Then things would be very pleasant and friendly, because he would start to question her about this or that aspect of her life, about her father's work and his beliefs, and the state of the weaving industry. He was a great one for finding things out. I don't think he was ever bored in his life. He seemed remarkably knowledgeable about all manner of things, but anxious to know more, and it struck me that he was genuinely intrigued. It made me pleased for him and pleased for her as well, that he was taking such an interest in a country lassie and her family.

'Tell me about the shawls,' Thomas said. 'Isn't that what your father is making just now?'

There was a depression in the west of Scotland silk trade at the time but an Edinburgh manufacturer called Paterson was putting a lot of work in the way of the Glasgow and Paisley weavers. Sandy Caddas had told me all about it one evening when I had sat with him over his ale and his pipe, and I had mentioned it to Thomas.

Now, Jenny spoke to Thomas with easy familiarity. She had confessed to me that, although she had been shy of him at first, he had quickly put her at her ease. 'Why yes. He is weaving shawls for ladies, sir. Mr Paterson has been wanting copies of Turkish Shawls.'

'And what are they?'

'They have fantastic figures woven into them. They're very beautiful but they are difficult to make and they take a lot of time and trouble. Father says he's never paid enough for them.'

'No working man ever thinks he is paid enough for what he does.'

'And maybe that's the truth,' I said, lifting my head from my book.

'Aye, maybe it is!' he agreed, smiling at my ferocity. 'So the Edinburgh ladies want Turkish designs do they, Jenny?'

'Aye and lovely damask shawls with a black weft and a crimson warp.'

'You wear one such yourself, don't you?'

'I do. My father made one for me.'

I observed that her face was alight with pleasure, although whether at the thought of the shawl, or with surprise that he should take an interest in such things, I couldn't say.

'Perhaps I'll ask him to make one for Marion,' said Thomas, smiling at her enthusiasm. 'Do you think she would like one?'

'For your wife? Oh yes.' She started to laugh, although I could not see that he had said anything so very funny. 'He has a few on hand and perhaps you could come one day and look at them and take your pick.'

'A very good idea! I will have to take care and choose my time carefully. I think I should like to meet your father, Jenny. He sounds like an interesting man.'

'Oh he is! Isn't he, William?'

'He's a very clever man. And he's been very kind to me.'

The weavers at that time were – as they are, even now – well educated, well read and thoughtful, but back then they were also to a great extent their own masters, prosperous and independent, and that has very much changed for the worse now, for all but the favoured few who saw the way things might be going. They were skilled and ingenious and those that owned their own looms or even a small weaving shed with several looms and had some skill in designing, like Jenny's father, could command high prices for their work, however much they might complain about costs.

Although he did not exactly broadcast the fact, I was well aware that Mr Caddas was a radical. This was something that had shocked my mother, but certainly would not have shocked my father, although he would perhaps not have gone so far as to voice his support. Events in France had made such a position precarious in the extreme. Along with his companions, Sandy Caddas had taken shares in the purchase of a weekly newspaper, so that he knew what was going on in the world outside the narrow interests of his trade. Such things, as he was fond of remarking, would sooner or later affect his trade, and he wanted to know about them before that happened. Like I myself, he had a strong sense of justice and of injustice too. He did not like the way the world was arranged and he was brave enough to say so. I admired him for that.

Besides that, he would cultivate his garden, growing kale and potatoes for the table, leaving the flowers and herbs to Jenny. But he was almost as interested in botany as I was. I think this was one of the things that fascinated Thomas, because he was always quizzing Jenny about her father, his beliefs, his habits, and within the space of a few short visits, he seemed to have found out much more about Sandy Caddas than I had discovered in the space of as many years.

There was one thing only that made me jealous, and it was a strange thing to be envious of, but I remember it all the same, remember my resentment. Thomas could always make Jenny laugh in a way I never did. He had that talent: a dry way of making an observation that you would suddenly realise was very funny. Jenny was quicker to see this than I. I would see her chuckling to herself and realise that he was making fun of me, mildly, and then I would start to laugh too and he would look from one to the other of us with a pretence of surprise. 'Have I said something amusing?' he would ask innocently.

Once, he brought a box of sugar plums into the library, and we finished them between us, like greedy children. Another time he had a wooden crate of some foreign sweetmeat that had the scent of roses about it, a scent and taste that lingered on the tongue long after you had finished eating it. I was not so fond of this, but Jenny thought it was wonderful, and he gave her the rest of the box to take home with her so that her sister could have some as well. He told her it was as Turkish as the shawls her father was making and that was why he had bought it.

Sometimes I would walk her home but from time to time she would stay in Thomas's house because she had promised Marion she would finish some piece of work or other. They would give her a bed betwixt and between the servants' quarters and the family rooms, making her very comfortable, so she told me. And once or twice, she said that Thomas had actually taken her home on horseback, when her father was expecting her but it was too late or the weather too inconvenient for walking.

Then she would steal her hand into mine and say, 'But I would rather have ridden up in front of you, William. You know that, don't you? He's a very kind gentleman to be sure, but I would rather have ridden up in front of you.'

Which was a strange thing to say, because not a horse did I possess, nor ever had possessed one, nor was ever likely to, so far as I could see.

▨ ▨ ▨

My own Jenny, my grand-daughter, has just come into the room, bringing with her a posy of late flowers from a neighbour's garden: mostly lavender, past its best, with the blooms whitening on the stem, a few tiny rosebuds and some ragged sweet peas and pinks.

'I picked these for you, grandfather,' she says.

She has brought over the brown and white pitcher from the new Bell's pottery, which is a great fascination for the ladies. Her mother bought the pitcher only a week ago, very much the fashion she tells me, and Jenny is intent on filling it with water and stuffing flowers into it. I do not think her mother would be very pleased to see to what use she is putting this new and treasured possession. But who am I to disappoint her when she is so intent on the task? The flowers are already wilting from the heat of her starfish fingers, so it is as well that she is putting them in water. The smell of them is very sweet.

Jenny, my other Jenny, grew all of these in her garden. When I close my eyes and breathe in the scent of sweet peas, I am back there again, sitting with my arm around her waist. Sometimes, when there was dried lavender to be rubbed, to make into lavender bags for her linens, I would help her. The scent, astringent and heady, would stay on my hands for hours afterwards.

Even now, the scent of lavender always reminds me of those days and that peculiar, uncertain feeling when everything was in a state of flux. I knew that I would have to find other work, I knew that this would be my last year in the college garden, a garden that had meant so much to me, a place that had been my home since infancy, and yet I could not be unhappy. In fact, it was something of a relief to be leaving at last, and I was very excited about the future. With every month that passed, my problems seemed to be resolving themselves. Thomas had raised the matter as promised, and his uncle was quite amenable to the Ayrshire plan. There was a small problem of the cottages, which had to be made habitable, but he was confident that before our lease and my garden work ran out in Glasgow, we would all be able to go to Ayrshire and settle down there together. A little later, as soon as practicable, Jenny and I would have a country wedding in the village kirk and all would be well.

'Leave it with me,' he said.

And I trusted him.

I would be sorry to leave Glasgow and even more sorry that I would not see Thomas so regularly as before, but I was confident that our friendship could and would continue. He was in the habit of visiting his cousin often. How much more frequently might he come when he could have a hand in laying out and improving these large grounds and gardens? I knew he had plans for us and thought that when I was working there too, his uncle, who was very lazy in such matters, and his cousin, who was a sickly soul, would give him a free hand. There might even be the possibility of the long dreamed-of expedition to collect plants, a small expedition perhaps, not to China, which would be a great and dangerous distance, but perhaps to France or Italy. And to me, who had not even seen very much of Scotland, and for whom the Isle of Arran had been a voyage of discovery, France or Italy might as well have been China, so exotic were the visions conjured by those names in my imagination.

The rest of the family was in a fair way to prospering. Bessie had moved out of the scullery and was now a housemaid and very proud of the fact. Moreover, she had the trust of the cook, who seemed to be teaching her all she knew. The younger girls were shaping up too. I thought that Susanna would never rise beyond her work as scullery maid. I worried about her because she was still clumsy and never seemed very happy, especially now that she was separated from her sister. But Jean had lately been taken on as lady's maid to the younger daughter of the house where she had been in service. There was little between them in age and it was the girl's own choice, I think. She wanted a maid she could confide in and, for all her shortcomings, Jean was a sweet-natured lass with a face that invited confidences. We all thought she would do very well in the household. As for my brother James, he was fast becoming a useful under-gardener, absorbing knowledge as a sponge absorbs water, stronger and more capable than myself.

Of all the boys, Johnnie was still hankering after ships, making plans for when he was old enough to go to sea. Although my mother disapproved, I was inclined to let him go when the time came and follow his heart. Once a man is smitten with that fever, or so my uncle John had told us, there is nothing to be done about it, there is only salt water will cure it. Only Rab was still a sickly soul, nine years old and never thriving. Each winter we thought we would lose him and each winter – with Thomas's help – he struggled through to see another spring. There was a dogged determination about him that seemed a useful substitute for health and he was an uncomplaining lad with great reserves of self-sufficiency for all that he was so often unwell. My mother cosseted him as much as she could. He was her baby and she loved him.

But since, apart from Rab, all my brothers and sisters seemed to be off our hands, or very nearly, Jenny and I could begin to look forward to our marriage. Her father had already declared his intention of settling a reasonable tocher on his daughter, should she find a 'man she wished to marry' as he would say, with a wink in my direction. In fact, the dreaded dismissal from the gardens was proving to be a blessing in disguise and I was looking forward with a certain amount of complacency to a happier future than I could ever have hoped for.

CHAPTER TWENTY-SEVEN

A Departure and a Puzzle

I have racked my brains since. Was I so very foolish, so unseeing? Was there even the smallest hint of what was to follow? But I can find none. She was always her ordinary loving self with me. She gave me not a single hint of the storm that must have been taking place in her head and in her heart. Afterwards I found myself wondering, are all women like this? Can all women dissemble so completely, when there is something quite different going on behind their eyes? To believe that, of course, would be to call into question every single friendship, every courtship, every marriage. How could you ever trust a lassie again? Well, I did find myself thinking like that for a time, until I brought myself up short with the realisation that you must trust somebody or life itself would become unbearable. But from time to time, I still find myself considering the conundrum, albeit with feelings less sharp, less painful than I once endured.

Are lassies so used to disguising their true feelings, brought up as they are from birth to be pleasing to everyone except themselves, to accede to all demands, to consider themselves so much less than the menfolk in their lives? I sometimes think that must be the case. But then, so often they are bought and sold, so who can blame them? *The tocher's the jewel*, as the poet Burns wrote. And so many men are but *knotless threids* who will slide away from lassies at time of need, so how could they be otherwise than dissembling? That a woman can tell you one thing with wide open eyes and a candid face, like a flower – that a woman can do this but be hiding so many shameful secrets, cherishing them deep inside her – that is the revelation from which I think I have never quite recovered. And even now, I am at a loss to know why she did it, how she could bring herself to do it, when I had given her all my trust and asked for so little in return. Besides, there was another betrayal to consider. Another dissembling. Even more monstrous, because there was far, far less excuse.

I watch my own wee Jenny now, arranging her flowers, a little crossly because they will not go the way she wants them. The lavender is too spiky, the late sweet peas too fragile and the one is warring with the other in her pitcher. Her cheeks have grown very pink. She tut-tuts, sighs, putting one hand on her hip as her mother sometimes does. I tell her to take them all out and start again, putting the flimsy sweet peas and the pinks in first and then coaxing a few of the stiff lavender stalks among them. I would try to do it for her but I know she would not accept my help, would flounce off in a temper, so I have to content myself with telling her what she might do to remedy matters, knowing that she will either take my advice or fall into a temper anyway.

She looks at me for a long moment, frowning and pursing her lips, and I have no idea what she is thinking either. But on this occasion at least, she decides to take my advice, hauls her flowers out, splashing water on my table and my books, which I have to mop up with my handkerchief, and begins all over again, as I have told her. This time she makes a passable attempt at a pretty arrangement. She is satisfied with herself and with my help and consequently with me for the time being. So she smiles at me. Which is reward enough.

'There now,' she says. 'That's done!' The scent of sweet peas, lavender and cloves fills the room, and I am back there again in Jenny's garden, knocking on the door, come to call upon her as we had arranged a few days previously. Thoughtless and happy. One of those moments in life when you look back and think, 'That was it. That was the very second when everything changed.'

I was surprised when Sandy Caddas came to the door instead of Jenny, his face literally contorted by something. Worry? Anger? I couldn't be sure but my stomach turned over with anxiety at the sight of him. What was wrong?

He ushered me in and I could see Anna sitting at the table, a grubby handkerchief screwed up in her fingers. She seemed nervous and I noticed that her eyes were red. She had been crying.

'I only came to see Jenny.' I was embarrassed by their discomfort. Had there been an argument of some sort? Was I the cause of it?

He stared at me for a moment. 'She's not here,' he said. 'She's gone away.'

I was thrown into confusion. 'Gone away?'

'Did she not tell you?' He said the words almost accusingly, but my stare of blank astonishment must have convinced him that I knew nothing. I was completely unaware that anything was amiss. If it was amiss.

I shook my head. 'No. She said nothing. We were supposed to be meeting here today.'

He sighed, motioned me to sit at the table, poured out a mug of ale. Anna seemed disposed to talk, but he silenced her with a glance.

'William!' It was not often that he used my first name. Mostly he called me nothing, although he always spoke politely enough. 'William,' he said, again, 'Can I be blunt with you? I'm sorry I have to ask you this. What are your intentions towards my daughter?'

I was momentarily surprised by the question. But there was only one answer. 'Marriage, of course,' I told him. 'You must know that, Mr Caddas. I am hoping that as soon as I am properly established down in Ayrshire, with Doctor Brown's help, I will be able to offer Jenny a home. I have wanted to wed her this long time past. You must know that.'

'And does *she* know that?'

It seemed a very odd question. Why would Jenny not know it?

'Of course. We have spoken of it often. She will tell you herself. You only need ask her. I thought she must have spoken to you about it.'

He had no reply to this, which fairly astonished me. I found myself blustering on, like a fool. 'I was only waiting for a word from her that you had no objection to the match and I would have asked your permission myself. Where is she?'

He sighed deeply. 'It's no matter, son. She's only gone away for a few weeks. Gone to stay with relatives.'

I couldn't disguise my surprise.

'But she never told me that she was going away. When was this decided?'

He glanced across at Anna, who regarded him in silence with large, frightened eyes.

'She has gone to her cousin's house. In Dumfries.'

'She never told me she had cousins down there.'

'They have never been close, until now.'

'Then why …?'

'They have asked her to stay. The old lady is unwell and needs nursing and they are a busy household. Jenny volunteered. She's a good lass. You do know that, don't you?'

I had never heard tell of these Dumfries cousins, but then I too had cousins whom I seldom saw.

'Sir,' I said, after a moment's thought. 'Sir, I must ask you, at the risk of upsetting you. Have you done this to remove her from me? Do you not agree to our marriage? Do you disapprove of me in some way?'

He was shaking his head, but I continued.

'I am well aware that I have been dismissed by the college, but Dr Brown will vouch for my honour and my hard work. The position there had become untenable for me, as you must know. Now he has found me work as a gardener with his uncle in Ayrshire. There will be a home for my family there too and for my wife, when we are wed.'

He shook his head again. Managed a thin smile. 'William, I would be very happy to agree to your marriage. I would be glad of it, in fact. You seem like a nice, steady lad to me and I think you will do your best for her.'

'I will, I promise I will.'

'She is very precious to me. But no. This is something quite different. She has gone away to … to do her duty by her family. She will return at last and when she does, I hope that you will still … I hope that you will want to marry her. That you can resume your courtship of her and we will talk about her tocher in the meantime. I can do that at least.'

'The tocher can wait!' I said, angrily. 'Jenny would be just as dear me without it. With respect to you, sir, she can come to me penniless in her shift if she likes, and I will still love her and do my best for her. But if you tell me where she is, I can perhaps write to her and reassure her. If you think it is in any way necessary.'

'Well yes. Perhaps you could write to her. But not immediately, William. You see, she was torn between her duty to go and her desire to stay here. And I think that a letter from you at this precise time might do more harm than good to her peace of mind. Do you understand me?'

'I think so,' I replied, cautiously. But I spoke out of politeness only. I didn't understand him at all.

'When a little while has passed and we have more idea of how long she might be away, I will tell you where she is, and you might write to her then. But not now, lad. Do you see? Not for a wee while.'

I was very puzzled, but I agreed. What else could I do? I couldn't imagine what manner of family illness might have made Jenny depart so swiftly for the south of the country. And a long, arduous journey it was too, by postroads over mossy moors, most of which were – so the stories went – infested with bandits and gypsies. You had to have permission to travel down there, through the extensive lands owned by the various factions of the great but turbulent Kennedy family. Twixt Wigtown and the Cruives of Cree, so the old rhyme went, you could not pass unless you courted a Kennedy.

'The minister gave her the necessary letters of permission,' he added, as though reading my thoughts.

'But how has she gone?' I asked, thoroughly alarmed now. 'Good God, sir, has she gone on foot? It is such a long way. And she should have been accompanied. Was there nobody to take her? How has she gone?'

'No, no,' he said. 'Calm yourself, man. She has gone by the weekly coach. It transports the wool from the south, and takes the weaving back, and I managed to secure her a place inside the coach. She will be safe enough. With her letters of permission from Mr Blackie, and a little siller in her purse, she will do well enough. And one of her cousins has agreed to come some of the way to meet with her.'

I was somewhat relieved, but still puzzled. I finished my ale and got up to leave. He shook my hand, but he would not meet my eyes as I left the house. I didn't understand it at all and to compound my discomfort, when I got to the bend in the track, Anna emerged like a sprite from behind a tree. She was panting because she had run to intercept me. She stood there, glancing behind her, all poised to run back again instantly if her father should come looking for her.

'William!' she hissed. 'William, she didnae want to go! I saw her leave. They made her go. She didnae want to go, but they made her! My father and Nancy from next door. They made her go and she was greetin' so she was. Greetin' so that I thocht her heart would brak' in twa!'

I put out my hand to detain her, to question her further, but she had heard some noise, real or imagined, from the weaving shed. She slipped through my fingers and was gone, running like a young hare back towards her father's cottage. I thought I saw Gilbert's weaselly face, peering at us from behind a wall. But perhaps I was mistaken. I wondered briefly if I should go back, confront Mr Caddas, demand to know the truth. But I knew that he would tell me nothing else and I thought it unwise to antagonise him. So I went home.

I needed to confide in somebody, and Thomas was the obvious person, but I felt a faint reluctance to do so. It seemed too personal a problem to discuss, even with a man whom I had come to think of as my best friend. I got the length of his house, not knowing where else to go, but the housekeeper told me the family had gone to Edinburgh to visit Marion's brother and would be away for a couple of weeks. I found myself hoping that Jenny would be back by then. I should have told my mother and I did tell her a sketchy story, half truth, half lies: that Jenny had warned me she might be going away to help with a sick cousin, that she had been called away suddenly because the cousin was worse but would return as soon as possible. If my mother found anything strange about this, she didn't remark upon it.

That night, and for several nights after, I lay awake, trying to puzzle it all out. Finally, I sought out my sister, Bessie, as soon as was practical and confided my misgivings to her, telling her the whole of the strange tale, right down to Anna's whispered warnings.

'What do you think?' I asked her.

We were sitting in the kitchen at the house where she was in service. Mistress MacTaggart, the cook, was taking an afternoon nap in her room. Young men were not generally allowed in the kitchen, but as Bessie's elder brother I had privileges beyond the normal rules of the household. The family were out and the kitchen was quiet and private, although Bessie was meant to be cleaning the big copper moulds that hung there and were used for making celebratory jellies and shapes. She had a pile of cut lemons and some silver sand and she was rubbing away at the moulds with sand-filled lemons, greatly to the destruction of her fingernails. She listened while she cleaned. The moulds had bizarre shapes, like castles or strange fruits. The smell of lemons was very strong in the air and brought Thomas to my mind, and the time he had made me my whisky toddy, when I was so ill. The time he had rested a cool hand on my forehead. I found myself wishing he were here now. Wishing I could confide in him.

'It might be exactly as her father told you. Why would he lie to you? What reason would he have?' Bessie asked.

'I don't know. I can't think of one.'

'She had promised to help out with a sick relative and was summoned to the bedside quite suddenly. Perhaps she didn't want to go, since it meant being away from you. Anna may have seen her in tears, but that would mean nothing. Only that she will miss you as much as you will miss her.'

'Do you think so?'

She regarded me steadily if a little sternly. 'Well, could there be any other explanation? Ask yourself!'

'What do you mean?'

'Oh William, you know what I mean. The reasons why young women are sent away from home are generally to do with the state of their bellies, are they not? And I don't mean that they have eaten too many green apples!'

I was shocked by her forthrightness, but that was typical of Bessie. I think I must have blushed, because she laughed at me.

'You know exactly what I mean, don't you? Lassies are sent away when they have a whaup in the nest! Especially when there is no man prepared to marry them. But everyone knows you would marry her tomorrow if you could. So I see no problem that would occasion her being banished.'

I must have blushed scarlet because she looked at me inquisitively, pausing with a fresh half lemon in her hand. She was meant to be dipping it in silver sand, but she put it to her lips and sucked at it momentarily. Then pulled a face, licked her lips, dipped it in sand, and commenced her cleaning again.

'Could that be the reason? Only you know the answer, William!'

'No. No. We never … never. There is no possibility.'

'Are you telling me the truth?'

'Yes. Of course I am. She's a good girl. And I never pressed her to more than a kiss or two. I thought it was better to wait.'

I was surprised that my sister knew anything about such matters, but maids will talk to each other I suppose, and I have heard tell that kitchens are very robust places, in big houses at any rate.

She grinned at me. 'In that case, you have nothing to fear and nothing to worry about. I think her wee sister is just mischief making. I never saw a lass more in love than Jenny Caddas is with you. She has burst into bloom like an apple tree since she has been in your company. She has gone south to fulfil a family obligation and that's all. Good for her. When she returns you may be that much closer to being able to marry her. In your place, I think I would do as her father says, cherish the thought of her, and wait until he tells you that it is appropriate before writing to her.'

❑ ❑ ❑

Which was what I did. It was all I could do. But it didn't prevent me from worrying. And eventually, a couple of weeks later, when the Brown family had returned from Edinburgh but when there was still no word of Jenny, I confided my worries to Thomas, although without going into too many details.

He seemed very surprised and a little perturbed. 'So that's what has happened to her!' he said, frowning. 'We wondered where she had gone, Marion and I. She left some work all unfinished, you know.'

'She should not have done that. They should have told you. It would have been a courtesy, surely.'

'Well, if there was a sudden illness ... And besides, we were in Edinburgh at the time.'

'Her father says she's in Dumfries, helping to nurse a sick cousin.'

'For how long?'

'I don't know. He can't say.'

'It must be something serious. And if so, it's impossible to predict. Why don't you write and ask her about it?'

'He won't give me the direction.'

'Why not?'

'He says it will upset her and make her homesick.'

He pursed his lips. 'I suppose that's possible.'

'He says that when she comes home again, he'll start to think about her tocher and that we should be wed.'

'He said that to you?'

'Yes.'

'And you agreed?'

'I would marry her tomorrow if I could.'

'Then you've nothing to worry about, William.'

'I'm worried because she left without saying goodbye. And her sister told me that she was crying and she didn't want to go.'

'But she was leaving you. And she didn't know for how long. And she was being hurried away without being able to say a proper goodbye to you!'

'You're right. I know. But it worries me all the same. And to be frank with you, I miss her.'

'Well, we miss her too,' he said, thoughtfully. 'Very much. We miss seeing her sitting in the library, perched on the window seat with the sun in her hair. We miss the way she would sometimes sing when she was sewing. I loved to hear her sing. She had the sweetest, clearest voice I have ever heard, and that includes all the fashionable young ladies who think that they have a voice because they have learned to string a few conventional notes together. Oh those interminable musical evenings, William. You should thank the Lord that you never have to attend them!'

It was another thing I had never noticed, not consciously. But it was true. She would sing as she stitched, love songs mostly but sometimes lullabies.

'She could sing "Waly Waly" till it brought a tear to your eye,' he added, and then, much to my embarrassment, he started to sing the old song of love and loss himself:

'Tis not the frost, that freezes fell,
Nor blawing snaw's inclemencie,
Tis not sic cauld that makes me cry;
But my love's heart grown cauld to me.

When we cam in by Glasgow toun,
We were a comely sicht to see;
My love was clad in the black velvet,
And I mysel in cramasie.'

I had never yet heard Thomas sing, but his voice was deep and clear and he could carry a tune. I can hear it yet: those bleak words and that eerie melody which seemed to bring a breath of sadness into the room, a sadness that lingered long after the notes of his song had died away.

'But had I wist, before I kist
That love had been sae ill to win,
I had lock'd my heart in a case o' gowd
And pinn'd it wi' a siller pin.

And O! if my young babe were born,
And set upon the nurse's knee,
And I mysel were dead and gane,
And the green grass growing over me!

CHAPTER TWENTY-EIGHT

Dumfries

Radical. Of the root. There is some correspondence, surely, between the radical movement and the work of the gardener. Is it that he sees how all things grow in their proper time? How all things have equal value but different properties. A garden, to be truly a garden worth cultivating, needs due measure of different plants: flowers, vegetables, soft fruits, trees and shrubs, large and small. I was reading, not only about gardening and plants and their properties, but there were other books in Thomas's library, books about the rights of man; works that changed not just my knowledge but my thinking as well. He had a handsomely illustrated volume of the poems and letters of Robert Burns and it was obvious where the poet's sympathies lay, although he had been but a cautious exponent of radicalism. Like most of us, he had a wife and family to support, the fear of poverty ate into him, and he also knew a bit about patronage. So many of us are caught between the knowledge that lies deep in head and heart and the pressing demands of our everyday lives.

All of this stood me in good stead later on, when I left gardening forever and entered into the world of books and bookselling. Where did I get the wherewithal for such an undertaking you may wonder? Well, I got it from my father-in-law. Always of radical tendencies, he wholeheartedly embraced the movement with renewed vigour. I run ahead of myself, perhaps because of a very reasonable desire to leap over the events of the following few months, a desire not to come to the point. But I have to return to the tale, and it must be told just as it happened.

From Jenny there was complete silence for some weeks. I worked away in the gardens, a little sadly to be sure, because I was aware that the future care of all my beloved trees and plants would fall to somebody else. But I was making plans with Thomas, plans that involved moving myself and at least some of my family to Ayrshire. And there was a certain excitement in that, or would have been, if I had been able to take my mind off Jenny for more than a few hours at a time. I would visit her father and he would give me word of her, a carefully balanced tissue of caution and hope. He was sure that she would soon be coming home but he couldn't say when.

At last, I demanded that he give me the direction to her cousin's house in Dumfries. And because he could see that I was on the verge of losing all patience with him, he agreed.

I can see him yet, sitting at his table, with his head bent, writing it down for me.

'Write to her,' he said. 'She is but a poor correspondent where I am concerned, but she may write to you. Tell her that we miss her. We'd be glad to have her home again. Tell her that she should come home again as soon as she can.'

After that, I sent her letters whenever I could, writing them in Thomas's library, using Thomas's paper and his pens. At long last she replied, but her letters were few and far between and disappointingly short, a few lines in her neat, childish hand, telling me that pen and paper were at a premium in the house, as were candles to see by, so she would not be writing very often. She was well, although her cousin was still very ill. Dumfries was a pretty town, but she wished that she were at home. She would never fail to ask after my family, her father and Anna. When I can bear to reread them — for I have them yet, buried deep inside my desk, thrust to the back of the secret drawer concealed by a lion's head carving – I can see that they told me almost nothing except that she herself was well. But not happy. She never mentioned that she was happy and I sensed that below her reassuring words, something was very much amiss.

⊞ ⊞ ⊞

In October I decided that enough was enough. We were in the mild spell that often comes to the west before the onset of winter, much like now, as I write these words, before the rains begin in good earnest. There was yellow stubble in the fields, the leaves were turning to liquid gold and there was a breathless quality over the land as though it were pausing before winter, sighing for summer, but with a wee spice of anticipation for the coming spring about it all the same. So do all green and growing things fall in with the seasons. Sometimes it seems to me that it is only we human beings who battle against what should be our deepest instincts.

But there, I have become ridiculously philosophical in my old age and I am quite sure that I thought of none of this back then, when I was a daft young man, and wanted only to see Jenny home again so that we could make plans for our wedding. All I thought was that we were in for a spell of fine weather, perhaps the last before winter, and I must seize the initiative and find out what was detaining my girl in Dumfries, before travelling became thoroughly impractical. Faculty would not be pleased at my absence, but then there was little they could do to me since they had already dismissed me. James knew fine what he had to do in the gardens and urged me to go and leave everything in his hands, which were capable enough.

And so I took myself off to Dumfries. From Thomas, I borrowed a horse called Meg, like Tam O' Shanter's mare, the one that lost her *ain grey tail* to Cutty Sark. I sent James to make the request lest Thomas should question me too closely about my journey. Having made the decision to visit Jenny, at last, I think I was afraid my friend might try to dissuade me from travelling. He lent me Meg very gladly, although I was but a poor horseman, and bounced up and down upon the placid animal, giving myself the most amazing pains in my back and thighs. Every so often, Meg would turn her head and look round at me with an expression of dismayed disbelief on her features, if a horse can possibly do such a thing. It was comical in the extreme and greatly endeared the animal to me. The journey, even along the postroad, was arduous, and I marvelled that Jenny had undertaken it, although she had been in a coach, which would have been easier. But then I had to take stabling for Meg at coaching inns each night – the horse was better accommodated than I was – and I found myself sleeping in the least expensive and therefore most bug- and flea-infested rooms, on filthy straw. There was little I could do to prevent the loathsome creatures feasting off me, but I closed my eyes to the discomfort and thought of Jenny. When I was outside the town of Dumfries, I stopped, stripped off my soiled linen, washed in a fast-flowing and icy burn and changed into a more respectable shirt which I had kept clean for the purpose, so that her relatives would not wonder what manner of vagabond was coming to their door.

I stabled my Meg at another inn. I think we had been something of a trial to each other, but she seemed to have grown fond of me, surveying me with weary patience when I came to saddle her up each morning. Still, I'm sure she was glad enough to be rid of me for a spell, finding herself warm and well fed in a good stable. Then I wandered about aimlessly, clutching the paper upon which Sandy had written his direction. I could not make out the maze of unfamiliar streets at all but, at last, I found a ragged boy with a grubby face, crouching on a street corner, tossing pebbles in the air and trying to catch them again. By dint of promising to give him a penny for his pains, I had a guide to the very doorstep.

It was a tumbledown stone cottage with a mouldy thatch, like a worn-out wig, in a back close of the town, and I would never have come upon it without the child's assistance. A thin line of smoke, a pencil stroke across the sky, went up from the chimney. The little lad grinned at me and tested the coin between his teeth – God knows what he was testing it for but I suppose he thought that it made him look like a grown man – and then swaggered off.

'Mind the auld yin!' was all he said, glancing over his shoulder. 'She'll gie you a sair dunt on the heid as soon as look at ye!'

With this awful warning ringing in my ears, I knocked on the door. What 'auld yin' I asked myself? But then, I knew Jenny had been helping to look after a sick old lady. I had timed my visit for a very respectable hour of the early afternoon. I thought I would be able to talk to Jenny, perhaps even walk out with her for a while, spend a night at the inn where I had stabled the mare, or even at their house, if her relatives allowed, and then return to Glasgow, with the benefit of having reassured myself that all was well with her and that all was well between the two of us.

CHAPTER TWENTY-NINE

The Mistress and the Maid

I don't know quite what I expected but it certainly wasn't what I found. My worries were all centred upon the thought that Jenny might have changed towards me; that she might have met some other lad, down in Dumfries – a wealthy weaver perhaps, or a prosperous young farmer – and have changed her mind about our betrothal. What I didn't anticipate at all was the skivvy with coal dust and sores on her face who answered my knock and ushered me into the front room. It was a parlour kitchen where a woman, who contrived to be both plump and hard-faced at the same time, looked upon me with profound suspicion. I would have put her at something over forty and it struck me that she must have been the wee lad's 'auld yin'.

She wore a black wool dress that was stained and draggled, and she had a yellowed mutch covering a head of greasy, greying hair. She was sitting sewing. It looked like another rusty black skirt that she was mending, crudely darning with long stitches in black wool, and she had a bowl of some kind of gruel beside her and a cup of ale. There was a fire that seemed to give out no heat whatsoever, smouldering faintly in the hearth. It struck me that the thin line of smoke I had seen from outside, rising through the air, must have come from this inadequate fire. Although the day was not cold it seemed a peculiarly cheerless room, and the woman seemed an equally cheerless individual. My heart sank.

'Mr William Lang,' said the skivvy, poking her head round the door and then withdrawing it precipitately, as though afraid of receiving blows just for the indiscretion of announcing me to her mistress. She motioned me into the room and trotted off as fast as her spindly legs would carry her.

The woman looked me up and down and went on with her stitching.

'Aye?' she said. 'What are you wanting, lad? There's nae work here. And I don't give charity to beggars.'

'I am no beggar,' I replied, trying to maintain my dignity. 'And I have no need of work, or even lodging. But I am come on business of my own. I am looking for Jenny Caddas.'

'Oh you are, are you?'

I cannot rightly describe to you the expression that crossed her face at the mention of Jenny's name. It was some unfathomable mixture of cunning, caution, shame and, yes, distaste. I know that it made my insides clench with some nameless fear, a premonition of disaster. And regret too. I should have come sooner, I thought. I should not have trusted her father. I should have come sooner. It is too late. But too late for what, I could not rightly have told you.

'She and I are to be betrothed with the blessing of her father,' I continued. 'But she has been gone from home for so long now, albeit the reasons were all of a charitable nature. And we are worried about her!'

'Oh, you are, are you?' she repeated, gazing at me, her thin lips twisted into a sneer.

'I will be starting a new position in Ayrshire after Candlemas, and thought that I should seize my only opportunity to come and visit her, so I would thank you to tell her that I am here, as I am sure she will be very pleased to see me.'

'Aye. I am sure that would be the case,' she said, slowly, putting down her sewing and squinting up at me in the gloom. 'So, tell me. You'll be the gardener's son from Glasgow. Is that it?'

'Yes. I am. And a gardener in my own right, not just the gardener's son.'

'Aye, aye, Mr High and Mighty. And you want to marry the lass?'

'I've told you. We have her father's blessing. We hope to marry as soon as I am set up and have a decent home to bring her to. I have been promised a cottage in my new position.'

I don't know why I felt the need to justify myself to her. I owed her nothing. But I think I had some idea of placating her, or at least making things easier for Jenny.

She stared into the fire and I could have sworn then that a momentary pity crossed her face. It was extraordinary how transparent her features were. She was an ugly enough woman and yet she could not dissemble. Her feelings were clearly visible on her face for all to see.

There was a silence in the room, which I again felt prompted to fill with explanations, in case I had not made myself clear enough. 'Her father told me that she was called here to help nurse a sick cousin. I have been writing to her, and she has been writing to me.'

She gazed up at me then.

'And when did you last have a letter from her, son?'

'Some time ago. I have been on the road for several days. But it must have been a couple of weeks before that. A note just, telling me that she was well and looking forward to seeing me on her return. But she did not say when that return might be and, in consultation with some of my friends and hers, I decided that I would come and satisfy myself as to her wellbeing.'

'Friends, eh?' she said.

'Yes. She has influential friends, and so do I!'

Even to myself, my voice sounded ridiculously formal to the point of pompousness.

'And here you are.'

'Here I am. And – begging your pardon, madam, if I offend you – but it is high time she was at home with her family again.'

She hauled herself to her feet, setting down her sewing, the rusty black skirt, on a small table by her side. She smelled of smoke and camphor and stale sweat. She went over to a jug and poured me a cup of ale. I had expected it to be thin and sour but to my surprise, I found it was very good.

'The trouble is,' she said, and then hesitated. 'The trouble is that she isnae here.'

Again I felt it, that terrible sinking in heart and stomach. 'What do you mean, she isn't here? Has she gone home then?'

Had our paths crossed? Had she finally been allowed to return to her father? I had deliberately not told him what I was planning on doing, so he would have had no opportunity to deter me from coming. But perhaps she had already been on her way home, even as Meg and I were plodding our weary way to Dumfries. As I thought about this, another, more sensible part of my mind realised that I was clutching at straws. She had not returned to her father's house. If she had been on her way home, she would have written to me to tell me so. She would have been so pleased to be free at last, that she would have let me know well in advance.

I drank my ale, for I was very thirsty, and stared at the woman. We exchanged names and, with curious formality, we shook hands. Her name was Mary Strachan. She was some relative of Jenny's mother, a cousin of some sort. I never did establish the proper relationship, whether first or second cousin, but it didn't matter. I saw it again, that strange, shifty look cross her face. And then she said, 'Well she's no' here, son. That's all I can say for sure. She's no' here.'

'But she was here?'

'Aye. She was here. But she's no' here the noo.'

'So, where is she?'

She shrugged, shook her head. 'How should I ken? The lassie upped and left in the middle of the night and that's a' I ken aboot it. Never tell't a soul where she was going or why.'

'But she *must* have. She must have left a note of some sort. How could she just leave, all unprotected? In the night! Where would she go? She must have told somebody.'

'Well she didnae. She was neither use nor ornament while she was here and noo she's gane. And that's the lang and the short of it. So ye can away back to your gairdens and tell her faither that I did all I could do, but nae mair.'

She picked up her sewing, turned her face to the fire, which continued to give off a little light but small heat, and commenced her stitching again, jagged stitches of black wool like her own broken teeth. Not a word more would she say to me, but when I stood rooted to the spot, she presently rang the bell and the skivvy edged into the room, keeping her back to the wall.

'Show the young gentleman oot, Rebecca,' she said. And that was all she said. Short of physical violence, which believe me, I contemplated, I could not have made her tell me more.

⊞ ⊞ ⊞

What would you have done? What would I have done now? Well, as an older man with a certain gravitas about me, I think I would perhaps have managed to coax the truth out of her. As a young man with no gravitas whatsoever, there was nothing for me to do except leave the house and make my way back to the nearby inn, with a view to hastening back to Glasgow with all speed. Perhaps Jenny would be there before me.

It was while I was half-heartedly eating a stew whose chief ingredients seemed to be ragged and unidentifiable vegetables mingled with suspicious pieces of gristle which put me much in mind of elderly horses like Meg, that I saw the skivvy, Rebecca, loitering about the doorway.

'The mistress fell asleep in front of the fire, and I slipped out for a minute, but she'll skin me alive if she finds out I've been talking to you.'

'Then tell me quickly. Tell me what you've come to say.'

'Only that they were far from kind to the puir lassie. That woman and her worthless husband, deil tak' them for a pair of greedy beggars. There was little I could dae. But they had her sewin' away for all she was worth, night and day. The mistress would tak' the things away and sell them, but never a penny did she gie to your lassie. She said it was to pay for her bed and board. And they had her daein the washing an' all an' feedin' the chickens they keep oot the back. She was mair o' a skivvy than I am, if you ask me, for a' that she was faim'ly to them.'

I sat amazed, my spoon clutched in my hand like a dagger.

'But what about her cousin, the lady that was so ill? She was sent to help with the nursing, surely?'

The lassie looked at me with scornful pity. 'Whit cousin?' she said. 'Whit lady? There's nae ladies in that hoose, except maybe for your puir lassie. And what nursin' are you talking about? There's naebody sick in that hoose. Ah weel, sick in the heid mebbe.'

'I don't understand you.'

'I speak as I find. It was cruel to have a lassie in that state workin' day and night, and nae wunner she went aff. I'm tellin' you, if I'd had mair courage, I'd have been aff tae. I'd have gane wi' her. She said, "Will ye come with me, Becky?" but I didnae have the courage. So she went all by herself, God love her. It was about a week ago. She left in the middle of the night, taking her bundle wi' her, and a wee bit breid and cheese that I had saved for her, and a few bawbees that she took from the jar in the kitchen to buy mair breid on the road. And that was the last ony of us saw of her.'

I felt my heart contract in my chest.

'But where did she go?' I asked. 'Did she tell you where she was going?'

'Are ye daft?' she said.

'In God's name, for what reason would she set off all alone? Why?'

'Ach,' she said, as if I were a simpleton, which indeed I think I was. 'Only just to seek the faither of the wean. Whit other reason could there be?'

CHAPTER THIRTY

Coming Home

The weather had broken. All the long, uncomfortable way back to Glasgow, with the old mare plodding along and the autumn rains tumbling down the back of my neck and hers, the stench of damp and dirty clothes compounded the sour smells lodged in my nostrils and the discomfort of the itches and scratches of flea-infested inns along the road. All the way, I hoped and prayed that she would be back in her father's house by the time I arrived.

I took the horse to Thomas's stable without seeing anybody but the lad who took the reins from me. Meg had picked up speed, the closer we came to Glasgow. I think she could smell home and she positively cantered into her stable with the steam rising from her coat. I paused only to change my clothes at my own house, to grab a mouthful to eat and drink, to counter all my mother's arguments that I was weary from the road and should sleep first – all true, but I could not do it – and set off again for Jenny's house. It was late and very dark by the time I rapped on her door. Her sister Anna came to answer it, ladle in hand. The room smelled of cooking, and her father was seated at the table over his evening meal: a bowl of stew with a mound of potatoes floating in the gravy, a loaf of bread, a slab of white cheese. She had been serving him and herself, ladling the stew into wooden bowls. He looked up, startled by my entrance.

'William! Come in and sit yourself down,' he said. 'Here, Anna, bring the lad something to drink. He looks fair worn out.'

'I am.'

I sat down in the proffered chair. No point in antagonising the man from the off. He knew more than he had told me, for sure, but perhaps he didn't know everything. As I rode back to the city, I had had more than enough time to consider the matter from all angles.

He gestured to a stone flagon on the dresser, and Anna poured whisky into a small glass. It was good whisky, but not something he dispensed lightly. Not like Thomas.

'Drink up. You look half starved with the cold.'

'I've had a long journey.'

He looked startled at that, as well he might. 'Journey?' he asked. 'What journey?'

'I went to Dumfries. I was sick of half truths, Mr Caddas, and so I thought I would find out for myself just what was happening with Jenny.'

He had the grace to blush. He glanced across at Anna, and I saw that she looked puzzled. She was not in on the secret then. Or perhaps she had been told only the fiction of the cousin who was in want of a nurse.

'Here,' he said, suddenly. 'Anna. Take yourself off next door for a wee while.'

'But I haven't had my supper yet,' she said, plaintively.

'Nancy will give you your supper, lass. Say I sent ye. I have serious business to talk about with William here. Just tak' yourself off next door for a while and leave us in peace, hen, there's a good lass.'

She went, frowning and none too happy about it, but she went.

He followed her to the door, watched her go along the lane, watched her knocking on the low door of Nancy's cottage and saw her admitted before he allowed himself to come back in and sit down at the table. He pushed his supper away from him, untouched, but poured himself a large measure of the spirit and refilled my glass. We sat in silence for a moment, during which he rested his elbows on the table and rubbed his eyes with his fists, like a wean.

'Ye should have asked me before you went, lad,' he said.

'I asked you often and often and you wouldnae tell me.'

'So you ken why she went?'

'I do now.'

'I thocht just at first the wean was yours, William.'

'Did you?'

'Why would I no'? I was angry enough, Will, but she declared it wisnae yours at all, only she wouldnae tell me the name of the faither, no matter how I pressed her.'

'Then she told you the truth. If there is a wean, it isn't mine.'

'God forgive me, Will, but I said tae her, why would she no' tell you it was yours anyway. Many a man has brought up another man's child in blissful ignorance, and since you were so obviously fond of the lassie, I saw no reason why you should not do the same.'

'You would have had her lie to me?'

'God help me, I would. But I thought only of her wellbeing. I was feart that you would reject her, and I'm sure she was feart of that herself. Why would she no' be, given the circumstances? I said "He's a good lad. He'll stand by you if you only tell him the wean's his." That's what I said to her.'

'And what did she say to that?'

'She said she couldnae and that was that and I was not to press her further.' He saw my nod. 'You're not surprised?'

'No.'

'And when I did press her further, she tell't me she could-nae dae that for the simple reason … because you and she, you and she …' His voice trailed off. He was very flushed, his hands clenched on the table.

'She told you the truth in that at least. We did naething but hold hands. Whiles she would kiss me, maistly on the cheek and once or twice I kissed her back, maistly on the lips. That was it. I have small experience with the lassies, Mr Caddas, but even I ken that ye cannae get a wean that wey.'

'So she tellt me and blushed as she said it. But somebody was not so shy and who that man was, she wouldnae say.'

'Some weaver lad maybe,' I muttered. 'And maybe married? Eh?'

He cast me a swift, stern glance as much as to say, 'why blame the weavers?' but he could not deny the possibility. There were lads and men too, in and out of the weaving shed most days, and Jenny was a pretty lass.

'So, we made a plan,' he said, ignoring my interruption. 'We made a plan that she would go to stay with these cousins in Dumfries. When once the wean was born, she would decide what to do. I said I wouldnae force her into anything. She could find a home for the wean down in Dumfries – her cousin said she would see tae that herself – or keep the wean if she wished. And I would not turn her away from my door. But I knew she was still fond of you. I thocht she might want to let the wean go and come hame and marry you. Besides ... there's many a slip. What if she lost the wean and had ruined all her chances with you for naething?'

How did I feel? I can't rightly say. There was shock right enough. Oh and anger. I could feel rage at the duplicity of it all, boiling up inside me. But alongside it, there was this stream of terrible sadness, like water flowing among boulders. It hurt the heart of me. Had she not trusted me enough to tell me of her predicament? But perhaps she had been right. How else would I have reacted if not with anger at her news? I could do nothing but picture her confusion. Mr Caddas's confession enraged me too, but then it occurred to me that in his position I might well have done the same thing. He loved his daughter, none more so. Not even myself.

There filtered back into my mind the question that must have been exercising her father too. If the child was not mine, then whose was it? I couldn't begin to imagine. I thought I was the only lad she saw, but I found myself wondering if there had been other lads she chatted to over the garden wall, other lads who might have helped her to take a swarm of bees or shelled peas for her or gathered lavender with her. And suddenly I remembered that Mr Caddas himself had only half the story, and I had better tell him what I had come to say.

He pre-empted me. 'How is the lass?' he asked. 'Is she well?'

I shook my head. 'I have no idea.' ·

'You didn't see her?'

'She was not there.'

'What do you mean?'

'Exactly what I say. She was not there. They treated her very badly, those cousins of hers and yours. I cannot imagine that they were blood relatives or, if they were, she is naething like them. I had the sorry tale from a servant of the house. They worked her half to death. And so she left. She must have been quite far gone. With the baby I mean. I have asked after her along the way. There was no sign of her along the road, no word at all of her, and believe me, I asked. But then I was some days behind her.'

I had made a nuisance of myself with questions about Jenny. Nobody had seen her.

He had already leapt to his feet, the chair falling over behind him. He began to pace up and down the kitchen.

'Gone?' he said. 'But where is she? Where has she gone?'

'Mr Caddas, how should I know? I thought, hoped, prayed even, that she would be at home with you, but I assume that there has been no sign of her here, either.'

'No. None whatsoever. Where is she? Where is she?'

I could see that the same sense of helpless panic was invading his mind as had already invaded mine. If she had not come home, where in the name of God had she gone? To search for the father of her child. That's what she had told the skivvy, Rebecca. Had she found him? How would he have reacted? Was she with him, or had he cast her out too? It didn't bear thinking about, now, when the year was falling rapidly towards winter.

Sandy Caddas had turned pale and then so crimson in the face that I feared for him. I thought he might have a seizure. I made him sit down, gave him more whisky. 'Where is she? Where can she be?' he kept muttering.

'I only wish I knew.'

He seized my hand. 'William – dear God in heaven – what shall we do? How can we find her?'

'I don't know. I don't know where she's gone. I hoped she might have come back to the city. That I would find her here. But she isn't here either and she did not come to my house, for I have been there already.'

'What can we do? If we spread the word, she will be ruined. Her reputation in tatters.' He looked at me piteously. I had always thought him so wise and strong, but he crumbled before my eyes.

'I care nothing about her reputation, sir. I would marry her with or without it.'

They were very fine words, spoken in the heat of the moment, but I wondered afterwards if I had really meant them. Well, perhaps I should give myself the benefit of the doubt and maybe I would have seen it through, if I was indeed the fine, honourable man I thought myself.

'You're a good lad.'

'Aye. Maybe. But that doesn't help us in this predicament. First we have to find her, see her safe, make sure the child is safe. Reassure her.'

'Would you really be able to bring yourself to care for another man's child?'

I honestly didn't know. How could I tell? The thought was so new to me. But there was the idea at the back of my mind that it wasn't the wean's fault. No child could help the accident of its birth. So perhaps I could. And it came into my head that I would rather have Jenny Caddas with another man's wean than no Jenny Caddas at all. So I said, 'Maybe. Maybe I couldn't and maybe I could. But first we have to find her. All that matters now is her safety.'

'What will we do?'

His bluster, his confidence, was all gone. 'What will we do, William?' he repeated, miserably.

'I don't know.'

We sat there like a pair of eejits, drinking whisky with thoughts and suggestions whirling around our heads. I needed to speak to somebody else about this, but who? My mother would be so shocked that she would be no help. Besides, there was something in me that shrank from betraying Jenny's secrets to her. I thought it was exactly the sort of predicament in which I would have turned to Jenny herself for advice. She would have been wise and thoughtful, and she would have told me what to do and where to turn.

And then it struck me that I could perhaps turn to Thomas for help. I would not want him to tell Marion about it, but he knew when to keep quiet. He liked Jenny, had been kind to her, loved her work. Out of regard for me, if nothing else, he would keep his own counsel. Besides, he was a doctor and used to keeping confidences. But he was an influential man, with many colleagues in the town. He would know how to make discreet enquiries. If anyone could find the means to lead us to Jenny, then he surely would.

I told Mr Caddas that I would make careful enquiries through certain contacts of my own, but without making it particularly clear who those contacts were, who I would be consulting. I thought he would be mortified to know that I would be confiding his family's shameful secrets to the likes of Thomas Brown. How could I explain about our friendship? How could I explain to him that I knew I could trust Thomas with my life, never mind with these secrets? So I told him only that I would make enquiries, and would tell him as soon as there was news. That maybe he had better go about the streets of the town himself and see if there was any sign of Jenny at all. And this he agreed to do.

CHAPTER THIRTY-ONE

Repercussions

I went home to my bed if not to sleep, and the next day I got on with my work, which had all fallen behind in my absence, but what could they do to me? They had already dismissed me and it would be well-nigh impossible for them to replace me before Candlemas. Nevertheless, I worked with a will and set James and Johnnie and the other lads to putting right all the many things they had neglected while I had been in Dumfries. Later in the day, when I felt I had control of the gardens again, although by no means control of myself, I took myself off to Thomas's house to tell him all that had passed.

As ill luck would have it, he had visitors. Professor Jeffray and his wife were there, for dinner. I had forgotten, of course, that they ate much later than we did, particularly when they were entertaining. I could smell the appetising scent of roast meat and hear Jeffray's great braying laugh from the dining room, although I never got a sight of him, and I felt more like an intruder than I ever had in this house before. For once, I felt like the common gardener I was, standing at Thomas's door with my cap in my hand and despising myself for the sense of inferiority that came over me at that moment. I think I always had the fear that one day Thomas would avert his gaze from mine for good, come to his senses, renounce our friendship. I don't know why I was like this with Thomas in particular. I was never so unsure of myself with anybody else, but Thomas seemed to open within me a positive abyss of uncertainty.

The maid, new to the household, didn't invite me in, but looked askance at my muddy boots and went to fetch her master. Thomas came to the door and – surprised to see me, but welcoming as ever – pulled me inside. I think he would actually have asked me to join them, but I felt the full weight of the dirt in my fingernails and my shabby clothes. I stood there like a gowk, turning my cap over and over in my hands and telling him that no, I wouldn't come in to spoil their evening. Thomas felt badly about it, that was plain to see, but Jeffray was an influential man and no great friend to me either. It was certainly better if I didn't meet him. And besides, it would ruin Marion's party. And Thomas would have rued his unwise behaviour, I'm sure. Jeffray would have seen to that.

'I have to ask for your advice. But I won't do it tonight,' I told him. 'Tomorrow will do. There's not a thing that can be done tonight, after all.'

He seemed intrigued. 'Advice about what?'

'No, no. Tomorrow will be soon enough. But I need to talk to you. I need a friend's help. Maybe you would come to the garden? Tomorrow? Maybe we could talk then?'

'Aye. Aye, of course.' He seemed torn between embarrassment and curiosity, but I think he could tell from my manner that it was a serious matter. 'What's wrong, William?' he asked. 'At least tell me what's wrong?'

'We'll speak about it tomorrow. It's about Jenny.'

'Jenny?' He seemed very surprised. 'Have you spoken to her at last?'

'I went down to Dumfries to see her. It was for that reason I needed the horse. Did you not guess?'

'You said she was helping to look after a sick relative. I wondered whether that was where you had gone, but your brother would tell me nothing definite.'

'Well, he was under instructions to be circumspect. I didn't want the likes of ...' I glanced into the hall. Jeffrey's voice could be heard relating one of his interminable stories. 'I didn't want the likes of the professor enquiring too closely about where I had gone.'

'I was worried about you.'

'I went south.'

'Why didn't you tell me?'

'It was between me and Jenny.'

'And is all well in that quarter?'

'No. No, Thomas. Nothing is well. But we'll speak about it tomorrow.' I could hear Marion now, calling for her husband from the drawing room. Perhaps she needed some leavening in the steady flow of Jeffrey's tales, which were all to do with himself and his own cleverness.

'I need your advice,' I said. 'You know Jenny well enough, and I think you are fond of her.'

'Of course I am. She's a lovely lass.'

'Aye. She is.' I almost said, 'she was', God help me. Why was I tempted to say it?' She was fine and well. I had to cling onto that fact. She must be fine and well.

'And a very clever young lady.'

'Aye.'

But not clever enough, I thought. Not nearly clever enough.

'Marion has grown very fond of her too,' he continued.

'Please!' I found myself touching his arm. 'Say nothing to your wife about this. Not yet a while.'

He frowned. 'Why? Has something happened to her? What is amiss, William?'

'We'll speak of it tomorrow.'

I turned to go, just as Marion came out into the hallway in all her party finery, a flowing muslin dress like a fountain of water, a dress that was scattered with flowers, each blossom embroidered in glowing silks. I looked at her and could think only that Jenny must have stitched those flowers. That she would never have

232

been able to spare the time to make such a gown for herself, but that she would have looked very beautiful in it. She would have been much more beautiful than Marion, who was quite a thick-set woman, and had an air of awkwardness when she moved in the delicate fabric.

Not long ago, I saw a copy of a painting by an Italian artist, Sandro Botticelli. It was in a book just, for I have never travelled abroad to see such things and cannot imagine that I will ever do it now. The painting was called *Primavera*, and among a number of lassies who were dancing as naked as nature intended, there was one in a gown covered with flowers. Flora she was, a goddess of the spring or some such, very tall and fair with flowers in her hair and around her neck and on her gown. It reminded me of the gown that Marion wore that night. But it was Jenny I could fancy wearing it, for the girl in the picture was most astonishingly like her. Even after all these years, I found myself gazing at the picture and remembering Jenny.

Marion seemed surprised to see me. 'William? What are you doing here?' she asked, controlling her anger at the interruption to her party when she saw me. Maybe she noticed the distress which I was at such pains to conceal. Marion Jeffrey was nothing if not kindly. A nice woman. I still think of her as a nice woman: brusque and forthright to be sure, but you always knew where you were with her. And it was not in her nature to dissemble. She would sooner give you the unvarnished truth than tell you a lie. And that is a good quality, if a little uncomfortable to live with.

'I'm away now, Mistress,' I said, with an attempt at a smile. 'I brought a message for the doctor here, that's all. But I'll not interrupt your party any longer.'

I turned and left them, standing together on the threshold, still not altogether pleased with my own diffidence. I felt inferior in that company and I didn't like the sensation. I could assume only that it was the presence of Jeffray in the other room that had made all the difference. I don't know what Thomas told Marion, nothing about Jenny I suppose, because you could always rely on him to be discreet. They went back to their party and I went home to another restless night, although exhaustion gave me a few hours of sleep at last.

▫ ▫ ▫

The night was intensely cold and the following morning the frost was everywhere, inside and out, papering all the windows of our house with ferns and feathers. It was the kind of weather that always brought the fumes from the type foundry down low into the garden, covering everything with a bitter fog that left a metallic taste on your tongue, but we soldiered on, covering our faces with woollen mufflers which allowed us to breathe more easily. Later in the afternoon, though, there was a blink of sunshine, the fog lifted a little and Thomas came into the garden and sought me out. We went into the old but 'n' ben where I kept the tools. It had once been a dwelling but was now little more than a tumbledown store. Still, it had a fireplace and a chimney, and we gardeners would often set ourselves a fire there with dead wood from the garden so that we could heat up ale to warm us, or a pan of porridge maybe. Whiles we would roast apples in the embers and float them in our drinks, where they would explode and froth up into a foam of sweetness on top of the ale. I poured a couple of mugs of the cider I had made with last year's harvest. I heated up the poker till it was red and glowing and plunged it into each pewter mug while it hissed and spat and made the drink very palatable. Then Thomas and I huddled up close to the fire, holding the mugs in our fists, and holding our fists out to the blaze. Mine were blue with the cold. Thomas had on a pair of gloves but he was still shivering.

Full winter had descended on us quite suddenly. The leaves, which had turned all shades of orange and gold, had blown down into hillocks in the recent gales and were lying about the gardens. The students ran and jumped and tumbled through them, laughing like younger boys than they were. I watched their careless joy with something very like envy. I hardly remembered that I had ever felt that kind of elation – except perhaps as a wee boy just, when I had run through the gardens and been conscious of nothing save the strength and speed in my own legs. I had a vivid memory of running, running, running so quickly through the gardens and among the trees, that I think I forgot my own body altogether.

Even now, as an old man, I can remember that feeling. I remember the wind rushing past my ears and the sense of breaking through some barrier so that my feet hardly seemed to be touching the ground at all, so that I thought I was like to fly, and I can call to mind the utter elation of it, of that new sensation, even when I stopped, panting, surprised by how far and how fast I had come. Strange how even rheumatic limbs can keep the memory of such lightness. But all too soon, unrelenting hard work had been my lot, and the effort had doubled after my father died. The sodden earth had rooted my boots to the ground as surely as if I had been one of my own trees.

Then Jenny Caddas had been my salvation. Well, Jenny and Thomas, always Thomas, who had shown me what it was to be the valued friend of such a man as he. But for a long time now, it seemed to me that Jenny had been the sun in my sky and the moon that rose over my nights. She had been my joy and now she was my intense sorrow and I didn't know what to do with all these unfamiliar and unmanageable feelings that flooded my mind: anger, worry, resentment, disappointment. They filled my head and spilled over and I didn't know what to do with any of them.

We sat there, Thomas and I, ower-warm at the front, freezing cold at the back, as is so often the way of it in winter, and I told him about my visit to Dumfries in search of Jenny. I described her terrible cousin and the skivvy Rebecca, the story she had told me and the lies and evasions of Jenny's father. The whole sorry tale, the fact that Jenny was with child but was now nowhere to be found, came spilling out of me. I heard his sharply indrawn breath at the news, saw his sudden frown, but then he sat there, listening quietly, as was his wont, while I came to the end of my story.

Once or twice he patted my shoulder or my knee. I saw grave concern in his eyes. He looked deeply troubled, sad and anxious but there was no censure, certainly. He got up and walked over to the crumbling window of the but 'n' ben, gazing out across the wintry garden.

'How can I help you?' he asked,. 'What would you like me to do?'

'I don't know.' The truth was that I felt helpless in the face of such a situation. 'I would have her back, you know. I would marry the lass tomorrow, if I thought it would set everything to rights.'

He came back and sat down again, staring at me.

'You would marry her? Even with another man's baby in tow?'

'Aye, with another man's baby and all. It would make no difference to me.' As I gave voice to this, I realised that it was the truth.

'Then you love her most truly, William.'

'I think I do.'

'She's a lucky lass to have you. There are few such men in the world.'

'I would think myself lucky to have her for my wife.'

'But you have to find her first.'

'I have to find her first. It cuts me to the quick that she did not see fit to confide in me.'

'But it would have been a difficult thing for any lassie. And there is no word of her at all?'

'Nothing. Not a sight of her, nor a sound of her. No word of her on the road anywhere. I stopped at all the inns, the best and the worst of places. I asked everyone I met as I rode back to town. But then, who would notice her? And even if she has won back to Glasgow, she has disappeared and I have no way of knowing where she might be!'

He set his mug on the hearth, got up again and began to pace about, frowning, kicking stones over the uneven flagged floor, hugging his arms around his body to warm himself up. The wood in the hearth burned down quickly and gave out a subdued heat. I threw another couple of logs onto the embers but they were too green and a thin spiral of aromatic smoke went up from them, giving off little heat.

'God help the lassie,' he said. 'God help her.'

'Don't say such things.'

'Did she have any friends, other relatives maybe? Is there anywhere at all she might be?'

'Oh there were lassies in the village, but nane that will admit to having seen her. Or if they have, they aren't telling. And what reasons would they have to keep silent? I'm so worried about her, Thomas.'

'You must be.'

'It's like this dreadful ache, here in my chest, and I don't ken what to do with the pain of it.'

'My dear friend,' he said, leaning across and embracing me. 'My dear friend.'

'I should have confided in you sooner.'

'You should. You should.'

'I have kept it to myself for too long, but her father told me very little.'

'Well, now that I know, what can I do of a practical nature? How can I help? It's a delicate matter, Will.'

'It is indeed.'

'If she has found some shelter where she can have the child and then plans to return home, it would be a terrible thing if we were to destroy her reputation through too specific enquiries. On the other hand, if she is alone and in need of help ... good God, what a dilemma!'

'I could kill her cousins with my bare hands for the cruel and greedy souls they are.'

'Why did they offer to take her in the first place?'

'Exactly what I've been asking myself.'

'They seem to be wretched hypocrites, that's for sure. But perhaps they wanted to make use of her skills for their own ends and cared not what became of her.'

'Despicable creatures.'

'What does her father say to all this?'

'Not a great deal. He blames himself and yet his intentions were all for the best. I know only that she has never been near her father's door since she left Dumfries, and that worries me beyond everything.'

'It looks very grave.'

'She might avoid me out of shame. But he knew fine what her condition was, and I would have thought that she would return there if anywhere. There has been not a word of her in the village either.'

'I could make enquiries, you know. Careful enquiries.'

'Do you think that wise?'

'There are discreet people. A scant handful who are known to help poor women in her condition. As a doctor, I am aware of them, and I could ask, if you think it might help.'

'Anything might help, Thomas, anything at all. Her father is wandering the streets in search of her to the neglect of everything else. God knows what he has told Anna about the whole affair. I would spend my time looking for her as well, but I have my work and I have tried the patience of Faculty for long enough. I will go when I can, but I thought that perhaps you might be able to narrow the search in some way.'

'I'll see what I can do.' He sighed heavily, shaking his head. 'In fact, I'll go now, this minute. Courage,' he said, as he left. 'Courage! We'll find her yet.'

❑ ❑ ❑

He did what he could. Made discreet enquiries. Sent me here and there, to this or that house. And went himself, I suppose. I think he did that for me as much as for Jenny. Once, I found myself in a poor hospital, the rooms filthy and smelling of a terrible mixture of blood and vomit and worse, hellish with the moans and groans of the sick and dying, for whom almost nothing could be done. She was not there, nor had she been, thank God. There was no sign of her. A wheen of filthy houses and streets had sprung up in the town over the past few years in response to the demands for housing for the vast numbers of people who were employed in the new manufactories, incomers from the Highlands and Islands, and from over the water in Ireland. Sometimes, when I found myself peering into rooms that never saw the light of day, stinking, bug-ridden rooms and passages that led from other windowless rooms and passages in a drab and deadly succession, all leprous with damp, I thought that I had found myself in some hellish labyrinth, an underground warren where only troglodytes might live. A vulnerable lassie might go missing in this maze and never be found again.

Days passed and then weeks, and still there was no sign of her. I grew weary and her father grew wearier. He looked terrible. He seemed to have aged ten years in the space of a few weeks. Anna said hardly a word about her sister. To our surprise she was often to be found in the weaving shed, keeping Gilbert and another lad, a new younger apprentice called Allan, hard at work, so that the business should not be neglected in her father's absence, showing a capability that we had not suspected she possessed. I think Gilbert had a soft spot for her, but she treated him briskly enough, making it clear that she would stand no nonsense from him. She seemed to have grown up overnight. When she was not supervising the lads, she cooked and cleaned, washed and kept house, making things as easy as possible for her father. From time to time, he returned, sick and heart sore, only to go out again after dark and trawl the fetid streets, taking nothing with him lest he should be robbed, always a danger for an older man going into places where his face was unknown.

It was easier for me. I think I looked what I was: young and strong and well able to take care of myself. All my years as a gardener had lent me a certain wiry presence and I thought that I was not in any great personal danger, particularly since I took James's dog, Queenie, with me, a great, grey, shaggy beast – a poacher's dog, I suppose, although I did not like to enquire too closely what my brother did with her on those occasions when he would venture out into the countryside. Often he would return with a rabbit for the pot and sometimes a pheasant and we did not question that either. I had confided in him to some extent, telling him that Jenny had gone missing and I must search for her.

'You'll tak' Queenie then,' was all he said, and she would accompany me, walking at my heel with her long-legged, rolling gait. She was a gentle creature, so long as she knew you, but with a look of something savage about her and a mouthful of yellowing teeth, which she was not above baring at suspicious strangers. Once a couple of men edged too close to me with menace in their manners, but when Queenie slunk out of the shadows, growling low, ears laid back, her hackles bristling, her lip curled and all her teeth showing, they raised their hands and moved off, backwards.

It was a sad and sorry business, and I think that for all that I had lived in Glasgow for so long, I had not been aware before just how many lassies, some of them little more than children, lurked on the streets of this city, displaying their borrowed or stolen finery, foolish clothes that showed their breasts and their ankles to passing strangers, all of them willing to sell themselves for a wee bit siller, or even for a drink or a loaf of bread. But then most likely they were not willing at all. Most likely some man lurked in the background, forcing them to do it. Or the grim prospect of starvation offered them no alternative. And there were always other men willing to take advantage of their desperation in return for a few moments of pleasure, cheaply bought, soon forgotten. We do not see until our eyes are opened, do we? We hurry on by and never notice, until something changes our perspective.

CHAPTER THIRTY-TWO

Chain Saws

Even now, looking back on it, I am not entirely sure why Thomas took me to that place at that particular time. For sure, our debate about the respective merits of physic and surgery (with its necessary adjunct of dissection) had rumbled on for a little while, but without ever causing us to quarrel as we had once quarrelled over Hunter's book. Thomas knew how I felt about Professor Jeffray and his inherent showmanship. He knew I was all for physic — even after my own failed apothecary venture — and so was he, otherwise he would not have been lecturing in botany, would not have been so interested in the medicinal properties of plants.

So many hours in Jenny's company had only served to reinforce my preferences. She had a hundred remedies, most of them distilled from the contents of her garden, and she had instructed me in their use. In fact, some of them had been put to very good use indeed for our Rab. I would almost go so far as to say that they had been instrumental in his survival: the poultices and the potions she and Thomas brought for him, the medicines that seemed to loosen the tightness in his chest and bring his fever down. He would never be robust, but we had great hopes of our move to the country, great hopes that the fresh air and good food would finish the work that Jenny's and Thomas's medications had begun.

Over the years, we had indulged in many friendly debates, Thomas and I, about the possibility of repairing the human body as one might fix some complicated machine, as Jenny's father repaired his loom, making parts for it, oiling this or that component, carefully watching the way it worked and making sure that all was in good order. Thomas believed that, in time, this would be possible for the human body as well. But, so he said, the medical men had to know what went on beneath the skin, how all these processes worked.

I found myself acknowledging the truth of it. I can still acknowledge it now, when such things have become fairly commonplace, but there was something in me that shrank from it all the same. It seemed to discount something else, something vital. Lord knows I have never been a passionately religious man. I had gone to the kirk on the Sabbath, right enough, because I had no choice but to sit shivering and yawning through interminable sermons. My daughter-in-law would still have me go and threatens now and again to set the holy beagles on me, but I plead the infirmities of old age, my rheumatism which prevents me from attending. To tell you the truth, I am but rheumatic north north west as the melancholy Dane might have put it, but the excuse serves me well enough.

It has aye struck me that God, if he exists, has done me and mine few favours. My successes have mostly been earned by the diligent work of hands and mind together. But all the same, whenever Thomas and I were discussing these things, I could not help but think that perhaps in examining the processes which animated the human frame, the surgeons failed to realise – or perhaps too easily forgot – that there was something else, some spirit that enlivened and illuminated this piece of walking, talking meat.

I suppose that was one reason why Thomas had almost persuaded me that dissection was permissible, if only as a means to a desirable end. He never failed to remind me that he too believed in the existence of that same spirit. He had told me one or two stories about the value of surgery, without ever going into any of the more gruesome details, but he always stressed his own belief that some synthesis of the two, surgery and physic, might be advisable, that perhaps surgery should be attempted only where physic had failed.

For myself, I could not look impartially on these things, could not see the blood and bones without thinking of all the other things that made up a man or woman, the hopes and dreams and fears that constituted the experience of each of them, the friendships, the affections and enmities. When Thomas talked of this or that cadaver, I could think only that it had once been a living, breathing person who ate and drank, who walked and slept, who kissed and danced and wept and perhaps dreamed of a better life. Could not even these, the lowest among the low, once have had hopes for a better life? And were they not, each man or woman, and no matter how abased at the end, still unique in the world, and different from all others? But Thomas told me that he agreed with me in all particulars save one. You must remember that I was young and reasonably unfamiliar with the sight of death at close quarters. To be sure, I had observed the deaths of my father and my baby sister, but that was all. It strikes me that Thomas had sat at many a bedside to see the soul slipping away from the body, as I myself have done since. Oh, it never becomes commonplace. Familiarity does not breed contempt. But you grow accustomed to such things and doctors sooner than most.

'The difference between life and death is profound,' he would say. 'It is one thing to respect the remains because of what they were in life. To give those remains a decent burial wherever possible. But the body, the cadaver, is a shell. The spirit no longer has need of it. And that being the case, why should we not investigate its inner workings, if it may help others to survive and thrive, like your Rab and so many others? Who knows when poor souls like him may have need of treatment while they are yet in life? Isn't that true, William?'

I could not disagree with him.

And so it was that when he came to the garden on that chilly afternoon – a clear, cool day it was – and carried me off with him to Professor Jeffray's dissecting rooms, to see the chain saw in use, I went with him. All reluctantly, but I went with him. I had never yet been to view a dissection, although he had tried to persuade me from time to time. 'You will see if you come, William, that it is by no means so dreadful as you believe it to be. We should all face our fears. And then they will lose the power to harm us. Besides, I have a great wish that you should see the chain saw. It is a very fine and humane invention.'

He thought it might very well, in modified form, be of some use in the Ayrshire gardens where he expected me soon to be working, but his real interest lay in its potential to ease the suffering of patients that might become so acute that they died under the blade, especially those wounded in war.

'I am told that Jeffray intends to use it today. I have his express permission to attend and bring you with me. It will be a popular event. If the saw can cut through bone, then it can cut through green wood as well.'

'But you could have told me all this without taking me along to see it for myself!'

'You can have one peep at it, Thomas, and then, if the whole process still revolts you, I promise you that you can be out of the viewing gallery faster than you can say knife.'

He could see that I was wavering, as I invariably did when he set his mind to persuade me of something.

'Come. We shall both lurk near the back, and then you can go and I can stay, as we both please. But I would certainly like you to see this machine, because I feel it has very many uses other than the rather grisly reason for its invention!'

The professor had indeed designed the chain saw (one of two such saws which were invented at precisely the same time in the later years of the last century) with a very specific kind of operation in mind, but when Thomas had told me about it, I had thought how useful it might be to have such an instrument, in order to trim awkward branches or clear persistent undergrowth.

Many years after the events I now relate, I came across Jeffray's own account of his invention and a fascinating document it was too, although even reading it at that distance in time set my teeth on edge somewhat.

'I had an opportunity,' Jeffray wrote, about a particular amputation that he must have been observing, 'of seeing an attempt made to cut out a piece that was diseased, near the middle of the thigh bone. To do that with the common saw was next to impossible. A saw, therefore, was prepared, of a different kind, to rasp the bone across, without hurting the flesh; but the difficulty that attended the execution of this operation, the time spent in performing it, and the pain which, notwithstanding all the care that was taken, the patient seemed to suffer, made such an impression on me, that I could not rest from thinking of some method by which bones might be cut out more easily.'

When I read that, I think I revised some of my ideas about the professor. While the very idea of cutting out bones with ease from the living flesh still revolted me, his intentions seemed wholly admirable. He wished to alleviate the suffering of his patients and so he made a drawing of a chain saw that he thought might be useful in speeding up the whole process. As soon as he could afford the venture, when he was first appointed to the chair of Anatomy and Botany, he had a specimen of his design manufactured by a London jeweller and it was this instrument he wished to demonstrate in Glasgow. I have pondered long and hard about this over the years. Did Thomas want only to show me the new saw? Did he want to take my mind off my own troubles for an hour or two? Was it some failure of his imagination? And then I ask myself, was there some less straightforward motive? Did he still remember what he thought of as my over-reaction to the Hunter book, the book with those distressing illustrations that I had found in his library? We had agreed to disagree about it and move on, which is what I sincerely believed we had done. But now, looking back on it, I wonder if it rankled with him just a little, wounded his intellectual pride, that his friend with whom he was in such concordance about all else, still, to some small extent, disagreed with him upon this one matter, a matter, moreover, about which he was confident that he was right. But I see that I must give him the benefit of the doubt and perhaps he simply wanted to persuade me once and for all of the gravity and value of surgery. I cannot fault him for that. He believed in it. Perhaps he thought that I would be persuaded and then we would be in agreement on this, as in so much else.

If so, he over-reached himself. Whatever goddess watches over such things, Nemesis herself, perhaps, gazed sternly down at him, smiled her thin smile, and pointed her finger directly at him. Never in a million years could he have foreseen the consequences of his decision to carry me off to the professor's dissecting rooms in College Street on that cool winter's day.

These dissecting rooms, by the by, had long assumed a kind of notoriety in the mind of the public, the mob, I suppose you would call them. The unpredictable masses, composed of men and women very like myself, were as suspicious of them as I was, more so perhaps. On various occasions then, and in the future, the superintendent and a number of tall mounted police officers, with their swords much in evidence, had to be called into attendance to prevent the common folk of the town from entering the dissecting rooms and destroying them and everything contained in them. There was a certain amount of horrified censure expressed in the drawing rooms of the gentry about all this, but I had a deal of sympathy with the general outrage. It was a popular superstition – and I think remains so to this day – that the sawbones, as the surgeons were called, would seek live victims for their dissections and that there were many unscrupulous people who were in their pay and who would look for helpless victims, those poor souls who could be entrapped, carried off and dispatched, and all for the convenience of some distinguished professor of surgery and his rabble of students.

Bodysnatching was widespread and, worse than that, murder

has certainly happened since then in Edinburgh, with the case of the notorious Burke and Hare. When bodies were in short supply, the pair seemingly decided to take things a step further and manufacture the goods themselves. I suspect it may also have happened more than once in Glasgow, although there is no proof of such a crime occurring here, and I would certainly never go so far as to accuse Jeffray of such a thing. But it is on record that the resurrection men would cast their net very wide, travelling out to remote Ayrshire villages where folk might be less cautious and more trusting than in the town.

I think at heart Jeffray was an honourable man, according to his own beliefs, if a trifle over-enthusiastic in the pursuit of knowledge. But then, what good scholar is not over-enthusiastic in this way? What good gardener too? Or bookseller for that matter? So as you see, time has mellowed me, save in one particular only. But that single thing I could not forgive. It was not Jeffray's fault. But I must needs lay the blame somewhere, and I was not at fault either. I run ahead of myself only because I cannot bear to think about what happened next. But I see that I must. And so I can only tell it plainly and baldly as it happened, neither seeking to embellish it with spurious emotions, nor reducing it to less than the horror it undoubtedly was.

▨ ▨ ▨

The dissecting rooms were wicked cold. The stone itself seemed to exude a chill that had nothing fresh about it, but more the quality of a subterranean cavern where the air had lain stale for many years. There were no fires to lighten the atmosphere, for the cadavers demanded cold conditions for their preservation if they were not to stink to high heaven with the stench of their own corruption. There were the surgeons, the professor and his assistant, all in their long aprons that reminded me oddly of the aprons we gardeners wore, but smeared with the rusty brown of dried blood, rather than the deep brown of dried earth. There was the smell of blood in the air. I remember that. A faint, sickly scent of blood, like a flesher's shop.

The gallery was full, mostly of students, a rowdy crowd and much inclined to jeer, although the professor quelled them with a glance. I saw that Thomas's presence helped to quieten them, because most of them attended his lectures and he was as popular as ever. There were, besides, various gentlemen of the town for whom this was something of an event, a rite of passage into adulthood. If you could watch a dissection without swooning like a woman, then you were a man indeed. It had become a popular pastime, like going to see a play I suppose, but more masculine and robust than such feminine pretences.

The body lay ready on the slab, covered with a sheet. It looked rather small and insignificant to be sure, with the linen bunched and heaped over it, but a wee thing sinister as well, as though the vivid imagination might detect movement there among the mounds and folds of creased linen. In spite of the cold, there was another faint smell in the air over and above the smell of blood, and I knew that it was the odour of putrefaction, which was already setting in. The body must be some few days old. I was trying to avoid looking in that direction again, but Thomas nudged me, and I saw that Professor Jeffray was holding up the saw, which was what Thomas had wanted me to see, a hand saw with a finely serrated link chain. The professor was explaining how the instrument could be very useful for a process called symphysiotomy and that was what he was going to be demonstrating today.

'Symphysi – what?' I whispered to Thomas and he looked at me, frowning for a moment, nonplussed in a way that I had never seen him before.

'It is used to increase the size of the pelvis. When a woman is having great difficulty in childbirth. Such things can be life threatening. But I think there is a process of dividing the ligaments of what is called the symphysis – down there – which will allow the child to be born more or less naturally.'

'But would such a process not be fatal to the mother?'

'No. Not fatal. Not always. It is painful. But it is less dangerous to the mother than a full caesarean from which many women die, even though the child may be saved. So it is deemed to be a useful procedure, although I'll allow it can have unpleasant after-effects.'

'What kind of after-effects?'

'Some women have extreme difficulty walking afterwards.'

'Dear God!'

'But anything that helps to alleviate the dangers of childbirth is useful.'

'Maybe so.'

'William, I had no idea that Jeffray was demonstrating this procedure today. I thought it was an amputation merely! Perhaps you should go now.'

I could see that he was mortified, although trying hard to disguise it. I think he would not have brought me had he known.

I decided to spare his feelings. And in truth, I was very reluctant to stay.

'Well,' I told him. 'Now I have seen your chain saw and admired it, albeit from a safe distance, I think I shall take myself off back to my garden!' I spoke with a determined attempt at light-heartedness. 'And you are right. There may be uses for it in the garden, but it would need to be a much more robust instrument altogether and not such a delicate thing, although I can see that it might be of some value for pruning small specimen trees.'

Even as I said that I turned back to glance at the instrument in question, only to see the professor's assistant pull the sheet from the stone table with its gruesome burden, like a sacrifice to some heathen deity.

Flax. Spun flax. Dirty withall, like flax that has lain in a muddy pool. A fountain of fair hair, falling around a pale face, so pale that it had a greenish tinge, like a fish left too long on the slab. It seemed as though the men who had placed the body there could not resist arranging the hair. It seemed to have taken into itself all the life that had fled from its possessor. It was the hair I recognised but I could not help myself. I stared at the body, long enough for my eyes to travel downwards over the breasts, the swollen belly, the slender legs, and back to the face. Then one of the students standing behind me let out a little whoop and a whistle. 'Sonsie!' he said, with morbid appreciation.

CHAPTER THIRTY-THREE

Afterwards

I turned towards the student who had whistled. I would have struck him, given the chance. God knows what my face must have told him, because he recoiled in horror and my blow missed him. I grasped him by the shoulders and thrust him aside, bruising him I'm sure, and then I was running down the stairs and out into the street, gasping for the town air that suddenly seemed blessedly cool and clean and fresh, heaving as though I would never fill my lungs with enough of it. I was coughing and gasping, striving to shift the stench of mortality that filled my nostrils at the sight of my darling Jenny, lying on that slab, stone cold and naked, exposed for all to see.

It was a sight that I would never ever be rid of again.

I could feel the tears starting in my eyes and the revulsion that rose from my stomach into my throat and made me want to vomit. But no sooner did I get command of myself with some monumental effort than I was aware of Thomas beside me. He too was weeping, sobbing and choking. Indeed he was so unlike himself that in the middle of my own horror, I found myself wondering if he might be having a seizure.

'Jenny, Jenny, Jenny,' he kept saying.

It was true then, and not some terrible figment of my imagination. It had been Jenny, there on the slab, my Jenny, with the child still inside her, Jenny upon whom the professor had been about to demonstrate his brutal procedure, slitting her open, for the edification of a group of careless students and the entertainment of a handful of men about town.

'I knew nothing!' he was saying. 'Oh, William, I swear I knew nothing until you told me! Why didn't she come to me? Why didn't she tell me? Why? Why? Dear God, she should have told me!'

I looked at his tormented face. I saw the tears streaming down and the colour all gone, except for two bright spots of red on his cheeks. He had his hands over his mouth and he was retching. And then he leaned against the outer wall of the dissecting rooms and threw his head back against the stones, banging his skull there, until you could see a patch of blood and hair on the stone.

I put my hand out to him in alarm at his vehemence. 'Stop it!' I said. 'Stop it, Thomas! You're wounding yourself!'

'I should do more than wound myself! It's my fault. Dear God, man, don't you see? It's my fault! God help me, what have I done? What have I done!'

I looked at him again and a dreadful calm came upon me. I had a sudden bizarre thought that it was like Mr Caddas's weaving loom when everything fell into place and the true pattern emerged from the confusion of flying shuttles and coloured wools. The scales fell from my eyes and I saw just what a fool I had been. I had assumed – with no evidence of any other liaison – that the father of Jenny's child was some weaver, perhaps a married man, and that was why she would not name him. Well, I had been right in one particular at least. He was a married man. I thought of all those occasions when Jenny had been invited to stay at Thomas's house to do this or that piece of work: the dress for Marion, the drapes for the bedroom, the waistcoat for Thomas. I thought of his charm, and the attention he had paid to her. I thought of how his attention had made me feel, how I would have done almost anything to please him. How flattering it must have been for a young woman like Jenny! I saw it all with astounding clarity: Thomas, casually enchanting her. My Jenny, adoring him, following wherever he led her.

When had he first taken her to his bed I wonder? Had it been often, or only one lapse? I knew that Marion went to Edinburgh to visit her family, taking the children with her. Had there been occasions when he had contrived to be in the house overnight at the same time as Jenny, with his wife absent? There were other servants in the house, of course, but that made it look all the more respectable. If he was circumspect, nobody would have suspected. Jenny herself had told me how they were so kind, the Browns, because they gave her a bed chamber of her own, a small room with its own fireplace and a good fire to keep her warm in the evenings, even though she would have expected to be sharing one of the maids' rooms up in the attic with the other lassies.

It flashed before my eyes in an instant. Jenny had been carrying Thomas's child. By the time he found out, she had been away to Dumfries and — what seems so much worse to me now — he had taken the decision to do nothing about it. When she went missing he had deluded himself into thinking that she had found shelter elsewhere. He must have been worried that she would return with or without the child. And equally worried that she would not return at all. But perhaps he had hoped that she would return with the child, that I would do as he expected (he knew me, to that extent, better than I knew myself), would find it in my heart to take Jenny in marriage and bring up the child as my own.

What he had not expected, of course, was that in her desperation and misery, she would leave Dumfries and come back to Glasgow, seeking the father, intending perhaps to throw herself on his mercy. God knows what would have happened if she had reached her destination. Would Jenny have confessed all to Marion? Would she have been believed? Would Thomas have managed to intercept her? And what then? Maids who 'got themselves into trouble' (a curious expression with a flavour of impossibility about it) were seldom believed when they named the fathers of their ill-gotten weans, particularly when those fathers were gentlemen. It would have been easier for Marion to believe me to be the culprit in spite of my protestations of innocence.

But then it struck me that what was commonplace – and deemed to be generous – was for the gentleman in question to arrange a marriage with some trusted servant and set the young couple up with a good dowry. Sometimes the child might be fed and clothed and educated as well. I have no doubt at all that, even if Jenny had turned up at his door in her shift, this is exactly what Thomas would have done. Marion would have been hurt and angry but she would have accepted the situation. I saw all too clearly that I would have been cast in the role of trusted servant. I would undoubtedly have married Jenny. But the friendship between Thomas and me would have been damaged beyond repair, and I think he knew that too and wished to avoid it, if at all possible.

Eventually I found out a few more details of her death, although even reading about them was painful beyond belief. The journey back to Glasgow had taken her a very long time and who knew what privations she had suffered along the way? She had fetched up at the door of a house of correction, not too far from Thomas's house, exhausted and in pain. I managed to establish this much later, writing to Professor Jeffray for such information as he could give me. He replied soberly, with kindness even, offering no false solace where none was to be had, and I respected him for that, ever afterwards. He was a better and much more compassionate man than I had given him credit for. She had gone into labour with the child, dying of exhaustion and shock before she could even give birth and taking her unborn infant with her. The correction house had contacted the professor, who had asked them to keep an eye out for just such a 'specimen' – a woman dying in late pregnancy or early childbirth, upon whom he might demonstrate the efficacy of his chain saw in the terrible process of symphysiotomy. The infant had been a girl. I hadn't asked, hadn't wished to know, but Jeffray had mentioned it himself in his letter, referring to Jenny and the child as 'the mother and her baby girl' without further explanation.

But all that came much later. For the moment, I could see only that I had been cruelly betrayed by the best friend I ever had. The realisation struck me like a physical pain, like a blow to the chest. Thomas stretched out his hand to me, but I cast him off and then — because I really think I might have killed him if I had stayed — I ran away into the streets of the town and down towards the river. I came to myself only much later on that day, in the countryside where I had been wont to gather specimens for him, sitting on a stone beside the burn where we had once guddled for trout and weeping as if my very heart were broken.

CHAPTER THIRTY-FOUR

False Friends

He tried to speak to me on several occasions. I think he wanted to make some attempt to explain, but I wouldn't listen, would neither see him, nor speak to him. He had betrayed Jenny in the worst possible way, but more than that, he had betrayed me. I thought I would never forgive him. He had betrayed himself as well, the ultimate betrayal for a man who thought of himself as the possessor of an enquiring mind: he had refused to believe the evidence. Even when I had told him that Jenny was expecting a child, I think he had somehow managed to deny the very possibility that the child could be his. Perhaps he thought I was lying about the chastity of my own relationship with the lass. I don't know and the time for asking him such things is long past. All I know is that when you lose a friend in this way, a man you have loved deeply, as I loved Thomas, when you see that he has betrayed you in this, perhaps the worst of all possible ways, it somehow calls into question everything about your life. Nothing can ever be the same again. You can be sure of nothing, trust nothing and nobody in quite the same way again.

It is as if you have sailed through life, encountering problems and difficulties to be sure, but always with a strong undercurrent of friendship to bear you up. When it is removed as swiftly and suddenly as my faith in Thomas had been removed — and by his own actions at that – you find yourself sinking into some vortex of pain. It was a sickness deep inside me. I think I would have more readily forgiven Jenny than I ever forgave Thomas. For her, perhaps, it would have been a momentary lapse. He would have charmed her as he charmed everyone who came into his orbit. He was a powerful man, and powerfully attractive to men and women alike. Her body would have betrayed her and I could not blame her. If it was true of the lads, why not of the lassies? She was beyond interrogation. How could I do anything but forgive her?

But Thomas! Ah, I still think Thomas ought to have known better. He ought to have known *me* better. He ought to have thought of me and remembered what I was to him and he to me. And so I splashed and struggled through life for a time, drowning in a sea of self-pity. How could he? How *could* he? I would walk out into the countryside so that I could howl the words aloud, screaming them against the wind. But there was no answer save the rooks that shrieked their chorus, swaying above me in the trees, like sailors perched aloft. When the rage inside me became too much to bear, I would go down to the great river and watch the women doing their washing along the banks. There was something soothing in the sight of them with their buckets and baskets, their aprons and skirts kilted up above the knee, their sturdy legs and strong arms, something soothing and timeless in their repetitive movements, the necessary treading and pummelling of linen, the rinsing and folding. They looked askance at me at first and there were jeers and catcalls, but I think they grew used to me, thought me some kind of lunatic, but harmless enough withall. Sink or swim. Sink or swim, I thought. Well, eventually, I swam. I survived.

But it was entirely down to my own efforts and when I came through, staggering onto dry land, finding my feet again, I knew that not only would I never trust Thomas again, but I would never trust anyone so completely and wholeheartedly as I had trusted him. He had persuaded me to think the best of him. Well, more fool me. And I was minded of something my father had once told me. 'Fool me once, shame on you. Fool me twice, shame on me.'

Of course, I would find it in my heart to love again. I have made a good life for myself and those who won my affection. But never again would I give that affection so fondly and freely as I had once given it to Thomas and to Jenny, without the perception that it was but a precarious thing at best, that I could no more judge the truth of others by my own faithfulness than it is possible to judge one growing season by another. Nothing is safe. It can all come crashing down in an instant.

Except now perhaps. Except with my grand-daughter, Jenny. Who loves me with such unfailing and wholehearted devotion that I cannot help but return it. I expect nothing in return. I love her without any desire for return of love. I will love her self-lessly, and whatever fate brings, till I die. There is nothing she could ever do, physically or morally, which will alter that. Which should, I suppose, teach me something. That in order to truly love another being, we must expect nothing whatsoever in return. We must love selflessly, and entirely without hope of reward. I would give my life for her without a moment's thought, and I know that this commitment to her has been my salvation. It is this, perhaps, more than anything else, that has allowed me to remember the whole story, to accept Thomas's gift to me and to sit here reading his final letter to me. But first I must finish my tale, tell you what happened immediately after the events of Professor Jeffray's dis-secting rooms.

Sick at heart, I at last recovered myself sufficiently to return home. My mother could see that there was something terribly wrong. Rab came and offered me a drink of ale, and put his hand on my knee. 'You're awfy sad,' he said, and I agreed that I was indeed 'awfy sad', but it was nothing that he had done and noth-ing that he could remedy either. When he was settled for the night in the box bed in the wall, all cosy and warm against the wintry draughts, my mother tried to quiz me about the events of the day. I told her nothing except that Jenny had died. She had been on her way home from Dumfries and had met with some terrible mis-fortune. Even that small manipulation of the truth almost choked me. When she tried to question me further, I begged her to be silent, for I knew no more than that. I was too busy thinking about what I was going to do next. I would have to tell Mr Caddas that his daughter was dead. I would have to tell Anna that her sister was dead and I was not relishing the thought. I couldn't possibly explain any of what had happened, and my mother was stricken into silence by her own shock and sorrow at the news.

I made up my mind that I would have to leave the college garden at once, but would go and throw myself on the mercy of Faculty, asking them if my mother and brothers might remain in the house for a few months until I could find myself other work, and set up some kind of establishment, however meagre, that would house them. And this they agreed to do, not wanting to be responsible for casting my family out onto the street. They did it, I think, in memory of my father and not as a favour to me. They did not enquire too closely as to the reason for my sudden decision. Perhaps they thought I had already found work elsewhere. Perhaps they simply didn't care. There were more weighty, more scholarly matters on their minds. But it occurs to me to wonder, at this distance in time, whether Professor Jeffray, knowing something of what had passed, and perhaps guessing much of the rest, had a hand in the matter, and tried to make things easier for me. As I said, I fear I may have underestimated his good nature all along. He was a better man than I thought him. A far better man than Thomas.

The following day I went to see Mr Caddas, only to find that he already knew. Coming to his senses somewhat, Thomas had retrieved the mutilated body from a mortified Jeffray. Without explaining anything of his role in the affair – which was perhaps just as well, for Caddas would have killed him if he had known the truth – he had offered his condolences to the bereaved father and insisted on paying for a decent funeral. Much against his inclination, Caddas had accepted. In the normal course of events, he would have had no trouble in paying for the funeral himself, but his resources were all exhausted because he had spent so long in the fruitless search for his daughter.

Thomas had the good grace not to attend the funeral or, if he did, he lurked well out of sight at the back of the kirkyard. I did not see him there but after the bleak service I went down to Jenny's wintry garden and with the cold bringing tears to my eyes, I told the bees. The hives were silent, dormant, lifeless, and if any heard me, they gave no sign. Caddas, as was only to be expected, was devastated by the death of his daughter. Soon after, however, he married his neighbour, Nancy Mackenzie, the widow he had been courting for so long. I think their mutual grief – for she had treated Jenny as her own daughter – drew them even more closely together and eventually they achieved a kind of contentment. I hope so, for he was a good man and these events were none of his doing.

Anna was no fool. She knew that there was more to the tale than met the eye, but she could not fathom the way it truly was and was forced to accept the version of events that her father had given her. He believed it to be the truth himself and I never told her anything different. The story went like this. Jenny had been with child, but the child was not mine. If the child had been mine, I would have married her with all speed. I would have married her anyway, but she was not to know that, because she had insisted upon going away. She had been badly treated by her cousins in Dumfries, but had told nobody because she felt ashamed of herself. She had decided to leave that town and come home. Too late, I had gone to find her. Perhaps our paths had crossed but we had not met. She had been taken ill on the way and fetched up at the house of correction, where she had died of some fever contracted on the road. Thomas, who had been looking for her at my request, had found her there before she could give birth, too late to do more than send her home in her coffin and arrange for the funeral.

One more thing I did. I took my precious book, *The Scots Gard'ner*, from its high shelf, parcelled it up and sent it back to Thomas. I put no note with it. I put his name on the parcel and sent James to deliver it to the house. Except for the time when I returned the money to him, that was the last occasion upon which

I ever wrote his name. James was told to say that there was no reply expected, and to come away immediately, which was what he did.

CHAPTER THIRTY-FIVE

Loose Ends

That last tissue of truth and falsehood is the version of events my wife had always known and I'm sure she continued to believe it until the day she died, some five years ago now. It feels as though it were last week and I still miss her. I still go to the kirkyard from time to time and find myself unable to believe that she is lying down there, where I too will follow her in due course.

But it was not the whole truth. And I have waited this many a long year to come to the whole truth of the matter. How can I explain? Until that moment, when I saw Jenny lying upon the dissecting table, the whole of my life for many years past had been concerned with growing things, with the care and nurture of plants and trees. Well, my green time ended with Jenny. Since then, I have worked with books and dusty manuscripts and the truths contained therein, the wisdom of words. And sometimes, I have found myself following a perilous path indeed, for words and books and pamphlets can lead you into trouble as surely as affairs of the heart. I have often found myself negotiating that narrow pathway between my principles and the safety of myself and my family. They hang men for their beliefs, for their writings and even for their thoughts, but not, I think, for tending their gardens.

Do I regret the loss of that green time? Of course I do. I sometimes think I would give half my life to be back there, wandering through the countryside, gathering plants for Thomas with the prospect of meeting Jenny on the way home. Or to be back upon that hillside on the Isle of Arran, carefully loosening the earth from around the roots of a tiny whitebeam that clings to life on the edge of a precipice. But perhaps because of all that I have read and learned since, perhaps because of the dangers and the injustices I have known in my life, there is that in my mind that baulks at the prolongation of lies and half truths any longer.

I did not, of course, go to Ayrshire to work for Thomas's uncle. How could I? How could we be on any kind of footing ever again, not servant and master, not friend and friend, not even remote acquaintances? All that was at an end, and I could not even bring myself to think about him, let alone mention his name. Whenever he came into my mind – and during those first years it was more often than was either comfortable for me or conducive to any kind of peace – whenever he came into my thoughts I would deliberately swerve away from the very idea of him. At last I thought about him infrequently, and that was a relief to me.

I remained in the city, and although I would hear about him from time to time, because he was fast becoming a man of some consequence, I did not see him. This was something of a miracle, but then Glasgow was growing quickly over those years, we moved in quite different circles, as we always had done, and our paths never crossed. It would have been easier for him to seek me out than vice versa, but he did not do it and so I must assume that he never wanted to do it. But some years later, I heard that he had left the college and had moved to his uncle's house in Ayrshire, where he was amassing a great collection. This hurt me for a while, all unreasonably, until somebody told me that his collection was not of plants and trees, but of fossils, the petrified remains of ancient life forms.

For myself, I was despairing of ever finding suitable work, but at last, perhaps because of my love for books, rare in a young man of my station, I got work with a printer of somewhat radical persuasion. The position came to me through Mr Caddas who, being a man of great good sense and widely read too, had many connections in that line. Besides it was in his best interests that I should flourish, because some time after Jenny's death, I found myself keeping company with her sister Anna.

It was not my intention. It began as a simple continuation of our friendship. We were both grieving and I think we were a comfort to one another. We wanted to remember happier times, wanted to talk about the Jenny we remembered, full of life, full of ideas and skills and small but wonderful ambitions: to create beautiful things, to sew flowers and grow flowers and to make people well. In talking about Jenny, we were healed, after a fashion, and through this quiet healing we drew closer.

I had known Anna since she was a child and thought of her like that, until one day I looked at her and found that she had become a woman. I saw that she was looking at me as a woman looks at a man she loves. And then, having waited a decent time, we were married, with the blessings of my mother and her father. I flatter myself that the match gave both of them a certain amount of pleasure, although Sandy Caddas was never quite the same again. Even though he seemed happy enough with Nancy, sometimes you would find him weeping for no obvious reason. Once, when I had made a clumsy attempt to comfort him, he had told me, 'Just leave me be for a while. If you find me in tears, just leave me be, lad. The thought of her comes into my head and I miss her. But it will pass. It aye passes!'

Many of my brothers and sisters are gone now and I miss them too, Johnnie most of all. Johnnie grew up and went away to sea like his uncle, and never came back, like his uncle. He never made old bones, and I think it broke my mother's heart, because she was not the same after and didn't survive him by many months. The night he died, she frightened us all by waking us with a great shriek, wailing, 'Johnnie's gone, Johnnie's gone!' and so he had, taken by some foreign fever. When she came to her senses, she said that she had seen him. He was standing at the foot of her bed, shaking his head as though regretting something, and then she knew, even though it was a good long while until the news reached us in a letter.

James worked in the gardens for a few years more – my exclusion evidently did not include him – and lodged in the college, so that he should be close to his work. Later, he got work out at Gilmorehill, in the gardens of a big house there, married, and had a large family. They all lived in a certain amount of cheerful squalor and he died there a few years ago. His surviving children are all grown and he had a great number of grandchildren as well, at least some of whom have become gardeners in their turn. In due course, one of them came to the house and presented me with a fat pineapple and I found myself shedding a tear in memory of my father, even as I tasted the sweetness of it, and laughing at the absurdity of life in general.

The two younger girls seemed to be well settled, for a while at least. Then Susanna ran off with a footman and was never seen again, although many years later, a short and somewhat travel-stained letter arrived from the Carolinas. In it she said that she was well, was married and 'as happy as can be expected', whatever that meant. I wrote back to the direction given on the letter, but she never replied. It hurt me a little to think that of all of us, it was clumsy Susanna, who could not even sew a straight seam, who had attained my ambition of exploring, Susanna who had smelled the scent of exotic flowers under foreign skies.

Jean followed her mistress as lady's maid when that young woman made a good marriage and moved to her new home in the Highlands. A few years later, my sister married a highlander, a ghillie on the estate I believe, which was a good match for her, but she died in childbirth with her firstborn, which was a great tragedy for her husband and a sadness for all of us.

Bessie lives yet. She made the best of her opportunities, as my mother was always advising her and anybody who would listen. We expected her to become a cook, but instead, she became a lady's maid and then a housekeeper. Her mistress had, it seems, made a good marriage, and Bessie prospered along with the family. She never married, which goes a long way to explaining her survival. Childbirth claims so very many of our wives, sisters, daughters, in spite of all our medical men can do to remedy it. For many years she was housekeeper at one of the big houses near the Green and wore smart clothes over her well-corseted figure and preferred not to remember that she was once a scullery maid. Now she lives in a cottage provided for her by her employers, styles herself Mistress Elizabeth Lang, and acts as though she is a great lady in somewhat reduced circumstances. Her own 'lady' visits her from time to time, and then they squabble over their memories, like elderly sisters more than mistress and maid. I have heard them at it and envied them such lifelong friendship. You would never guess at her beginnings when you see her in the town, or in the kirk of a Sunday morning, with her stylish bonnets, even in old age, a new one for every season.

Rab and my mother came to live with me and Anna in my new lodgings, which consisted of two rooms over the printing business. After my mother's death, Rab remained with us. To our surprise, he flourished in this new, bookish environment. He was always sickly and short of stature, but – in the manner of creaking gates that hang longest – he lives yet. He and my wife grew as close as brother and sister in time. She loved him and he confided all his troubles, such as they were, in her.

He worked in the book business with us for many years until, again somewhat to our surprise, but greatly to our pleasure, he married a pretty, capable and kindly widow called Euphemia, fathered two sons of his own to add to her three daughters and lives close by. I think all of this astonishes even Rab himself. He expected very little from life and life has heaped unanticipated riches upon him. He is very well respected as he goes about the town, always with a faint air of disbelief and his nose in a book. We meet often for a drink and a chat, mostly about the books that are his passion. I could not have predicted any of this. But life has a way of springing these surprises. When my master in the book business died, I took over from him and made a success of the business. We print, we publish, we buy and sell books. The very smell of books is in my nostrils and I think it is now in my bones as much as it is in Rab's and I will never escape from it, nor would I want to.

Which is not to say that sometimes I do not have a hankering after the life I might have lived, after the possibility of travelling and exploring, of gathering plants and seeds and bringing them home. I have regrets too and they are very profound. I mind in the twenties and thirties, when they were planting up the town green with trees of many kinds, how much it hurt the heart of me, a sensation of envy and regret so powerful that it made my head ache. I have made the very best of what I have, you must understand that. But often, when I lie awake at nights, with the sounds of the city stilled at last, I sometimes get the strangest sensation.

How can I explain it to you? But I see that I must try, even if it seems like an old man's folly. It feels at those times as though I have somehow missed my way. As though I have been a wanderer down all these years. Not unhappy with my lot, but still a wanderer for whom some other destination was intended, but who has lost his way. It is as though something was planned for me, some pathway I could not find, could not take. Perhaps some god frowned on me for an instant. Some pagan god of the woods, Pan himself maybe? A jealous god, for sure. But it also seems to me that there might be some other incarnation of myself, the man who followed that pathway among the trees, among the green and growing things, the world of plants and their magical, miraculous properties. Is he any happier than I am? Who knows? Perhaps not. For nothing stays constant. Everything changes in time.

I have no way of contacting that other me, of speaking to him, of seeing where he is and what he is doing. He is a stranger to me and I to him. I might have the odd pang of envy, but there is nothing to be done. All I know is that it is the strangest feeling and it makes me profoundly sad, a melancholy that lasts all the next day and sometimes longer, a nostalgia for some paradise lost, some door slammed shut and locked against me, some entrance to an enchanted garden that I cannot now find and will never see again, not in this life, at least.

CHAPTER THIRTY-SIX

The Letter

But what of the letter that Thomas enclosed with the book? Well, I made myself read it, although I confess I waited several days before I could bring myself to take it from its hiding place, unfold it and spread it on my table.

> *My dear William,*
>
> *I can say nothing that will make things right between us because I know now that nothing can ever do that, even though so many years have gone by. We cannot reclaim the past and should not even try, although I wish with all my heart that we could have spoken earlier. I return your book to you at last. You sent it back to me, but now, at the end of my life, I must return it where it belongs as a token of my continuing affection for you. I did a great wrong to you and to the woman you loved. But you must have wondered why I did not admit my fault earlier. You must have thought the worse of me for it. I have suffered with that knowledge all my life, without being able to remedy it in any particular, for fear that you would think I was seeking only to justify my actions. Now, at the end, none of this matters. So I can tell you.*
>
> *The reason why I did not confess everything to you at the time, was that I had some hopes — vain hopes I now see, for God help me, my thoughts were all on you and our friendship and our future travels, and*

not on the poor lassie — I had some hopes that all might yet be well between us. That Jenny had found some kindly house where she might give birth, that she would come home bringing the child with her, that you would marry her, without ever discovering my part in the deception, for how could she possibly tell you? I thought at first that you might believe the child to be yours, but when you told me that could not be, I hoped, nay, I was sure that you — the loving, honourable William I knew — might marry her, child and all, without ever discovering the truth of its parentage. It is the kind of secret that many women have carried with them to the grave. My work as a doctor had taught me that, at least. I hoped that you would decamp to Ayrshire, where I might visit you. Where I might join you in due course, since I was well aware that my uncle had only one son, and he, God help him, was in very poor health. I hoped that this house might ultimately come to me, as in fact it did, not from any motive of greed, but because I thought that the two of us might do wonderful things with the gardens here.

I must ask you to believe me, although it may seem incredible to you, when I say that I had no thoughts whatsoever of continuing the affair with Jenny. I do not know why I even began it, although you must also try to believe me when I say that she was a willing partner. There was no coercion involved. And I thought that this solution would be best for all concerned. I believed that I would be able to do my duty by the child, paying for its education, much as a loving uncle might, that I would be able to retain your friendship, which I valued above all else and, if you can believe me, still do. That I would be able to achieve some sort of peace with Jenny, for whom I always had the highest regard. I constructed such dreams, such castles in the air. Can you imagine?

Reading over this now, this letter that I have written, these many years later, I can see that you will be filled with disbelief. Your face comes before me, with all your innate intelligence and scepticism. But I ask you to try to remember the man you knew then, and for whom, I believe, you had some affection, just as he had such fondness for you, such dreams and ambitions for the pair of us.

Why did I do it? If you have asked yourself that a hundred times, believe me when I say that I have asked myself the same question a

thousand times and more. Why? How could I do it to you of all people,
to a friend whom I never wished to hurt or harm in any way? I could
say that it was a momentary lapse, but that would not quite be true. I
was very fond of her. I charmed her, thoughtlessly. She was enchanted
for a brief spell and so was I. I think you never fully blamed her, and I
hope you never will. But that is not the whole of it. Had she been any
other lass, no matter how beautiful, how accomplished, I think I would
not have fallen. But your lass. Yours. Why did I do that? It was a kind
of lunacy. I confess it, William. I would watch you and I would feel
that I knew you better than I knew myself. But then I would become
all unsure. Could it be true? Did I ever know you at all? I think there
was a part of me that wanted her because she was yours, but not out of
envy. I think I wanted, needed to know what you knew, felt as you did,
to get inside your mind in all possible ways.

Is this credible? Is this not the very essence of what I was, back then?
Thoughtless, sometimes. But full of dreams and imaginings. Wholly
impulsive, wholly loving, ever hopeful that I could turn the world the
way I wanted it to be. My dreams were so very real that I never wished
to wake from them. Well, well. My self- love was my downfall in the end.
But worse, it caused the death of an innocent young woman and her
child. My child. And a most terrible and unforgivable injury to you,
my dear companion. You must believe this if nothing else: I have spent
a lifetime repenting of my folly. I wish to God you had written to me
before this, for I had not the courage and now I think I do not have the
strength to see you again, but wanted only to send you these words.

Your fond and loving friend, as ever,
Thomas

Well, I did read it with a certain scepticism. But I also asked
myself, was this not the very essence of the Thomas I had once
fancied I knew well? We were three points of a triangle. And afterwards, when passion was spent and reality intervened, my poor
Jenny would have presented herself and her condition to him as
a problem that had to be solved to everyone's satisfaction. The
logical solution, as he saw it, was that I should marry her. Then

everyone would be happy, not least Thomas Brown. But he had reckoned without Jenny's pride, Professor Jeffray, his chain saw and his dissecting rooms.

Thomas must have fallen ill, mortally ill, not long after he wrote that letter, or perhaps he was already feeling the first stirrings of whatever killed him. But he had written it, put it inside the book, parcelled up the whole and directed that it be sent to me upon his death. No sentimental deathbed reconciliation for Thomas. That was not his way. I could see that now.

And so I come to the end of my story. And I hope that you can understand why that terrible book, *The Anatomy of the Human Gravid Uterus*, brings back such an agony of mind, brings back to me the image of the lovely soul that was Jenny, with the child, Thomas's child — why did I not realise for so many years what a sudden and unimaginable horror that must have seemed to him? — still inside her, laid bare upon that table for all to see, for Jeffray to approach, wielding his chain saw, demonstrating its efficacy in such cases. It will not do. I cannot think about it, for even now, it makes me sick and angry and like to vomit. So instead I turn my attention to the book that Thomas saw fit to send back to me, the old gardening book that we had once pored over together and that I had returned to him in a rage. I read the lines that are obscurely comforting still.

'Choose your seeds from the high, straight, young and well thriving. Choose the fairest, the weightiest, and the brightest for it is observed that the seeds of hollow trees, whose pith is consumed, do not fill well or come to perfection.'

Was he but a hollow tree? For he certainly did not come to perfection. But neither did I, so perhaps I was always overly cautious, never quite sturdy enough.

'The black cherrie is a tree that I love well. There is a sort at Niddrie Castle whose fruit is preferable to any cherrie. I take it to be a soft heart cherrie but it's a great bearer.'

A soft heart cherry. That was what I was, back then when we used to recite the words as one might recite poetry with a friend.

I could remember it as if we had spoken the lines only yesterday, blithely, thinking of our old age as something so remote as to be unimaginable.

'Gather their fruit when full ripe, eat of the fleshy part and lay the stones to dry a little.'

We were young and strong and full of hope for a happy ending, just as my grand-daughter Jenny is still young and strong, with a head full of dreams and possibilities for her own magical future.

'Some trees there be that will not bear of themselves till they be old, but if you cut off the head of the shoots and then take out some great boughs, if you mind your time and do it with discretion, you may force your tree to put forth buds and bear.'

Our minds were so very much in tune. We were like two halves of the same fine fruit, Thomas and I. We had thought to plant trees, like weans, and watch them grow. We had thought, perhaps, to force each other to put forth buds and bear knowledge. And so we did. But as well as the knowledge of good, we found the knowledge of evil. And in the end, trees are no substitute for people.

▯ ▯ ▯

There is a last great truth that comes to me now, as I sit here in the autumn of the year. It is a truth that has lurked at the back of my mind for a long time; one that I never wished to bring out and examine in the light of day. Untenable you see. I never thought to do it until now. At this time of life you feel, oddly, that everything matters but nothing matters very much.

I loved Jenny Caddas, that's one truth. And I missed her. I miss her yet. But all the same, if you were to ask me what it was that made and sometimes still makes me wake in the night with a sense of regret that feels like an amputation, a lost limb that aches fiercely, bitterly, then I cannot in all conscience say that it is the thought of Jenny. My feelings for her have mellowed through time. My grand-daughter, who looks more like her great-aunt than her grandmother, comforts me, brings her before my eyes, heals the thought of her.

I loved my wife. That's another truth. We were absolutely faithful, throughout the long years of our marriage, and perhaps what's more important, we were always kindly to one another, each making allowances for the other. I have nothing to reproach myself with, now that she has gone.

So it is not Jenny or Anna that I think of at those times. It is something quite different. And I tell you, without guilt or even very much surprise, that it is Thomas I think of. It is our friendship, the affection that lay between us once, perhaps most of all those days of intimacy and ease on the Isle of Arran or in the college gardens, among the trees. I think of the attachment, the fondness that was all lost, all wasted, like some exotic flower, trampled underfoot. It is the thing that he betrayed, as I could not. What pains me most is the absolute certainty, even now, that I would not have so betrayed him, no matter what the reason. I would have died first.

I think afterwards that he blamed me for my lack of forgiveness, for my persistent distrust of him. But he did not understand the full extent of the wound that lay deep within my heart. Or perhaps, as he tried to tell me in that last letter, he hardly thought of it as a betrayal at all, but as something that he was driven to do by his need to put himself in my place. Can I bring myself to believe that? I would certainly like to do it. The wound healed over, in time, but the ache of it is with me yet. Whatever motives and excuses he may have had, nothing can change that. He was a good man, even a great one, but I still think that my affection for him was stronger than his for me.

Or do I? Was it not simply different? What comes to me is the thought of what was lost, of all that we might have done, the places we might have gone, the work we might have achieved together. None of which is in any way to devalue what I have, which is very precious to me. You must understand that. We are like that, we

273

human beings. We can regret what might have been, even while loving and cherishing and holding fast to what we have.

So I confess, it is the thought of Thomas that sometimes makes me wake in the night with a sense of regret so profound, so bitter, that it is like a physical pain in me and I shift and squirm with it and must light a candle and bury my nose in a book so as to be rid of it. What's for you won't go by you, my mother would have said. Looking up at the night sky, you will maybe see a shooting star and sometimes it seems to fall to earth and sometimes it seems to hurtle past and travel on its way to another time and place. But I am not sure which is which, whether that star is myself, or whether it was Thomas, who hurtled past me, dazzled me, blinded me to all else and then travelled on his way.

And still he comes before my eyes. My dearly beloved friend. Not the crabbit old man he no doubt became. How would I know? I never saw him again. But tall Thomas, with his grey eyes, his strong limbs and his warm smile, as he walked into the garden in search of me, Thomas, talking to me of thistle and valerian and sweet honeysuckle. Thomas, admiring the wayfarer tree and laughing uproariously at the thought of the students trying to set fire to it, and the vision of me chasing them with a spade and swearing at them. Thomas, full of ideas and ideals. Thomas, who loved to teach, and talk, who loved, more than anything, the imparting of knowledge, which is not always the same thing as wisdom.

My Jenny has just come into the room.

She looks at me and says, 'You're sad!'

I tell her that I have dust in my eyes. Dusty old books just.

She loves books too, and often asks me to read to her, but I tell her that she must not devote all her life to them. No. I tell her that she must be out and about in the world, breathing the fresh air. She can enjoy her books if she wishes, but she must not elect to live life at second hand. Books are but a poor substitute for experience, no matter how painful. I do not think she understands me yet, but she will, in time, God love her.

Now she takes up my linen handkerchief and wipes my eyes with it, much as I sometimes wipe her own when she weeps over her small troubles.

'There now,' she says. 'Is that better?'

And I tell her that it is. That all is well. That we will put the dusty old books away for the time being, and perhaps I will come down into the garden for a walk, before supper, for I may be in the winter of my years, but it is still a fine, golden autumn and besides, the very essence of spring is here beside me, tugging at my hand and, however much the city has grown, tonight the air out there among the trees seems very sweet.

AUTHOR'S NOTE

Some of this story is based on truth. There was a gardener in Glasgow called William Lang. There was a lecturer in botany at the old college of Glasgow University whose name was Thomas Brown, and the celebrated anatomist Professor James Jeffray did indeed ask him to undertake the botanical lectures in his stead. It is clear from existing correspondence that William Lang and Thomas Brown, who were not very far apart in years, struck up a friendship. It is clear that Thomas valued the work William did in collecting plant specimens for him. Later, when William found himself struggling to cope with a polluted garden and the necessities of providing for a widowed mother and younger siblings, Thomas Brown defended him from the complaints of Faculty, as far as he could. The book which so shocked William is all too real as is the old book about gardening. I have included a select bibliography of the books and websites I used in my research, in case any reader might be interested in the historical details. For the rest, although I hope it is a vivid recreation of the time and place, it is entirely fictional.

I would like to thank my family and friends for all their encouragement and understanding as ever but especially Michael Malone and Cally Phillips. Many thanks are also due to all at Saraband, but especially Sara Hunt, to my editor Ali Moore, as well as to The Society of Authors for years of advice and support. My thanks, too, to Rebecca Quinton for pointing us to the perfect sampler to illustrate the cover. Finally, a special mention must go to all the 'Authors Electric', best of online friends and bloggers.

BIBLIOGRAPHY

A.D. Boney. 1988. *The Lost Gardens of Glasgow University*. Christopher Helm.

Eric W. Curtis. 2006. *The Story of Glasgow's Botanic Gardens*. Argyll Publishing.

Sir James Fergusson. 1972. *Balloon Tytler*. Faber and Faber.

Carol Foreman. 2002. *Lost Glasgow*. Birlinn.

Henry Grey Graham. 1937. *Social Life of Scotland in the Eighteenth Century*. A & C Black.

Elizabeth S. Haldane. 1934. *Scots Gardens in Old Times*. Alexander MacLehose and Co.

William Hunter and Jan van Rymsdyk. 1774. *The Anatomy of the Human Gravid Uterus*. Birmingham (accessed in Glasgow University Library).

Latta and Millar. 1904. *The Kingdom of Carrick and its Capital*. John Latta.

Ann Lindsay. 2008. *Seeds of Blood and Beauty, Scottish Plant Explorers*. Birlinn.

Vincenzo Lunardi. 1786. *An Account of Five Aerial Voyages in Scotland*.

Martin Martin. 1994. *A Description of the Western Islands of Scotland, Circa 1695*. Birlinn.

Mary McCarthy. 1969. *A Social Geography of Paisley*. Paisley Public Library.

Robert D. McEwan. 1933. *Old Glasgow Weavers*. Carson and Nicol Ltd

Alexander Murdoch. 1921. *Ochiltree, Its History and Reminiscences*. Alexander Gardner.

John Reid. 1683. *The Scots Gardener*. Introduced by Annette Hope. Mainstream. 1988.

Norman Scarfe. 2001. *To The Highlands in 1786*. The Boydell Press.

'A Significant Medical History'. The University of Glasgow website (under the "about us/history" section).

Margaret Swain. 1955. *The Flowerers*. Chambers.

'The University of Glasgow Story'. The University of Glasgow website.

James Walker. 1895. *Old Kilmarnock*. Arthur Guthrie and Sons.

About the author

Catherine Czerkawska is a Scottish-based novelist and playwright. She graduated from Edinburgh University with a degree in Mediaeval Studies followed by a Masters in Folk Life Studies from the University of Leeds. She has written many plays for the stage and for BBC Radio and for television, and has published nine novels, historical and contemporary. Her short stories have been published in many literary magazines and anthologies and as ebook collections. She has also written non-fiction in the form of articles and books and has reviewed professionally for newspapers and magazines. *Wormwood*, her play about the Chernobyl disaster, was produced at Edinburgh's Traverse Theatre to critical acclaim in 1997, while her novel *The Curiosity Cabinet* was shortlisted for the Dundee Book Prize in 2005.

Catherine has taught creative writing for the Arvon Foundation and spent four years as Royal Literary Fund Writing Fellow at the University of the West of Scotland. She has also served on the committee of the Society of Authors in Scotland. When not writing, she collects and deals in the antique textiles that often find their way into her fiction.

house, when was that?" She tapped her fist against the top of her forehead. "Yesterday?" Another tap. "Yes, I'm sure it was yesterday."

"When?"

"Why, you didn't see her? I'm sure you were home. Your car was in the driveway."

70

AFTER GOLDIE WENT HOME I nuked a frozen dinner and sat down to eat and check my e-mails. The pile of unread discussion-list digests was depressing, so I deleted them all unread, along with several opportunities to donate my life savings to Nigerian widows and to assist a friend who had lost her wallet while traveling in Europe between last night, when I saw her at Dog Dayz, and now. *Do people really fall for these schemes?* I wondered. Then I googled *poison hemlock*.

Goldie had been correct. The active toxin in poison hemlock was an alkaloid related to nicotine. *Coniine* to be precise, in case I ever made it onto *Jeopardy*. I didn't find much about hemlock killing people other than Socrates, but there was plenty of information on livestock poisonings. Assuming that it affects most mammals in similar ways, the signs of poisoning by poison hemlock sounded all too familiar. Within a couple hours of eating the plant, the animal becomes nervous and uncoordinated. Didn't Connie say that Abigail was a regular jitterbug before her class, and that she was stumbling around on her heeling pattern? Eventually the animal becomes unable to breathe, and its heart rate slows. A vision of Abigail's stricken face filled my mind.

The sites I checked also said that while the plant's toxicity is lower in the spring than later in the growing season, it's probably also more palatable when young, although they mentioned a "mousy smell" from the crushed leaves. So it would be easier to slip it into some ... "Oh my God," I mumbled. "The cream cheese." I pictured the flotsam of Abigail's breakfast, including the remains of a bagel and remnants of a spread full of ... what? I'd assumed it was spinach or dill or something. Yes, dill, I smelled dill, I remembered. And mice. The spread had made me think of mice.

I dialed Jo Stevens' number.

As her phone rang I read that the ancient Greeks considered hemlock a "humane" means of execution. How civilized. I wondered whether Abigail would agree.

———

Dog Dayz was hopping with people and dogs preparing for upcoming obedience trials, and all the usual suspects were there. Unless they were top ranked, and dead. Jay was full of energy and not so full of attentiveness, so we had a happy but not exactly accurate session. But what the heck, we do this for fun. If my dog sits a little out of position but acts happy, that's a perfect performance to my mind.

Sylvia Eckhart, her Cocker, Tippy, in tow, strolled over and asked after my mom. I filled her in, and she assured me that Mom's right to her chin had caused her no serious damage.

I was packing up my dog treats and other equipment when I saw Giselle Swann charging me from the direction of the back door. Her head was thrust down and forward, her face was magenta, her shoulders slightly hunched and her two hands balled into fat fists. *Look out*, yelled the little demon on my left shoulder. *She thinks your red sweatshirt is a cape!*

I faced her straight on. "Evening, Giselle."

"How could you?" She stomped her right foot as she pulled up in front of me. "How could you? How could you do that to me? Abigail was my friend!"

"Uh, what's the problem, Giselle?"

I noticed movement in my peripheral vision. Marietta Santini was speed-walking our way, no doubt hoping to prevent an all-out bitch fight. I use the term in the canine sense. Every breeder I've ever talked to says that if a fight breaks out in a multi-dog home, they'd much rather it be among dogs—males—than bitches. Boys fight for status, and they can certainly hurt each other, but tend to do a lot of posturing and pushing and then forget about it. When two bitches fight, each wants the other gone, one way or another. I, on the other hand, had no desire to fight Giselle, and didn't much care where she was.

She stood in front of me, puffing and shifting from one foot to the other, glaring not into my eyes, but somewhere in the neighborhood of my chin. I hoped it hadn't sprouted a new hair. "The police came to my house again. They asked me a bunch of questions."

"They asked me a bunch of questions too."

"Everything okay over here?" asked Marietta.

"You sent them, didn't you?" Giselle lowered her voice to a growl.

"Giselle, no one sent them." Marietta crossed her arms and cocked a hip. "They're investigating. They're talking to everyone who knew Abigail and Suzette. They talked to me, too."

Giselle shifted her glare to Marietta, then right back to my chin. "I know you told that detective to question me. You'll be sorry." She turned her head toward Jay for a moment, then charged out to the parking lot.

Marietta squinted and pointed the stiffened, splayed fingers of both hands at my face, cackling, "You'll be sorry, you and your little dog." She relaxed her limbs. "Weirdo."

"What in the heck was that all about?"

"Fear. Jealousy. Guilt. Hallucinations." She grinned at me. "Who the hell knows with Giselle?"

"Do you think she'd hurt a dog?"

"I doubt it." Marietta pursed her lips. "On the other hand, if anybody looked at my dog that way, I wouldn't let him out of my sight for a while."

71

THURSDAY MORNING SEEMED TO bring, for once, a normal day. I stopped by the nursing home, but Mom was sleeping, so I didn't stay. Jade Templeton assured me that she was doing fine, and that it was sometimes better to let people settle in before visiting too often. *What difference does it make,* I wondered to myself, *when most of the time she has no idea who I am?*

Jade also said that Mom was enjoying the garden, and had assumed the role of garden director, telling the other residents as well as the staff how to plant, weed, water, and whatever. She might not know my name, but the Latin names of hundreds of plants were no problem. Other than that, it was business as usual for me—a five-mile walk on the River Greenway with Jay, phone calls, mailings, and miscellaneous. I skipped agility class, and by nine p.m. my brain was pooped.

I tried to focus on the boob tube before bedtime, but couldn't find anything I could stand to watch that I hadn't seen before, so I put on my old k.d. lang *Torch and Twang* CD, and lay down on the couch. I had my head propped on a couple of pillows, my feet tucked between Jay's cozy belly and flank, and my own belly blanketed by Leo's rumbling furry circle of heat. Despite my roiling thoughts and emotions, I must have been a picture of contentment as I opened my newly arrived issue of *Nature Photography*. But my brain wasn't ready to abandon current events, and when I found myself rereading the same paragraph for the fourth time, I gave up on the magazine and closed my eyes, my thoughts on the troubles in our little community of dog lovers.

Was Abigail right? Was Greg having an affair? Was he going to leave her for Suzette? But Connie said Abigail had hired a PI who said Greg wasn't fooling around. Maybe Abigail lied to Connie. I mean, if she was reluctant to say her dog was neutered, how would she feel about her husband's philandering? And where did Giselle fit into all this? Did she really think she'd get Greg if Abigail and Suzette were both out of the way? And what about Francine Peterson? Why in the heck was she lurking around?

The telephone shocked me out of my meditations. My limbs jerked, Leo flew off my belly with a yowl, and Jay leaped off the couch with a "Bfff," slid across the hardwood floor when his paws hit the throw rug in the center of the room, and gave me a "what the heck?" look. I made an effort to control my breathing, and picked up the receiver.

"Hiya!"

"Oh, Tom."

"You sound disappointed." He sounded disappointed.

"No, no! The boys and I were vegging out and the phone scared the bejeepers out of us. Sorry!"

We did the "how was your day" thing, and then Tom cut to the chase, inviting me to his place for dinner on Friday.

No, I thought. *You don't need that complication, not before these murders are solved,* but I heard myself ask, "Can I bring anything?" Meaning something I could pick up and pop open to serve.

"Yes. Drake says to bring Jay. Otherwise we're all set."

I hung up, and Jo Stevens's words came back to me. I had to watch what I ate.

I was halfway back to the couch when the phone rang again. Jay was already snuggled back into his corner cushion, and at the other end Leo was doing kitty yoga, back leg extended behind his neck, so it was just as well that I didn't need my spot back for a few more minutes.

Connie didn't waste any time on preliminaries. "I found out what Greg was up to at the travel agency."

"What are you talking about?"

"Remember when we saw Greg at the mall? Coming out of Travelfair?"

It took me a moment, but I remembered.

"Okay, so, he wasn't planning a trip. He was returning tickets."

"That makes sense."

"Yeah, it would if the tickets had been for him and Abigail," she replied slowly, with a tease in her voice. "Who do you think was going to Bermuda with him?"

"Tell me."

"Suzette."

"Suzette Anderson?"

"You know another Suzette around here?"

"How did you find this out, anyway?"

"Old high school friend manages the place. I bribed her with Abby Brown's chocolates." My salivary glands went wild at the thought.

"You're one devious woman."

"I prefer to think of myself as practical."

"You could have a bright future as a detective."

"You never know. If my wrist gives out from one too many Poodle trims, I might need a new career."

"You bring me anything from Abby Brown's?"

"I thought you were dieting?"

"I'm always dieting. Chocolate could be on my diet." Part of my brain was trying to recall whether I had any stashed anywhere. "So, anyway ... Greg and Suzette?"

She didn't say anything.

"What about the private detective that Abigail hired?" I asked. "You said he nixed her suspicions that Greg was having an affair."

"Abigail could have been lying. Maybe she knew but didn't want to let on."

Someone was lying, that was for sure. "I had that thought too. Or maybe the detective had some reason to lie. Or maybe he was incompetent."

When I got off the phone I went back to the couch and thought about the latest news, leaning back against the Aussie-face tapestry pillow, my right hand stroking Jay's silky head, my left scratching behind Leo's ears. Who says I can't multitask?

72

I DON'T THINK OF myself as a morning person, and was shocked to find I was up with the sun again Thursday morning. Jay and I went for an early walk to beat the heat, which was intensifying by the day.

The River Greenway led us into the rising sun, which danced among the leaves of tulip poplars, sycamores, black walnuts, beeches, and several species of oak and maple. A fine gray veil drifted over the murky surface of the Maumee, and the wooded banks fairly screeched as bluejays and crows called each other names. A farm field to the north of the trail showed a faint scatter of soft green shoots over the surface of the dark soil. Corn or soy beans, no doubt. Last year it was beans, so this was probably corn. We met only a handful of early joggers and cyclists.

A splash in the river caught our attention and I watched a pair of wood ducks paddle out of sight under some low-hanging branches. Cerise redbud and ivory dogwood blossoms, luminous in the morning light, danced beneath the hardwood canopy along the riverbank. An Indiana May morning at its finest.

The sirens of the river and woods urged me to linger, but I had things to do. Breakfast for Jay, and a quick shower, and I was on my way once more to Shadetree Retirement Home.

Jade Templeton met me at the front door. "Janet! So nice to see you. Mama is doing fine. She's out in the garden. I just came from there."

We walked through the common area where my mother had behaved like a berserker. Was it only three days ago? Two men played checkers by one of the floor-to-ceiling windows that flanked the French doors leading to the enclosed courtyard. An elfin little man with a fringe of white hair around his bald and spotted pate snoozed in a wheelchair toward the center of the room, and a cherry-cheeked woman with tightly curled too-black hair and an electric-yellow velour jumpsuit looked up from her book and fluttered her fingers at us. We exited the room through the French door.

Mom was busy at what appeared to be a brand-new flower bed. It was raised for easy access for gardeners in wheelchairs, or folding chairs like the one Mom sat in. Great idea, I thought. I could use a little less bending over in my own garden.

"Hi, Mom."

She didn't react, so I touched her lightly on the sleeve. "Oh, hello. I didn't hear you come in, dear." For a moment, I hoped she might be lucid. But then she carefully wiped the fresh soil coating her old, familiar garden gloves onto her light blue sweatpants before pulling her hands from the gloves and extending one in my direction. "I'm Elaine Jones."

Jones was her maiden name. It hadn't been her legal name for more than half a century. I worked to keep my voice upbeat. "Mom, it's me, Janet."

She went back to planting her bedding plants, gloveless now. She seemed to have this plot of raised soil all to herself. Two women and a man worked companionably at another bed, and at the third, a young volunteer aid steadied a gentleman whose hands shook too much to plant his tomato seedlings by himself.

Mom's aesthetic abilities were intact, judging by the way she arranged the baby plants. I imagined the bed as it would be in a month. Plastic name tags identified the contents of the plastic containers, and there were no dainty pastels in mom's selections. I knew there would be no symmetrical rows for my mom, either. I watched her anchor the center of the bed with purple and pink cleome and tall white cosmos. Around those she planted sweeps of crimson zinnias, electric-blue ageratum, and clear-yellow French marigolds. A froth of white alyssum played in the spaces where the colors met, and the borders were edged in vinca vine and blood-red, purple, and white trailing verbena that would soon drape the outer edge of the box like a curtain on a Gypsy caravan. This tiny garden promised me a glimpse of the mother I used to know.

I watched her work for a little more than an hour, enjoying the warm sun and the Big Band music playing softly in the courtyard. I felt calmer than I had in many days, reassured that my mother would be happy here, at least in the warm months.

By the time I left, Mom was focused on patting handfuls of mulch into place around the plants. She acknowledged my goodbye with a dismissive wave.

Jade called to me as I walked through the front lobby. "Wait, child, I'll walk you out." She caught up with me and asked what I thought.

"She seems as happy here as she was at home. And she's safer."

"Your mama is a sweet lady. I wish I'd known her before."

I nodded.

"So, the reason I wanted to talk to you, your mama showed me some pictures of your dog, and she got all teary-eyed. Your dog and other dogs. She had a bunch of dog pictures, all in a little box. So I wondered—why don't you bring him to visit sometime. Your mama would like that."

"How strange." Jade looked puzzled, so I went on. "Oh, the timing. I've been planning to do something along those lines. In fact, I'm taking Jay to Indianapolis on Saturday to be tested for his certification as a therapy dog. That will make him official, you know?"

"That's great then." Jade's smile was back. "We have some other dogs that visit, and our resident kitty, Thomas, but it's always nice to have one more. And your mama loves that dog. What's his name? Laddie, I think?"

"His name is Jay. But she thinks he's Laddie, a dog she had before I was born. Sad."

"Oh, no, not sad." Jade wrapped an arm around my shoulders as we walked. "Memories of love are a measure of grace." She gave me a squeeze. "In the end, love is all that matters in our lives." She was right, of course, and who better to love than those who love us as our dogs do?

73

A MESSAGE TO CALL Jo Stevens was waiting on my answering machine, so once I got squared away, I picked up the phone, tagged the detective's voice mail, and thought about sorting and dumping some of the magazines and junk mail that had invaded my living room.

Thinking was as far as I got. Leo bounded in with a little yellow foam ball in his mouth and mrowled at me. I was bound by duty as a cat servant to sacrifice a tidy house in favor of play. Jay watched from the safety of the couch, more out of regard for his tender nose than for politeness. Leo is quite the defender of his little foam balls.

When the phone rang, I expected to talk to the detective, and was surprised by the voice at the other end.

"Janet, it's Ginny Scott. You have a minute?"

"Ginny! Yes, sure. How's Fly?"

"She's a sweetheart. Moved in as if she'd never been gone. Seems to be looking for Suzette from time to time, but overall she's fine. She's eating, so that's good."

"Great."

"I wanted first to thank you again for bringing her to me. I probably couldn't have picked her up for another couple of weeks if I'd had to go to Fort Wayne. That would be an all-day trip."

"Oh, no problem. I'm always looking for a good excuse to get to different places with my camera."

She jumped ahead to what I suspect was the real reason for her call. "Something odd happened last night."

"Oh?"

"Francine Peterson called. All friendly and gushy. Asked me 'How's that lovely bitch of yours?' I must be slow, but I hadn't a clue who she was talking about. I have six lovely bitches!"

Spoken like a true dog woman.

"She went on and on about how gorgeous Fly is. I was tempted to say something about all the trash she put out back when Suzette declined to breed Fly to Pip, but I held my tongue."

"That must have been hard."

"I guess I was curious about where Francine was headed. Anyway, I didn't say much. Just let her blather on."

"Did she have a point?"

Her voice turned to a snarl. "She wanted to buy Fly."

"Did she make you an actual offer?"

"Oh yeah! Very generous offer, couched in all sorts of crap about how hard it is being a responsible breeder and what a nuisance it is to take back an adult puppy that someone else has owned for several years, complete with a story about one she took back that caused chaos in her kennel." I was dying to hear how much the offer was, but Ginny was wound up. "I told her I don't consider my puppies to be nuisances, no matter how old, and that the only time there's chaos among my dogs is when I have a tennis ball or food bowls."

"I know this is rude, but I'm dying to know—how much did she offer?"

"Four thousand dollars."

"Whoa! You're kidding!"

"Nope. I was blown away. She talked about breeding her to Pip, so she must not know he's neutered. I'm sure she figured she could sell puppies from Pip and Fly for a pretty penny."

"I can't see Greg agreeing to that."

"She claimed she's getting Pip back."

I remembered the scene at Abigail's funeral. "I doubt that."

"Yeah, me too."

"I take it you turned her down."

"I'd as soon cut my arm off with dull thinning shears as let that woman get her hands on one of my puppies."

That seemed perfectly rational to me.

"I'm really not such a big gossip, but I can't stand Francine. I didn't care for Abigail, either, God rest her soul, but at least she was good to her dogs and responsible about breeding. But you're right there where the investigation is going on, and I don't know why exactly, but I thought you should know about this."

"Okay. I mean, I'm not involved in any investigating," I ignored Janet Demon rolling her eyes and whispering, *yeah, right,* "but I'll mention it to the police detective on the case. She'll know better than I do whether it's important."

74

JAY AND LEO AND I went out to the backyard for a game of tennis ball. We each have our special plays. I try to fake Jay out, and he gives me his "How lame is that, trying to fake out a dog?" look. Then I throw it, and he races across the yard after the bouncing yellow fuzz, and another ball of yellow fuzz flies out from under the forsythia jungle in the corner, races after the dog, counts coup on Jay's fanny, and races back to the leafy lair. Then Jay grabs the ball, spins toward the forsythia and charges toward the cat hunkered under its lowest branches, where he lets out a ball-muffled brrffff. Then he brings me the ball so we can do it all again.

I heard the phone through the open window and ran for the door. As I picked up the receiver, I glanced out the window. Jay danced from foot to foot at the back door, panting. His expression pleaded, "Wait! Wait! The game isn't over!" Leo was strolling along the fence line, showing how much he didn't care.

Jo identified herself. "We've confirmed that the chisel we found is the tool used to slash your tires."

"Did you catch the fiend who did it?"

"Not yet. But we lifted fingerprints from the chisel."

"That's good, right?"

"Only if we identify a suspect. Or it's someone with a record."

I must have looked disappointed.

"It's not impossible that the prints will lead us to the culprit."

"But not likely either, right?"

"Turns out this chisel is really high quality. You know anyone who would have reason to have a good chisel?"

"Not really."

Must have been something in my voice, because she pressed me, so I told her that I'd heard that Francine had a mobile repair business of some sort. "But judging by the beat-up old van she drives, I don't know how much she's into high-quality equipment."

Jo let a beat go by, then went on, her voice pitched slightly lower and faster. "Look, I have no hard evidence, but you and I both know that the tires are linked to the stuffed dog and that both are somehow linked to the two dead women."

My heart rate increased by half. "Wow. Hearing a cop put my thoughts into words makes them even scarier."

I excused myself to let the beasties in and to collect my thoughts. Jay guzzled from his water bowl, but Leo was nowhere in sight. Probably prowling the perimeter. I'd have to retrieve him when I got off the phone, but for now I got back to Jo. "It makes sense that everything's connected, but I don't know what I have to do with anything."

I heard a noise in the living room and walked to the doorway leading there from the kitchen. Leo was on the front porch, balanced on the ladder back of my rocking chair and patting the window with his claws. He'd have to wait a minute. My home is electronically challenged and I still have a phone with a cord. It didn't reach to the front door.

"You've had both the dead women's dogs in your possession, right?"

"Well, yes, but not for long. I had Pip for four or five days, but everyone knew that was temporary. And I had Fly for a couple of hours, in my car."

"Still a link. And you knew both of the women. And you seem to know all the other players." She added, as if she'd just thought of it, "And you take pictures."

"Pictures. You mean that someone thinks I've taken a picture of something that I don't even know I've seen?"

"Look, you need to be careful, okay? And not just about what you eat."

"What do you mean?"

"I don't want to scare you, but the bloody dog toy and the attack on your tires suggest more violence is possible than simply poisoning." Having watched Abigail suffer, I wasn't sure I'd call poisoning "simple," but I let that thought go and listened as Jo continued. "Whoever's doing these things is getting more desperate, so maybe you're on to something without knowing what it is. Frankly, Janet, I think we have a nutcase on our hands, so you need to take these threats seriously. Be careful, lock your doors, and watch Jay and Leo. And if you feel remotely threatened, call 911 first, then call me."

In my rush to get off the phone and go bring Leo into the safety of the house, I forgot to tell her about Giselle's hissy fit or Greg's travel plans or Ginny's phone call. I really had to start making lists. I stepped out the front door, but Leo was no longer on the porch. I called his name, which usually brings His Excellency in at a leisurely stroll. He can't appear to be obeying, of course, but he does come when called. Usually.

Okay, sometimes.

I went in, grabbed a can of salmon-flavored treats from the cupboard, and went back outside. I left Jay in the house—he was entirely too focused on the fishy smell coming from the can to be of any help. Why do cats have to pick the worst possible time to play games? Then again, Leo didn't know there was a killer on the loose.

I walked around the yard, peeking under shrubs and into other hidey holes, calling and rattling the treats, but no cat appeared. Today was evidently not a come-when-called day, and after a twenty-minute tour of the front, side, and back yards, I went inside. I popped a salmon treat between Jay's slavering jaws and told him, "The little booger was probably hunkered down out there watching me and laughing his furry little butt off."

75

THE DOORBELL, FOLLOWED BY Jay's deep "boofs" from the direction
of the front door, jolted me out of bed the next morning. The one
morning in recent history that I'd actually slept until a decent hour,
mostly because I'd been up several times during the night calling for
Leo, and now some fool was ringing my bell. I glanced at my watch,
pulled on a pair of sweatpants, and combed my hair back with my
fingers. Turned out 6:49 was only a semi-decent time to get up, and
obscenely early for a visitor. Panic clutched at my mind.

I should have used the peephole before opening the door since
no rational person would come calling at that hour, unless they bore
devastating news. I mean, what's the point of having a reasonably
secure locking system that you open right up for bad guys? But it
was way too early to think, so I slipped the chain, flipped the deadbolt, grabbed Jay's collar, and pulled the door open.

Detectives Stevens and Hutchinson were on my porch.

"Ohmygod. Who's dead now?"

Hutchinson had his badge out, as if I wouldn't recognize him. "Can we come in?"

I took half a step backward, holding Jay's collar and my breath. Jo Stevens smiled at me and shook her head. "It's not that kind of a visit."

Jay stopped barking and leaned into his collar, stretching his neck toward the detectives, sucking in their scent while his body vibrated from his wriggling tail nub to his shoulders.

Hutchinson glowered at Jay. "Call off your dog."

"Oh, for crying out loud." Jo pushed past him and stepped into the house, giving Jay a scratch under the chin. Her partner followed, puffing up his chest as he glanced at Jay.

"You don't like dogs much, do you, detective? I'll put him outside if he scares you."

"I'm not scared," he lied.

Jay was no longer interested in Hutchinson. He stood in front of Jo, eyes sparkling and fanny wriggling. She rubbed behind his ears.

I peered out the door before I closed it. "You didn't happen to see an orange cat out there, did you?" They hadn't. "Leo's been gone since I talked to you yesterday."

Hutchinson hitched up his pants. "Look, we're not here to chat about your pets. We have a missing suspect to find."

76

Jo glared at her partner but spoke to me. "I'm sure Leo will show up when he gets hungry. Probably needed a night on the town."

I wanted to agree with her, but Leo wasn't an on-the-town sort of guy. What would be the point, since he was neutered? "It's not like him." I led them through to the kitchen, let Jay out the back door, and surveyed the backyard. No Leo. "Coffee?" I asked, turning back to the detectives. My hands needed something to do that didn't ruin my cuticles.

"That would be nice," said Jo.

I got busy with the coffee scoop and asked, "Do you work every day?"

"Seems like it. We're covering for a couple guys who are off."

Hutchinson dragged a chair out. "Mrs. MacPhail, where is Greg Dorn?"

"Ms."

He harumphed at me.

"Why ask me?"

"He's wanted for questioning in the murders of his wife and his mistress."

I turned toward the detectives. "Mistress?"

Jo glowered at Hutchinson, the look on her face suggesting that she'd smack him if she had to, and he shut up for a moment. "We need to find Mr. Dorn. He isn't at home."

"We're not really friends, just acquaintances." I finished setting the coffee maker, moved a couple of photo boxes and some files out of the way, and signaled them to sit at the table.

"Did Mr. Dorn plan to leave the country?" Hutchinson was nothing if not slow.

"How would I know?"

"So you're not aware of any plans he might have had to leave the country?" Jo asked softly.

"Look, I don't know the guy that well. Saw him with his wife at dog events sometimes, and I took care of Abigail's dog for a couple of days. That's it. I'm not privy to his plans. I heard some rumors that he might have been planning a trip before…." Suddenly my mind was spinning. Why would Greg kill Suzette if they'd been planning a Caribbean tryst? "Before?" asked Jo.

"Before what?" asked Mr. Charm.

"Well, before Suzette died." I sighed. "I heard that he cashed in some tickets he had for himself and Suzette. But I don't think…" I let Jay back in and served the coffee. "I can't imagine Greg killing anyone, especially his wife or Suzette."

Hutchinson pulled a beat-up spiral-bound notepad part way out of his shirt pocket. The end of the wire caught in the fabric, stretching out the bottom few coils and tearing the top hem of the pocket. He wrestled it free, tried to push the wire back into a coil, flipped the notebook open and scribbled something, and tried to pat the pocket flat against his chest. It defied his efforts, but Jay took the chest patting as an invitation and before I could intercede he had his front paws on the man's shoulders and they were nose to nose.

Everyone froze, and then I recovered enough to reach for my dog. "Jay! Off!"

But Hutchinson surprised me. His hands came up tentatively to Jay's cheeks, and he looked into the dog's eyes, and he said, "Nah. It's okay." His shoulders relaxed, and he slowly ran his fingers along Jay's copper cheek markings and, his voice softer, repeated, "It's okay."

Jo looked away from her partner and shrugged at me, then cleared her throat.

"Do you have any ideas about Greg's other friends, anyone who might know his whereabouts?"

"Sorry." Hadn't I just told them I didn't know him all that well?

"We haven't been able to locate any of his family." It was a statement, but there was a question in it.

"I don't think he has any family around here. I don't even know where he's from, now that I think about it. But how do you know he's gone? Maybe he just wasn't home when you were there."

"Oh, he's long gone." Hutchinson gently lifted Jay's feet from his chest and lowered the dog to the floor, then shoved his partially wired notebook back into his torn pocket. Jay sat beside him and rested his chin on the man's knee.

Jo explained. "We executed a search warrant early this morning." *Early? Had to be the crack of dawn,* I thought. "There's no sign of him. It certainly appears that he's gone out of town."

I watched several tiny bubbles spin in the whirlpool I stirred in my mug. "What about his car?"

"His car was there, and the van."

Jo carried her empty mug to the sink. Her partner stroked the top of Jay's head, and seemed reluctant to let the moment go. Finally he looked at me, his expression softer than I'd seen it. He seemed about to say something, then looked again at Jay, and stood up.

No one spoke on the way to the front porch, where I told Jay to lie down. "Are the dogs there?"

Jo looked at her partner, then at me, and shook her head.

"If the cars were there and the dogs weren't, I'd say he took them for a walk. How long were you there?"

"Forty-five minutes, maybe. We just came from there."

"Well, I bet he was just walking the dogs before work."

Hutchinson pulled a battered business card from his inside jacket pocket. "Call if you hear from Mr. Dorn or learn his whereabouts."

"Are you going to arrest Greg?"

Jo confirmed that there was a warrant for his arrest. Hutchinson's phone chirped. He bent and stroked Jay again, then headed for the car as he opened his phone. Jo watched him, and said, "That was interesting." She looked at me. "Cut him a little slack. His wife ran off last week with some biker dude."

"I didn't want to admit this to your partner…." I said, and Jo turned and looked me in the eye. "I'm a tad scared. I mean, someone killed Abigail and Suzette, and I knew them both. I probably know the killer."

Jo completed the thought. "And the killer knows you, and doesn't know how much you've figured out." I nodded at her. "And whoever it is knows that you've been talking to us." She glanced at the black sedan parked in front of my house. "So be alert and be cautious, okay? And again, if you think something's wrong, call 911. Or me, if it's not an emergency." She bent and scratched Jay's chest. "If I were you, I'd stick close to this guy for a while."

I watched her get behind the wheel of the black car before I stepped back inside the house with my dog. We started for the kitchen, but I backtracked to lock the door.

77

As soon as I was dressed I called the AKC's Companion Animal Recovery and left them my cell number on the off chance that someone would find Leo and scan him for a microchip. He might even still be wearing his collar and ID tag. Then I set out to look once more for my cat. I drove first to Kinkos and copied a flyer I'd made with Leo's picture and vitals. I handed them out at Animal Control, then the Allen County SPCA shelter, where I looked at the cats in the holding areas and filed "lost pet" reports. Then, consulting the pages I'd ripped from my phone book, I drove around to every vet office north of downtown and handed out more flyers. I've always thought that putting a distraught face with a report is better than just a phone call.

I tacked more than a hundred flyers to every bulletin board and lamp post I could find, and handed them out to my neighbors. I even got permission from the principals of all but one school in the area to tape copies to the exit doors for a few days, since kids were more likely than most adults to notice an animal wandering around.

I couldn't think of anything else to do to help Leo find his way home, and I realized that I was close to Greg's house, so I decided to run by and see if there was any sign of the other lost boy. Just as the detectives had said, Greg's cars were both in the driveway. I parked on the street, and checked for lurking Yugos as I got out. Not a soul in sight.

I went to the front door and rang the bell. No barking. A newspaper was lying in its plastic wrapper at the edge of the porch, and I picked it up and looked at the date. This morning. I tried to peek through the decorative glass of the door, but everything was distorted, so I didn't learn much. There was no sign of movement inside the house, though, so after a few minutes I set the paper back down by the door and walked around to the side of the house and through the gate into the backyard. No dogs, no Greg. I climbed the bluestone steps to the patio and tapped on the French door, just to be sure. The umbrella was up on the patio table, and a plate and half-full glass of diluted-looking tea sat under it. Odd that Greg would leave them out if he left, but maybe he was tidiness challenged. Like me.

From the patio I stepped onto a lawn that felt like thick carpet beneath my feet, not a weed or errant leaf in sight. The flower beds looked as if someone had edged them inch by flawless inch with nail scissors. I walked toward a building about the size of a two-car garage at the back of the yard. Clay pots were neatly stacked along one side under a row of narrow windows, all in the shadow of an enormous ash that must have been on the property before the house was built. An overhang shaded a wooden porch along the front of the building. I stepped onto it and knocked on the door. As I expected, there was no reply.

I stepped off the porch and went to the front-most window on the side and tried to see in, but the interior was too dark to reveal its secrets. I tried the other windows, too, but got the same results. I stood and looked at the lake behind the yard for a few moments, then headed back to the house. The blinds were closed on several windows, but I did manage to peek into the master bedroom. Nobody home.

I was just rounding the front corner of the house when a cold spray of water hit me in the back and sent me scuttling forward. I turned and look, half expecting to see Greg standing behind me with a hose. Instead I found myself staring at an automatic sprinkler that had popped out of the ground and assaulted me.

"Perfect," I muttered, twisting as well as I could to wring out the hems of my pants and shirt. On a hunch, I opened the mailbox on my way by and sure enough, a hefty pile of mail hadn't been picked up. I glanced up and down the street, not sure what I was looking for, but all was quiet. Too quiet, I thought. No kids out playing, no forgetful old ladies out gardening. No signs of life at all.

I glanced at my watch and was shocked to see that I'd used up most of the day. My reflection in my driver's side window looked like a drowned rat. The perfect look for a dinner date. *Date? Who said this was a date?* But who was I kidding? I was really starting to like Tom, and guessed this was as much like a date as it could get. Oh, well, I'd worry about my hair when I got home. At the moment, I admitted to myself, I was more worried about Greg and his dogs and, of course, my cat.

78

I ALMOST CANCELLED DINNER with Tom to stay home in case Leo showed up, but Goldie insisted I needed to go and promised to check my yard every hour or so and to let Leo in and call my cell phone if he showed up. Still, by the time I changed out of my damp clothes and fixed my hair and face, I pulled into Tom's driveway a quarter hour late. Tom was in the open front door before I was out of the van. Drake sat at his side, holding the stay command but vibrating with excitement. He and Tom wore matching grins. Tom also wore his ever-popular just-right jeans and a white shirt, sleeves rolled to his elbows and top button open to reveal a hint of brown and silver chest hair. With a little air brushing, he could pose for the cover of a romance novel.

Tom ushered Jay and me into the house. I wanted to linger near the kitchen, where the aroma of simmering tomato and basil and something I couldn't identify wrapped itself around me like a warm embrace. But Tom wisely hustled everyone straight through to the breakfast nook, where he opened a sliding door and shooed the dogs out before they clobbered anything, especially us. They took off through the yard, careened around two Adirondack chairs set under an enormous pin oak, and zoomed away to the far end of the yard, each snagging one of a dozen balls scattered across the lawn. We stood on the deck and watched. I didn't know about Tom, but I wasn't interested in being slammed in the knees by my fifty-pound Aussie, let alone his seventy-five-pound Labrador pal.

"Gee, I guess they're glad to see each other."

"And I'm glad to see you." Tom moved half a step closer to me. I got a whiff of a subtle, spicy fragrance, and fought off an impulse to make him lie down. Lucky for him, he kept moving. "But I'm not going to run like a maniac around the yard. How about a drink. Wine, beer … that's probably all I can scare up except a dribble of Bailey's."

I followed him back into the family room, placed my order, and looked around while he disappeared into the kitchen. The room was tastefully comfy in a masculine way, and tidier by far than my place ever is. The deep-brown leather couch was well broken in but nowhere near shabby, and little Janet Angel whispered in my ear, *Good guy. He lets his dog lie on the couch.* A large nylon chew toy once shaped like a Y lay beside a needlepoint pillow with a black Lab on it, one arm of the Y-bone gnawed to a pointed nub and the other arm on its way to the same state.

"Here ya go." Tom handed me a bottle of Killian's Red, then grabbed the bone and tossed it onto a big round dog bed snuggled up against the side of an antique roll-top desk. He grinned at me. "Dogs!"

"Hey, you've been in my house. Toys-and-hair-are-us."

"Wouldn't have it any other way." He set his bottle on a coaster sporting—what else?—a black Lab. "Make yourself at home. I'll start the pasta."

One wall of the room had a red brick fireplace flanked by built-in bookcases crammed from hearth-to-ceiling with books and a few knickknacks. A rough-hewn mantle held a pair of pewter candlesticks and about a dozen bronze, brass, and pewter Labrador Retrievers of various sizes. A large, very good oil of a black Lab in a field on a snowy day, a faraway look in his eyes, hung over the mantle.

My mother always said that you can tell a lot about a person by the books on their shelves, so I took a look. Low across the left-hand bookcase was an eclectic assortment of poetry. This is a science guy? Above the poetry was a shelf of nature and travel memoirs, including some of my golden-oldie favorites—Eiseley, Erlich, Lopez, Dillard, Chatwin. Good stuff. Above that, it was all fiction, modern and classic.

"See anything interesting?"

"As a matter of fact, I do." I took a sip of my beer as I turned toward his voice and almost spewed it back out.

79

TOM WAS DECKED OUT in an oversized chef's hat and an apron that said "The chef is not responsible for dog hair in the food" under a comedic black Lab. He struck a pose, nudging the hat flirtatiously. "Like my outfit?"

"And me without my camera!"

"Christmas presents from my kid." He winked, and something just south of my stomach did a flip-flop. "Need another beer?"

Hey, drink up! Janet Demon was on alert. *You can blame the booze for anything that happens.* "I'm fine, thanks."

He saluted, and went back to the kitchen. I moved to the right-hand bookcase. There were tons of paperbacks, mostly thrillers, some sci fi, on the bottom shelf. A row of anthropology and botany journals, a number of field guides to trees, mushrooms and fungi, birds, bugs, and flowers, and several volumes on training retrievers. The next two shelves were home to ethnographic monographs, including such classics as Turnbull's *The Forest People* and Mead's now-controversial *Coming of Age in Samoa*, both of which I'd actually read in an anthro class way back when. The rest were more recent and focused mostly on Mexico, Spain, and Central and South America. I took another swig of Killian's, then went cold as I examined the top shelf. Book after book on poisonous and medicinal plants. *Run* was my first reaction. *Don't be silly,* whispered Janet Demon. *His interest is academic— he studies plants and shamans and such.*

I heard the back door slide open. "Whoa! Give me that! No sticks in the house!" I walked to the kitchen doorway. Jay and Drake had their muzzles deep in a big stainless-steel water bowl, slurping and dripping, Drake's thick tail wagging away, Jay's little nub wriggling. Drake quit first and settled with a grunt onto the cool vinyl floor. Jay flopped down next to his new buddy and sighed.

The table was set, informal and inviting. A rough-woven table cloth of robin's-egg blue flecked with bits of white, yellow, and red supported honey-colored stoneware plates. The plates supported dark brown salad bowls, and not-quite-matching dark brown rough-woven napkins underlay heavy stainless place settings. A handmade clay pot held a splashy assortment of blooms and foliage, garden and wild flowers mingled with greenery.

"You know, if the research and teaching doesn't work out, you may have a future as a restaurateur."

Tom wrinkled his nose as he delivered a wooden bowl brimming with dark and pale greens, crimson grape tomatoes, golden bell-pepper bits, and brown-black olives. My reptilian brain hissed something about how easy it would be to hide noxious herbs in a mixed salad, but was interrupted when Tom said, "I was a waiter— or what do we say now, server?—off and on in college. Enough restaurant work for me, thanks. I prefer to do my serving at home."

"Here I thought you were strictly a rough-and-tumble Labrador Retriever sort of guy. Figured you lived on beef jerky and trail mix."

"I have been known to eat baked beans out of a can, standing at the sink and watching hockey on TV." He cocked his head. "Does that restore my rough-and-tumble image?" *What the heck*, I thought. *So have I, except for the hockey.* "Would you like wine with dinner, or another beer?"

I figured I'd better stick with the beer. I can't mix my alcohol and pretend to be rational as convincingly as I could a decade or two ago.

Tom set a golden-brown loaf of warm, garlicky bread in front of the flowers, and served vermicelli topped with a thick sauce that made my mouth water.

"What's that fragrance that I can't place?" I asked.

"Wet dog?"

"Noooo. That I can identify, thanks. No, sort of, sweet? Like licorice?"

"Ah. Sorry, secret ingredient. You'll have to wait until I know you better."

Yeah! Shouted Janet Demon. *In the biblical sense.* I felt very warm.

Before he sat down, Tom set two bowls of freshly grated cheese on the table. "Romano on the left," he rolled the r, "and Parmesan on the right." He sat down, flicked his napkin open with his left hand, and tucked it into the neckband of his shirt. "I don't know why I wear white when I eat tomato sauces. You'd think I'd learn." He grinned at me and lifted his beer. "To us." I could drink to that, I thought, until he pushed the cheeses toward me and said, "Pick your poison."

80

Tom's eyes widened and a deep furrow dug into the spot between his eyes as soon as the word *poison* left his lips. "Bad choice of words. Sorry!"

For half a heartbeat I thought of forgoing the cheese, then decided that even if I were a failure at judging people and he was in fact a murderer, he wouldn't be dumb enough to kill me in his own home. Besides, he covered his own generous serving of pasta and sauce with a thick blanket of both the Romano and the Parmesan, rolled a fork full of pasta against a spoon, and gobbled.

The remains of the evening passed without major incident other than my periodic non-menopausal hot flashes. The sauce more than lived up to its aromatic promise, and my taste buds were ecstatic and my stomach over-extended by the time we cleared the table and let the doggy boys pre-wash the dishes before loading them into the dishwasher. What the heck, the steam sterilizes, and even if it didn't, I figure I'm more likely to catch something from someone handing me change in a store than from well-cared-for dogs licking some dishes. Apparently Tom agreed.

All the way home I could taste the goodnight kiss Tom planted right smack on my lips, leaning in through the window as I fastened my seat belt. It was a simple brush of lips on lips, but I couldn't get it out of my head and was almost home before I knew it. Either I was entering my second adolescence, or I'd been celibate way too long.

I turned west off Maysville onto my own criminally dark street and once again cursed the neighbors who won't sign the street light petition. The moon wasn't up yet and the dark was impenetrable, and I barely saw the van parked on the wrong side of the street across from Goldie's house. "Shit!" I whipped the wheels to the left, missing the other vehicle by a foot or so. "What kind of idiot…" I let the thought subside along with my adrenaline level. Jay shifted in his crate, and I tried to see him in the rearview mirror, but the gloom was too thick. "You okay back there, Bubby?" His body thunked down in the crate.

I parked in the driveway, grabbed my purse, and walked to the back of my Caravan. Goldie's porch light popped on and her screen door banged. She came scurrying over, carrying two glasses and a bottle of Amaretto. "I brought the booze, and I want to hear all about it!"

"Any sign of Leo?"

"I'm sure he'll be back in the morning ready for a nice breakfast and some catnip. He's nobody's fool."

"No, I guess not," I said as I got Jay out of his crate. We were halfway to the front door when he turned toward the street, the hair standing out from his neck, ears pricked, nose thrust forward and

310

twitching. Even with my limited human senses, I could tell that something was moving in the shrubs across the street. He whined softly.

"Come on, it's just a raccoon," I sped our progress toward my front door, my hand firmly wrapped around his collar. Goldie held my screen door open with her elbow while I wrestled with my keys.

"Whose clunker?"

I pushed the door open and ushered Goldie and Jay into the house. "No idea, but I almost creamed it on my way in." I glanced toward the dark street, then closed and locked the inner door. I could have sworn I saw a flicker of movement across the living room floor where shades of gloom fought for dominance, but Jay didn't seem to find anything amiss. I decided I was paranoid. *Of course,* whispered the little voice in my left ear, *that doesn't mean someone's not out to get you.*

81

ANOTHER MORNING ARRIVED WITH no sign of Leo. Goldie promised again to check my yard and answering machine hourly and to call me if Leo showed up or if she heard anything, so I decided to proceed with my plans to drive the two-plus hours to Indianapolis for today's Delta Society Pet Partner test for Jay's therapy-dog certification. The tests are few and far between in our neck of the woods, and there was nothing more that I could do at home to find my missing cat.

If I'd had to pick a morning for a road trip, this would be it, except for the shadow that Leo's absence cast over my world. The sky was a soft, clear spring blue laced with delicate high-cirrus wisps. The long curve of I-469 that encircles Fort Wayne to the east ribbons through a twenty-mile stretch of farmland laid out like a massive quilt. The patches were newly tinted in the tender greens of sprouting corn, soy, timothy, and alfalfa, the fence rows stitched in willow, trumpet vine, and Russian olive. The whole green world still glistened under a sheet of dew that the morning sun had not yet lifted. I tried to remember the whole of e. e. cummings' poem of thanks, but it was buried too deep in memory, and all I could come up with was the beginning ... *I thank you God for most this amazing day: for the leaping greenly spirits of trees and a blue true dream of sky.* Add a warm-eyed dog, and it was prayer enough for me.

———

I pulled into the parking lot at the church where the test would be held about twenty minutes before our appointment. We had the second time slot, so I fluffed up Jay's bed hair with a pin brush, pulled my tote bag from the front seat, and walked my dog to an enormous ginkgo in the grassy strip between the parking lot and the street. When Jay had watered the tree, we followed the hand-lettered "Delta Test This Way" signs through a bent-willow gate and down a winding path of red bricks laid in a herringbone design.

Pink and yellow columbines, white candytuft, electric blue forget-me-nots with sunny yellow eyes, and a riot of late-blooming daffodils in pale saffron, deep gold, oranges, and whites danced from the edge of the path to the church wall on my left, and right to a hedge of forsythia, gone green but for a whisper of gold still clinging here and there.

I checked in with the volunteer who was assisting the tester. My paperwork was all in order, so there was nothing to do now but wait. The assistant said the first pair had arrived a little late and they were running about ten minutes behind. I took Jay outside and pulled out my cell phone.

Connie answered on the first ring and asked, "Have you heard about Greg?"

I told her about my visit the previous day from Stevens and Hutchinson.

"They came here, too. Said they're talking to everyone from Dog Dayz. Must have been right after you saw them. I'm so upset. What do you think?" She sounded pretty calm to me, but that's Connie. "They seem to think Greg killed Abigail and Suzette. I know we talked about that, but really, I don't believe it." We were both quiet for a moment. "I guess we all have our breaking points though."

"I don't believe it either."

Her voice dropped to conspiracy volume. "But you know, he might have killed Abigail to be with Suzette, and Suzette found out, so he had to kill her to keep her from ratting him out."

"'Ratting him out'?"

"You know what I mean!"

Neither of us spoke for a moment, then Connie said, "I'd put my money on Giselle."

I held the phone out in front of me, but there was no text message indicating that I'd heard wrong, so I put it back to my ear. "Is there anyone you don't think is involved?"

"Oh, please!" I could almost see her roll her eyes. "Giselle's in love with Greg. Maybe she figured she'd do away with the competition."

Giselle is a bit off, I thought, picturing the witchcraft books strewn inside her car. *She could have been into potions for more lethal pursuits than love. She did get pretty testy with me. But murder?*

"So I take it you don't know where Greg is?" I asked.

"How would I know?"

Jay put a gentle white paw on my knee. I massaged behind his ear and watched him tilt his head into my hand and close his eyes. *Why can't people be more like dogs?* I wondered, not for the first time. I told Connie where I was and promised to call later.

82

WHEN I WALKED BACK into the church, I saw the first pair of Pet Partner candidates, a frail wee man who looked like he could use a little therapy himself and his tiny mixed breed with long black stand-away hair like a Pomeranian on a long body slung low over short, bandy legs. The tester was wrapping up the paperwork. The little dog waved the long fringe of her tail and sneezed at Jay. She took a step toward us, her round little head tilted to her left and her bottom incisors gleaming from her undershot lower jaw. I asked if it was okay to pet her, and her owner beamed. "I should think so! Lulabelle passed her test!" He had dark, round eyes not unlike those of his companion. I grinned back at him, had Jay lie down, and knelt to pet Lulabelle.

Our test took about twenty minutes, and Jay sailed through. He wasn't happy about the part of the test in which a couple of people holler at one another, something that occasionally happens in therapy situations. But he responded as expected, staying where I told him to sit, and looking at me as if to ask why those people were so upset. When all the i's were dotted and the t's crossed, Jay and I backtracked along the brick pathway and headed for home.

Three hours later Jay polished off his supper, and we went looking for Leo again. I checked under and behind the shrubs, and into every nook and cranny I could think of in the backyard. Goldie leaned over the fence and said she'd walked the yard every hour to be sure the yellow guy wasn't waiting to be let in, but no luck. I told her I was going to try again to see if Jay could find Leo's scent trail. The old one would be getting weak by now, but if the cat had walked around the yard when we weren't looking, I should see some change in Jay's tracking behavior. At least I hoped so. Goldie said she'd like to watch and would meet us out front.

I took Jay into the house, snapped a retractable leash onto his collar, and grabbed the towel that lined Leo's favorite napping basket. Normally I'd put a tracking harness on Jay and use long line to run a track, but this one should take all of about forty-five seconds, so I stuck with the basics. On the front porch I held the towel for Jay to smell and gave him his tracking command—"Find it! Find Leo!" He gave the towel two quick little jabs with his nose, then sniffed around the front yard. We had only started tracking training a couple of months earlier, but I was sure he understood what I wanted, because, as he had two other times since Leo went missing, he followed his nose to a patch of ground between a pink shrub rose and the vinyl siding beneath the living room's picture window. It was one of Leo's favorite vantage points when I was working in the front garden.

Jay's eyes sparkled with anticipation. I slipped him a cheese-flavored training treat, showed him the towel again, and told him to "Find it." If I hadn't had a good grip on the handle of the retractable leash, I'd have been standing alone in the yard, because Jay took off again like his furry britches were on fire, nose to the ground and tiny tail wagging. As he had the other times, he raced around the side of the house, sticking close to the foundation. At the gate to the backyard he sniffed back and forth, made a quick about-turn, and shot across the grass to the edge of the driveway. He took a few more sniffs and a tentative lick, and finally sat down and looked at me as if to say, "Okay, end of the line, this is where I get my reward." Just like before.

I popped a couple more treats into Jay's mouth. Goldie folded her arms across her body and pooched her mouth out in a thoughtful O. "Is that what he did before?"

"Exactly. Except the first couple of times he did a lot more grass licking at the end of the track."

8 3

GOLDIE WENT HOME WITH a thoughtful look on her face, and I loaded Jay into his crate in the Caravan and slid in behind the wheel. I had a craving for a nice big salad, and Scott's grocery on Stellhorn has a nice big salad bar.

I swung by the vet clinic thinking I'd stop in and tell Connie we passed the Delta test. They're open Saturdays until 5 P.M., and Connie works a lot of weekends when she's not at dog shows. There were no empty spaces in the parking lot, so I pulled to one side of the lot, behind a row of vehicles, and let the engine idle while I dialed my cell phone. The receptionist said Connie had left for the day. I tried her house and cell numbers and left "call me's" on both voicemails. Odd for Connie to be completely out of touch. As a professional show-dog handler, she liked to be available for potential handling clients.

I tried for a three-point turn, but there wasn't much room and I had to add a couple extra points to get the Caravan facing out again. As I maneuvered through the final backward leg, I noticed a battered

red cargo van tucked into the corner space behind a shiny new conversion van. If it wasn't the rust bucket Francine Peterson drove, the two of them were littermates. I backed up a little further for a better look.

Why would Francine come to Fort Wayne for a vet? Then I noticed the license, not a plate but a temporary paper tag sheathed in plastic and taped to the back door.

You really are paranoid. There are lots of rusty old red vans. Janet Angel harangued me all the way to Scott's grocery store and then home, reminding me that, among other things, it's one thing to be careful, another to be obsessed, and I was treading darn close to the boundary. Then again, who wouldn't be obsessed with finding answers with two acquaintances dead, another missing, not to mention my cat, and my dog poisoned.

I grabbed my tote bag and salad, unloaded Jay, and locked the car doors. I even remembered to relock the front door when we got inside the house.

On the drive home I'd decided that if anyone was likely to know where Greg was, it would be Giselle. Not that he would tell her, but she seemed to have an inclination for stalking so she might know anyway. I didn't relish a conversation with her after our last one, but decided I had nothing to lose, so I looked up her number and called. Just as she picked up, I noticed that my answering machine was blinking at me.

———

"I'll tell you what I told your friends, the police." Giselle's delivery was stronger than usual. "I have no idea where Greg is. And if I did know I don't think I'd tell you."

319

Okay then. For once she wasn't speaking in the interrogative. Maybe the police interviews were building her confidence. Or maybe she was just pissed, a possibility she reinforced when she slammed the phone down without saying goodbye.

I pushed the playback button for my message. The voice was female, I was pretty sure, but pitched too high, like a fake voice, a cartoon voice, and a little fuzzy, as if she was speaking through a wool muffler. "Keep your nose in your own business and your cat will find his way home. Keep sticking it where it doesn't belong and who knows..." The recording ran silent, and then the voice came back. "You might find more dead than toy dogs." The ice in those words blasted like brainfreeze through my skull, but the taste in my mouth was definitely not ice cream.

I tried to wrap my mind around the threat as the machine whirred through the rewind. Then I replayed the recording, my gorge rising. I replayed it several more times, searching the voice, the inflection, for a clue to the speaker, but no bells rang. I hit the save button, and punched in Jo Stevens' number on my cell. By the time I had left her a message, my eyes were stinging and my heart was doing aerobics.

I considered calling Goldie, but changed my mind. Why worry her? What I really needed was a nice stress-reducing lavender bubble bath, so I rechecked all the doors, then ran a tub full of water as hot as I could stand it with double the recommended bubble bath. What did I care if it left bubble marks on the tile around the tub? I dropped my clothes in a heap between the toilet and the vanity, pulled my hair off my face with two alligator clips and a headband, and sank into the hot water. I was leaning back into my inflated bath pillow when the phone rang.

I decided to ignore it until I heard Goldie's voice. "I know you're there, Janet. Pick up the phone … Tum tee tum … Come on, Janet, pick up the phone …"

Goldie never hangs up if she knows I'm here, so I climbed out of the hot water, wrapped an almost-big-enough towel around myself, and shivered and dripped my way down the hall and across the living room. *Good thing I closed the blinds*, I thought. I reached for the phone, and heard the answering machine click off. Bzzzz. Goldie had hung up.

———

"You never hang up like that!"

"Oh, hi Janet. I thought you were in the bath or something."

"I was."

"Oh, dear. Are you covered?"

"Yes. With goose bumps."

She giggled. "That's not enough, dear."

"Very amusing. So were you checking to see if I was taking a bath?"

"My, my, aren't we grumpy." She clucked a couple times. "No, dear, let me tell you why I called."

Why didn't I think of that? I bit my tongue.

"You know," she seemed to be thinking aloud, "if I had to guess, I'd say Leo was bound for the backyard when he saw someone or something. With food. Remember how Jay was licking the grass?" She started tapping something against the phone. "You know what a social butterfly and chow hound, if that's the right thing to call a cat, he is. I think the trail ends because someone fed him something and picked him up."

84

Jay and I were out the door at four a.m. to search again for Leo before I left for my photo shoot near Culver. As I watched him work his nose along this end of whatever track he was following, Goldie's hunch about someone feeding and grabbing Leo echoed in my brain, and it rang true. I knew I should tell Detective Stevens about the threatening message on my answering machine, but was afraid she'd tell me not to make the drive. I'd made the commitment a couple months earlier, and at least one litter of baby Labs was supposed to be there for portraits. There wasn't much I could do at home, and Goldie had my cell number. Besides, I needed the money.

The Northern Indiana Hunting Retriever Club practices once a month at various ponds and lakes in a big rectangle from Michigan (the lake), south to Kentland on the Illinois side, east to the Ohio line around Decatur, and north to Michigan (the state). I enjoy the variety of terrains contained in those ten thousand square miles, from the flat, rich farmland of west-central Indiana that once lay deep under ancient Lake Chicago, to the rocky ravines and rolling hills laid out by glaciers in the northern tier ten millennia ago, to the fertile soils farther to the east, once the bottom of the malarial Great Black Swamp.

My destination was a small private lake not far from Lake Maxinkuckee. I loaded my equipment and my dog into the van. I hadn't planned to take Jay, but I wasn't about to leave him home alone after that phone call. Besides, no one would begrudge him a swim when the retrievers finished. A little more than two hours later I pulled onto a grassy berm and parked behind a white Suburban. The back doors stood wide open and two Labs, a chocolate and a black, watched me from their crates, tongues lolling and tails thumping.

The air shook off the chill of night as daylight took hold, so I chucked my jacket, pulled my sweatshirt off, and put the cotton jacket back on over my T-shirt. I grabbed my tripod and my camera, popped the back of the van and checked that Jay had water, then struck out across the uneven field toward the shore some hundred yards to the east. The sun had cleared the tops of a clump of young willows weeping along the far bank of the pond, but dew still lay heavy near the ground, and the shin-high quackgrass and foxtail soaked my pants and shoes. Several people waved or nodded as I reached the group of some dozen retriever fans and twice that many dogs, mostly Labs, several Goldens, one Standard Poodle, a couple of Tollers, three Chesapeakes, a Curly, and three Flat-coats.

I had no more than set my camera bag on a canvas chair offered by Collin Lahmeyer, president of the club, when a mass of wet, dripping black hair and solid muscle jostled me. I looked down into two sparkling eyes and gently took the sodden goose wing offered in welcome.

"Gee, thanks, Drake." I examined the gift, and handed it back to the sopping dog. He liked it a lot better than I did.

"Drake! Come!"

The big Lab turned toward the voice, glanced back at me as if to apologize for leaving so soon, and ran to Tom. Together they came over, Drake at heel now, and Tom grinning. "Nothing so friendly as a wet dog, huh?"

I grinned back, running my hand down my faded T-shirt and my well-worn jeans with the fraying seams. "And me all dressed up, too."

"Leo come home?"

"No."

"He's not in the habit of going awol?"

"Miss a meal of canned salmon? Not on your life."

"Maybe someone took him in."

"Or just plain took him." I told him about the message, and was on to Goldie's theory when we were interrupted by a sharp whistle. It was Collin, seeking everyone's attention. He explained to the assembled handlers that I was taking photos for possible sale to magazines, calendars, and books, then let me say a few words. I handed out release forms and business cards with my web address for those who wanted them, and promised I'd have the proofs online by the following weekend. A little foolhardy, but I find that a short deadline gets my fanny in gear. Besides, the sooner I post the proofs, the more likely people are to buy prints and CDs.

As I slung my camera case over my shoulder and picked up my tripod, Tom took me by the arm and said, "Call the detective."

"Okay, I will."

"Now, Janet." A flashback to Chet at his bossiest made me start to bristle at Tom's words, but when I saw the concern in his eyes I knew that his tone was one of care, not command. I unslung my bag from my shoulder, pulled my cell phone from my pocket, and punched Jo's number in, thinking I might as well put her on speed dial. She didn't pick up, so I told her voicemail about the latest warning, then turned the sound off on my phone.

I spent the next three hours taking hundreds of photos of retrievers doing what retrievers do best—leaping into water, swimming, carrying training bumpers and birds, shaking water out of their coats and onto people, racing through high grass and brush, and generally being the happiest dogs on earth. Tom took Jay for a couple of walks so I wouldn't have to stop shooting.

The Lab puppies arrived mid-morning, and their breeder fastened three exercise pens together with clips to let the little guys take care of the Three P's of Puppyhood—play, pee, and poop—as nature dictated. There were eleven of them, six blacks, five yellows. They really were babies, only six-and-a-half weeks old, roly-poly, and utterly smoochable. I could hardly put them down long enough to take their pictures, but I forced myself and got some nice shots, singles and groups, and then the whole gang having their first swim outside a wading pool. People put their dogs in their vehicles, all wide open for ventilation, and came to enjoy the puppies. The breeder created a "buddy system," with a volunteer assigned to keep track of each puppy so none of them would wander off when they were out of the pen. As we wrapped things up with the puppies, Tom recommended that she check everyone for suspicious lumps under their clothing before anyone was allowed to leave, especially himself.

I stowed my equipment in my van, got Jay out, and let him run ahead of me to the lake. He and Drake greeted each other with polite mutual fanny sniffing before they bowed at one another and took off in big, joyous loops around the field. Tom stood at the edge of the lake and called to get Drake's attention, then pitched a fat stick far out over the water. Both dogs saw it fly, and hit the water running. Drake grabbed one end of the stick first and Jay got the other end, facing the opposite direction, and they swam in a spiral around one another.

Tom pitched another stick off to their side, and Drake let go of the first one in favor of the second. Jay made the bank, where he dropped his treasure at Tom's feet and shook the water from his coat. Tom raised his left arm to shield his face, and flung the stick back into the water. Jay went for it, swimming out as Drake came in with his prize. Tom threw Drake's stick far into the field this time, then did the same with Jay's when he delivered his stick to shore. For the next ten minutes, Tom kept the two dogs retrieving, sometimes on land, sometimes in the water. By the end all three were grinning, panting, wet, and dirty, and supremely pleased with themselves. Male bonding at its finest.

Tom offered me lunch at a nice little café in The Village at Winona, an artsy community south of Warsaw and about halfway home, but I took a rain check. I was hot, covered with muck and plant matter, and worried about Leo.

I should have stuck with Tom.

85

I left the retriever club training session and headed north into Plymouth on U.S. 31, stopped for a red light, and glanced at the signs at the intersection. If I continued north, I'd wind up in South Bend. Behind me to the south was Rochester. Why did that ring a bell? The light changed and I turned east onto U.S. 30. They were working on this stretch, I remembered, on Wednesday when I met Ginny Scott in Valparaiso, and the new blacktop surface was a vast improvement over the old bumpity bump concrete that was there before. I'd been telling myself for years that someday I'm going to take the Great U.S. 30 Road Trip all the way from Atlantic City to Astoria, Oregon. Abigail and Suzette's unexpected departures had me thinking that I should do the things I've always planned to do now, since we never know how long we'll have, and I decided as I drove that I should plan this road trip and do it, right after I took the first aid class I'd been planning to take since who knows when. I also remembered why Rochester sounded familiar. That's where Francine lived.

About five miles further east I found myself catching up to a semi that was actually sticking to the speed limit, probably because this stretch of U.S. 30 is notorious for its speed traps. Thinking I'd pass him, I glanced into my rearview mirror and my stomach contracted. The front grille of something big was barreling toward the back of my Caravan, closing the distance between us with alarming efficiency. I couldn't speed up without ramming into the blue and gold Alphonse Trucking logo blazoned across the doors of the semi, and a pale-gold Toyota Corolla blocked the lane to my left. The shoulder was filled with orange barrels still waiting for the highway department to pick them up. There was no escape.

I lay the back of my head against the headrest on the off chance that it would save my neck, and hoped for the best. There was nothing I could do for Jay except pray, and vow to rearrange my van so the crates would be in the center, away from a rear-end hit, if we got through this without injury. At least he was in an airline-approved crate, which was better protection than if he'd been loose.

We were approaching a crossroad. Could I make the right turn at 60 miles per hour without rolling over? I had a cinematic image of my van skidding sideways in a too-fast turn and going airborne over the drainage ditch that surely paralleled the pavement. These county roads all have them. No reason this one would be any different. And at this speed, that's where I'd land, in turtle position. We'd both be hurt. Or dead. I glanced once more at the mirror and realized that the turn option was moot. Whatever was behind us would make contact before we got to the corner.

I prefer not to close my eyes when I'm driving, but I couldn't see that it would matter much under the circumstances. My shoulders curled toward my sternum and my arms petrified against the steering wheel. *Please let the crate hold up, please let Jay be safe* ran like a mantra through my mind. My fingers started to cramp, and I couldn't stop my teeth from biting into my lip. Rubber squealed against concrete. *Please, please, please.* I murmured a slow count to give my spinning mind some traction, squeezed my eyelids tighter, and braced for impact.

86

By the count of three I was still rolling down U.S. 30, unscathed. I opened my eyes. A squeal of tires pierced the air to my left. The sound seemed to be moving away from me. I checked the mirror. Just open road. In my peripheral vision I saw the Corolla fall back, horn blaring but apparently unscathed. I turned to look. The speed demon had somehow squeezed between me and the Corolla without creaming either of us and was passing me on the left. The camera in my mind worked in spite of my fear, taking in a rattletrap old cargo van with rust eating the edges of the wheel wells. The back side door was dented, and binder's twine coiled through the handle to snake into the vehicle between the door and the frame. The driver was all but invisible behind a screen of dirty windows and reckless speed. My first impression was that it was a redhead. *Francine?* But doubt reared up. At that speed, without a clear view, I couldn't be sure. And anyway, how would Francine know where to find me?

We shot through the intersection. The cargo van shimmied back and forth in the left-turn lane, then rocketed through the intersection and veered back across the passing lane. It disappeared from my view in front of the eighteen wheeler.

Four miles further down the road I followed the Alphonse semi into a truck stop, pulled around the big rig, and parked in front of the store and restaurant. I had to will the muscles of my hands to unclench and let loose of the steering wheel, and my thigh muscles to relax. I turned off the engine, thinking I might have to toss my cookies. Instead I draped both hands across the steering wheel at twelve o'clock, pressed my forehead against them, and waited for the adrenalin to seep away. I had to check on Jay, but I couldn't get my limbs to move. All lucid thought faded as a visceral wave of relief rolled through me.

I was startled out of my moment of gratitude by a tap on the window. A wiry guy with a couple day's worth of whiskers was leaning toward me, a worried look on his face and an Alphonse Trucking cap on his head. I rolled down the window.

"You okay, ma'am?" He pulled the cap off, revealing close-cropped sandy hair that matched his stubble.

"Yes, thanks, I'm fine."

"That's good. An' just so's you know, I called 911 on that guy. Told 'em what he done back there. Damn fool like to kilt someone." He gave the rim of my open window a pat, and straightened up. "Don't know that they'll catch 'im. He turned off back there, pulled off on one of them county roads." He straightened up and took a step back. "More'n likely drunk."

"Him? You could see the driver?"

He ran his fingers and thumb up and down the sides of his jaw bone and thought about that. "No ma'am, I couldn't see that good.

But dang fool driver like that more'n likely some young buck. Most women ain't that dumb."

A man of wisdom.

"You be safe now, ma'am." He touched the rim of his cap with two fingers, nodded, and walked into the truck stop store.

You be safe, I thought. *That's what I'd like to be.* But I was starting to wonder if we were safe anywhere.

87

JAY WAS FINE. I walked him on the grass on the far side of the parking lot for a few minutes, then walked myself around the truck stop store for ten more, sipping coffee that I feared would put hair on my chest and looking at "scenic Indiana" ashtrays, mud guards with glittering buxom women, megaboxes of Milkduds, yard-long jerky sticks, and various other gifts from the road. Oddly enough, the coffee calmed me, and I finally got back on the horse, mine being a blue Grand Caravan. We were home, safe, an hour later.

I had hoped that Leo would also be waiting when I got there, but no such luck. I stripped off my mucky clothes and took a quick shower, pulled on some gray knit pants that have seen better days and a long-sleeved faded navy henley, and went to the kitchen to feed Jay. It was only three o'clock, and technically he eats at five, but what the heck. It had been a long day, and he isn't fussy about his schedule, as long as the food isn't late. Early is good.

While he snarfed up his kibble, I peeked out the back door and felt my heart rise at a hint of orange movement on Goldie's side of the picket fence. I opened the door and stepped onto the patio, calling. As soon as Leo's name was past my lips, though, I realized that I was looking at orange tulips swaying in the breeze. The hope that floated my heart for a moment dripped into heavy sludge around my ankles, and I went back inside.

Jay scoured the stainless bowl with his tongue, then nudged me in the pants pocket, so I let him out. I fished my cell phone out from under a bag of freeze-dried liver treats in my tote bag, slipped my feet into some grubby old tennies I keep for the garden, and joined Jay in the yard. I hit Goldie's speed-dial number, which seemed pretty silly when I could just walk over and knock on the door, but I was busy shaking the shrubs again. There was no answer, so I folded the phone and put it in my pocket. The elastic in the waistband was so old and frail I wasn't sure it would hold against the extra weight, but other than feeling an ominous little droop in the right side of my drawers, nothing happened.

Jay and I pottered around the yard for an hour before we went back inside. I considered checking the fridge for signs of food, but why kid myself? I wasn't going to cook an actual meal just for me when I could have a well-rounded dinner of English muffin with grape jelly followed later in the evening by cheddar-flavored popcorn. That gave me my grains, fruit, dairy, and veggie. A big hunk of chocolate and I'd have all the important food groups covered. Dark chocolate. Just last week I heard a doctor on National Public Radio say that dark chocolate is good for us, and if it's on NPR, it's good enough for me.

Restlessness was getting the better of me and I was in danger of doing some dusting when my cell phone rang. As I pulled it from my pocket and opened it, I had a quickie fantasy conversation with

Leo, calling to tell me to pick him up at a cat house on West Coliseum, where he was being held captive as a sardine inspector. But it wasn't Leo, and I realized that I must be exhausted to be making up tales like that.

It was Giselle, which took me a minute to figure out from the marginally coherent bursts of English scattered between hysterical sobs and screams. "Calm down! I can't understand you."

"Okay," she squeaked. "I'll try?"

"Giselle?"

"Yes, yes, it's me, Giselle?" *Don't ask me!* I thought, another heart-rending sob ringing in my ear. "I can't believe he's dead! I don't know what to do? There's blood, so much blood."

88

FOR A TERRIBLE MOMENT I thought Giselle had found Leo, and my heart crawled into my throat. But then she said, "I'm at his house? Janet? I'm here, and he's dead, and ..." She sounded like she might not be far behind him, whoever he was.

"Giselle, stop. Take a deep breath. Who's dead? What house?"

"Greg!"

"Greg? Greg Dorn?"

"Yes, yes, Greg Dorn! What other Greg?" Her voice pitched higher and faster as she spoke. "Greg's dead! I'm sure he's dead. What am I going to do?"

A chill swept my body. "Have you called the police?"

"The police?"

I reached for a tissue to wipe away the tears that were spilling inexplicably down my cheeks, and forced my voice to work. "Look, Giselle, you have to call 911. Get an ambulance and the police." Despite my lack of concrete information about whatever she'd seen, I clung to a scrap of hope. "He may not be dead."

"They'll think I did it!" she protested. "I didn't! I didn't do it!"

"Okay, look, don't touch anything. I'll be there in ten minutes. Wait for me, okay?"

"Okay." Sob. "I'll wait. I knew you'd know what to do."

Yeah, I know what to do. I hung up, wiped my eyes and nose, and wondered vaguely why I was crying for Greg. But it wasn't just for Greg, I realized, but loss and senseless death, and for my mom, for my poisoned dog and my missing cat, and my own fear of being hurt, and a boatload of other sorrows, great and small. I pressed my thumb and forefinger against the inner corners of my eyes, sucked up a lungfull of air, and, not so sure that Giselle would follow through, dialed 911. I gave them the Dorn's address, then found Jo Stevens' card on my desk and called the cell phone number she'd jotted on the back. I loaded Jay into his crate in the back of my van and took off.

I was a block from Greg's house when I realized I was still wearing my crappy don't-leave-home-in-these pants. Oh well, my undies were clean and free of holes, in case of incident. Like the elastic in my ratty old pants finally giving up. *Or murder?*

89

SIRENS SOUNDED IN THE distance as I popped the back hatch of the Caravan, now parked in a circle of shade in front of Greg Dorn's house. "You have to stay here, Bubby." Jay slumped onto his bed and lodged an appeal with the droopiest eyes he could manage.

Giselle sat on the top step leading to the front porch, her feet on the bottom step. Patches like big red plums blotched her face, and black streaks radiated down her cheeks from her eyes. Her bangs stuck up and out in all directions, as if she had been pulling at them in desperation. I wondered vaguely why they looked so rigid when Giselle's hair never seemed to benefit from hair care products. She shoved the last bite of a chocolate eclair into her mouth as I climbed the porch steps, sobbed at me by way of greeting, and ran a sticky hand through her bangs. *Ah, that's her hairdressing secret—the holding power of sugar.* Giselle reached for another goodie from a white bag on the top step.

"Giselle. What happened?"

"I don't know?" She burst into ragged sobs, and followed up with a choking, coughing fit.

While I waited for her to recover I pushed the pastry bag out of the way and sat down next to her. A police car skidded to the curb. I reached over and took the donut from Giselle's hand. She'd gone limp at the sight of the police, and didn't resist. I handed her a napkin from the bag, and suggested she pull herself together, then got up to greet the fresh-faced officer who walked up to the porch. His nametag identified him as L. Baker. I wondered if he was old enough to drive. His partner, an older guy who might or might not pass his next annual physical, stopped back a few yards in the lawn.

"We have a call about someone being injured?"

I explained that I'd just arrived, and tilted my head toward Giselle. She had pulled her feet up to the step below the one she sat on and had her arms on her knees, her face buried in their ample bulk. "Giselle?"

"Mrmff?"

"Come on, Giselle, give us a hand here. Where's Greg?" I glanced at the cop. His expression was completely neutral, and he seemed perfectly willing to let me deal with the incoherent woman on the porch. "Giselle!"

"Back..." sob, gasp, "backyard. Sh... sh..."

I wondered why she was shushing us, but you never know with Giselle. The cop was watching the ambulance pull in and didn't seem to notice. "What happened, ma'am? An accident?"

"N...n...no. H...h...h...he..." She started to cry.

"Giselle, what happened to Greg?" I shook her arm enough to make her gasp.

"Blood. There's so much blood. Stabbed."

339

Baker turned, placed a hand on his holster, told the EMTs to stay put, and gestured for his partner to go around the house the other direction.

"Shed. He's in the storage sh ..." Giselle tried, but she muffled the final word in more sobs.

I called after Baker, "She says he's in the storage shed." I had another thought, and ran a few steps after the cop. "Officer, there could be two dogs in the yard. Don't hurt them! They know me, I can get them out of the way!"

He nodded and gestured for me to stay back. He had pulled his gun. I retreated to the porch with Giselle.

"I have to tell you something?" Giselle looked at me out of the corner of her eye.

"Yes?"

Before she could continue one of the EMTs approached and asked if Giselle needed their assistance. Taking in the crimson shade of her face and the sheen of perspiration, I understood his concern and asked if she wanted them to check her out. She shook her head.

When the EMT had retreated, Giselle murmured, "I sent you that e-mail." I had no idea what she was talking about. "I just wanted you to leave Greg alone, because ..."

Oh, that *e-mail,* I thought. "The one telling me to butt out?"

She nodded. That explained why, at Abigail's funeral, Greg had acted as if he hadn't just sent me a snotty e-mail. He hadn't.

"Okay. Forget it." I let her relax for a moment, then asked, "Where are the dogs?"

"Hrmph?" She had retrieved the bag and was eating again, between sobs, and a blob of something gooey peeked over the edge of her lip.

"Pip and Percy. Where are they?"

She stopped chewing and turned wide eyes my way. "I don't know?"

"Was the gate open when you got here?"

She dropped half a donut back into the bag. "No? I didn't think of that? I forgot about the dogs when I saw Greg?" She looked at the front window of the house, sniffing and gulping. "They should be barking, huh?"

90

A BLACK TAURUS PULLED up behind the ambulance, and Detectives Stevens and Hutchinson got out and started toward us. Giselle had stopped sobbing and eating and sat hunched, rumpled and streaked with makeup, half her bangs now hanging in her eyes, the other half still sticking out at odd angles.

Jo wrinkled her forehead at Giselle. "Are they in the house?"

"Backyard," I said.

"Right." She turned toward the side of the house, looked around for her partner, and called "Hutch!" He was at the back of my Caravan, talking to Jay and stroking him through the crate wires. *Maybe there's hope for the guy.* Jo gestured to her partner to follow, and turned to me and Giselle. "You both stay put."

We sat in silence for about ten minutes. Jo finally reappeared with a pale-faced Officer Baker tagging behind. Baker conferred with the ambulance crew while Detective Stevens pulled her notebook and pen from her pocket and joined me on the bottom step.

"Ms. Swann—it is Ms. Swann?" Giselle murmured her assent, eyes wide, and Jo continued. "Ms. Swann, I understand you found Mr. Dorn?"

Giselle nodded hard enough to throw tears into the air.

"Did you move the body, or touch it?"

"No?"

"Are you sure?"

"Yes, I never moved him or touched him?" She sucked in a ragged breath, and went on in a barely audible voice. "I just opened the shed, could tell he was d … d … dead." She punctuated her pronouncement by blowing her nose.

"And Janet, did you touch or move the body?"

"I haven't been back there. I just got here a few minutes ago. I've been here with Giselle."

"Neither of you touched or moved Mr. Dorn?"

How hard is this? I stifled Janet Demon—this was no time for a smart mouth. Giselle and I shook our heads.

"Right." She played twenty questions—when did Giselle get here, did either of us see or hear anyone or anything unusual, could we think of anyone who might want him dead? I wasn't exactly full of useful information, and Giselle didn't seem to have anything to add.

"And what were you doing here, Ms. Swann?"

Giselle looked like she might swoon under Detective Stevens' scrutiny. "Huh?"

"Why were you here? And what were you doing in the shed?"

Giselle's face twisted and she sniffed and choked all at once, but then she regained some control. "I, you know, wanted to see if Greg needed anything?"

Jo Stevens continued to gaze at her, quiet, waiting.

343

"I went to see if maybe he was in the back, and I opened the shed, the door, you know, to the shed, to see if he was there, and…."

"Was the door unlocked?"

"Huh?"

Jo softened her tone a notch. "Ms. Swann, was the door to the shed locked or unlocked?"

"Locked?"

"Yes, was it locked?" Jo apparently hadn't yet caught on to Giselle's interrogative affirmatives.

"Uh-huh."

"You have a key?"

"No? I mean, you know, I know where they keep, I mean, where he keeps it under the windowsill, and I, you know, thought Greg might be in there working or something?"

I wondered whether Giselle realized what she was saying. If Greg locked himself into his shed and didn't open the door to her, he was hiding from her. Assuming he was alive at the time.

Jo met my gaze. "It was locked when we were here looking for him. And he's been dead a while." She looked at the sky and shook her head. "Damn it."

Was he in there, dead or—worse—dying, when I was here snooping around the shed?

"Oh, man, I can't believe it, you know?" mumbled Giselle, addressing her knees as far as I could tell. She looked up at Jo and asked, "Can I go home? I can't stand this?"

"Not yet. We need to get your statement before you leave."

Giselle appeared to be on the verge of collapse, but agreed to wait to give a statement. She asked if she could get some tissues from her car and, permission granted, hauled herself up, using the wrought-iron railing for support. She grabbed her pastry bag and schlumped down the sidewalk to her car, which for some reason was parked across from the lot next door.

Jo called to Giselle, and caught up with her in a few long strides.

"Ms. Swann, why did you park over here?"

"Hunh?"

"Why didn't you park right in front of Mr. Dorn's house?"

"Oh." The confusion left Giselle's face. "There was a car there."

"A car?"

"A van really. Looked like, I dunno, a work van."

"Work van?"

"You know, like a plumber or carpenter or something. I figured Greg was having some work done?"

"Was there a sign on it?"

"A sign?"

The detective spoke slowly. "Why did you think it was a work van?"

"I dunno? It was kind of beat-up looking, you know? And the paint was faded, and it was one of those vans with no windows in back, like it's full of work stuff, you know, equipment?"

"Right." Jo jotted something in her notebook. "What color was it?"

"I dunno. Sort of b … b … brown?"

Sort of brown. *Could sort of brown be sort of rusty red?* I wondered.

Jo patted Giselle's shoulder. "Okay, try to relax, Ms. Swann. An officer will be with you in a few minutes." Giselle snuffled and coughed and seemed to study something on the ground.

Jo came back to the porch, leafing back through her notes, looking for something. I interrupted her. "Are you sure Greg is dead?"

"Oh, he's dead."

I started to tell her about Francine's red van, but she was dialing her cell phone. As she waited for a response, she flipped through her ratty little notebook, seemed to confirm something, and tucked it back into her pocket. "Ellen, we need a whereabouts on a Francine Peterson." *Great minds.* Jo gave a description of Francine's cargo van, the license number, and Francine's address and phone number.

"Giselle mentioned blood. I take it he wasn't poisoned like Abigail and Suzette?"

"We can't say he wasn't poisoned until we have the autopsy report, but I have a hunch he didn't *die* from poison." I waited for the rest, and got a taste of Jo's grim sense of humor. "I have a hunch that the chisel shoved through his eye took care of that."

91

NEITHER MY LEGS NOR my voice seemed to be working properly, so I let myself sink into a moment of silence on the concrete step while Jo once again scribbled in her little notebook. My vocal cords eventually recovered, and I told Jo that there was no sign of the Dorns' dogs, and that wasn't normal. I asked if we could check in the house, and offered to take both dogs home temporarily if they were there.

She called for Baker to clear the house before we went in, which was fine with me. I didn't relish a chisel in *my* eye. Officer Baker came out a few minutes later. "No sign of the dogs, but someone made a mess of one of the rooms. Looks like a home office. Down the hall." He pointed to the left, off the foyer.

I followed Jo through the glorious entry and down a wide hallway. I got a glimpse of my dream bathroom, complete with shower stall, huge Jacuzzi tub, skylight, and an antique fainting couch. Okay, the fainting couch isn't in my dream. But then, my dream bathroom isn't in my house. Now I knew why. The Dorns had it.

I almost bumped into Jo in the doorway to a room at the end of the hall. The Dorns' home office looked like a spring windstorm had hit it. A drawer marked "Dogs" stood open in the rosewood filing cabinet next to an antique desk that commanded the center of the room. Books littered the oriental carpet in front of the now-empty built-in floor-to-ceiling bookshelves. Crystal paperweights, pens, framed photographs, a leather blotter holder, and pads of paper and sticky notes were heaped on the floor at one end of the desk. A burgundy leather wingback chair lay on its side in front of the room's one window.

The top of the desk was hidden under file folders, some open, some closed, the contents spilling out. It looked a lot like my desk.

Beyond the mess on the floor was a wall covered with framed photos, many of them awards pictures taken at dog shows, obedience and agility trials, and, judging by the crook in Abigail's hand in a few photos, some herding trials. A couple of the photos had fallen, and some hung askew, the glass in one of the frames radiating across the image like a spiderweb of shards as if something had scored a direct hit.

I squinted at that one. It was one of the few non-show photos, a shot of Abigail and Greg in hiking attire, smiling and holding hands against the rocky red architecture of Monument Valley. Pip and Percy sat in front of them.

"Either Mr. Dorn had serious housekeeping problems since his wife died, or someone was looking for something." Jo followed my gaze to the photo. "Something significant about that picture?"

"Not really. But it must have been taken recently."

"How do you know?"

"Abigail wore her hair long and straight for years." I looked back at the short, curly style in the photo. "She just cut it, I don't know exactly, but not long ago."

"Well, if they weren't getting along, they sure put on a good show for the camera." She was right. They looked happy and relaxed with one another.

I looked back at the mess on the floor. "Can we see what the open folders are?"

"We can't touch the room until the crime scene techs finish with it." She eyed the desk. "Stay here." She tiptoed between the papers on the floor and read the label tab on a folder that lay open and empty on the desk. Then she retreated to the door. "It says 'Pip'. That's the dog, right, the big show star?"

"Yes, the Border Collie. Obedience star."

"Also a scribbled note, looks like 'DHA' or 'DNA.' Any idea what that might mean?"

Several possibilities scurried through my mind, so I let myself think out loud. "Parentage verification. Or checking for markers for certain inherited diseases, maybe, but I don't know the ins and outs of Border Collie DNA testing for disorders. I've heard that there may have been some question about the accuracy of Pip's pedigree, that maybe his breeder lied about his parents, you know, who they are. Maybe Abigail had his DNA checked against his parents, or siblings, or even offspring if he had any."

Jo listened intently. "You mean like paternity testing for dogs?"

"Exactly. Paternity and maternity. The AKC actually requires dogs who are bred a certain number of times to be DNA-ed so that offspring can be verified if a question comes up, or if a buyer wants to do that for some reason."

"Wow."

"Yeah, just takes a cheek swab, you send it in and the lab compares certain markers to relatives, or supposed relatives. Or in some cases they can look for disease markers."

"And if Abigail was doing this, it might worry someone?"

"Well, not if everything was on the up and up. But if his breeder falsified her application to register a litter or two, then yeah, if the DNA doesn't confirm parentage, she could lose her registration privileges and be fined, and they'd publish her name so there goes her reputation." I thought about Francine's nutty, almost panicky, behavior. "I've heard that Francine invested a lot of money in importing two dogs, well, you know, a dog and a bitch, to revive her breeding program. If she did lie about Pip's parents, and she was found out, she'd lose not just her rights and reputation, but a pile of money as well. And she'd be open to lawsuits."

Jo wrote madly for a few moments, flipping a page, another. Then she asked, "What else would be in his file that isn't there now?"

I thought for a moment. "Registration papers, health records, pedigree, his competition record, photos. Like that."

"Papers. Those would be valuable? Like if someone wanted to sell him or use him as a stud dog?"

"Well, sort of. But the papers are registered to the owner, or owners."

"And if someone wanted him for breeding?"

"But Pip's neutered!" I reminded her.

"I know, but you said Abigail kept that a secret, right?"

"Oh, I see." I thought about that for a moment. "But to register his puppies, the sire's owner has to sign an application. So stealing the papers doesn't mean much, unless someone forges the signatures. But Pip's well known in Border Collie circles. Everyone knows who owns him, and who doesn't, so ... "

"Right." She wrinkled her forehead. "So what's this all about?"

I had nothing more to offer out loud, but I planned to find out what I could about litters and puppies that Francine had registered.

Jo guided me back down the hall, past my fantasy bathroom, and out the front door. "I'll put out an alert on the dog."

"Dogs." I corrected. "Greg also had a little Poodle named Percy." I started to give her a description, then ducked back in the door and pointed to a framed photo of the curly little guy.

I got Jay out of the Caravan so he could relieve himself while Jo called in the descriptions of the dogs. She walked to the curb and gave Jay a scratch under the chin before he hopped back into his crate. Jo told me she'd notify the shelters, and I offered to get the word out to the BC and Poodle rescue organizations as well. She told me to let her know if I heard anything.

I drove home in a deep, dark funk. Did someone really kill Greg and steal Pip and Pip's papers in hopes of using him at stud? Was Abigail about to reveal a more insidious secret entwined in the strands of her dog's DNA? If so, Francine stood to lose her reputation, her registration privileges, and some serious money. Greg would have to know about Abigail's suspicions, and Suzette may have been privy to Abigail's hunch as well. Now they were all dead. And with a flash of panic it occurred to me that Giselle, too, might know about Abigail's concerns, or the killer might think she did, and she might be in danger now. I pulled out my cell, found her number in my old calls, and left her a message to be careful.

It all seemed crazy. But then, anyone who kills three people is crazy by definition, right? Francine fit the crazy bill from what I'd seen. Did she have Pip and Percy? What about Leo? The thought made me shudder. And Greg's death? She might catnap Leo to frighten me off, and that had to be her in the cargo van scaring me out of ten years' growth. But why would she take Percy along with Pip? And if she didn't have the missing pets, where were they? The dogs could have wandered off through an open gate, although I'd have expected them to stay as close to Greg as they could. Leo could have wandered off, too, for that matter. I didn't want to believe that, but it was possible. I knew two things for sure. If I got him back, Leo was an indoor cat from now on, and I wasn't letting Jay out of my sight until someone got to the bottom of this.

92

As eager as I was to look into Pip's DNA records, I had other things to take care of on Monday morning. Jade Templeton and I had agreed on Monday for Jay's first nursing home visit, although his certification wouldn't be official until I had the paperwork back from the Delta Society. Jade understood that, but a local magazine was doing a story on Shadetree Retirement Home, and Jade was hoping to spotlight several life-enrichment programs going on at the home, including animal-assisted activities, garden therapy, art and music therapy, and a fledgling program in which preschoolers visited a select group of residents two days a week. Considering how welcoming Jade had been despite Mom's best effort to get herself expelled before she even moved in, I couldn't say no.

I'd tried to reach Giselle several times during the previous evening with no luck, but finally got through to her mid-morning. She said she'd be watchful and careful.

The magazine's photographer was supposed to be at Shadetree at 4:30, so in the morning I had tidied up the hair on Jay's tail, ears, and feet with my thinning sheers, smoothed his nails with a Dremel, and bathed him. Then the two of us headed over to Mom's house. Bill was already there, elbow deep in a beat-up cardboard file box.

"Gad, her files are like her cupboards."

I glanced at the wastebasket sitting next to the file box, filled nearly to the brim with paper.

"I take it she kept everything?"

"Even the envelopes everything came in. In no particular order, of course." He pulled a stapled packet of papers out, riffled through them, and got up. "Okay, finally, her long-term care policy." He looked closely at several pages, took a deep breath. "Thank God, it's paid up and current." He looked at me, relief palpable in his eyes. "I was afraid she might have let it lapse."

We spent the rest of the morning cleaning out files and putting together paperwork we might need soon. For lunch we had tomato soup and crackers on the patio, and caught up a bit. The tension of the past few months was gone, the decision about Mom made and action taken. It was nice to have my brother back, even if he could be a pain in the butt.

After lunch Bill mowed the lawn and tidied up the yard while I packed up the canned goods for him to take to the food bank, straightened the house up a bit, and finally headed home to prepare for our semi-official therapy debut. At four o'clock I made one final pass over Jay with a brush, tied a new red cowboy bandana around his neck, hooked up his leash, grabbed my tote bag, and we were on our way.

The sun hunkered behind a leading phalanx of gray thunder bumpers, and a hard southwest wind rippled the flag in front of Mr.

Hostetler's house across the street, holding the stripes almost horizontal. The temperature had dropped twenty degrees since noon, and when I stepped out the door, I decided I'd better take a jacket. I put Jay in the Caravan and ran to the front door. As I fiddled with my key, I noticed two startling reflections in the full-length window flanking the door. The first was my hair. I'd forgotten to comb it. That was scary enough, but the other reflection made me forget to breathe.

A cargo van crept along the street behind me. I almost turned around, but thought better of it. I stepped into the house, grabbed my camera from its case on the coffee table, and gently parted the sheer curtains with the lens. The vehicle was more rusted maroon than red in this light. As it surged ahead, I clicked off three or four shots.

It didn't make sense, though. Why would Francine Peterson be hanging out in Fort Wayne, especially if she had killed Greg. She knew the police could be looking for her. And why harass me? I didn't have Pip, or anything else she could possibly want. Then again, the woman did seem to be a few pixels short of a complete picture.

———

"You did what?" Jo Stevens sounded angry.

"I followed it. Or tried to." I sat in my Caravan, still looking around as I spoke into my cell phone. "I couldn't find it."

"Are you *nuts*?" She scolded, then shifted to a lower-pitched, much scarier voice. "You see something, you call me or Hutchinson or dispatch, you got that?"

"Okay."

"Seriously, Janet. What were you going to do if you caught the van? This isn't funny—you want to end up like Greg, with a carpentry tool rammed through your brain?"

93

A HUGE RAINDROP SPLATTED against my windshield, followed by another, and another. Not exactly a downpour, at least not yet. Just enough to smear the film of road gunk when I turned the wipers on. I tried the washers, but got only a few bubbles at the base of the windshield. *Note to self: check the washer fluid more often.* I turned the wipers off. I could see better through rain than through smeared road gunk.

Ten minutes later I drove through the South Anthony railroad underpass, a stretch of road I've always hated. The street dips beneath the tracks, and stone pillars split traffic into lanes so narrow that I swear they scrape dirt from anything wider than a bicycle. Decades of exhaust have coated the whole affair with a stinking black patina. It always makes me want to get in and out as quickly as possible, even in bright daylight. Two blocks further south I turned into the Shadetree entrance and found a parking space close to the building—a good thing since the raindrop scouts were joined shortly by a cavalry of their friends. I didn't care if I got drenched,

357

but I didn't want all my hard work on Jay's coat ruined before his photo op.

Jade skipped my usual hug, squatting to greet Jay with an ear rub and an "Oh, what a beautiful dog." Jay responded by gathering as many scent clues as possible from her face, and she giggled. "Those little whiskers tickle!"

"Is the rain going to ruin the outdoor shots?" I asked when she finished smooching my dog.

"All done except for the dog visit, and we'll do that inside." She led us into the common area, where fifteen or so residents were gathered. Their apparent awareness of their surroundings ranged from full to none. Mom was snuggled into a green high-backed armchair, flipping through the new issue of *Fine Gardening*. She glanced our way without any sign of recognition, and went back to her magazine.

Jay snapped his leash tight, his rear end wagging wildly. I let him take me to her, not a hint of hesitation in his step, though being a stranger to my own mother gave me pause enough for both of us. Jay laid his soft white chin across Mom's arm. She let the magazine fall to the floor, and tenderly cradled the dog's chin in her left hand, stroking his head with the other. "Laddie." Her voice was love itself, and my eyes filled.

The moment was brief, lost to the arrival first of an old gentleman with bushy silver hair and eyebrows that extended like wings past his temples, followed by another old man and woman. They paid me no attention at all, just reached out to touch the dog. I felt a light fluttering at my elbow, and turned to see a wren-like little woman with wispy gray hair and a sharp little nose. She chirped, "I like your dog," then turned and flitted away.

We made the rounds to visit other residents, and Jay tolerated wheelchairs, walkers, oxygen tanks, and palsied hands as if he saw them every day. Renee Koch, the reporter who was writing the article, followed along, asking questions of me, Jade, and some of the residents. The photographer clicked away, alternating his shots with peeks at his watch. I took a jab at conversation, but he didn't seem exactly thrilled with the subject matter, or with a jabbering woman old enough to be his mother.

I was saved the trouble of a polite withdrawal when an old man playing solitaire at a table by the window squealed "Ooh-ee! Looka that!" He pointed out the window, where a premature dusk had settled in under a dome of indigo clouds. Sheets of rain pounded the sidewalk in front of the common room, and sporadic bursts of wind shot the rain, clattering like BBs, straight into the window glass. A jagged electric gash tore the dingy sky, trailed within seconds by a rolling boom that made my teeth rattle.

The photographer checked his watch one more time, yanked a green poncho over his head and camera, and looked at the reporter. "Time to go."

Rene apologized to Jade for having another appointment.

"You could wait for the rain to let up, child!"

Renee turned to where the photographer had been, but he was already out the door. "It's okay. He'll pick me up under the over-hang."

We watched her go, and Jade turned to me. "I am not letting you take that dog out in that rain." The emphasis of her concern didn't escape me. "You sit down." She steered me toward a couch next to Mom's chair. "I'll get us some coffee."

Mom was engrossed in her magazine, although when Jay lay beside her and rested his chin on her foot she did bend over to stroke the top of his head. "What a good boy, Laddie." I may as well not have been there.

The rain retreated to a sprinkle twenty minutes later and the clouds dispersed, although the light was growing dimmer as evening came on. To the west another battalion of angry-looking clouds threatened to move in. I said goodbye to Jade while several residents told Jay to come back soon. I stopped in front of Mom. She grabbed the hair on both sides of Jay's neck, pulled him to her face, and kissed the space between his eyes. "I love you, Laddie." She still didn't look at me.

94

I was about to turn right out of the Shadetree parking lot onto Anthony when I saw a line of red taillights creeping into the underpass. They seemed to stretch a full block, the last one in the lineup idling a couple of car lengths past the intersection north of the nursing home. The road was alive with water, swirling and grabbing at wheel wells, arcing away behind the cars like long, fluid fins. If drowning is my destiny, I'd rather not fulfill it in an oily underpass, so I turned south on Anthony, cut west to Lafayette, and then north through downtown. The rain and wind were picking up again by the time I turned east on State, and night settled over the city like a shroud.

The traffic lights were out all along State, at Reed, Maplecrest, and Lahmeier, adding to the challenge of the windblown obstacle course. Cars slowed and wove back and forth between lanes, dodging big tree limbs and crushing small ones. Three or four garbage cans rolled around the street, spinning this way and that, as if a giant cat were knocking them from one lane to another. I thought of *my* cat and hoped he was safe and dry.

So far people were civil, taking turns at the cross streets. I crept through the last uncontrolled intersection before my turn, inching up to 35 mph, which seemed to be fast enough for everyone except the vehicle on my rear bumper. Its brights bounced off my mirrors into my eyes, and I couldn't see what it was, but the height of the lights said truck or van or SUV. Big. For one paranoid moment I thought it was that cargo van again, and for some reason Connie's admonition that "it's not all about you, Janet" came screaming into my head. As much as that had stung, she was right, and not every wacko driver was out to get me. At least I hoped not.

I tried slowing down to get the fool to pass me. When that didn't work, I sped up to 40. All I could see in my mirrors was the blinding brightness. I used a couple of expletives when the lights followed me around the corner onto Maysville.

The turn onto my street was half a block away when I put my signal on. I was tapping my brakes and hoping the jerk wouldn't hit us when a sheet of newspaper splatted against my windshield and diverted my focus from the truck on my bumper. I hit the down button on my window and reached into the maelstrom to try to pull the paper out of my way, but a morsel of newsprint tore away in my fingers, leaving the bulk glued to the glass. *Great! They'll find us dead in a papier-mâché car.* The wipers tore at the paper, shredding a little more with each swipe until I could see enough to make the turn if the nut on my tail didn't rear-end us first.

For a couple seconds, the lights stayed put, then suddenly swung to the left as I skidded around to the right. I checked my rearview mirror again, but there was nothing to see. I glanced over my left shoulder and got a quick impression of a big-wheel pickup. Not a cargo van. *What is it with idiot drivers lately?*

I pulled into the garage, turned off the engine, shut the overhead door, and leaned my head back against the headrest. I realized that I was panting, my lungs trying to catch up with my heart, and I forced my muscles to loosen as the tension oozed from my arms and legs. A headache had sunk its fangs into the base of my skull and was nibbling its way up the nerve paths to the top. The timer on the light from the overhead-door opener ran its course, and the garage went dark. Jay shifted in his crate and gave a little whine, bringing me back to the moment.

I got out and felt my way around the front bumper to the light switch on the wall. I didn't want to raise the overhead door again, so I popped the back of the van and let it rise slowly to a forty-five degree opening, the leading edge braced against the inner surface of the garage door, leaving an opening just big enough for me to crawl under to open the crate. Jay rolled his eyes up to look at the low-hanging hatch, and carefully hopped to the concrete floor. I slammed the hatch shut, and we retreated to the comfort and safety of the house.

I checked in with Goldie. Still no sign of Leo. I shed my wet clothes, toweled my hair, and put the kettle on for some tea. Blackberry sage, my comfort brew. Jay snarfed up his dinner in record time, but looked at me like I was nuts when I offered to let him out. I could see his point. The rain had lightened to a sprinkle, but the wind whipped the forsythia and lilac branches into a frenzy, and thunder rumbled somewhere to the west. I'd hold it awhile too if I had to go out there to pee.

I dialed Connie's number, but there was no answer. I wondered to her machine whether she'd heard about Greg, although I figured that Giselle had no doubt called her. There was nothing much on the television, and my headache seemed to be settling in for the night, so I decided to drug myself, take a nice relaxing lavender bubble bath, and hit the sack.

I fished around the bottom of my purse for some naproxen, but couldn't find any. Then I remembered the bottle I keep in my training bag, along with gourmet cheese-and-liver training treats, an emergency collar, and a lot of stuff I forgot about long ago. I started pulling things out of my bag and setting them on the end table by the couch, next to the old dumbbell I'd put there the previous week. Goldie would razz me again if she saw it still sitting there. I pulled out some notes and maps from tracking sessions. Several bungee cords—you never know when you'll need one. Finally I dug out the naproxen bottle.

I took two naproxens, went to the bedroom, and was pulling off my soggy pants when Jay started barking like a mad man somewhere in the front of the house.

95

JAY USUALLY QUITS BARKING when I tell him "Quiet," but not this time, so I pulled my pants back up and went to see what was happening. He bounced around the living room window, his hair standing straight out around his neck, booming a warning into the darkness around us. I tried to see through the glass into the night, but couldn't make out anything except frantic branches and their shadows cavorting in the scattered lights.

"It's okay, Bubby. Just the wind." He gave me a "You can't fool me, I know you're scared!" look, but he quieted down except for an occasional soft *brffff*.

The adrenalin from the drive home had left me a bit woozy, and my head was about to explode, so I went to the kitchen and half filled a bowl with ice cubes and water, carried it to the living room, and set it on the floor by the couch. Then I trudged to the bathroom, pulled a washcloth from the towel rack, trudged back to the couch. I dunked the cloth into the ice water, wrung it out, and folded it in half. As I stretched out on the cushions, I lay the cloth across my forehead, pressing the soothing cold into my scalp line and temples, and lay as still as I could. Finally, the headache flinched and loosened its hold on the back of my skull, giving me some hope of a reasonable night's sleep.

Forty minutes later I was feeling a lot better, but the whine and clatter of the wind through the kitchen vent was making my nerves itch, so I dragged myself off the couch and down the hall to my bedroom.

My little respite on the couch wasn't nearly so relaxing for Jay. He had spent the entire time torn between lying next to the couch to keep an eye on me, as always, and running to bark at the kitchen door, then back to me every time I told him to be quiet, a most un-Jay-like behavior. The wind was making us both weird.

"Where's Leo, Bubby?" I asked my dog. I put on some old but clean sweatpants and a T-shirt and checked outside both doors once more. I was pulling the covers back on the bed when all hell broke loose. Something crashed outside the kitchen door, followed by a jarring wham into the door itself.

Jay barked frantically, looking at me for instructions as I ran into the kitchen. I held on to his collar and opened the door. "Leo?" I called, hoping against hope that he would pick this hostile night to return to us.

A maple branch sprawled across the patio, its main arm a foot or so in diameter, its smaller tentacles reaching toward the house. It saddened me to know that the big old tree was damaged, but I told Jay, "Look, Bubby, it's just a big stick." I closed the door and locked it, and decided to double check the front door while I was at it.

By the time I crawled into bed I was wide awake again, so I snuggled in and opened my book. Jay plastered his back against the length of my blanketed leg and heaved a sigh. The normal routine is for me to read and for him to fall fast asleep, but every few minutes he raised his head, ears swivelled toward the front of the house. I rested a hand on his flank. He rolled his hip tight against me, but kept his attention on the door.

A nearly imperceptible growl vibrated in Jay's throat, raising the hairs on my arms. I was about to get up and see for myself what was beyond the bedroom door when Jay rested his chin on his crossed paws, letting me off the hook. The storm was still roaring around us twenty minutes later when I stuck a piece of tissue between the pages of my book, set it next to the lamp, and turned out the light.

I was floating very near slumber land when Jay's barking jolted me back to full consciousness.

96

JAY STOOD ON THE bed, and it shook every time he let out a booming *buroof*. I should know by now to listen to my dog, but the shock to my adrenals had brought my headache back with a vengeance, and I took Jay by the collar and hustled him down the hall toward the kitchen. I flipped the switch for the hallway light, but nothing happened. *I told you to replace that bulb,* whispered the voice from my pompous side.

Jay tried to pull me into the living room, growling and barking, but I hauled him through the dark to the kitchen and out the door. "Go out and pee, and have a look around. Then maybe we can get some sleep!"

I groped for and found the light switch by the door, but it made no difference. No lights. *Storm must have knocked out a transformer,* I thought, until I noticed that Goldie's back porch light was on, as it often was all night. My circuit breaker must have tripped.

I turned toward the laundry room, felt my way past the kitchen table and chairs, hoping not to catch a toe on a chair leg, and followed the smooth surface of the wall into the gloom of the windowless laundry room. My fingers hit the cool edge of the dryer, drifted to the right, touched the wall, and ran over the vinyl wallpaper until they found metal. I felt for the pull ring and yanked the breaker box open, then realized that I had no idea which breaker was where. I needed some light.

I backtracked into the kitchen and slowly made my way to the counter. I opened the first drawer to the right of the sink and felt around, trying to remember whether anything sharp lay waiting to stab me. The biggest hazards in the drawer were probably a couple of pens. As my fingers closed over the hard plastic flashlight handle, I thought I heard something behind me.

I stopped, listening into the dark. *Must be the wind.* I picked up the flashlight and tried it. No go. *Note to self: replace flashlight batteries.*

I fumbled in the drawer again, and my fingers closed over a small cardboard box. I pushed it open and felt inside. Two matches. *Another note to self. Renew supply of matches.*

Jay was raising hell outside the door. It wasn't his usual "let me in" bark, but more serious, a prolonged medley of deep-throated boofs and high-pitched squeals. "Quiet!" Knowing he didn't like the wind but puzzled by the panic in his voice, I hollered that I'd be right there.

My fingers fumbled further into the drawer and were rewarded by the feel of a cylinder about four inches long. I pictured its scarred red surface and blackened wick, and was glad I'd kept it though its tabletop days were done. As I'd told Goldie many times, you never know when something may come in handy. I put the candle stub in my pocket and edged back toward the laundry room. I was just starting to pull open the matchbox when a stunning pain knocked all thought out of my mind.

97

THE PAIN SEVERED ANY commitment I had made to clean up my language, and I swore like a lady pirate as I leaned against the door frame and bent to massage my poor little piggies. Jay leaped and banged against the kitchen door, barking and squealing, and the flap on the dryer vent clattered and whined erratically in the wind. I knew my headache was back when a fist of pain clutched my skull, unsheathed its claws, and sank them in.

Suck it up, MacPhail. I let go of my toes, straightened up, and tried to focus on the job at hand. I gently nudged open the matchbox. My fingertips caught one of the matches and pulled it out. I slid the cover over the inner box, felt for the striker paper, and stroked the head of the match along the rough surface. A couple of sparks, nothing more. "Crap!" I struck it again, harder. The head of the match snapped off, flared and arced like a fairy's comet, and fizzled before it hit the floor.

I dropped the useless bit of wood and carefully retrieved the remaining match from the box as I moved back into the laundry room. I held my breath and laid the head of the match against the striker. And stopped.

That sound again, a hint of sound really, not quite there, a whisper, like metal against cloth. I stepped backward out of the laundry room and listened. No sound, but something.

I backed further into the kitchen and inclined my head toward the living room, straining to hear. The kitchen window offered a dim glow, but not enough to reveal whatever the deep shadows concealed. Visions of maniacs danced in my mind, their heads aglow with incandescent red hair.

My cheek grazed something cold and hard. The phone. I picked up the receiver and pushed Goldie's speed dial button, listening for the ping ping ping of the electronic numbers. Nothing. I pushed and released the phone cradle, and listened. Still nothing. I knocked the cradle up and down a few more times. Dead.

Jay scratched and barked and banged at the door. I remembered the dead receiver in my hand, and plunked it back into the cradle. Never had the lights and phone both pooped out together. I felt along the top of the counter until I found my cell phone, but it was dead as well. I'd forgotten to recharge it. Again. A shot of panic flashed through me, and I wanted my dog beside me. If there were anything—or anyone—inside the house, Jay would know long before I would. Maybe he did know. Maybe that's what he'd been trying to tell me. My head throbbed and a razor of fear slashed into my gut.

I found the back door and pulled on the handle. It wouldn't open. The deadbolt had apparently slipped into place when I let Jay out, or maybe I'd turned it unconsciously. I grasped the deadbolt's knob and twisted, heard the click as it opened and caught. As I reached for the door handle, a new shock of pain bit into the base of my skull and coiled upward until my whole head was in its grip. It squeezed, and then the world went black.

98

I CAME TO ALMOST as soon as my face hit the cool vinyl. Jay was still outside the door, barking nonstop, his voice pitched high and verging on hysteria. I heard a shuffle and the squeak of a shoe sole on the vinyl behind me.

I scuttled across the floor on my hands and knees, trying to get to the back door, but froze at a bone-jarring report close at hand. It ended with the tinkle of glass shattering in the kitchen door and a sharp yip from outside. *Oh God, don't let him be shot.*

I ducked my head, cradling it in my left arm and wondering which throb would be the one that exploded my skull. Through the fog of pain and fear, my mind registered the sound of Jay barking again, loud and strong as ever. *Thank you, God.* I scrambled away from the back door, toward the living room.

"You'll be sorry you ever stuck your nose in my business." The threat came in a snarl barely louder than a whisper. I couldn't identify the owner.

I wanted to ask who it was, but decided to shut up for once on the off chance I'd be invisible in the dark. If I could get to the front door … I heard Jay's claws scraping the back door, his frantic yips ripping through my heart. *Please don't let him get hurt.*

As I edged through the doorway from kitchen to living room, I got my feet under me and rose into a crouch. I figured I could move faster that way while keeping myself a tough target. I sprinted toward the front door. A blast from the gun, the bounce of the bullet off the steel front door, the muffled finale as the drywall absorbed the ricocheted shell. I stopped in my tracks, revised my exit strategy, and turned back into the room.

"I see you, you nosey bitch!"

I knew the voice.

Another shot sounded like a cannon in my small living room.

"How will killing me help?" She might be beyond reason, but it was the only weapon I had for the moment.

"Shut up!" Click. "Shit!" Click, click. A bunch more clicks.

A shadow flew across the room at me, snarling, "I don't need a gun to deal with you!" Then why did she seem to be raising one above her head like a club?

"You don't have to deal with me!" I took a step back, forgetting that the couch was behind me, and tripped, sprawling backward onto the soft seat cushions. "It's too late! You can't get away with it now."

"Yes, I can," she growled. All my senses were focused on the crazy woman in front of me, but some corner of my mind registered that the front door had opened. Or did I imagine it? Then she was on me, like pure energy. She planted a knee, sharp as a spade, against my thigh and pinned me into the couch. Bone pressed into my flesh, through it to my own bone within, and I wondered vaguely whether the bruise would show if I died in the next minute or so.

I saw her gun hand slam down toward my head, but was able to block it, wielding the tapestry pillow like a shield over my head. The impact knocked the pillow into my nose, filling my sinuses with bubbling pain.

I peeked from behind my shield in time to see her raise the gun once more, and was preparing to block her again when an inhuman caterwaul shocked the night, a wail calculated to turn blood to jelly. In the next instant the air in front of my attacker erupted in shadowy frenzy as the woman jerked upright, away from me, and whirled, her screams almost a match for the first one.

I dropped the pillow and tried to get up. Big mistake. She whacked with the gun at her own thighs, acting as if an army of fire ants had climbed up her pants, and in her flailing caught my brow bone with an elbow, sending a galaxy of stars cascading through my head. The gun thunked against the oak floor, the sound nearly lost in a stream of curses, snarls, and more howls.

"Janet?" Goldie's voice was almost drowned out, but I heard her.

"Here!" I panted, trying to get out from behind the maelstrom in front of the couch and onto my feet. I'd almost made it when I was smashed back into the cushions. A second set of snarls, pitched lower. I felt long fur against my hand. Jay. He'd unlatched the back door again.

The bones of my foe's rear end dug into my gut, and her arms windmilled in panic. Her left hand slapped at her thigh. A beam of light hit us, quivered away, returned. I was vaguely aware that it came from Goldie's hand, which was shaking too much to keep the flashlight steady, but steady enough to reveal the source of the blood-gelling screams.

99

LEO WAS LOCKED ON to my assailant's thigh, his fur standing straight out, ears flat against his skull, lips pulled back to let his fangs do their work, claws extended through cotton capris and into the flesh beneath. He sounded like he was possessed.

Jay had a grip on the intruder's arm just below the elbow and was trying to pull her off me, or her arm off her torso, whichever came first. Low, rolling snarls erupted from his throat, all business, primeval, like nothing I'd ever heard from him before. Blood ran down the attacker's arm where the dog had clamped on. It dripped and mingled with the gore that soaked the fabric of her shredded left pant leg.

The more Jay tugged on her arm, the more she pulled into me, knocking the air back out every time I managed to suck some in. I punched at her back as well as I could manage, pinned as I was to the couch. She shoved me farther toward the armrest. I braced my right hand against her and pushed, groping blindly toward the end table with my left, seeking a purchase, a way to pull myself free.

Leo let out a new unearthly sound, part growl, part battle cry, shrill hate and anger, as he dodged a blow to the head. He flinched and loosed the hold he had mid-thigh, swatted at the offending arm, and reattached himself with a vengeance higher up. One paw slipped between the woman's legs and sank daggers into the soft flesh at the top of her inner thigh. The other flexed wide and gripped her buttocks. He worked his back claws like pistons, shredding the bloodstained cotton and ripping the skin beneath. The light beam danced erratically, but I saw my little tiger sink his fangs through the flimsy fabric once again, prying loose more barely human keening from the woman in his grip.

My head felt like a kettledrum, noise and heat and fear beating it raw. I pushed once more against the small of my attacker's back, and managed to slip partway out from under her. I had no plan, and acted on pure pain and reflex.

I extended an arm toward the end table, fingers flexed, and heard something fall away, clatter to the floor, and roll. The naproxen bottle. I pictured the table, trying to build a map in my mind, and reached further, feeling in the dark. My fingernail brushed something hard.

A long howl erupted from the body on top of me. My attacker arched and shifted backward, emptying my lungs again as she came down hard.

Something white flashed forward and down from behind my head, past my eyes. I heard a dull hard *thwack,* and then the world went slow. My bloodied foe stopped mid-scream, swayed for a moment, and, with a little shove from my right hand, toppled to the floor.

Leo released his grip and flew straight up, changed direction mid-leap, and came down running. His tail stood high and straight, fluffed out like a feather duster as he let out a yowl and disappeared into the bedroom. Jay gave the arm he held a test tug to be sure its owner was out of the fight, let it go, and jumped onto the couch, planting his paws on my shoulders and his elbows against my bruised ribs as he whined and licked my face.

"That'll teach her!"

I pushed Jay partway off and looked at Goldie, silhouetted like a spirit against the open front door, her long silver hair loose and wild, her free hand raised in a fist of victory.

I glanced at the body sprawled in the beam of Goldie's light on the floor in front of me and felt a pang of regret. As I tried to push Jay off the couch and raise myself into a sitting position, I realized I had something in my left hand. I felt its familiar shape and heft, moved it into the light, and waggled my big clunky spare dumbbell at Goldie. "I told you this might come in handy."

100

I GOT THE LIGHTS back on and fished my cell phone recharger out of my tote bag, but before I plugged the phone in, Goldie said, "I already called that detective."

"You did?" Sure enough, I heard a siren somewhere in the night.

"She gave me her card a few days ago when she stopped by and you weren't here."

Goldie picked up a handful of bungee cords from where I'd left them on the end table. She rolled the intruder onto her stomach and secured her hands behind her back, then wound another cord several times around her feet. My attacker was waking up by the time Goldie propped her back against the couch and bound her knees together.

"What are you doing here, anyway?" I asked Goldie.

"Jay was raising such a ruckus at the back door, and your lights were out. I knew something was wrong."

The woman on the floor let out a string of expletives, ending with "hurts." Her clothes were torn and bloody, barely concealing the lacerated flesh underneath. She started to say something, but stopped when two uniformed police officers rushed in, Jo Stevens on their heels.

"Why, Connie?" I asked softly. She didn't answer. She tried to toss a strand of blood-soaked hair out of her eyes. I stepped toward her. She flinched from my hand, then let me push the hair behind her ear. I looked into her eyes, and a stranger looked back. Then she turned her head toward Jay, and her expression softened.

"I'm sorry I used you and Leo to scare that nosey bitch. I wouldn't really have hurt you."

A rocket of anger exploded in my mind. "Not hurt them? You poisoned him and kidnapped my cat! Did you take Greg's dogs, too?" I didn't realize that more people had entered the room, or that I had stepped toward her again until I felt the back edge of Detective Jo Stevens' arm cross my chest.

Connie continued speaking softly, ignoring me in favor of Jay. "Your biscuits weren't poisoned, sweetie." Jay cocked his head at her. "I would never do such a thing. I put mouse bait out in my garage. That's where the mouse came from. I put it in the pantry," she turned toward me and went on, "while you were putting the grooming supplies away. And Leo was perfectly safe." Conflicting emotions seemed to dance across her face, but I couldn't see anything like affection or friendship, and a sledgehammer of loss smashed into my heart. Then Connie's eyes filled with the light I knew and loved, and her voice went soft. "I thought I could scare you off. Should have known better, you're so damn stubborn."

I didn't know what to say to that.

"I took Pip and Percy so they wouldn't have to smell that bastard's body rotting or go hungry if no one found the sonofabitch for a while. I'd have found them all good homes."

Sorrow gnawed at me as I realized I might never have known what happened to my cat, or to Greg and Abigail's dogs. I looked at Goldie. "Where was Leo, anyway?"

"In that clunker van in the street. I heard dogs barking so I took a look."

"The van was open?" asked Detective Stevens

"Not exactly. One of the back doors was tied shut with twine. I squeezed my arm in far enough to unlock the front, and then popped the locks. And there was Leo, in a crate, looking like a wildcat. There are a couple more dogs there, too, and a bunch of luggage. That black and white guy you had here, and a Poodle."

Jo signaled one of the officers to go check the van.

Goldie continued. "Leo was a yellow streak to your front door when I opened his cage, and wild to get into the house."

"How *did* you get in?" I asked Goldie.

"Door was unlocked."

"No! I know I locked it."

Connie made a face. "Key under the geranium pot. How creative."

I looked at her, and tried again. "Why, Connie?"

Connie's face went livid. "I waited for that bastard all these years while he had his fling."

"Fling? Connie! Greg and Abigail were married more than twenty years."

She bared her teeth at me, twisting against her restraints. A siren sounded in the distance. "When they separated, I figured my wait was over." She snarled again, collected herself, and went on, "And then the stupid bastard ruined it all."

"What?"

"Stupid sonofabitch thought Suzette killed Abigail," she hissed. "I thought *you'd* blame her for Abigail's death," she glared at Jo, "but the police didn't get it, and Greg got it wrong."

My head was spinning now as well as pounding. "But I thought Francine…" My thought trailed off. "You killed Abigail?"

Connie sounded suddenly like a woeful little girl. "I've loved that man all my life. I got tired of waiting. I thought when he moved out it was finally my turn."

"But they…"

"Yeah, yeah, I know." She shot me a look. "They were redecorating, for crying out loud."

Another question struck me. "Why do you have Francine's van?"

She looked at me like I was the village idiot. "I bought one like hers. And a stupid red wig. I knew if you kept asking questions, and thinking about it, you'd figure Francine did it because of the DNA tests. I knew you'd be on 30 that day, coming back from the lake. I just wanted to piss you off enough to make you blame Francine."

"You did my tires, too?"

I took her glare as a yes.

"And what about Greg? I mean, if you loved him…"

Her eyes went watery. "I went to see him. Told him I'd waited all these years." She sniffed a couple of times. "I told him I killed Abigail. I did it for him, for us, and he just went crazy, started screaming that he thought Suzette did it. Then he started bawling like a baby. Said we'd have to turn ourselves in." She was talking very fast now. "He said he'd never loved me and he started to call the police, to confess about Suzette and tell them about me, and the next thing I knew the chisel was in my hand..."

Connie went quiet, Goldie and I exchanged looks of sympathy mixed with horror, and Detective Stevens directed one of the police officers to arrest Connie. As he stepped toward her and started to read her her rights, I asked, "Greg killed Suzette?"

Connie winced as she was pulled to her feet and cuffed, then nodded. "I think the chisel was meant to be there." Her voice had turned to a monotone that spooked me more than her screeching had. "Then you wouldn't back off, and I knew you weren't really sure about Francine, and that was a big problem. With Tom around you'd find out about me and Greg and put it all together." The venom was back in her voice. "You may be nosey, but you're not stupid."

I wasn't too sure about that at the moment.

An ambulance pulled to a stop in front of the house. The cops escorted Connie out the door for her ride to the hospital and then the jail. She resisted at the door and turned her face to me, a glint back in her eye. "I don't think you'll get Leo into a cat carrier for a while. But if you need to, he's a slut for sardines."

101

THE SUN NESTLED INTO the trees along the Maumee River, and flights of crows and smaller birds swooped over the brown water and called to the coming night. Barely a day had passed since Connie's arrest, and the world along the river went on unchanged, indifferent. Jay and Drake drew their retractable leashes full length as they searched both edges of the Greenway path, back and forth, back and forth.

"I didn't know Connie still carried that torch for Greg." Tom spoke softly, and my eyes filled. We walked in silence for a few minutes, watching the dogs and reeling them in whenever anyone else happened along.

I elbowed Tom, trying to lighten my dark mood. "So, Mr. Toxic Plants, what do you think she used?"

"The police mentioned alkaloids?"

I nodded.

"And Abigail had coordination problems, and trouble breathing... Did anyone mention a funny smell?"

I thought back to Abigail's gear at the show, "I found cheese spread that smelled sort of mousy."

"Poison hemlock?"

"Very good. Yes. Goldie nudged that one out of her before they took her away. Connie made Abigail some 'special' spread for her bagels."

"And Suzette?"

"And was Greg really involved with Suzette?"

"No. Yvonne filled me in on that, too. Seems Abigail introduced Suzette to an old family friend when they were in the Bahamas last year, and they fell in love. Yvonne said their parents opposed the marriage. Hers didn't want Suzette going so far away, his had someone else in mind. So they were keeping their plans for a small summer wedding with close friends quiet."

"What about the tickets?"

"Yvonne said Greg and Abigail always flew separately, so Greg and Suzette were going on one flight, Abigail and Yvonne on another."

Tom guided me off the path to a bench overlooking a bend in the river. We sat, and the dogs lay down in the shade. Tom took my hand in both of his and traced the lines in my palm, sending a flight of butterflies spinning among my internal organs. I asked myself whether they were there because I didn't want to get too involved, or because I did, and I had no answer. Jay rolled onto his back and leaned his ribs against a sapling, and I envied him the simplicity of life in the moment. At least that's how we assume animals live, although I'm not always sure that's right. My philosophizing was interrupted when Tom asked, "And I take it Connie hadn't planned to kill Greg?"

"She seemed genuinely shocked that he wasn't thrilled that Abigail was out of their way, and angry that he'd spoiled it by killing Suzette and, worse, wanting to come clean to the police. She said it was satisfying to stab the son of a bitch with his own tool."

"Ouch."

"A little Freudian, huh? And very Connie. You know, she even bought herself an engagement ring. She said Greg gave it to her, but the police found a credit card receipt in her purse."

"What will happen to the dogs?"

Jay rolled onto his side, and Drake stretched himself so that one front paw touched one of Jay's.

"I spent today on that. Connie's dogs all have co-owners, so they'll take them. They're at the clinic in the meantime."

"And the DNA business?"

"Ginny Scott, Fly's breeder, talked to someone at the Border Collie registry and she said both they and the AKC were already investigating Francine. Apparently some of her puppies have been DNA tested and the results didn't line up with the dogs she claimed were their parents."

"What will happen to her?"

"She'll no doubt lose her registration privileges and Border Collie club memberships. What reputation she still had among BC people is shot. And Ginny said there's talk of a couple of lawsuits from other breeders who bought pups from her or bred to her dogs and now have pedigree disasters."

"Her dogs?"

"Ginny said Border Collie rescue groups are standing by to take them if necessary. They'll neuter them and find them new homes."

"What a mess." Tom shook his head and clucked softly. "And what about Greg and Abigail's dogs?"

The man was gaining hundreds of brownie points in my book. To my surprise, few people had shown much concern for the fate of all the dogs affected by the murders and scandals. "They're at my house for now. Ginny is going to find Pip a home. And it turns out that little Percy is a certified therapy dog and visited a nursing home every week. You won't believe which one."

"Not where your mom is?"

"You got it. Jade Templeton wants him. She's wanted a dog for a long time, but didn't think it fair to leave one alone for the long hours she works. She loves Percy, so she'll adopt him and he'll be her dog, and he'll go to work with her. She has to clear it with the board of directors, but doesn't think that will be a problem. Their resident cat has worked out really well."

"Speaking of cats, is Leo happy to be home?"

I thought of my little orange man. "He curled up against my head and purred all night."

"Lucky guy!" Tom grinned and stood. "It's getting dark, lady and gents. We should head back." The dogs jumped up, and I eased myself into a stand, trying to ignore my aches and bruises and wondering how people on TV bounce back so fast from getting punched and shot and run over by trains. I was a wreck from a little couch wrestling.

My thoughts were cut short when Tom pulled me close, searched my eyes, and traced my lips with a touch as light as a whisper. He laced his fingers into my hair and cradled the back of my head, and then kissed me, slowly and thoroughly. Warring currents of lust and panic surged through me, and I didn't know whether to lie down right there or run like hell.

I barely felt the solid ground beneath my feet on the way back to the parking lot. My thoughts bounced around in my head like numbered balls in a lottery machine—*I don't want to get involved with anyone. Why didn't I shave my legs this morning? I can't get close and then go through the pain of losing him. This may be the man I've looked for all my life. I like my life the way I've created it. Change is good.*

Janet Angel and Janet Demon piped up in harmony, reminding me that life is like an obedience trial, and if I don't send the entry, I'll never get the title. *Of course,* I argued back, *I won't lose, either.* I thought of my disastrous relationship with Chet and the few uninspiring flubs since then, and of a photo I took years ago of two paths diverging in a wood of shadows and light.

Once again, Tom grinned and brought me back to the moment. "By the way, you owe me some portraits of my dog, and I intend to collect. So don't make a habit of putting yourself in harm's way."

Good thing I didn't make any promises.

ABOUT THE AUTHOR

Sheila Webster Boneham has been writing professionally for three decades, and writes in several genres. She has taught writing at universities in the U.S. and abroad, and occasionally teaches writing workshops. In the past fifteen years Sheila has published seventeen nonfiction books, six of which have won major awards. A long-time participant in canine sports, therapy, and other activities, Sheila is also an avid amateur photographer and painter. When she isn't pursuing creative activities or playing with animals, Sheila can be found walking the beach or salt marsh near her home in North Carolina. You can reach her through her website at www.sheilaboneham.com.

WWW.MIDNIGHTINKBOOKS.COM

From the gritty streets of New York City to sacred tombs in the Middle East, it's always midnight somewhere. Join us online at any hour for fresh new voices in mystery fiction.

At midnightinkbooks.com you'll also find our author blog, new and upcoming books, events, book club questions, excerpts, mystery resources, and more.

MIDNIGHT INK ORDERING INFORMATION

Order Online:
• Visit our website www.midnightinkbooks.com, select your books, and order them on our secure server.

Order by Phone:
• Call toll-free within the U.S. and Canada at 1-888-NITE-INK (1-888-648-3465)
• We accept VISA, MasterCard, and American Express

Order by Mail:
Send the full price of your order (MN residents add 6.875% sales tax) in U.S. funds, plus postage & handling to:

> Midnight Ink
> 2143 Wooddale Drive
> Woodbury, MN 55125-2989

Postage & Handling:

Standard (U.S. & Canada). If your order is:
> $25.00 and under, add $4.00
> $25.01 and over, FREE STANDARD SHIPPING

AK, HI, PR: $16.00 for one book plus $2.00 for each additional book.

International Orders (airmail only):
> $16.00 for one book plus $3.00 for each additional book

Orders are processed within 12 business days. Please allow for normal shipping time.
Postage and handling rates subject to change.